# LOVE

## ON THE SPRINGS OF
## MY TIME-TRAVELLING BED

### BY

### RICHARD HAPPER

JonesCat
PUBLISHING

Published by JonesCat Publishing Limited
Edinburgh

Copyright © Richard Happer 2016

ISBN 978-0956242860

Design and typesetting by Iain Sangster

If you've ever made a terrible mistake
and been very glad that you did,
this book is for you.

Invented a time-travelling bed today. How else could I shag Lucy Sugar? She's a Hollywood star. Absolutely gorgeous. White hot property. Just won an Oscar for playing that four-fingered concert pianist. Whereas I'm living in a brewery in Edinburgh, 5,161 miles away. So it's not going to happen now, you see? But there was a time when we were very much on. She completely fancied old Freddie. She'd have plonked herself on his bobby and ridden him home like a champ. If only I hadn't... hang on, don't think like that. No point in going there. Besides, I'm engaged as well. So I really couldn't shag her now. Hence the time-travelling bed.

Engaged.

Shit, sounds weird when you say it. Weird when it happened too. Just last night. And doubly weird 'cos the Penster asked me.

Five o'clock in the afternoon and I'm down in the lab working on the wind-powered photocopier. Thorny problem – very. How to stop the paper blowing away. Ideas not flowing, so I was having a little refreshment. To stimulate the synapses, you understand, when...

RING RING

What the hell?

RING RING

Scrabble for the phone.

RING RING

Find it behind my bottle of Merlot. In an empty sweet and sour King Pot.

"Hello?"

"Hello, honey!" bubbles a female voice.

"Hello, my love," I say. "Good day?"

"Oh, ups and downs, you know. That little wretch in 3B threw up in the sandpit again."

"Aha," I grunt, cradling the phone in my shoulder as I pour a top-up into my S Club 7 mug.

"But then, in the afternoon, I was chatting with Mr Greaves over lunch and-"

"Listen, honey, I'm at a really important juncture right now. Can we talk about this later?"

"That's why I phoned, Freddie!"

"What?"

"Come and meet me in Ambrosetti's," she coos. "Hanover Street. Below that bar where the footballers go."

"Um... why?"

She giggles. A real high-pitched wobbly giggle. Like she's nineteen again or something. "Just come, Freddie. Half an hour." Another nervous giggle and she hangs up.

Have to say, I'm not pleased. Do my best work in the early evening. My breakfast has settled, the wine has kicked in and my levels are just about right. So it's with a few huffs and puffs that I get up from the drawing board and search round for some underpants.

An hour later I'm walking down the steps into Ambrosetti's. Open the door. Sublime smells hit me like a wall. Noises too – clinking of cutlery, raucous sizzling from the open-walled kitchen, shouts from chefs and heavy, heavy chatter. Place is full. Crammed, in fact. Difficult to get my bearings. Stand just inside the door feeling very awkward. Diners begin to clock me. Look at their eyes. They know I feel awkward. Which makes me feel even MORE awkward.

Smarmbag waiter approaches. Gives me the once-over. Yanks his nose in the air. Doesn't like the look of my Teletubbies T-shirt.

"Yay-ess, sarr?"

"My girlfriend's here," I say.

He looks blank.

"Yay high," I add, lifting my hand to the level of the chest hairs visible through the largish hole in said T-shirt. "Mousey hair."

Smarmbag waiter raises one eyebrow. It's a tiny expression but it manages to convey the following: "How remarkable. I cannot possibly imagine someone who looks and smells as you do being allowed to walk the streets, let alone having a girlfriend. Nevertheless, I do remember seeing a respectable-enough girl sat at a table on her own, so, considering the possibility that you are some rich eccentric, I will lower myself to serve you on this one occasion."

"Zees way, sir," he says, and spins on a leather heel.

Past the really nice tables, through an arch. A sharp left and down a steep stairway into the basement section. Ceiling very low. Practically have to bend double.

Whole thing's making me feel very uncertain.

But there's my old gel. Little face buried in a huge menu. Gnawing on a breadstick like a hamster. Bless her.

She looks up.

"Hey hun!" she squeaks.

"Hey you," I say, leaning down.

Kiss kiss.

Take my seat. Right beside the desert fridge. Not much room. Have to shuffle my tiny wooden chair. A gang of tira misus looms evilly over my shoulder. There's a yellow rose in a glass vase on the table in front of me. My hands reach for it. Start fiddling. Don't know why.

Smarmbag waiter puts a menu beside me. About to glance down at it when I notice...

There's something different about the Penster. She's not looking at me like she usually does. And there's something else. Something fuzzy...

"It's so hard!" she says. "There're so many nice things."

Can't think about food, though. Still trying to work out the fuzziness. It's making my skin prickle.

"Um..."

Smarmbag waiter coughs.

"Look at it, Freddie!

"Huh?"

"Your menu, honey."

"Right."

Glance down. Oh bloody hell. Beckon the Penster towards me. She leans forward. Whisper:

"Have you seen the price of this shit?"

"Don't worry about it, Freddie."

"Twelve pound fifty," I say. "For a fish."

The smarmbag waiter bends at the waist. Leans his head down between us. Swivels to look at me. Swear I can smell his moustache.

"Eet a-comes on eets own salver wit' a saffrrron anda why-ate trrruffle soce," says the waiter.

"Don't care if it comes on its own bloody yacht," I mutter, "I'm having the soup."

"Oh, Freddie, come on!" laughs Pen. "My treat."

Your treat. This is definitely weird. There's something bigger in the room here. Bigger than this menu. Than the waiter. Than both of us. Something so big and so close and so fuzzy that I can't see what it is.

"Alright," I sigh. "I'll have the fish."

"Me too," smiles Pen at the smarmbag waiter.

The smarmbag waiter bobs and takes our menus. Slithers off to the kitchen.

"You okay?" she asks.

"Fine. Cool. Just not sure what the hell we're doing here, is all."

She swallows. Pushes a stray lock of brown hair away from her face. Takes a breath. So the thing is there for her too. She can't look at me.

"Freddie." She swallows again. "I sat with Mr Greaves at lunch today, and he–" she looks around the restaurant. "–he told me a secret."

Her mouth twitches. She looks down at her gnawed breadstick.

"Old Dr Stephanou is retiring..."

She pauses. Pushes the breadstick to one side. Takes another breath.

"...so they're after a new head of department. And..."

Still she isn't catching my eye.

"... they're going to offer it to me!"

She smiles.

Then she does something very odd. Pen reaches over the table and takes the rose from my fiddling hands. Looks at it for a second. Then she passes it back to me. Puts it in my hands and clasps her fingers round mine. Everything goes very, very quiet.

Then, finally, she looks directly at me.

"Freddie, will you marry me?"

And that's when I see the thing. It's in the lines. The tiny lines around her eyes that I never noticed before.

My little mouse is looking old.

She gulps. Says in a croak:

"Did you hear me?"

But I can't think straight. No way I can take this in. All I can think about is the hugeness of those wrinkles round her brown mouse eyes.

"Marry you?" my mouth manages.

"Why not? It's always been our plan, hasn't it?"

"Of course, of course," I mutter. "It's just that now isn't the best time, cash wise-"

"But that's the fabby thing. I'll get a raise with my promotion!"

No, this isn't right. Everything's going even fuzzier. Like I've put on someone else's glasses.

"M-m-maybe when I've sold the patent on the Unboiler-" I stammer.

"Oh, Freddie, you're always about to sell something-"

"What do you mean by that?" I snap, sitting upright.

"Nothing, nothing," she soothes.

And it's speeding up too. Like I've put on someone else's glasses and then got on a rollercoaster. Need to slow things down. Words. They can slow it. Got to say something, anything, get that tongue moving...

"Weddings cost a lot, you know," I say.

Pen leans right forward. Grips my hands even tighter. Cries:

"Oh, sweetie! You're all that's important to me. I don't care about a big do. Well, of course it would be nice, but not every girl can get married in a castle with hundreds of guests and champagne. We could do it our way. Find a beach up on the west coast, a little hotel. Dairloch maybe. Fish and chips and our family and friends and... the kind of fun you don't have to pay for... oh, Freddie, say we can do it!"

And she just hangs there. Her face furrowed to all hell. Looks in pain, like she's maybe stubbed her toe under the table. God, those damn lines. Like little bunches of cuts. What the hell are they? Not just age. What? Shit. Now I really see.

Mouse's face is full of fear.

Soon as I notice that, my heart lurches in my chest. Eyes twitch. Forehead goes tight. Hot all over. Can't bear to look at her. Drink the entire jug of water. Still can't look.

"Well?" she says, her fear eating her up.

Whole of my back goes itchy. Flick my eyes around the room and realise that EVERY FUCKER IS WATCHING ME!

The pressure's unbearable. Want to yell, want to tear my clothes off, want to flip the table high in the air with mighty paws when, to my own astonishment, I hear this coming gently from my mouth:

"Okay."

Pen looks confused.

"Okay what?"

"Okay, I'll marry you."

Her eyes shine.

"Really?"

"Absolutely, my little potato wedge. My idea of fun."

Well, the poor creature literally explodes. Tears, hugs, ice-cream kisses, hell of a mess. Chorus of cheers from paying punters. Clapping aplenty. Smarmbag waiter tries to sell us champagne. Not falling for that one.

Apparently we eat the meal, but I don't remember it. Reality's a blurred reflection of itself. Next time I come to, we're in a cab. Mouse more like an electric octopus. Promising.

Barely in the door back home and we're at it like bunnies on Benzedrine. Filling the house with love. Magnificent. First blowjob in nine months, would you believe. Followed by hot, close, loving rumpy. Very much felt like the right thing. Went to bed not unhappy. But then this morning...

~

Pen's bounced to work. Kiss kiss, love you madly my husband to be, there's so much we have to talk about, can't wait to see you later. More kisses, smile a mile wide and she's off. Mouse floats out the door and down the canal towpath past the brewery.

Ten minutes later I'm fixing a relaxing breakfast in my underwear. Shreddies. Shit, no milk. Going to the shop would involve putting on clothes. Arsed. Can't be. Decide to use cabernet sauvignon. Sorts the hangover out nicely, but does make cereal look a bit like afterbirth.

Watching Richard and Judy. No I'm not. Only manage to stick it for five then reach for the remote – Finnegan's starting to freak me out again – when up flips a report about the Oscars. Ceremony was last night. Actresses flashing parts of the body I didn't know existed. Maybe I'll watch this a couple of minutes more.

Smiles and legs and cleavages and more smiles and legs and Toni has come with Tom and who is going to win and who cares I'm bored again so grab the Frank again and-

There.

She.

Is.

Fucking look at her. Like sunshine poured in a dress. Heart flips in my chest. Lungs spasm. Brain seizes.

Course, I knew she was an actress. Who doesn't? She's been famous for a couple of years now. Broke through that horror movie about the boss from hell – The Zombie in Pinstripe Just Ate Daniella's Brain. Played the cute little photocopier girl. Didn't get her brain munched until the sixty-ninth minute and stuck it to a couple of zombies with the staple gun. Top effort, I say.

Been quite a buzz to see her up there. Often tell people in the pub – I nearly shagged her you know. Catch up with old friends – you see Lucy's doing well for herself? Yeah, she's up there all right. Hey, Freddie, didn't you nearly shag her once? That's right, dude. I nearly shagged her once. Had that conversation a fair few times. Fun. Feels good – I nearly shagged a star. Very much the man.

But today, it tears my heart out.

Yeah, I nearly shagged that girl. But more importantly – now I never will. Pen was my first and she will be my last. That is that. I will die having shagged only one woman. Because

I.

Am.

Getting.

Married.

Of course, it's not like I was ever going to shag Lucy now. I mean, what did I think? That she'll be on location in Scotland one time, doing a thriller about fucking oatcake farming or something and she'll be winding down having a drink or two only she won't go for a cocktail in some posh bar, she'll keep it real and go for a pint of eighty in the Diggers where I'll be butchering a Sudoku as I sip my Deuchars and she'll come in, golden sunlight suddenly flooding the high windows, and the place will stop, all the guys like totally focused as she scans the smoky room, head high, savouring every devouring stare and then our eyes will meet and she'll walk up to me – not you, pal, me, me, me – her incredible breasts swaying like caramel puddings, and she won't say a word, she'll just lick her ripe lips, wink one insanely blue eye, toss her superblonde hair and stick her hand down my North Face zip-offs–

Okay, so maybe I did think that. But only for a moment. And like I say, that's past now. Had my chance, blew it. Twat that I was I fucked it up. Ended up copping off with Pen instead at the Midwinter Beach Ball and that was great – here I am, about to marry the girl. College sweethearts. Almost as romantic as it gets–

But look at her!

On the telly there. Look at her breasts, her legs, hair. Her perfectly glamorous features taunting me from the screen. They were inches from mine once. Centimetres. Millimetres even. Naïve, cocky, idiotic young TWAT. If only I'd... I don't know. Done something different...

And then the strangest thing.

The air gets fat and still. Only sound's the squelch of disintegrating wheat lattices.

It drops into my brain. Complete and perfect. The best idea I will ever have.

Fling the remote to one side. Got to move fast. Got to get to B&Q.

~

A six-armed monkey god couldn't have got as much in that trolley in as short a time as I did. My hands fly, sweat pours, trolley groans, fathers pull children from under my speeding wheels. Out of breath, get to the checkout. Girl in the orange dungarees looks a bit scared when she sees me. Strange thing – must have been served by her a hundred times, but never really noticed how nice she is. Boss eyed and spotty, sure, but there's something about the way her eyebrows are hoisted in fear. How her lower lip droops open, quivering. Breasts so pert they make her nametag sit squint. Tempted to pull my trousers down and show her the old boy right then and there. Bad idea. Police involvement not helpful to plan. So I hand over Pen's VISA card and blow that joint.

Outside in the carpark and a wind is getting up. Starts to rain a little – oily, clammy drops. Trolley skids – old man with a hydrangea – shit, out of the way, you fool!

Uh oh.

Help him up. Apologise – keep it brief. Got to get going. Rain thickens on drive back, traffic abysmal. Frantic to get back to the lab – can't let this one get away. Jesus, now only one wiper working – wrong one, of course – have to drive with my head out of the window like a lobotomised labrador. Not good for barnet. Plus, car not performing, get home and smoke pouring from bonnet. Rain hissing into steam on the screaming metal. Silly arse, I've gone all the way in first gear.

Hah! Who cares? Genius sings in my blood.

Rain thickening rapidly. Abnormally dark for this time of day. Not that there's much light in our flat at the best of times – we live behind a vast brewery in an old lockkeeper's cottage on the canal. Cottage is dwarfed by angry chimneys spouting vapours. Pen wants to move but the place has magnificent cellars. Used for storing barrels some centuries past. Now make a perfect lab, connected to the basement of our cottage by a little tunnel that no one knows I know about. Besides, I quite like the smell.

Drains outside the cottage full with scum from the brewery overflow. Slip, slide, skid, flip flat on my back – narrowly avoid cracking my head open. Above me the sky growls a warning. Growl all you like, pal, I got work to do.

My legs are going like pistons as I ferry the kit in and down to the lab. First major question - what am I going to back in time in? My shaggy brown armchair? It would be a nice ride, but it's practically falling apart. The kitchen table? Sturdy, but difficult to hang onto if I hit any megamagnetic waves. I'm all set to go for the bath, until I remember I have never worked out where the stopcock is. Flooding Pen's cork tiles would get me in serious hot water. What can it be... ?

And that's when I realise. Not only will the brass frame give excellent nucleic stability in the temporal vortex, but it's damn comfy too. So comfy in fact that I often find it hard to get out of. It's perfect for my purposes. Our bed. One problem – the thing is an heirloom. Pen's great great Aunt Bazouki brought it all the way from Tangiers in a herring smack. Never mind, I have no choice. Think of something to tell the mouse later.

Dash up to the bedroom and wrestle our bed downstairs on

its side, only taking out a handful of banister struts. Clatter down into the cellar and through to the lab. Severe difficulty getting the damn thing in the door. Have to bend the frame a little.

Lab is a shitpit of deconstructed consumer electronics, empty claret bottles and Pot Noodles. Halves of hoovers, tubes from tellies, widgets from washing machines, all randomly mating in the half darkness with several of my own aborted creations... my digital golf clubs, the atomic dog neuterer, my machine for making tartan shortbread (what a market that would be). So many ideas, so many lost and lonely hours.

All got to go.

Gather up a tarpaulin and haul the whole lot outside into the dark wet yard. Rain even heavier now, big metallic drops hurting my skin through my sopping clothes.

KKKRASH!

Length of gutter smashes to earth beside me, shattering into rusty shards on the paving slabs. That was close. Sure that guttering was secure... Nevermind, can't hang around. Back inside – quick – to stand panting, my breath hanging in the air before me in icy puffs. Catch a view of myself in a broken piece of mirror. Physically, I may resemble a six-foot-six cat that just got flushed down the lavatory, but there's an intensity, a true fire in my eyes that thrills me. And I stop for a second-

-and just pause-

As a terrible confidence surges through me like a wave, and that's when I know for sure.

This is my time.

Inspiration's pouring through me like the rain in the gutters. Pull the bed into the middle of the room. Throw open every toolbox, empty every cupboard around the central space and start to build. Circuits, motors, tubing, solenoids, resistors, crystals: I don't see them, I sense them. My hands frantically trying to keep speed with the pace of my creation. My fingers are covered in oil and dirt and blood from a thousand plier nicks, but I don't care. Haven't felt this good in a long time. A long, long time.

And my baby is coming to life.

Every idea sends an atomic shot of adrenaline surging through my system. What's the time? Is it getting dark? Who cares? Fire up the sodium burners.

Pen comes home from work at some point and calls down to me. She's made coq au vin and wants to talk. Probably about wedding dresses or something, but I really don't know, because I barely hear her. And as she knows better than to come down to the lab, I can work undisturbed. Scoff half a donut that I find in the spanner drawer and continue.

"What are you doing with the bed, Freddie?" comes a plaintive call.

"Building a time machine, my little feather duster," I reply.

"Oh, Freddie," she says with gentle impatience. "Do you have to do that now?"

"Ah, most definitely."

"Where am I going to sleep?"

"The bath?"

"But–"

"Use the sponge as a pillow. Be comfier than you think."

Sssmasch! Tinkle!

A window's blown in. Swirling rain whips in through the jagged hole. Wind howls round the room. Knocks me sideways. Bash my head. Painful, goddammit.

"Honey, I have to bring these ideas to life before it's too late!" I yell up the stairs, then slam and lock the hatch. Put some Green Day in the stereo and Pen fades away. The rain is muted. We're rocking again.

And through the night I go.

On and on I work, fuelling myself with Chilean pinot noir and Starmix. As the rain outside gets harder and the night deeper, I begin to dance as I work. A spin here, a head bang there. Fun, but hot work. Take off everything apart from my underpants. Then they too have to come off.

Hours fly. The sun comes up, Pen goes to work with a

faint "Bye, sweetie". The only constants are the rain and my inspiration.

Everything is possible now. How to modulate the temporal magnetism? Not a problem – attach a proton extrapolator. What about the possibility of a charmed quark surge? Easy, just reverse the flux through a zeiss gate. Won't that polarise the gravitational overspill? Forget it! Run a pair of tronic conduits in parallel, increase the quantum flow, change the sheets and voila!

One inter-era double divan.

Can it really be? Have I created a time travelling bed? Yes. Am I really a genius? Double yes.

Arms windmilling, I run out into the street to tell the universe.

"I am the spawn of da Vinci and Edison" I sing, the rain thrilling my cavorting limbs. "And that cunt Dyson is history!" Roll my eyes and dance and sing some more, forgetting I am naked. A commuter looks at me fearfully from beneath his umbrella, but I don't care.

And then, disaster. With an almighty fucking KABLANNNGG!!! the sky over our house is ripped in two by a crazy scar of white-hot fire. The lightning bolt blinds me for a terrifying moment. Stagger, bashing into parked cars, cracking my shins on the curb. Then I curse as a creamy skid tells me my toes have connected with dogshit. When my sight returns I see the chimney pots are shattered, the TV aerial is melted and all the lights are off. Dash inside.

The lab is dead black. The air is thick with the acrid tang of burning plastic and roasted glass. Gag on the stench as I scrabble for the fusebox. Lights back on. Frantically check the bed. It can't be - it seems fine. The UV diodes are sound, the catalytic corkscrew is undamaged – even the sheets are still clean. I turn it on and –

FUCK! The lights blink on once and then dim to black. Power is good, but the readout screens are dead. The motherboard is fried.

That was the only computer I have. Even Pen's Switch card

can't afford another one. This is a complete disaster... It's not fair. So close and it's taken away from me... will things ever go my way? Not again. Please, not again.

This is the worst possible news.

But there's nothing else for it.

Going to have to go to work.

~

Ballantrae's is an astonishing labyrinth of a bookshop. The size of a department store, its six floors of crumbling gothic stonework have grown over the centuries to occupy a whole city block opposite the university.

Should have been in two hours ago. Impressive lateness even by my standards. New personal best, in fact. Sneak in the fire escape, up the back stairs, grab my timecard. Cut through the canteen, dispose of timecard in a large pan of hot custard. Stow my bag in my staffroom locker, walk along two passages and up three twisted staircases to very confidently slide onto the sales floor.

Ancient History section is where I work – one of the dozens of sections up in the Cunninghame Loft, the shop's many-levelled maze of attic floors. Aisles here branch like veins in a cadaver. Rooms have sprouted their own warrens of sub-passages and hidden nooks. Who knows where half of them go to. Found a dead law student in here once, turned out the lad had passed away in 1878.

Aisle upon towering aisle of creaking tomes press in on me from every side. My chest wheezes with the dust. Pick up a stack of books for shelving and head off to find Dougal. This is not tricky, he runs the Poetry section and is always stuck deep down his aisle, snout in a dusty book. I'm halfway across salesfloor 6F when a fierce hand grips my arm.

"Excuse me, young man," barks a metallic voice in my ear, "can you tell me where I'd find the Harry Potter section?"

Turn. Customer is a fat woman in pale coat buttoned very

tight. Dark brown scarf and hat. Customer looks very much like an enormous sausage, complete with HP sauce. She has a child, correspondingly upholstered. Child resembles chipolata.

Haven't got time for this.

Drop to my knees and take portion of sausage-skin coat in my teeth while making noise like lion.

Chipolata bursts into tears. Sausage's eyebrows shoot up and disappear inside HP hat. She loosens grip of my arm and flees in shock. Ha hah! Tactic successful. Jump to feet and nash off to resume my search.

There he is! My rotund quarry perches on a high stool staring vacantly at The Bell Jar. His too-small shirt has popped from his waist, freeing up a hefty baguette of doughy flesh that hangs over his straining polyester belt. There's a look of incredible sadness on his pudgy little face. Old boy needs cheering up. A quick recce and I locate a bulldog clip lying beside the nearest till and quietly palm it.

"Can you direct me to the Tennyson section?" I say.

"Certainly, sir-" he begins, and before he can turn round I reach across and attach clip to aforementioned baguette.

"Yow!"

Poor Dougal jack-knifes rapidly forward and headbutts the shelving, book flying from his pudgy fingers like a crazy bat. Customers pull their noses out of books to get a good eyeful.

"Hello, my hairy little pudding," I say, "how the hell are you?"

"That hurt," he says, slowly standing up and rubbing his nose. His voice is slow and heavy. The tiniest trace of a highland accent – but the lilt and sparkle it once had are long gone. Big brown eyes that look so mournful, like a spaniel that's just soiled in your slippers. Used to look very different. Quite a livewire. But he's been like this for so bloody long now, I can't possibly feel sorry for him.

"Just keeping you on your toes, Dougalicious," I say. "Listen, I need your help-"

He bends down and picks up the dropped volume.

"Freddie, can we do this some other time? I don't feel well."

Now he mentions it, he doesn't look at all well. His cheeks are drooping even more than normal. He looks like a dormouse that's eaten ball bearings.

"What is this?" I ask. "International Moping Day?"

He sighs. Smoothes the pages of poetry flat.

"It's the anniversary. Of when she... went."

Not that again.

"Oh right. Shit. Well, that's very sad. Really. And at any other time I would talk to you in great depth about this. But Dougal, this is urgent. Need your laptop, dude. Right now."

He sighs. His little bushy brows droop.

"What for?"

"Can't specifically tell you at this time, but what I can say is that you won't regret it."

He stares at me. Brows droop even further.

"No, Freddie."

Son of a bitch. Check left and right and then haul him into the darkest corner of the Alternative Religion aisle.

"How long have we known each other?" I ask, stabbing my finger in his face.

"A very, very, very long time," he says, sighing.

"So you know you can trust me."

"Hmmm."

"Gave you your stereo back the time I borrowed that, remember? "

"Yes, you did give me it back," he hisses, "filled with glue."

"Super-conducting resin–"

"For Christ's sake, Freddie, can't you just consider someone else's feelings for a change?"

And he turns away again. Why do they insist on pushing me? Drop one knee and launch myself. Good tackle. Not in the first XV at fourteen for nothing. Eventually get him to the floor and manage to pin him down.

"Give me your flat keys," I say.

"Mmmmppfffff!!" He's resisting. Fine. Go for his pockets. He wriggles like a ticklish anaconda in a feather factory, almost throwing me off, but I sit on his head and pull his hands away. There's a crack and a muffled yelp and I manage to thrust one hand in the front pocket of his cords, my fingers closing on the cool steel keys when suddenly I'm ejected vertically into the air.

Crunch down kidneys first on a stack of Russian philosophy textbooks.

Ooooooo.

Forgotten how strong the little fella could be.

Dougal stands up, dusts his corduroy trousers down.

"You're emotional, I can see. As is that mother over there. Have you been upsetting people again? What did you do to her?"

"Just took a little bite."

"Good god, man, why?!"

"Not eaten in twenty-four hours. Been inventing. Damn hungry. Customer resembled sausage," I explain.

In slow motion, Dougal covers his face with his hands, fingertips on eyes, palms on cheeks. He squeezes.

After a moment, he says:

"Calm down. Slow down. And explain, in as few clear words as possible, the reason why I should lend you my laptop."

Take a deep breath. Feel a bit shakey for some reason. I say:

"Disappointment with the Unboiler. Ran into Clive. Got engaged. Invented a time machine. Sort the whole thing out. Hence laptop."

"Okay, so you're going to need to give me just a few more words than that."

~

Probably should have explained this at the beginning. Whole story's a bit muddled up, sorry. So this happened yesterday...

A beeping thing is drilling into my brain. Thick fingers scrabble for tiny buttons. Peer at my phone.

Noon.

Why the hell would I set my alarm so early?

Look around for more data.

Slept in the lab again. My body is slouched in a swivel chair and my feet are propped up on a half-dismantled instrument panel in front of me.

Hell of a fog in the room, like I slept with contact lenses in. Don't wear contact lenses. Fog is in my head. Empty wine bottles lounge rakishly on my workbench. No sketchpads or notebooks around, so I can't have been using the wine to fuel an inventing session. Why was I in here?

The email!

Remember receiving it and getting very excited. So excited that only a large amount of wine and loud rock music could exhaust me enough to induce sleep. I think. What if my naughty brain made it up? Got to check the email. Wipe a couple of wine splashes off my trackpad and open my inbox. Nope, there it is, as real as my hangover:

To: freddiekeddie@gmail.com
From: t.fox@foxco.com
Date: 12.13pm 18 January 2016
Subject: Your prototype

Mr Keddie –

Thank you for the prototype of your latest invention, which you sent to our Kitchenware Team.

We are extremely keen to discuss the future of your idea with you.

Could you please come to present your device to our technical assessment board tomorrow at 1pm. Sorry to give you so little time, but this is the only day in the next month that our Managing Director will be in this office.

Most sincerely yours,

Marissa Piper
pp. The Managing Director
The Foxco Corporation

You beauty. World fame here we come. Sir Tom Fox, the founder and MD of Foxco got rich and famous for inventing the first washing machine in the world that doesn't judder like a motherfucker. Then one genius gadget after another. Today I get to pitch my invention to his den of dragons. No problem.

First, need to look the part. Can't go as I am – peach dressing gown with the rabbits on the back and the front burnt out. Eccentricity has always been an accepted part of an inventor's personal style; indecency might be frowned upon.

Head back through the tunnel and up from the basement into the cottage. Root through the few clothes I have for something interview-worthy. There's my Einstein-with-his-tongue-out T-shirt – not exactly formal, but it shows I have a role model. Man like Sir Tom will approve of that. It's winter, though, so I'll need a top layer and some trousers. Something on the smart side.

Of course! – my dinner jacket! Jacket's generally okay, if a bit tight around the shoulders, back, sides and front. Pull on the trousers. Damn moths have launched an assault on the left leg. Large area of my pasty thigh is visible. Dammit, what sort of brewery has moths? But I own no other breeks even half as dandy. What to do. Aha, a genius notion! Fossick in a sideboard drawer, find a chisel-tipped marker pen and use it to blacken a four-inch square section of my leg skin. Pull the damaged trousers up again and – the illusion is perfect! Well, the raggedy rim of the hole flaps a bit, and the marker ink is more green than black, but Sir Tom Fox won't be looking at my damn thighs.

Finally footwear. Well, this really is a Hobson's choice as for several months now the only shoes I have owned are the pair of over-sized yellow duck boots that I found in the brewery pump room.

Gulp some leftover Greek merlot for Dutch courage and head to the bus-stop.

~

Steel door. Set in a glass wall. Door is in the shape of a 'T' and an 'F' mating in an earnest logo. As I approach, the letters slide apart. Step through into an atrium four floors high. A waterfall pours from nowhere into a fish-filled pool. Apparently hovering above the pool is a large glass desk with a girl behind it. There's no one else about, so I figure she must be the receptionist. As I walk towards her, stepping stones rise up from the pool to meet my feet.

Pretty girl in glasses. Scythe of black hair slashes her face. Eyebrows by Picasso. In a vase on the desk in front of her is a large bunch of creamy magnolias.

"Hi there-" I start.

"We already have a window cleaner, thank you."

"Here to see Sir Tom."

The artistic eyebrows take off like two Harrier jump jets and disappear beneath the scythe of hair.

"Freddie Keddie," I say.

Looks me up and down. Checks her smartwatch.

"You're very, very late," she says at last.

"Moths."

~

Glassy, classy room. Big windows looking out on the snow-cloaked Pentland Hills. One blackout blind drawn down against the low winter sun.

My metal invention shines on an even shinier walnut desk. Other side of the desk are the girl in glasses and what seems to be a five-foot owl stuffed into a suit. In a chair set away from the desk, in the shadow of the blind, sits another figure. Must be Sir Tom. Famously secretive.

"I am Marissa. This is Dr Feldspar, our head of new technology. Our managing director is at the end. You have two minutes to tell us why we should invest in your invention."

"Okay. So... ah..." Feeling a bit hot in this damn dinner jacket. Odd itching tells me there might be some previously undetected moths about to emerge from my crotch area. Words aren't flowing as normal. Better step things up a bit. Stand up and throw my arms open wide. Yell:

"Embrace your privilege, mortals! For ye three be the only three humans to yet behold... the Unboiler! This will be a boon to cooks, chefs and ordinary households throughout the world! It will save energy, cut waste, reduce effort."

Silence.

"What does it do? you ask. And I'm glad you asked. So, you madam. Housewife. You know how when you're cooking vegetables you somehow always cook too much? No matter how carefully you follow the recipe there's always mashed potato left in the pan. Or some turnip that nobody wants. And sprouts. Jesus. Endless fucking sprouts. Too many for little children to eat. Am I right?"

More silence.

"And that food – those precious, if less than tasty vitamins – it all goes to waste. Which is money in the bin. Gas you needn't have used. Preparation time you can never get back."

Raindrops suddenly dapple the windows. As soon as they hit, they slide clean down the glass and leave no trail. Surface must have been treated with some revolutionary new coating...

electrostatic polymer perhaps, or... Got to concentrate! Must sell this!

"Well, my device will do away with all of that. You see, it takes that boiled food and, by passing it through a molecular field matrix and reversing the ionic polarity, returns your dinner to its raw, uncooked state. I call it, THE UNBOILER!"

Feldspar the owl gives his feathery head a little shake and leans forward from the waist.

"Thank you for your pitch. Mr Keddie," he says. "Most informative. But we must now be honest with you – we were so intrigued by your idea that we have already tried it out."

Could this really be? After all these years – success?

"And... it worked?"

"Yes indeed. A kilogram of boiled carrots was returned to its pristine state."

"Fantastic!"

"However, this displacement only lasted ten minutes and three seconds. Then the carrots once again assumed their boiled state. Mushy state, really."

"Great start. Not an insurmountable problem."

"You're right. But what is insurmountable, however, is that fact that when it 'unboiled' those carrots, your device shorted our main fuse, melted our transformer and blew a promising employee into the Royal Infirmary."

"So the Unboiler needs development. We can work on it." I nod to the figure beyond the table. "Tom Fox started off small."

'Yes, but he didn't start off mad. Mr Keddie-" Feldspar throws his hands up in the air- "I don't know what to say to you."

Now comes the voice from the shadows.

"Did you know... did you know that Paul McCartney left the Beatles when he was twenty-seven?"

My skin shrinks a little relative to my body, because I know that voice. Far-off but also hatefully familiar, like the shout of a bully from the far end of a school corridor.

"Funny thing isn't it, this time lark," continues the voice. "No ssssooner do you have it-" the voice extends his Ss, not in a lisp, but in a savouring hiss – "than it slithers away from you."

And the managing director's chair somehow slides noiselessly out of the shadows on unseen wheels, bringing into the light a slippery little codfish of a man.

Clive.

Ever-wet purple lips that when not talking always rest half-open in a hungry pout. Cold wet eyes that seem to be looking at a point behind the back of your skull. A sheen to the skin.

Clive may be the same as ever, but his togs have certainly changed a bit. Rolex strangling his bony wrist. Shiny silk tie. Suit as sleek as the back of an iPad. Probably cost the same as six months of my mortgage payments. Not that I pay the mortgage, that's Pen's bag. Still, you get the idea.

"Hi Clive," I say.

"Sssuper to see you again, Freddie."

He drops his wet hand into mine. All that money. Still couldn't buy himself a decent handshake.

"Have to ask," I say, pulling my fingers out from the inside of a slug. "What happened to Sir Tom?"

"Where have you been living for the last six months?" Clive sneers.

"A brewery."

"Is that sssso? Well, Sir Tom cashed in. Sold his company to a hedge fund. My hedge fund. One of my hedge funds."

Clearly wants me to ask how many hedge funds he has. Make me feel small when he tells me the answer. Not going to play that game. Best avoid the subject, particularly as I don't have the first idea what a hedge fund is.

"Which brings you here," I say.

"Oh no. I don't normally get involved at this level. But when I heard about this invention – and the incredible mess it made of my beautiful new facility – I had to come and see you. Catch up a little."

Ever get the feeling that you're in a conversation where the other person has a script and you don't? Me. Now.

"Came here to talk about the Unboiler," I say, deepening my voice.

"You look older, Mr Keddie," Clive continues in exactly the same tone. "Older than when I saw you last, obviously. That is to be expected. But also older than one ought to look at thirty-three. Perhaps it's your lifestyle."

Isn't listening to me. Has a point to make.

"I remember you were religious once, so you'll know that Jesus was crucified at thirty-three. Young, but he'd managed to accomplish a few things."

He's been thinking about this for years. Got to stop him making that point. Going to try going left field.

"Broccoli definitely works."

Clive pauses, purple lips pouting open. Got him! Oh yes, if we're going random, I can fig otter with the best of them.

But Clive recovers, swimming on.

"Einstein, who I see you are wearing on your undergarment, elucidated Special Relativity when he was just twenty-five."

"I'll accept that boil-in-the-bag curries occupy a greater volume when unboiled-"

Clive wafts a fin-like hand in the air and moves it in time with his syllables.

"However, thirty-three, the age we are, is a handy measure. It's a time by which a man ought to have made at least one leap along his chosen career path if, I feel, he is to get anywhere. Scientist, artist, tradesman; this rule holds true for all."

"-but they still taste okay."

"Did you know that Sean Connery was James Bond by our age? Being the hero. Getting the girls. Tailored in the best suits. Flying hither and thither. And here you are. Dressed like a refugee who's wearing the clothes the other refugees took off when the Oxfam truck rolled into camp."

Question now is how hard I can hit him by the time I get over the desk. Thinking about the angles when-

"Do you two know each other?" asks Marissa suddenly.

Clive's cod lips part in a futile attempt at a smile.

"We had a friend in common."

Now I see where this is going. Well, he's not going to get me there. Too close to home. Stand up. Shove my chair back. Turn towards the door and take a step towards it but my foot freezes in mid-air because somewhere an unseen button is pressed and a huge image is suddenly projected on the internal wall to my left.

My heart leaps in my chest like a salmon.

It's her.

She's on stage, clutching her Oscar, a split turquoise dress revealing the lines of her breasts and reflecting the magic of her eyes.

This is going to sound odd, because God knows I love the Penster, but just a glimpse of that picture causes a physiological short circuit in me. Short circuit in my cock, if I'm totally honest. Can't help it. Just can't.

Clive's mouth splits in his non-grin again.

"I see you still feel for her," he says. "Not surprising. She is - was - is still - quite, quite magnificent." He goggle-eyes the picture up and down, up and down, his slimy little tongue pinned between his fleshless lips like a flap of kelp. Suddenly occurs to me Clive might be happier in the ocean. Make mental note to take him down to Portobello beach sometime and shove him in.

"Look at young Marissa here. A beauty is she not? Yet nowhere near the equal of Lucy, you must agree?"

Streak of sadness blemishes Marissa's face.

"Don't agree to be rude," I say.

"Look at the way her lips hang open," he continues, pointing at the photo projected on the wall. "Like they're waiting for something... Reminds me of the time those lips were waiting for me."

Marissa's eyebrows disappear under her hairline again. Clive turns to her.

"Oh, didn't you know? It's true. My friend here will verify. We were at St Mary's university together. Lucy Sugar spent a term with us before she went to LA. Incredibly, this princess of the film world actually had quite a thing for Keddie here. It looked very much like he was going to make it with her. Wouldn't you say, old friend? It was in the blesssssed bag."

Clive slides one fin-hand into the other.

"And then, at the Midwinter Beach Ball, to the complete surprise of all concerned, he made a fox's paws of the whole thing. Ended up with a girl called Penelope, I don't remember much about her, a ssssweet sort of creature perhaps, but I'm sure even Keddie would agree, not fit to lace up Lucy's six-inch strappy sssssandals."

My heart stops pumping blood. Starts ramming white hot steel through my veins instead.

Clive leans forward on the desk, steeples his fins, licks his purple lips and says:

"So anyway, I fucked Lucy Sugar-"

Marissa shifts her weight in her chair.

"-and she was absolutely phenomenal." Clive slowly brushes imaginary dust from the lapel of his jacket with his left fin-hand. "It was really rather remarkable. Her breasts, for example, were sssssimply superhuman." Marissa crosses her legs. Leather squeaks as Clive eases back in his big chair. "But I shan't bore you with the sordid details. I'm sure you've imagined them yourself, Keddie, many times over in the past. What you may not realise, though, since I haven't seen you for so long, is that from that single electric moment on, Lucy Sugar became something of a lucky charm to me. She took me with her when she went to LA, if you remember. I was a producer on her first movie. That success brought more movies. We parted on the best of terms to focus on our careers. You can do more... interesting things... out of the limelight, I found. I moved into finance. Became an investor. And here I am. In front of you. After all these years."

He leans forward, stares right at me, his cold wet eyes wide open.

"You know what? I think my firm will buy your Unboiler. For £2.40. The price of a pint of cider in 2002."

~

"One thing I don't understand," says Dougal, "is if you managed to get across the table and land a punch on him, how come you're the one who's been beaten to a bloody pulp?"

"Security guard. Built like the rock of Gibraltar but somehow didn't see him. Bastard was hiding right in the corner by the blind."

Dougal looks at me. Finished filling him in. Don't know what the hell it is, but my eyes smart. They start to water. Hayfever, maybe. Odd in January, but there you go.

"It's really important to you, isn't it?"

"What?"

He sighs.

"You can borrow my laptop if you like."

Hoist myself onto my elbows. Wince with pain.

"Really?"

"As long as you let me watch the experiment. And there's no glue involved."

"Superconducting resin," I murmur.

"That too."

My ducts are definitely filling with liquid.

"Are you serious?" I manage.

"Come on," he says, "I'll buy you a coffee."

He puts his arm round me and lifts me to my feet. Feels so good I let it rest there, even when the pain stops.

~

Back at the flat and I'm hoping the Penster isn't home from work yet, so I have time to make preparations for Dougal's arrival and my departure into the past. Alas, just in door and I get hit by a supersonic love-crazed fiancée. She moves so fast down the hall I don't see her until she's three feet away at which point she launches herself at me, clamping her arms and legs around my torso like a grippy koala round a pencil. Flattened against the door, breath knocked out of me, smothered in kisses, hard to breathe – very.

"Mmmmggecgghhh Fffffff!"

"It's good to see you my darling husband-to-be. I've missed you so much today. Oh, kiss, me won't you!"

She hugs me hard, unfortunately twisting my throbbing shoulder.

"Ow-ow-ouch!' I yelp. "Much as I adore cuddles, my elegant little cover drive, I don't really think I have the time for this right now."

Long pause. Very pained look.

"I was only saying hello," she says quietly.

God, she suddenly looks old again. Wish I could come back in the front door and do that one again, but I can't. Best press on. Move away towards the cellar.

"Where are you going?"

"Work."

She moves round in front of me.

"Could we talk for a minute first?"

"What about?"

"Come into the kitchen."

"No time–"

"Please Freddie, I'm only asking for two minutes," she adds with her little brown eyebrows raised in hope.

Bloody hell, I feel like I'm ten years old again. It's Christmas day and I've been given a Meccano set. The best present ever. Unbelievable excitement. No sooner do I get it unwrapped than I'm summoned to go to Grandma's house. Have to leave the Meccano set agonisingly unplayed with under the tree as I'm whisked off for an afternoon of oversized sweaters and pan drops. Come back later and we've been burgled. Meccano set taken clean away. Hard lesson learnt very well: never ever, if you can at all help it, go to Grandma's house.

Glance eagerly down to the lab as Pen leads me through to the kitchen. Be with you soon, baby, I whisper.

"What?" she asks, turning her head.

"Wasn't talking to you," I say with a reassuring smile.

In the kitchen and a wall of hot sweet air flattens my nose as I enter. Fresh pastries cram every surface. There are acres of apple pies, bomb-heavy fudge brownies, empire biscuits dripping with jam and icing, donuts piled like treasure, and more scones than you can shake an éclair at. She loves her baking, but I've never seen anything like this before.

"I thought we'd have a little party," she says, crossing her hands in front of her pinny like a schoolgirl caught talking in class.

"What kind of party?" I say, "a wake for our arteries?"

"An engagement party, silly. Tomorrow's Friday, we could just have a few people over after work. You could make some punch, you like doing that." And she smiles at me.

"What few people?"

"I was thinking, Phil and Ruth, Pete and Clare, Mark and Jill..."

"See a pattern here."

"...and my parents would love to come."

"Oh God, no."

"Come on, Freddie, their only daughter just got engaged. Mummy is practically bursting with excitement. And Daddy wants a word with you.'

"Bet he does."

"He's over the moon!"

"Look, can this not wait? I'm at a crucial stage with my latest invention. You throw a spanner in the works now and it could put me years behind."

"But- but- people are happy for us. They want to share. And I'd love to-"

BRRRIINGG!!!

"I'll get it," I say, "stay here." And I dash out of the door.

Sprint down the hall, open the front door. It's the potato-faced wonder himself. He's depressed again. Can tell that because he's wearing his tracksuit. Shabby chocolate-brown number. Used to wear it when we'd run on North Sands together. But that was fourteen years ago. Fitted him well at first, but as he's got fatter over time it's stretched and frayed. Now it makes him looks like a big jobbie. But he always goes back to it when he's stressed.

'Got it?" I ask.

"Good to see you, too, Freddie."

"Come in!" I hiss, and bundle him through the doorway.

"You said come fast, so I didn't stop for tea–"

"Who is it, honey?" comes a plaintive voice from the kitchen.

"Oh, Pen's here. I'm glad," he says.

"Shush," I whisper, clamping my hand over his mouth. "Quick! Get down those stairs," and start bundling him down to the cellar. Too late. The kitchen door creaks open.

"Oh, Dougal!" Pen claps her hands together a few times. "How lovely to see you! Have you come for supper?"

Smile breaks over his pudgy face.

"Dougal's not here to get fatter," I say. "He's here to help me with my latest invention. Testing stage. Most important. Critical in fact." And I recommence shoving him down the trapdoor.

"He'll have some tea, though?" smiles Pen.

"Wine downstairs."

"Surely a little cake?"

"No."

"I'd love some cake," says Dougal, tearing my hand from his mouth with a vicious little swipe. "I'm sure Freddie can spare me for five minutes. And I want to give you these."

Little pudding only goes and pulls out a bunch of flowers!

"Oh, Dougal, they're lovely. How sweet of you! Come through."

Glare at the son of a bitch. "Make it quick," I hiss. He pretends not to notice as I follow them into the kitchen.

"Here, have a plate. Help yourself to cakes, I'll put these in some water and get the kettle on. How are you? You're looking well. How's your mum? Gosh, it seems like ages since we chatted."

"I know. It must be five months, Penelope. Too long."

"These flowers really are lovely Dougal. But you know, you should have given them to Freddie. After all, I asked him!"

Pause. Dougal looks confused.

"Asked him what?"

Pen looks confused.

"Asked him to marry me, of course!"

Longer pause. Yet more confusion on the face of the rotund one.

"You're getting married?"

"Of course... I thought... didn't Freddie say?"

She stares at me, eyes wide, hair going wild, panic rising.

"Of course I told him, my little Chelsea boot. He just forgot. Didn't you, Dougal?"

Dougal glares at me. Then sees the creased lines of hope in Pen's face. Good old boy wisely decides to lie.

"Sorry, Penelope, it's been one of those days." He looks at me with black eyes. "Why else would I have brought you flowers?"

It's a slim lifeline but Pen grasps at it. Poor girl really is desperate.

"That's okay, Dougal darling–"

"Well, time waits for no man," I say and push him – fat paws still clutching a plate of cakes – towards the door.

"Oh. Yes. You boys have work to do..."

"See you soon, Penelope," says Dougal simperingly.

Finally. The door is shut and we're heading down to the lab. Excitement jolts through me. Suddenly there she is again, peering down the trap at us.

"I almost forgot. Dougal, I know it's short notice, but we're having a little gathering tomorrow. To celebrate, you know. Nothing fancy. Just drinks. And some cakes, obviously..."

"Penelope, I wouldn't miss it for the world." And he winks at her like he's Cary fucking Grant or something. She smiles, and they wave. Christ.

Shove him off the step. He lands with a yelp and a crunch and

I slam the trapdoor shut behind us, shutting out Pen's squeaking concern.

"You're not making this any easier for me, you know," I say.

He dusts himself off slowly.

"I'm not sure this is the right time for this, Freddie."

"You saw what she's done with the cakes," I say, holding out my hand for his computer case. He hangs on to it. "What better time could there be?"

"Penelope's so excited about your engagement. I think she wants to chat. You know? Make plans and stuff. For the party, for wedding."

Spin to face him fully and jab a finger in his face.

"Listen, Dougal, you have to get a little perspective on this. She has baked some cakes – I have invented a time machine. Okay? All this cakes and parties bullshit can wait. And if you're so fucking keen on flowers, here..." Reach over to the mantel. Reach in between the stacks of empty Pot Noodle pots. Pull out the yellow rose Pen gave me last night. "...have this." And I open his mouth with one and jam the rose in with the other, then clamp his jaw shut. "Now come on, give me your laptop."

With hugely annoying slowness he takes the rose from his mouth. Looks at it very carefully like it's something precious. Then he places it carefully on the mantelshelf, clearing a little space for it amid the clutter.

"You've invented a time machine?" he says at last.

"Yes!" I snap.

"So it doesn't really matter if you spend an hour with her now, does it? You can just go back a little earlier in time when you turn it on. In fact, you could spend the whole evening with her."

"Hilarious," I say, and poke him in the belly. He exhales loudly and doubles up. Grab his computer and steer him gently towards an armchair.

Before Dougal has time to recover I put the laptop on Pen's pillow and plug it into the temporal displacement engine that hangs, like some crazy crustacean, from the opposite side of the brass frame, at the top of the bed. Then, while it boots up – POP! – I open a nice bottle of South African Merlot.

"You're going to travel in time in your bed?" wheezes Dougal as I pour some wine into a handy flowerpot.

"Pen's great great aunt Bazouki's bed, strictly speaking," I reply, gulping vino. "I hope you charged the battery," I add as I boot up the laptop and start a systems check. Outside I hear the rain start again.

"You want some of this?" I say, offering him the bottle. "It's the shit."

"No, thank you."

"Suit yourself," I say, and take another pull.

"So, Mr Time Traveller, when are you and Pen's great great aunt's bed going to?"

"Two thousand and two."

Can feel his dopey little mole eyes scanning me.

"That's two thousand and two, A.D.?"

"Aha."

Long pause. The silence is nice. But the rain is getting harder. A lot harder.

"Of all the eras in history, all the fascinating ages, you're going back fourteen years?"

"That's right."

Very long pause. The rain is now a wild pounding in the yard outside, clattering off the junk out there. Can still feel Dougal's eyes burning into me as I work. He's bugging me now.

"Why are you doing this?"

"For the glory of scientific discovery and the benefit of mankind."

"And the real reason?"

Stop working. Look up at him. And as I slowly say these simple words, to my own astonishment, my voice cracks a little:

"Can't you guess?"

And then all at once he gets it.

"Not Lucy Sugar!" he cries, and outside lightning smashes to earth with a deafening crash.

"Why not Lucy Sugar?!" I yell back as a crescendo of thunder rolls overhead.

"After all these years, I thought you might have finally forgotten her."

"How could I forget... that?

"So, what, you're going to go back in time and impress her with your big shiny time machine and finally get her to sleep with you? That doesn't strike you as a little insane?"

"Only ever prodding one woman your entire life. That's insane. Christ – even you've copped off with three. Four if you count that sympathy handjob from the backwards girl in Peebles."

"I did not... that is, she wasn't backwards... she had Asperger's... not that you can even say 'backwards' now... and anyway, you're avoiding the issue," he splutters. "The point is that you're about to defy the physical universe just so that you can cheat on Penelope, your partner of over thirteen years, the love of your life!"

"Are you mental?" I say. "Never do that to the Penster. Love the old sausage." I pause for a second, stare out at the rain. "But you can't deny that Lucy Sugar was... something else. Her tits were nothing short of miraculous. Deny that, go on."

Pause. Little donut says nothing.

"Exactly. And if only I hadn't buggered things up on the Three-Legged Pub Crawl, I could have shagged that miracle."

"It's getting engaged, isn't it?" soothes Dougal. "The surprise of the event has triggered a desperate panic reaction in you. It's okay, Freddie, it's totally understandable."

"It's not understandable at all, furball!" I say. "I can see no good reason at all why an eighteen-year-old virginal cretin was give complete control of MY life at a key moment. We both know what an absolute arse he was-"

"I quite liked the fella," muses Dougal.

"-taking stupid vows, refusing to listen to reason, sticking his stubborn head in the sand and missing golden opportunities. He missed his chance with that girl, Clive took it and look where we've ended up. Well, I'm going to rectify that. She's going to be my lucky charm, not his."

Dougal shakes his head. Laughs a little.

"I don't even know why I'm bothering myself. We both know time travel is completely impossible."

"Is it?" I say, and pull the sash cord that starts the initiation sequence. With a mighty growl the proton subtractor comes online. The bedframe begins to oscillate. Outside, the rain smacks down fatter than ever. The thunder rolls nearer.

"Frederick," he starts, his tone slow and serious. "Let's just say you do travel in time. If you sleep with Lucy Sugar, whether you do it now or in two thousand and two, that is being unfaithful."

"No, it's not," I reply, equally solemnly.

"Yes. It is."

Grab my wine bottle, raise my eyes to heaven and yell, "Is this the price of genius? To be surrounded by morons?" A searing double flash of lightning sears the basement onto my retina in negative form. The double crash of thunder that follows shatters my thoughts. It takes a long pull of wine to clear them. Turn to Dougal. "When did I start going out with Pen?" I yell.

"Er, first year. Two thousand and two."

"Right, but when exactly?"

"Fresher's week."

"That's when we met, yes. But we didn't get together until the Midwinter Beach Ball, at the end of term, right?"

"Right..."

"Right," I help him, "so if I can get him to shag Sugar before that, then..."

"Hang on," says Dougal. "If you can get who to shag her?"

"Him," I shout, pointing to a picture sitting on top of a Sweet and Sour Kingpot on the mantelshelf. Dougal steps over and picks up the frame. Wipes it off. Looks at it intently for a second, then stares up at me, his expression exactly like that of a hedgehog meeting its first and last Range Rover.

"HAH!" I snort, "now you get it, don't you? Now you see the genius at work here."

He's quiet for a moment as I set the gravitational neutralisers. The oscillations double in frequency. The rain is so loud now that we have to raise our voices to talk.

"Let me get this straight," he says slowly. "You have built a time machine to help your nineteen-year-old self get laid?"

Smile at him.

"It won't be cheating if my younger self does it," I say. "If I can get nineteen-year-old Freddie to rod Lucy Sugar before he hooks up with Pen at the Midwinter Beach Ball, bingo! – I will gain the memory of shagging her, but not the guilt of cheating on Pen, for the simple reason that I haven't done it. It will have happened before we got together. In two thousand and two. As well as the memory, I get the halo of success and the luck she gave Clive. You have to admit, Dougalicious, that's rare."

Little pudding can only stare. Knew he'd be impressed.

Eventually he says:

"At the very least, it's an unethical use of science–"

"You think Newton thought of gravity for ethics? You think Einstein came up with relativity for the Nobel prize? Balls! They did it for the fanny."

Gulp some wine, swipe my mouth with the back of one meaty hand and slam the bottle down.

"How is it powered?"

"Gravitational waves. Thanks to those yank physicists proving they exist, all we have to do is use them. These waves can stretch a planet out of shape in a femtosecond, so they can easily bump a double bed up a dimension or two. Just got to focus them."

"With... ?"

"A singularity."

"A black hole?!"

"Frig no! You mad? Nothing like that big. More nuggetty. About the size of... size of... well, your bell-end."

"A black hole the size of my bell-end. You are completely

insane."

"All we have to do is focus the gravitational waves using my innovative and stylishly finished Unboiler to initiate the singularity. When that stabilises between the zeiss gates, we will have a tachyonic anti-telephone – our wormhole. As long as it stays stable we will be displaced in time. When it decays, we return. Nifty, huh?"

"It's an improvement on the wind-powered photocopier, I'll give you that."

"You, my over-fed friend, are about to witness the biggest scientific breakthrough since the invention of the electric guitar! Now all we need is some source material and we're go. Pass me that box, will you?"

Dougal's too stunned to do anything but obey. He picks up the shabby cardboard box I was pointing to.

"What's this junk?"

"This 'junk' is everything I have from my university career," I say.

"Oasis posters and beermats, mainly," says Dougal, fossicking with a fat paw.

"Give it here, cretin," I say, snatching a bunch of papers. "I need this for the timeframe reference hopper. You see, this isn't Back to The Future. This is reality. You can't just type a date into some keypad and turn up there. This machine is designed to take a human being through time, so it needs a human reference point. An alkali solution of my first year matriculation card should do the trick."

Flick the card into a beaker and pour in the fluid. Outside, the rain is cracking down like nails from a Hilti gun. Thunder bangs furiously overhead.

"The machine uses sub-atomic dating to scan the source material and determine when it was created. Then it converts that reading into a magnetic field, magnifies it until it surrounds the entire bed, and then – and this is the important bit – reverses it through the wormhole created by the singularity, pulling whatever's inside the field out through time and space and guiding it to the source location."

Drop the cardboard on the floor and kick it under the bed. With a final triumphant swig I gulp down the last of the wine and hurl the bottle across the cellar to smash in a corner. And suddenly, oddly, I notice the rain has completely stopped. There's nothing. No drumming of falling water, no, grumbling from the heavens, no crashing lightning. Just Dougal panting loud over the silence.

Nothing left to wait for now. I tighten the cord on my dressing gown and climb on the bed. Nice and comfy. Always liked this bed.

"Well, Dougal baby, I will see you in about a quadrillionth of a second. Nothing will change to you, but I will have the memory of sticking my bobby in Lucy Sugar's pert little tumshy. Farewell."

Press the green button marked, "Let's rock!"

Nothing happens. For a long, long moment.

Press the button again.

Still nothing.

Kick the bromide optimiser. Yet again, zip.

"Fine," says Dougal. "You tried. Now can we go and see Penelope?"

And then there is the quietest little creak. A tiny shift of metal in the springs. Like Pen just turned over in her sleep. And from outside there comes a gentle 'pit'. Then another. 'Pat'.

It's raining again.

Humming starts somewhere beneath me. Bed begins to shake. Brass joints creak against themselves and the mattress springs groan. Then as soon as it started, the movement stops. There is one last little rattle, then utter silence.

Dougal smiles at me. "Did you really think-" he starts.

And then the entire bed leaps three feet into the air and with an almighty crack! eight giant white whips of writhing current leap out from the tops and bottoms of the bed posts. Dougal is flung tumbling through the air onto the wind-powered photocopier. The whips halt about three feet from the bed and then splay out as if on the inside of a giant sphere. They snap and twist, forming a living, surging network of veiny currents around me. Damn bed rocks around in the maelstrom like a drunken lilo, almost flipping me onto the deck.

Dougal gathers himself and looking across the room with fear on his face. The currents are leaping and cracking around the bed like demented snakes. With a deafening, surging pulse they double in intensity. The bed is in the middle of a crackling white orb that stretches from floor to ceiling and out around its sides.

Now the orb begins to oscillate, whumping in and out like a giant electric heart. The writhing currents accelerate into a wild white frenzy. Smile to myself – it's really happening!

Whummp! The orb suddenly contracts and white hot pincers squeeze my brain.

"Christ!" I bellow, "the reversal is starting!"

Haven't moved till now – too astonished – but the pain snaps me out of it. It's happening. Gotta work fast. Dive to the laptop. Hands fly over the keyboard, firing control commands to the pulsating machinery.

Whummp!

Yow! Another vice-like blitz of agony.

Whuummpp!

Fuuuck! It's getting worse.

"It's going too fast!" I scream. "Help me!" But the wondermuffin is too terrified to move. Shit, I gotta do this alone. Have to modulate the reversal or I am – quite literally – history. My fingers are a blur over the laptop keyboard as I try to change the settings. Concentration holds my body like steel guy ropes.

WHUUUMMP! Aaarrgh! Another violent contraction, another bolt of pain. Not long. Any second now. Got to complete the instruction…. hit enter… and suddenly music blasts my skull, resonating across the orb.

"What the fuck is that!?" I scream.

"ELO," squeaks Dougal. "Livin' thing."

"No shit," I bellow. "What the fuck's it playing for?!"

"You must have opened iTunes. You can shut it down again – just double click on the icon."

WHUUUMMMPPP!! The orb makes another soul churning contraction. It's now only just bigger than the bed. Any second now...

"It's a livin' thing, diddle iddle iddle oo, such terrible thing to loooose..."

"You shut it down," I yell.

And that's when Dougal's brain capsizes.

"Oo, hang on a sec," he says and calmly steps away from the bed.

"Where the fuck are you going?!" I scream.

The orb is changing colour now, from white to blue to blood red.

"Need to get the rose," he mutters, and makes his way across the room.

"What?!"

"It's a givin' thing, diddle iddle iddle oooo..."

Don't believe it. Silly idiot's going for the flower Pen gave me last night.

"What the hell do I need a rose for?!"

He shrugs his shoulders. "Luck, I guess," he says.

Suddenly the machine kicks up another level – the snakes are whipping so fast they blur into one shimmering electric mass.

"Leave it, you fat idiot! Get back here and turn this off."

But her keeps moving towards the flower – and cracks his shin on a wine crate. Stops to rub the bruise. God, I want to kill him.

A red light flashes on the display and the old police siren I bought from a junkyard starts up – shit, I know what that means.

"It's reversing!" I yell.

He pushes himself to his feet like Paddington Bear and stumbles through the clutter to where the yellow rose sits between an empty Kingpot and a bottle of Shiraz.

"KKERRRAACCCKKKKK!" My brain practically shatters. A tiny something has sprung into being in the direct centre of the orb. It's like a black dot – but it's not black as a colour, it's more like a complete absence of anything at all.

The singularity.

The air begins to swirl and spin and reality starts disappearing into it.

The music is intensified by the energy field. It's like molten metal pouring through my brain. My fury at Dougal is a hot fountain inside me.

"...tear your fucking ears off, you stupid bastard..." I mutter.

The swirling is getting faster. The wormhole is growing as spacetime is sucked in. It's now the size of a football. Move myself up to the top of the bed – but it's got the bottom of my dressing gown. My rabbits are disappearing into infinity. The room outside the orb is fading from view – I can just see Dougal reaching the rose.

"GET OVER HERE!" I scream.

He turns, walks back towards the bed and trips over the same wine crate, dropping the flower.

The wormhole is six feet across – I'm pressed right back up against the machinery at the head of the bed. Oblivion spirals towards my fucking face!

"Oh, for Christ's sake, Dougal-" I manage and then the universe implodes through my skull. Every atom in my body turns white hot. A thunderclap of infinite noise shatters my consciousness. My senses are stripped from my body. My soul is flattened. My self has shrunk to the size of a single point, and instantaneously expanded to encompass the entire universe. The circle takes me: I am nothing and everything.

Oblivion comes rushing at me from all around, insanely fast. My panic peaks. This is it. The end of everything.

"NOOOOOOO!!!!" I scream, and wrench my eyes open one last time...

...to see Dougal walking calmly into the orb, a yellow flower in his hand.

And then with a tiny pop! and a gentle hisssss, the blackness swallows all.

The North Sea is as grey as my habit. An icy-fingered nor'easter runs over the cold waves, up the beach and pokes into the gaps in my humble garment's crude stitching. My skin tightens. Shivers jerk my gangly limbs. It's unpleasant, I can't deny that. But it is a price I am willing to pay. For I have taken vows. Proud vows that can never be broken and which by their purity will give me eternal life. Yes, my spirit is sacred! Who needs bodily warmth when heaven awaits? I raise my chin into the wind, flip up my hood and stride up the beach towards the ancient university town.

St Mary's is such a perfect place for a life of contemplation and spiritual enrichment. A little Scottish seaside town, the air rich with the tang of salt and old books, a pair of beautiful beaches stretching like golden limbs on either side of a neat little harbour. Two hills to the landward side. A rack of rib-like little streets of shops and market stalls. Crazy old pubs down alleys and in basements. And the softly beating heart of it all – the weathered and wise college buildings.

The clock in the tall tower chimes twice as I pace through the quadrangle. Fat raindrops start to dapple the smooth flagstones that surround the rectangle of lawn.

Round and into a second, smaller quad lined on three sides with grey stone buildings. A single mighty yew tree, centuries old, fills the fourth side.

The building to my right is a large, stately structure, classical in its lines.

Two females step out of one of its doorways, almost tumbling down the steps in their laughter and closeness.

"Excuse me, daughter of Eve," I say, "can you tell me the way to the Administration Faculty?"

The females stare up at me for a moment, their eyes wide.

"Fi," whispers one of the girls out of the side of her mouth. "it's Jesus."

"Nay, sweet sister, I am not the Christ," I say, lifting my hands heavenwards in supplication. "I am but a poor friar sent out into the world of the unbelievers to spread our Lord's holy love. Tell me, have you felt the love of our Lord?"

The females say nothing else for a moment.

"He looks like Jesus, doesn't he, Fi?"

Fi looks me up and down and wrinkles her nose.

"If Jesus was a tramp."

The other girl laughs. I forgive them. They know not what they do.

"Tell me, your holiness, what you wearing under that robe?"

I ignore their laughter and walk on. It is a source of constant surprise to me that so many of my peers are so obsessed with sex. And particularly in such a calm, quiet, secluded place of learning, why is romance this first thing that comes into their heads? Why, look there, just in front of me - there's a carrot-haired youth goggling at a girl with tight white jeans and a fluffy sweater. His friend is staring at another creature in a sheer creamy blouse. The way the garment hugs the curves of her breasts in all three dimensions appears to have melted his brain, for his tongue dangles like a labrador's!

How wonderful that I am forever free of such base and time-wasting thoughts.

The Administration Faculty is in a basement of a crumbling building in a corner of the Old Quad. A secretary directs me down a flight of narrow stone steps. In the corridor at the bottom, three fellow freshmen are sitting on chairs I take my place at the end of the line. After a couple of minutes, another student exits the first door on the left holding a new matriculation card.

"Your turn," he says, and the next student in line steps up and enters the room.

When it's my turn I step slowly into the long, low room, brightly lit with artificial lights bouncing off a white backdrop and umbrella reflectors. The room is hot from the lights. At the far end of the room a half-open door leads to a smaller anteroom.

The photographer has a fat red face and he is clearly suffering in the heat. His eyes are watery and yellow, and his skin shines with oily sweat. His sparse ginger hair is trying its best to flee the whole awful scene, upwards. He slumps behind a large, box-like camera and barely moves his body as he beckons me forward with a tired wave of his sweating hand.

"Hurry up! Sit on the chair. Look at the camera. Okay, great, now - hang on, lose the hoodie, kid."

This is what I love so much about my calling; every day it gives me the chance to spread the Word to a fellow human still in ignorance.

"Peace find you, brother," I say, and I make the sign of the holy chin bandage of Saint Mungo at him. "Peace. This is not a hoodie, it is a habit."

"You reckon? It looks to me like you've taken your high school leaver hoodie, sewn an old kilt on the bottom then dyed the whole thing an unpleasant, and patchy, shade of brown."

Such heretical statements should never be engaged with, merely ignored.

"Nor am I a kid," I continue, "I am a friar. This habit is a symbol of the holiness of my order, of vows I have taken, and of my chastity."

The photographer slowly closes his eyes. When he opens them again they are noticeably more watery and yellow.

"Kid, the camera can't see your face. The whole point of the matriculation photograph is to get a shot of your face. So we know who you are."

"My calling is my character. I will matriculate fully robed."

The photographer lets out a long sigh.

"You know what, kid? I too have taken a vow. I have sworn to the university that I will take a picture of every sodding student they send in here to put on every sodding matriculation card. A picture of every student's sodding face. And I can't see your sodding face with the hood of your sodding habit covering it. So, if your holiness doesn't sodding well mind, can you lower your habit this one time?"

"As you are, in your own fashion, a man of honour, surely you will understand my reticence to lower my hood when I have sworn not to-"

"Jesus Christ."

"I am not the Christ, merely a poor, chaste friar-"

"All right, kid, have it your damn way. But don't blame me if no pub in town will serve you.'

FLASH.

The camera spits out a Polaroid-style print. The photographer peels the backing off and begins waving it dry.

"Wait there while I get this laminated," he says, and wobbles through to the anteroom at the far end. He clatters with a piece of machinery for a couple of minutes then returns, bearing my image neatly laminated onto a plastic card. The fact that my hood up is very pleasing, but I am a little miffed to discover that rather than looking suitably serene, what you can see of my face makes me look merely constipated.

"Now, if it pleases your eminence, could you push off to your hall and register with your subward-"

But he gets no further because something very, very weird happens.

The air freezes.

It doesn't go cold. Just absolutely dead still. Like every molecule, every atom instantly stops vibrating. Noise can't travel anymore. The singing of the birds outside simply drops away into nothing. Then there's a single unearthly 'whump', a super-bass pulse of incredible intensity – like an entire evening's disco got compressed into one microsecond of noise. My organs vibrate in my core. Lungs seize up. Brain is squeezed like a lemon. The air seems to contract and expand very briefly – except it's not just the air, it's everything I can see.

Reality skips a beat.

And then, just as suddenly, everything is normal. I breathe again. Thoughts flow. The birds are twittering again.

The photographer and I exchange a look – 'what that hell was that?' – and I'm about to say something when there suddenly comes a celebratory whoop from the anteroom.

We look round. Smoke is seeping round the jamb of the half-open door at the far end of the room. The air around it glows a sick orange. Scratching at my brain is an awful metallic whine, like robots being slowly tortured.

"I did it! I only went and fucking did it!" yells the voice in the anteroom. The tones are familiar and yet distant. An echo of an echo. It's the weirdest thing.

"Mah hair's on fire!" squeaks a second voice.

"Don't panic, my portly pal," says the first voice, which is now fully freaking me out. So familiar and yet so alien. The nearest thing to it is my father, but not now – before I knew him. Doesn't make sense, I know, but that's how it is – damn weird.

There's a rapid rustling noise beyond the door. Then the first voice speaks again:

"See? Nothing to fret about."

The photographer and I take a few paces nearer the anteroom. Our steps ring out on the polished wood floor.

"What's that?" says the second voice from the anteroom.

"Shit!" shouts the first voice. "Must be them. Move it – sharpish!" And there's a clattering of metal, the rattling of a window and much oofing and groaning.

I'm scared but feel drawn on towards the door as if by some supernatural power. The photographer and I take several more steps.

Smoke still pours from under the door. Now we're nearer I can smell a thick, sick burning smell – and the unmistakeable odour of stale alcohol.

Everything falls silent again.

I take a deep breath.

We reach the half-open door.

The heat is like a wall. The air feels like it has ground glass in it. My breath punches its way up my nose and grates down my throat. I cough and lift my sleeve to my face.

As the through-draught clears the smoke I see something very strange. Between the door and a desk with laminating equipment is a large brass bed. A huge, organic-looking mass of dripping pipes and smoking valves clings to the bars at the head end. The bed is contracting as we watch, the metal moaning as it does so. The sheets are smouldering. On one smoking pillow sits what appears to be a charred rose.

Now I see that a small basement window that lets out onto a rear yard is open. On the ledge outside the window sits a figure.

Another plume of smoke jets up from the apparatus. I wave my hand around to clear it. When it goes, the figure is gone.

"Sodding student pranksters!" says the photographer. "How the hell did they get this bed in here?"

It's thorny question, deserving serious consideration, but my brain is in no position to think on it. For it has been seized by something even more extraordinary: I only glimpsed it for a second, but I could have sworn that the figure on the ledge...

Was me.

~

I've been billeted in McIvor Hall, an immense building that used to be a hotel. Maybe it seemed more welcoming in that incarnation, but as a hall of residence is is daunting; the great grey structure looks more like an enormous old grey battleship, somehow run aground in the middle of a small Scottish university town. It overlooks the beach, longing for the day when it will once again slip happily to war at sea. Until then, it towers over the ancient fishing cottages and golf shops, slowly rotting.

Maybe it's all in my head – that incident with the photographer has been oddly unsettling – because as I approach the hall from the landward side I can see it's actually rather impressive. To reach it, you approach along a straight avenue with smart old townhouses on one side and a long communal garden on the other. The tall beech trees that line the border of this garden have resurfaced the pavement with a metallic patina of fallen bronze leaves.

This noble avenue terminates in front of the main entrance to McIvor Hall. There's a small turning circle for cars and taxis, beyond which grand sandstone steps swoop up a full ten feet to an imposing double oak door. On the sandstone pillar to the left of these doors is an ancient brass bell-pull. At the other side, McIvor Hall introduces itself to the world on an enormous plaque of the same polished metal.

The turning circle and the steps are now a bubbling swell of students and parents, the students washing up onto the steps like driftwood, the parents being tugged away again by the tide.

Weeping mothers, embarrassed daughters, confused fathers, impatient sons. Takes me an age to bustle through them all. Just get over it will you? As my Dad said, it's not such a big deal.

And people have so many bags. What have they got in there? I only need my tashi delek canvas bag and my thurible.

Finally, I battle to the top of the steps, push one of the big oak doors open and am about to leave this irritating chaos behind – when the second very odd thing of the day happens.

The air around me suddenly feels denser. And the fresh sea breeze dies in a second – the atmosphere is superstill. Like there's a storm coming. Then I notice that the frothing crowd behind me is being covered with a wave of silence rolling in from Hart Street. I try to move but my body feels like it's in treacle. Very slowly I turn.

To see an angel walking on earth.

Praise be to the great creator, for surely there can be no other explanation! She's unlike any creature I have ever seen – a girl apparently made of sunshine. Everything about her is otherworldly. To start with, she's wearing a white sleeveless summer dress. All the other girls are sporting jeans, jumpers and fleeces against the brisk Scottish September day. But she brings the heat with her and she carries this shift of white cotton like she's on a promenade in St Tropez.

The loose cut of the shirt would hide her figure, were it not so obviously stunning. Rounded, sensual hips that roll like adverts for WD40. A neat waist. White plimsolls. Then between shoe and skirt there is an exquisite stretch of honey-coloured calf – a colour you simply cannot attain if you spend more than six months a year in this country. Her dress flows up and in, tapering at her trim middle and hugging her figure from there on up. Which shows off her... breasts... Golly. Look at them. No, don't look at them, you savage! How can you debase this fine creature by staring so?! Remember your vows!

But sweet Jesus in a jumpsuit, will you just look at them. A base man would say they were perky. Obviously a friar would not observe such a carnal thing. Nor would he add the detail that they are so perky they appear to be levitating her dress, causing the fabric to jut up in an outrageous cotton-covered shelf. And they're full. So full they force the casual V cut of the dress wide open revealing a single sharp animal tooth on a thin strip of black leather cord dangling precariously above a plunging golden cleavage. Sworn to truth as I am, I will include these observations only to enhance the accuracy of my testimony.

Thus it also behooves me to mention that her hair is a light, lovely blonde. Which today she has chosen to wear in bunches. Bloody bunches. That's plain unfair. Constructing a prettier face would be impossible. Oval shaped, chin delicate and yet strong. Lips bursting with bright red blood. Sweet nose. Bet it's never produced a bogey. A hearty scarlet flush in the cheeks. Huge eyes the colour of mineral lakes in the high Andes, glaciers in Chamonix, shards of arctic iceberg. A thousand pure blue places I have never been.

So much for the parts. They're attractive, definitely. But the sum of them is so much more: because when she moves, when you're close enough to drink her all in, something even bigger than her mighty beauty hits you dead between the eyes.

It's not just her hair and her tanned limbs and her smile. Everything about her is golden: her expression, the way she carries herself, the confidence in her every move. This is a girl who is used to being at the centre of the universe. My life has been illuminated like a manuscript and I never want the light to go out.

The sea of people is parting in front of her as she steps royally down the shining metal carpet of beech leaves that Mother Nature has clearly laid for her favourite daughter. I swear, at this very moment the sun breaks through the mackerel sky and enflames the beech leaves, alchemising them from bronze to gold. Like a tractor beam she draws the eyes of each and every person as she passes. Girls stare. Men gawp. A stunned father drops a suitcase on his toe and doesn't even notice.

And as she walks she greets people in soft, strangely accented tones.

"'Ello," she says to a demure girl in a black polo neck.

"'Ow are you?" she asks an Asian guy.

"Hola, monsieur," she directs at a father with a pipe and

hydraulic eyebrows.

"Salut, fraulein," to his wife.

French, German, Spanish, Swedish... where's she from? Not this earthly sphere, that's for sure.

She walks up the steps now and her breasts begin to bounce. They're so firm they go in double time - twice up and down for each step. It's quite an effect.

She reaches the last step. She's only inches away from me. The light is blinding at this range. I have to drop my eyes.

"Why sank you," she says, "you are so kind."

And with a bounce and a swirl of her beautiful white skirt she's gone. Straight through the door I am still holding open.

And the world catches up with itself.

The crowd flows together, chatter starts, the air returns to normal. Was she really here? I have no answer. The holy spirit that lives within me is curiously silent. But I have to find out the truth. I square my shoulders and step in through the doorway.

~

A small vestibule turns at a right angle and opens into a huge, high-ceilinged room. This must have been the lobby when the hotel was frequented by Victorian holidaymakers; now it is a gathering place, communications hub and transit lounge.

To my right is a bank of six payphones, each with its own wooden armchair. Some homesick students are already calling home. Or ordering takeaways, more likely.

The wall to my left is peppered with pigeon holes for mail. Keller, Joan... Kelman, Andrew... Keddie Frederick - there I am! Wow. Reality check. I am at uni. Sort of forgotten that for a moment.

At the far end of the room, a magnificent staircase sweeps up to a landing with an enormous stained glass window. The glass depicts a mediaeval student about to be either given his degree or have his head cut off. Heavy lead lines make it difficult to tell.

But there is no sign at all of the Angel. Was she a mere vision? A fleeting embodiment of and ethereal spirit? Or, more wonderfully, was her substantiation on the earthly plane a permanent

51

hypostatisation? In which last case, it throws up some truly fascinating theological questions. What is her angelic purpose among us – messenger, destroyer, redeemer, forgiver? Has she recently taken this form, or has she lived with us for a while? If so, what life has she led? What company has she kept? What sort of things does she like doing? Reciting psalms, grabbing a burger, walking with a close friend along a windswept beach at midnight? Does she have a dog? Or a cat? What does her arse look like naked... ?

By Saint Casimir's sacred pouch of chastity! Where did that impure thought come from? An outrageous eruption from the cellar of my soul! I must regain my spiritual harmony. I shall assume that she was a zephyrous impermanence and return to my new life of peace and learning. Right, time to get my key.

I pace along the lobby looking for some sign of authority. At last I see a small wooden door painted a queasy shade of pea green. Painted upon it in red is some poorly executed lettering – "Subwarden's Office".

I knock.

"Do come in!" keens a thin, nasal voice. I turn the rattly handle and enter. The room is tiny. No window. Clearly never designed as an office. More a storage cupboard. But a desk (the old wooden school type) and two orange plastic chairs have somehow been crammed in. Opposite me, behind the desk sits a lengthy coil of wet male flesh. His hair is dank and dark, his face thin, but long and pointed. His head resembles a half-chewed toffee. A wispy, catfish-like moustache underlines the lumpiness of his nose.

"Good day," I say. "I am newly arrived within your residence and would like my key."

"Take a ssseat," he hisses, an eelish lisp completing his piscine demeanour.

The room's so small I have to put my thurible on my lap. As I squeeze in I notice that there's someone else in there. Beside a battered filing cabinet in the corner stands a short, spotty guy with the biggest pair of NHS specs you have ever seen. They're so big and his head is so small I wonder he doesn't topple over. He has a wispy moustache very similar to the manfish's.

I perch my angular frame on the tiny piece of orange plastic on this side of the room. My knees rise high above his desk.

The manfish extends a hand. I shake – and almost recoil. So limp and wet it's like grasping an eel. A none too fresh eel.

"Good morning," he says. "I am Clive Sleevewort..." And he pauses. Like I should have heard of him or something. "Subwarden of McIvor Hall," he adds. "The warden himself is on a sabbatical studying cleft-palated gibbons in Burkina Faso so I am, de facto, the boss around here."

He says "the boss around here" in a terrible attempt at a New York accent and then tries to smile, but it doesn't quite work. His features just sort of ooze round his face a bit. He's clearly been saying that to every fresher. Bet not a soul has laughed.

"I am known as Brother Fridericus," I say, "a poor and chaste friar of the Order of the Blessed Brothers of Burgundy."

Clive looks to the guy with the NHS glasses who quickly consults an enormous clipboard and then nods. Clive turns back to face me.

"You're down here as Frederick Keddie," he says.

"That was my pre-enlightenment name. I insist that you call me Brother Fridericus."

Clive he stands up, clasps his hands behind his back and, as he talks, starts to pace in front of the window. But the room's so small he can only take two steps before he has to turn around again.

"It seems incredible now, I know," Clive says, "but two long years ago, I was a fresher just like you. Confused, clueless, lost... until I found myself here. As you can see, McIvor has been good to me, it has valued my input and rewarded it with authority. And the reason? The reason is simply this-"

And he points to a long list of regulations pinned to the back of the door.

"Rules!" says his acolyte with a smirk of triumph.

Clive nods.

"Exactly, Matthew. Mr Keddie-"

"Brother Fridericus," I remind him, but he ignores me and continues:

"I would like to welcome you to McIvor Hall. I hope you will thrive here. But I should also like to advise you that we observe certain rules within these walls, rules that make living here better for everyone. The first is that we always follow our paperwork. You are down on this list as Frederick Keddie, so that is what you will be known as."

Oh, here comes the Angel again, back in my head. What sort of female friends does she have? Does she have a male friend? If she does, I bet he's cool. Muscley. And confident...

"Secondly, you must join in with life here, not cloister yourself away. We are your family while you are finding your feet in your first year at the university.

I'll bet he'd be the most confident git you've ever met. But he'd be the kind of guy who other guys would love to be. You'd burn to hate him but really you'd want him to be your friend. Like George Clooney in Ocean's Eleven...

Clive runs a fin-hand across his wispy catfish moustache.

"The best way to join in with life here is to adhere to my social programming schedule. You will find this to be engaging, self-improving and, of course, fun. In fact, you can see from this data that my aim this year is for McIvor to have more fun, per student, than any other hall at St Mary's."

He points to a framed chart on the wall. It is headed, 'Predicted Social Activity 02/03'. Below this is a bar graph, each bar labelled with the name of a hall. Up the y axis are numbers. McIvor's bar is the biggest. It is coloured yellow. "My social secretary is doing the rounds today – she'll take you through the activities I have planned. But-" and he points to the list on the back of the door again, "to conclude, I must insist that you read and remember these rules. They are pinned up in every room. They could save your life."

I don't mean to snort, but I do.

Clive leans in towards me, his black eyes oiling from side to side.

"For example, you will see that rule 17b(ii) prohibits all drug use and, indeed, smoking in any part of the hall."

"I don't poison my bodily vessel with any narcotics."

"But you are holding a bong."

"Bong?! This is my thurible. A sacred incense burner."

"It creates smoke, does it not?"

"Yes-"

"Then you can't use it in halls."

This guy is now really getting to me.

"My thurible is essential to my daily prayers. To prevent me using it is to subject me to religious persecution. I will have to report this to the university's chancellor."

"We don't have a chancellor, we have a dean! He made a mistake!" squeaks Glasses Matthew.

"You are right, Matthew, he has," says Clive. "But never let it be said that I was being unfair. Let him go now with his complaint to the dean."

"Maybe I will!" I yell, standing up so fast my chair topples over. But as soon as I'm on my feet I realise I've made a mistake. Clive and Matthew are smirking. I've lost my temper. Dammit, I can't think straight all of a sudden. What's the matter with me? How did I get myself into this corner? As well as chastity, I swore vows of charity and humility as well. I should be able to control myself, but this Clive person is sorely testing my faith.

"Maybe you will indeed," says Clive. "Or maybe you will simply take your room key from Matthew, go upstairs, make some new friends and have some officially sanctioned fun."

His deep-sea eyes glisten blackly. The scaly skin around his neck glistens.

I snatch my key from Glasses Matthew's hand.

"Fine," I say. "I'll go have some fun."

I push open the door with sudden violence and take a decisive step out into the huge lobby.

I stop.

Dead.

Standing right outside is the Angel, waiting patiently to get her key.

She steps up close to me. Her face is a handspan from mine. Her primrose breath warms my cheek. Somehow my brain has been instantaneously replaced with three pounds of scrambled egg.

"Bonjour encore," she says. Her cool blue eyes look calmly into mine. There is no hint of a hurry. She is relaxed. She is waiting for me to say something.

And from the corner of my vision I can see that everyone else in the great lobby is looking at me, waiting too. I can even feel Clive's stare burning into my spine from behind. But I can't consciously summon any words. Maybe my subconscious can help me out. And that's when, astonished, I hear my own mouth say this:

"I'm never going to be able to have sex with you because I've taken a vow of celibacy."

~

What an idiot. Why those words? Never asking my goddam subconscious another thing again. Forgive my blasphemy.

The burning shame of remembering it is even worse than I felt when I said them. Nothing to do now but trudge up to my room and perform a prodigious penance. Hit myself one thousand times over the head with my bible. That ought to do it.

I look at my key fob – room A2. Getting there is something of a pilgrimage in itself; McIvor is just as much of a battleship inside as it is outside. A labyrinth of long, thin corridors, split-level floors, hidden staircases and dark, dark corners, the décor is tatty. There's also a very funky smell permeating the whole place, like a hundred years of raging hormones. I must light up my thurible when I get to my room to mask it.

I stop to look at a map of the hall. There are four floors of rooms: A and C are boys, B and D girls. The sexes like layers in a cake. Refectory and games room in the basement. It takes me an age to find A2. This is because it's not beside A1 like I naively assumed it might be. In fact, there isn't an A1. There's just a dark, unpainted door. Nor is A2 beside A3. That's between A4 and A6a. Eventually I find it at the end of an astonishingly long and dirty sub-corridor that branches off beside A13c.

The once-white door has been criss-crossed into dirty greyness by the adhesive of a million hilarious notes. A2 is announced in ornate but filthy brass lettering.

The door is ajar. Soft murmuring comes from within. I push it open.

Beds, wardrobes, desks, chairs – two of each. But not a pair amongst them: each item of furniture looks as if it's been bought in different charity shop in a different decade.

It's a tatty room, but it's light. Gentle September sunshine rolls in from two magnificently proportioned windows. Almost directly below, a magical three-mile stretch of golden sand hems the ocean.

And at the far desk sits a young man. There has never been a human being who more closely resembled a Yorkshire terrier. Small, wiry. Bright little button eyes below hopeful eyebrows. His nose is neat and healthily moist. Luxurious red hair tufts everywhere.

Cross-legged at his feet is a girl. She's plump. Her folded thighs fill her jeans like over-inflated inner tubes. Still, she's very attractive. A lovely round face with high, dark arched brows and a fine nose. And there's a tremendous energy about her. Like she might spring to her feet at any moment and start dancing.

Between them, I can see a half-full cafetière and two cups nestling precariously on the soft duvet of the far bed.

They haven't seen me enter, and I realise that the girl is looking to the boy, waiting. He opens a folder on his lap. Pulls out a tatty piece of paper. A close-lined leaf torn hurriedly from a notebook. Holds it in front of him, clasped like a jewel in his little paws.

The girl waggles her big legs from side to side. Settling herself. She bends forward a little. Rests her elbows on her knees, her chin on her hands and tilts her face up.

The boy clears his throat. And begins to read:

> *"Softly now my soul departs*
> *And settles by your side*
> *To watch you where you're sleeping*
> *Taste the pillow where you cried*
>
> *I wish that I could wake you*
> *And dream into your eyes*

*But soon I must be gone, my love*
*I'm dying at sunrise*

*Call this a flight of fancy*
*A fiction I don't feel*
*And I'll fly again tomorrow*
*And prove my love is real."*

"That's beautiful, my darling," says the fat girl in rolling cockney tones. "Fucking beautiful is what that is," she adds, wiping her eyes.

He hands her a tissue.

"I'm glad ye liked it," says the boy.

Then he suddenly looks up.

"What do ye think?" he asks, brown eyes shining.

Wasn't ready for this. Bit lost. Forgot they could see me, for a second.

"Oh. I... um... I thought it was excellent." I say. "But I didn't mean to intrude."

"Ach, dinnae be silly," says the boy. "Ye're my roommate." He really rolls his r's and lilts his vowels. He says 'room' like it's part of vvroomm and he's a little chestnut motorbike about to whiz round in circles.

"I am?" I say.

"Whit else would ye be doin' here?"

He gets to his feet and crosses towards me. Holds out a paw.

His grip is warm and firm.

"Dougal MacDougal," he says.

I was about to say 'Brother Fridericus' but instead I reply:

"Freddie Keddie."

And we both smile. Quietly sharing the joy of finding someone with a worse name. Never happened to either of us, I imagine.

"This is Monica," he says, pointing to the cockney girl. She jumps up, surprisingly quickly and bounds over to stand very closely to Dougal, a lovely big smile on her face.

"Alright, my darling," she says brightly, pumping my hand passionately.

"Hi," I say.

There's a pause. She stands there some more.

"So are you two...?" I start, waving my hand between them and hoping someone will finish my sentence.

No one does.

"Are we what, darling?" Monica asks, cocking her head on one side.

"Are you... you know...?" and God only knows why I choose this word – "are you lovers?"

They both goggle at me for precisely three seconds then turn to each other and laugh.

"Ach no, man. Monica just popped by," says Dougal.

"I'm a second year, darling," Monica says, smiling. "I run all the social events in McIvor."

There's something about her mouth and the way her lips smack when she swears... I don't know for sure because obviously I've never had a blow job, but if I had had a blow job and knew what I was talking about, I'd reckon Monica was very very good at blowjobs. By Casimir, another of those extraordinarily awful thoughts! So much confusion today.

"Listen," continues Monica, "I was just saying to Dougal, I'm hosting toast later to get people partnered up for the three-legged pub crawl on Friday, and-"

"Three-legged pub crawl?"

She beams again. "The highlight of freshers week in McIvor, my darling. You hit every pub in town with one leg tied to a partner. By the time you get to the Union everyone's totally plastered. Best of all, it's in fancy dress! Bloomin' magic fun. I gotta make sure everyone's partnered up before then, so you will come, my darling, won't you?"

I look at Dougal. "You going?" I say.

"Course he's fucking going!" says Monica.

"Well, sure, I'd love to come," I say.

"Sweet," says Monica, moving to the door. "And great to meet you both," she adds before waving her hand high above her head and bowling off down the corridor.

"Ye want a coffee?" asks Dougal, reaching for his cafetière.

"Love one," I say, moving my luggage to my wardrobe.

I perch on the end of my bed and watch his sure little hands fill the kettle and measure the coffee. He moves so quickly and surely – there's a real rhythm to it. I watch for a moment, half-hypnotised.

"You really only just met her?" I suddenly ask.

Dougal pauses.

"Ten minutes ago. Why?"

"I just... it's that... you were reading her a poem. A poem you wrote."

He points to my thurible with his teaspoon.

"Ye never get a bit creative when ye're having a bowl?"

"Why does everyone think this is a bong?!" I reply. "It's my thurible, not a bloody bong!"

Dougal nods. Grins a little.

"So that's how it is," he says, then sploodges down the little plunger on his cafetière. Then he looks at me directly with his keen terrier eyes and adds:

"But you made your thurible out of a bong, didn't you?"

And I don't know what it is about his humble, honest countenance that makes me want to do this, but I tell him the truth.

"Yes I did. My old bong. Enlarged the burner. Perforated the bowl. Added a lid. Now my thurible."

"And yer habit – that's yer old kilt and a hoodie sewn together, right?"

"Y-y-yes. But how did you know it was a habit?"

"What else would a friar wear?" he says.

For some reason I want to hug this hairy little fellow.

He hands me my coffee. I had sworn off all narcotics, including caffeine, but its soft caramel aroma is enflaming my senses so I take a sip. Forgive me, Blessed Mungo.

"Delicious," I say. "Thanks."

"Take a seat," Dougal says, nodding to the bed. The mattress is firm, but yielding. My muscles relax of their own accord as I recline a little. It feels peaceful sitting here. This is the most peaceful I've been since I stepped off the train. And then I'm not sure why I ask this, because I'm not normally this nosy, but it just sort of pops out:

"So who was the poem really for?"

"Rrrruth."

He says it with such simple power. And the way he rolls that 'r'. Makes one name sound like a whole life.

"Who's Ruth?" I ask.

"My girl," he says simply, then reaches for the cup. He goes on: "Known her since she was four and I was five. Neither of us had any brothers or sisters. And when that's how it is on Corosay, well, we were schoolfriends, playmates, soulmates... we grew up together you understand."

"Where's Corosay?"

Dougal drops his eyebrows into a frown and leans back slightly.

"Whit de ye mean, 'where's Corosay'? It's an island off the island of Keilda."

"Um, where's Keilda?"

"Lord, man, ye've never heard of Keilda? Are you from Ooter Space or something?"

"Edinburgh."

"Aye, close enough." He hands me my coffee. "Keilda is an island off the island of Iona. Which is off the island of Mull – ye've heard of Mull, I take it?"

"I have."

"Right you are then."

"So Corosay's kind of remote, huh?" I say.

"Not when you live there. Then it's the centre of the world. It has everything you need. A beach, a harbour, a hill – even a shop."

"Golly."

"Ah, that beach... Sea Horse Bay we called it. The white sands, the green ocean, the dunes behind. It's a paradise I tell ye. We met there ye know. I remember the day more clearly than last year's sheep trials. Deep in the middle of one of those eighties summers. A real scorcher. I spent six weeks solid on Sea Horse Bay, I'm sure. One day I was paddling on the beach and I saw this little figure at the end of the bay. Wearing blue wellingtons and a straw sunhat. She had one of those nylon fishing nets on the end of a cane you used to get. I had one also. So I wandered over. She was dipping her net in a rockpool. Her jamjar was full of wee fishes.

She looked up and smiled at me and... I don't know quite what it was, but there was something so very comfortable about that smile that, well, I just went straight up and without a word put my rod in her rockpool too."

His soft brown eyes are misting. He stares out the window at the ocean, his fine little features outlined sharply against the tatty bookcase.

"Now yer man Freud would probably say that's all about somethin' in yer troosers, but as far as it goes with me it's about me an' her an' a rockpool."

He looks back into the room.

"From then on we were inseparable."

Then his shining eyes swing to the window again. I sense there's a part of him that's gone out to sea.

"And she's still there?" I say.

He looks at me. Smiles a little.

"You must be missing her," I add.

He takes a breath.

"Ye know what I did? Just last week. The day before I leave to come here. Everyone on the island throws a big party for me, the clever local laddie, making it to St Mary's. It's all getting' a bit boisterous, as these things are apt to do, ye understand. And suddenly she's there beside me – 'Dougie,' she says – that's her nickname for me, ye understand-"

"I'm with you."

"'Dougie,' she says, the breeze pushing her wild red hair around. 'I'm gonnae miss ye, ye know." And I looked at her see-green eyes and I said, 'Why, Ruthie,' says I – that's my nickname for her-"

"Yes. Go on."

"I said, 'Will ye come with me to Sea Horse Bay?'

"'Aye, Dougie, I will,' she says. So we go walking down there to the rockpool where first we met all them years gone by. And we stop for a moment to look at the wee sea creatures.

"We stand there just lookin' and enjoyin' the air together, and then I say to her, 'We've been together a fair number of, my love. 'Aye, we have that,' she says. 'Well,' says I, 'there's one thing I want to ask of ye.'

"'Dougie,' she suddenly says, 'Shoosh.' And she puts her finger on my lips. I take it away. 'No, my love, I really have to ask you,' I try. But again she stops my tongue. 'Please,' I start for the third time. Whereupon the lass looks all serious. Her eyes cloud and swirl like the stormy sea. 'No, Dougie,' she says simply. And I can see she means it. Can see it as plain on her face as I can see the deer on the hill. 'Just wait,' she says. 'I'll see you again in the spring. You can ask it of me then.' And she gave me such a lovely big smile that of course I had to drop it."

Dougal pours the coffee.

"What happened then?" I ask, edging forward on the bed.

He sighs. Takes a sip of his coffee.

"Well the next day I had to start my journey. And all the way I wished she'd let me ask her my question. I thought about it all the way on the ferry to Keilda. I thought about it as I walked over that island. I thought about it as I got the ferry to Iona. I thought about it as I walked over that island. I thought about it on the ferry from Iona to-"

"And what did you think?"

"As I was thinking about it on the train, I finally realised I had to ask her this of her anyway. It was up to me, not her. And of course I wanted to get off that train and straight back onto all those ferries. But the islanders had given me a send off. I couldn't go back without comin' here. So, with her not having a phone or suchlike, I thought I'd write to her and tell her how I felt. And you know what? It came out as a poem."

"That poem you read earlier?"

"The very fella. And yon writing business went so well that I decided to write some more. In fact, by the time I got to St Mary's, I'd fair decided to be a poet. The first thing I did here was buy this-"

He points to the cafetière.

"-an' these-"

He picks up a pack of cigarettes.

"-but there's strict rules against these, apparently. So I'm just going to keep drinking coffee and writing poems until spring time, when I can see her and ask her."

Golly. I suddenly feel very close to this wee Dougal fellow. Like we share something. And the way he's looking at me from under heavy brows, I want to let him know how I feel.

"It's okay," I say, patting his arm. I'm a virgin too."

"Ye what?"

"You wanted to ask her to sleep with you, right? Well, it's okay, I know how you feel. I haven't managed it yet either."

Dougal's eyes just about pop out of his head.

"Whit ye on about, man?! We've been at it since we were fourteen."

"Wh-what?"

"Bugger all else to do on an island that size."

"Right," I say. "Of course."

And suddenly I'm not so interested in what he had to ask her. Don't know what to say really. Dougal doesn't say anything either, mind you, just watches me for a long time with his bright brown eyes. After an age, he taps my forearm gently with a hairy paw.

"So how long have you been a friar?"

"Since the feast of St Gregor's Immaculate Consumption."

"I'm not so well versed in the days of our saints, you know. Was that a long time ago?"

"Uh... it's a very ancient celebration. Been marked every year for centuries."

"You've been doing this quite a while, then?"

As the Lord is my witness, I didn't want to have to tell anyone this. People are always so quick to rush to judgements. But now that it's this fellow asking, I feel strangely okay about it.

"Three weeks," I say. "Well, three weeks since last Saturday. So, three weeks and four days, technically."

"I see how it is," Dougal says, and gives me another pat. It's the most reassuring human touch I've felt in years.

~

As I unpack my few things and stow them in my wardrobe, I can't stop trying to work out just what the hell it is that I don't have.

Of course I'm happy with my vocation, but I can't help wondering why no rosy-cheeked young lasses pounced on me when I was fourteen. I mean Dougal's a nice guy and everything, but look at him: wild sandy tufts of hair all over the show, dirty little paws covered in ink and biscuit crumbs. Short. I bet his foreskin whiffs just as much as mine.

And he's fighting them off.

What is wrong with me...?

It's no good thinking like that. It's irrelevant when you're living the rest of life in a state of celibacy. But let's imagine – just for the sake of argument – that a female were to appraise me for the purposes of a romantic interaction. What would she make of me? Let's start with the positives. What have I got? Inventory of the assets. Height: yes. I am prodigiously well-endowed vertically. Six foot six, in fact. Breadth: not an abundance. Quite the opposite in fact. Weigh close to twelve stones. Official medical term: thin. Official playground term: Ethiopian stick insect. Looks: confused features saved from elephant-man disaster by an imposing jaw line. As attractive as your average Easter Island statue. Fingers: superbly long and agile. Could have been a fabulous concert pianist were it not for total lack of musical talent and dedication. Now, genitalia. Seems crude, but it's part of the package, as it were. Balls: big. Pre-calling comparisons with pornography suggested a bobby of average size but my pods are most definitely pendulous. Brains: recorded fact – A in Modern Studies. Certificate from Scottish Education Authority.

And that's about it. Not athletic, stylish or rich. Neither confident nor charming. No superpowers. Brains, balls, big fingers and height. Not exactly Bezalel, son of Uri, am I...

"You ready?" asks Dougal. "You're miles away."

"Huh?"

"We're due at Monica's," he says, tapping his watch. "For toast."

"Sure."

Monica lives in B2. It takes us a full ten minutes to navigate our way down there. When we arrive she's alone.

"Come in, my darlings," she says. "My doll of a roommate's just popped out to the all-night garage for some milk."

It hits me that this is the first time I've been in a girl's bedroom. It's directly below ours, so it must be pretty much the same size and shape. And it has two beds, two wardrobes and two desks just the same. But for all that our room might as well be on Mars.

This room is lovely.

Softness abounds. The chairs have cushions on them. There are spreads on the beds with squares in different textures and pastel shades. Vases of flowers calm my beating heart. A couple of lamps soften the lighting. A cork board is covered with multi-coloured timetables and lecture plans. A single small Coldplay poster is tacked up beside the bookcase.

But best of all, the room smells lovely. No room with a male living in it could ever smell quite like this. It's sugar and spice and Bodyshop foot soap and... I don't know, just nineteen-year-old girl. I want to stay here forever.

Monica bounces to the toaster which sits on a little table complete with red checked cloth.

"You gentlemen want some toast?"

"Yes please."

"That would be great."

"Sit down," she says, pointing to a tiny chair. I move a stuffed bear and something that's like a green pig but with giant ears and squeeze my angular frame into the rattan receptacle.

The door opens. And in comes her roommate holding a pint of milk.

You wouldn't exactly say she was pretty. You definitely wouldn't say she was ugly. But not pretty. Her nose is maybe a little too pointy for that. Her mouth a little small. Her hair curls down to rest on her shoulder like the tail of a happy cat, but it's as plain brown as brown can be. While her grey-green eyes remind me of the sea, it's the sea in a rainstorm on the wild west coast. Her upper body is slim, with only the faintest shadow of a bosom on a fold in her thick woolly jumper.

"Guys, this is Penelope," says Monica. "Penelope, this is Dougal and Frederick. Why don't you sit on the bed there next to Frederick and pour the tea?"

Penelope takes a faltering half step and scurries over towards me. The way she holds the milk in her hands and pushes her pointy face forward, she looks like a little mouse.

She sits on the other end of the bed from me. A delicate fragrance blooms around me. Suddenly feel a little hot. Have to shuffle my thighs and shift my bum a little.

"So, ah, where's everyone else?" I ask.

"Everyone who else?" replies Monica with a wicked smile. "Now Dougal," she says, "tell, me all about Corosay. Are there a lot of sheep there?"

He may not have one in this dimension, but on some other plane, Dougal definitely has a tail, and right now it's wagging like billy-o.

He leans in towards Monica.

"Och, there's a grand amount of sheep on Corosay..."

She mirrors him, their shoulders now closing out their conversation. I may not be experienced, but I know a set up when I see one.

"I don't know about you," says Penelope, "but I think we're being set up."

"What?" I splutter.

She colours a little.

"I said-"

"I heard what you said," I say. "What I mean is, did you just think that right just now?"

"I'm hardly likely to have said it if I didn't," she adds, reddening a little more.

"No no, I'm sorry. I don't mean to be sharp. It's just that I was thinking the same thing. The very second before you said it."

"Really?"

"I swear."

And she smiles for the first time – and I have to catch my breath. Because it's a fragile smile, but somehow it brings all her odd mouse features together. Her face is in harmony now. A delicate melody that makes me feel something new – completely relaxed in the presence of a female.

I return the smile. It feels like it's coming out a little satanic, but it's the best I can do right now.

"Would you like a cup of tea?" she says, holding up a white teapot with pink polka dots.

I lean a little forward and nod enthusiastically.

"Tea would be great," I say.

"How do you have it?"

"Milk, four sugars. Thanks."

She smiles a little more. "We have some Ribena if you'd like," she says.

I smile back.

"Tea's fine," I say.

I watch her pour the tea. She does it so precisely. No splashes, no bits of sugar on the tablecloth. With her neat mouse hands and pointy mouse nose, she looks like a character from a children's story book. I have to restrain a very strange urge to cuddle her.

She hands me a delicate cup of perfectly brown liquid.

"Thank you," I say. "So, um, what's your surname, Penelope?

"Cotton," she says. "Penelope Cotton."

"Then I shall call you... The Penster!" I say with a flourish.

The grey-green waters in her eyes eddy a little. "I prefer Penelope," she says evenly.

"Yes," I nod. "Penelope's cool. Goddess of fire, right?"

"Loyal wife of Ulysses," she says.

"Course, course. That's her. Knew that."

"No, you didn't."

What the hell? Is she serious? Is she telling me off? She looks serious. Check out her prim little face there. Oh no, wait. The corner of her mouth is twisting up. Trying to hide a smile. She's taking the piss.

I laugh. Her face sparkles. Looks so pretty all of a sudden. But man, that is one crisp sense of humour.

"Penelope, darling," says Monica, "put the toast on there's a love- oh, and ask Freddie about his bong."

I glare over at Dougal. What's he telling everyone about me? He grins naughtily and shrugs.

"It's not a bong," I say, turning back to Penelope. "It's my thurible. I have taken the holy vows of a friar."

"How interesting-" Penelope starts, slipping two pale slices of bread into the toaster that sits underneath her desk.

"Yeah, he's taken a vow of celibacy," brays Monica. "Like to see how long you manage to keep that one in this horny little hotpot of a town!"

"Madam, my vows are for life," I tell her.

"Ignore her, Freddie," says Penelope. "And tell me more – I'm curious, why are you here at university? Shouldn't you be in a monastery?"

She seems genuinely interested. How unusual. I feel myself moving a little closer to her along the bed.

"Ah, people often get the two mixed up. Monks cloister themselves in their monastery. But friars honour God by doing his work in the community. Holiness on the hoof as it were."

"How strange – they're really very different, but I never even thought about it," says Penelope. She smiles, and it is a smile that illuminates her whole face. "I should have been more curious."

Incredibly, she seems to mean it.

"Oh, don't worry, nobody really thinks about friars any more," I continue. "But they were once really important. An example – you ever had a cappuccino coffee?"

"Of course I have," says Penelope, smiling again. I have an urge to keep saying things to keep her amused, just so I can bask in that beam of hers.

"It has white frothy milk on top and dark brown coffee underneath, right?" I continue. "Well, the Capuchin friars wear a white hood and brown robe, and 'cappuccino' is Italian for little hood. So the world's favourite coffee is named after friars."

"I did not know that," she says, reaching out through the slightly open window to pull the butter in from the ledge outside. "And I suppose everyone asks you this but, apart from the whole coffee thing, what made you want become a friar?"

I pause for a moment to listen and gauge if things are safe. But the other two have lost interest in us and are talking about how incredible it is that Monica has never milked a cow.

"Actually no one has asked me that. They just usually laugh at me." Gosh she has bright eyes. "Well, the last couple of years I've been on my own a lot, what with my parents and the house and school and everything, and it made sense to make some order out of that. So I did a bit of theosophical research on, you know, the internet, and... here I am."

I don't remember anyone being so willing to listen to me that I think I have got a bit carried away. But she doesn't stare at me like I've grown a second head, which is the normal reaction to this sort of explanation. Instead she just nods, ever so simply, and says:

"It's hard to find a place to fit in, isn't it? Especially when things aren't going so well at home. And then, once you've found a little space and time in the world, it's even harder to move out of that zone. No matter how much things change."

"How do you mean?" I ask. But I know exactly what she means, so why I ask that I don't know.

"Well, look at my furry crew here," she replies, and she points to a startlingly large collection of stuffed animals behind me at the head of her bed. "I started making them when I was nine, in Craft Club with my mum. By the time I was fifteen I knew I should stop making them. Put these childish things away. Yet here my furry friends are. On my bed in university."

I look down at her little fingers still gripping the pale china of her teacup. For some reason I wonder if she's a virgin. Have those delicate digits gripped a throbbing cock? She seems so straight, and yet... there's something else... Or is there? Oh, I don't know. No real experience you see. Girl could be a nun. Girl could be what those in the know term a 'cock monster'. Impossible to tell with current data.

"Hob nob?" Penelope says suddenly, proffering a packet of biscuits. I take one and thank her, but add nothing else. Penelope takes one too, but doesn't seem like she's about to say any more either. We nibble a little in silence together, so I take a moment to look around at her animals again. There's a rather elegant pale green cat, exquisitely stitched, smiling at a cat joke it will never share.

I look back at Pen. She's sitting nibbling a biscuit, looking at me. God, look at her eyes. They're as deep and unknowable as the Corryvreckan whirlpool. And she's not examining me. Just looking. Contentedly?

This silence is awkward. At least, I feel it must be. Neither of us has said a word for, like, hours. But I don't feel that I should say anything. I mean, it's okay just sitting here like this. Strange, but okay.

Have to say something though. The other two are rabbiting on about sheep-dipping. Can't just sit here for the rest of the term drinking her tea and eating her bloody hob nobs. Actually, I think I probably could.

And what's the point in saying anything anyway? I could ask her about that cat. When she made it. Boy or girl? What's its name? But why? She'll think I'm a right helmet.

No, even though I can't think of anything to say, it doesn't bother me that I can't. It's okay just sitting here, in silence, drinking her tea and eating her biscuits. Really quite okay. And she seems quite relaxed – she's onto her third biscuit. I wonder if she thinks it's okay too. Hope so, because I-

"You got a partner for the pub crawl?" I hear my own damn mouth suddenly say. Traitorous trap of mine! Where the hell did that come from?! "If not," my own tongue and lips continue, "you could go with me." Didn't I just say I should keep my mouth shut?!! Jesus on Jackanory.

The conversation opposite us instantly stops. Dougal and Monica whip their heads round in unison. They're staring at us.

Penelope flames on – neck and entire head go bright scarlet.

I feel my face flaming red like hers.

What's she going to say? By Satan's fulgent backside, I suddenly realise I really care what she says.

She opens her little mouth to answer and-

KA-CHUNK!

The toaster pops up.

"I'd like that," says Pen.

And the smile on her face is so enrapturing that I feel like throwing off my habit right then and there. Vowing loyalty to her.

"Sorry to interrupt you two darlings," says Monica, "but I like to get my toast buttered while it's still hot enough to melt the stuff."

"Oh, sure, of course, of course," mumbles Pen. The softness that had filled the air is broken. Things are spikier again. Stranger and

more alien. Monica and Dougal shuffle over to our little corner of the room.

"Come on your holiness, say grace for us!" says Monica.

"I really don't think that would be appropriate," I say.

"Aye, come on, my man, you heard my poem, let's hear your rite," says Dougal.

His terrier eyes glisten. I sigh.

"I suppose I could recite the blessing of the Seventh Dolorous Transit of St Mungo."

"That's the spirit, lad!" says Dougal.

"But I'll have to light my thurible. And you will all have to discalc."

"Dis-what, darling?" squawks Monica.

"Discalc. Take your shoes off. It's very important."

Monica looks at me, with a slight cock of her head – a look I've seen many times before - but Penelope is smiling. She whips her slippers off quickly and nods at the others to do the same.

"I should also tell you," I add, "that the lack of any notes or melody is not due to any choral inadequacy on my part. This rite is intended to be monotone."

"To add to the solemnity," says Dougal.

"Exactly!"

On the inside of my habit is a little pocket, which I sewed into place to hold my most sacred accoutrements, as well as keys and other such worldly necessities. I reach inside and from it I extract a nub of incense and a cigarette lighter with a picture of Cyprus on it. I lift my thurible from round my neck and place it on the small table beside the toaster. The lid flips up easily, and I place the incense in the centre of the little metal indentation. A couple of sparks and the lighter flips into life. I touch the flame to the oily brown resin. In a few seconds it catches, glows red and begins to smoke. I flip the lid of the thurible shut and take its pendant cords in my right hand.

I stand.

The incense has taken surprisingly quickly, so I wave my thurible to get the aromas billowing and commence the rite.

"Ab auribus tuis mutavit aspersione pulveris os sanctorum

tuorum carissimi Mungo Sancti, et audias nostra uerba esuriit..."
I chant.

"See what you mean about the bloody tune, darling," says Monica, "it's not exactly Penny Lane is it?"

"Sh!" says Penelope.

"...a marmot de Cartusiam furatus panem..."

"Tell me, your eminence," says Monica, "is that thing supposed to put out so much bloody smoke?"

"...et ursus ex Avenione bibebant vinum..."

"And what sort of holy bloody incense is that – Afghani black?!"

Before I can point out that the smell may indeed have come from some remnants of ancient resin from the thurible's previous employment, an ear-cracking alarm goes off.

WEEEEEEEEE... WEEEEEEEEEE... WEEEEEEEEEEE!!!!!!

"What in the Lord's name is that?" asks Dougal.

"The fire alarm, darlings," says Monica. "Come on." And she moves to the door. "Hurry, darlings," says Monica over her shoulder, "when you live here you have to move quickly when the alarm goes off. That prick Clive runs a weekly fire-drill and he loves nothing more than catching people out." She smiles back to us, "If you don't make it to the muster point in time he makes you sit a fire safety exam."

"But I was just getting to the good bit," I say.

Penelope puts a hand on my shoulder.

"The bit you did do was still rather special," she says.

Oh, bless her and praise her, dear Mungo!

The narrow corridor concentrates the alarm noise into an unbearable whine. Monica paces along to the fire door that connects our spur to the main corridor. We pace single file behind her: Dougal, then Penelope, and I bring up the rear.

As we reach the fire door, I look past her through the glass. What's that? Is it... ? I can't be sure but I think I see giant pair of spectacles disappearing round the next corner.

Monica pushes the door.

It doesn't open.

She pushes again.

No joy.

"Must be warped," she mutters.

"Let me help," says Dougal, adding his weight to the push. His little shoulder connects with the wood a full five inches below Monica's.

The door still doesn't budge.

WEEEEEEEEE... WEEEEEEEEEE... WEEEEEEEEEEEE!!!!!!

It's like having an ambulance inside your head.

We look at each other. And all at once we all start to shove like crazy. The door doesn't budge an inch. I use my height to look down through the glass.

"It's a radiator," I say. "One of the big radiators is jammed between the door and that corner opposite."

"How the hell could a damned radiator fall off the wall?" snarls Dougal.

And it comes to me.

"He did this," I say.

"Who?" says Dougal.

"Clive," I say.

Monica shakes her head and laughs darkly. "He's a fucking tosser, I know, but I doubt he'd go this far."

But I know different. He did this to upset my serenity.

"Is there another way out?" asks Dougal.

Monica shakes her head. "We'll just wait till it's over out. The worst that happens is we have to sit through his fucking safety lecture."

But no, I'm thinking. I don't want to sit through his lecture. I really, truly don't. That would be like... an affront. What I'm going to do about it, I don't know... And then Penelope says really quietly:

"What if it's a real fire?" And she turns to me, her mouse eyebrows scrunched in fear. Woah – what was that? The weirdest feeling. Looking at her I'm suddenly aware that I'm responsible here. All three of them are looking at me. And rather than feeling scared by this, I kind of like it.

Which is when inspiration strikes.

"Follow me," I say and stride back along the corridor to the room.

I leap over to the window, climb on the desk, remove the curtain rail's end cap and slide three off the large brass rings off into my hand.

"What are you doing?" asks Dougal.

Penelope looks up at me, concern in her eyes. I smile back at her.

"Getting us down," I say, and to my own surprise, wink. She looks a bit startled at this, but also, I have to say, a bit impressed too.

Now I undo the little brass pins that hold edges of the window frame in place. Once they're free I remove the frame sides and, with a sharp heave, swing the window in.

I start to haul out the sash cord.

"Er, Freddie, my man-" starts Dougal.

"Don't just stand there, Dougal," I say, "pass me a knife."

Two minutes later I'm coiling sash cord into a little pile. I undo the thin rope that serves as the belt of my habit and pass two curtain rings onto it before reknotting it. Then I pass a loop of the main run of the sash cord through the pair of curtain rings, which I hold at right angles. Then I pass one end of the sash cord to Dougal, and I toss the other one out of the window.

I climb out onto the ledge.

It's a nice evening. The sun is setting. Standing on the edge of the open window I'm bathed in a warm golden glow. A gentle sea breeze tousles my forelock. Looking down I can see people starting to gather at the fire muster point in the car park behind the refectory.

Looking back in the room I see the three of them are sat in a little half-circle on the edge of Penelope's bed. They seem almost entranced by my activity. Dougal suddenly shakes his head and jumps to his feet.

"In the Lord's name, man, ye're not... ye're not... jumping out of the window?"

"Abseiling out of the window, Dougal. You know," I say with a smile to Penelope, "SAS style."

"Now correct me if I'm wrong," says Dougal, "but the SAS are trained professional soldiers. And would I be right in saying that ye, while being a grand lad and all, are not skilled in that manner?"

He has a point. But both girls are still staring at me, curiosity and admiration easily overpowering fear as the dominant emotion right now.

I pat him on the shoulder.

"We're all descended from apes, right? Got natural climbing instinct," I say, stepping onto the window ledge. A delicious blast of ozone-rich sea air chills my face. Seagulls call to me. Far below, the crowd is swelling on the tarmac. It'll be a full house. Someone notices me. Points up.

"Okay, when I have successfully descended to the ledge of the room below this one, I will give this signal." I hold up my hand and make the sign of Saint Iwig of Lindisfarne. "That's your cue, Dougal, to make fast the cord while I disconnect myself. I will then progress through the window and give two tugs. That is your signal to let the cord run free. I will then head up the stairs, clear the obstruction and bring you to safety."

They continue to stare. I brace myself. More people are pointing up.

"So, Dougal. If you could just wrap the end of that there cord around yourself, that would be magic."

"I'm doing nae such thing."

"Yes, you are," I say, stretching one leg out onto the ledge.

"But-"

He wants to complain some more, but he can see by my eyes that I'm going to do it. And he's right. I am.

"Don't worry, ladies!" I smile, "Freddie'll save you," And with a wink and a nod of my head I kick back into nothingness. For a glorious instant I am free of both building and gravity, and then suddenly, I drop. I see Dougal scrabbling to pass the rope round himself, then I'm gone.

The slack sings falsetto as it pays out. After a few feet there's a gentle tug as my weight is taken by Dougal. I slow down. Stop.

Then without warning there is grinding skid from above and with a sickening lurch I start to plummet again. Dougal's let go. Either that or he's rocketing across the room. I fly past the target window. Christ I'm going to throw up...

Suddenly there's a crash and I stop with a jerk that nearly cuts me in two.

"Oof!!"

The curtain rings yurk and mutter.

A muffled yelp from above informs me that Dougal has prevented my further descent misfortune by bravely jamming himself under the desk.

"Good work!" I yell up to him.

And there I dangle.

"Oh my God, are you okay?!" I look up. Pen is peering over the edge, her face knotted in concern.

I look down at my harness. The speed of the descent has buggered up my knot. The whole thing is a coiled nest of sash cord under tension. There's no way I can undo it.

"Can you lower me down?" I shout up.

"Mmmmfffpphhhhmmhhhh!!!"

Penelope leans out of the window.

"Dougal is caught up in the rope!"

Shit.

There's a definite hubbub rising from below. Most of the large crowd is now looking up to me as I dangle forty feet from the ground in the rosy twilight.

Suddenly the sash cord creaks.

There's a jerk, another strangled yelp from above and I savagely drop another couple of feet. I lose my balance – flip upside down. My head is now directly above the tarmac, my feet point to heaven. I'm facing out to sea.

A seagull wheels below my head.

The sunset looks so odd upside down.

The sash cord groans again. No time for sightseeing. I look up – the corner of the desk is coming through the window. That teuchter idiot is too damned small. We're both going to plummet unless I come up with something pretty spectacular. And since the best idea I've ever had has resulted in this current predicament, I am not optimistic. I will meet my doom on the roof of a refectory, like some confused anorexic suicide.

People are shouting from below. Something seems to be

happening.

Now the wind buffets me. I bounce smartly off the crumbling sandstone and return. The sash cord creaks suddenly and I drop a foot. I look down – or rather, up – at my rope belt.

My improvised harness has become entangled in the rope, forming one giant knot. Worse than that, my weight is pulling the whole lot down – or rather, up. The knot is moving over the top of my pubes and is beginning to crush my genitals.

The wind smacks me into the stone again. The sash cord groans. I can feel an unpleasant crushing sensation on my penis.

The shouting from down below is getting louder.

I look up to the window – Penelope is there, fingers gripping the rough window ledge, knuckles white. Her mouse face is knotted in concern. Her eyes shine with tears.

The wind drops.

I smile at her.

And then suddenly:

Fwwwaaaaappppiiinng!!!

My belt breaks.

I grab for the harness but gravity has already whipped it down my thighs. My insides lurch as I plummet head first towards the ground.

And rather than images of the heavenly afterlife, the sole thought that leaps into my brain is – Shit, I really am going to die a virgin.

And it's all going so slowly.

I hear a mass gasp from below and then there's no sound any more, and vision is on freeze frame. I look up at Penelope. See her mousey face torn with terror, her hands flying to cover her screaming mouth. Damn. I was getting to like her.

Oh well.

And then my spine is stretched.

My harness has closed round my feet. The cord pulls wire-tight, wrapping around my ankles and securing me like bait on a line.

Then, in one smooth, fluid movement, my whole habit drops down from my knees and over my head.

There's a cheer from the crowd below.

I'm not dead. But my pasty, skinny body is now exposed from

armpit to ankle.

I just have time to watch my pendulous pods flop over my cock before my shirt drops down over my head.

I hear the gasps below give way to giggles. And, more to my distress than my comfort, I see through the grey cotton of my habit the lights of an upside-down fire engine screaming in from the east.

~

A grim, Desperate Dan-chinned fireman plucks me off the face of the building with his cherry picker.

As I stand in the middle of the carpark, shivering inside and out, I feel the gleeful stares of everyone in hall. Their eyes crawl over my body like leeches. This is when the firemen decide that it's apparently necessary to cut me free from the last scraps of my dignity that reside in my habit.

A pea-faced paramedic hands me a marathon runner's foil blanket. I try to wrap it round my lower body, but it tears in the wind. Clutching its flapping scraps vainly to my body I climb into the back of the ambulance. Even here there's no privacy. Looking out I see hundreds of eyes glowing like sinister fires in the failing light.

That's it, I think, have your fill. It's the last time you bastards will see me. And I scurry round the end of hall to where it abuts the street's garden area. There I drop to the ground and sit shivering in the dark at the foot of a glum old elm tree.

"Bonsoir."

Huh?

I turn. Look up.

My God.

It's the Angel. Shining down at me.

"Please, would it be ça va for you if I sit down here?"

She has just sat down on a tree root beside me. The outside world is gone. It's like a million candles just came on at once.

"Zat was very dramatic."

Her vowels roll like breakers on palm-hemmed sands.

"So bold."

Feel like I'm gently swaying in a pleasant breeze.

"I really like your balls," she smiles.

Trees evolve. Continents merge. Ice ages come and go.

"Erm, what?" I manage.

"Your courage, your spirit. Your bravissimo!"

Look at her fucking dressing gown. Is that silk? Is she... naked under that? The way she's leaning forward I can see the inside edge of her breasts. Christ in a catalogue, look at the way they swell...

"My name is Luciana Sugar. But I like to be called Lucy."

She's holding out her right hand. I start to move mine – and feel my foil start to slide. I shrug a little in explanation. She smiles and nods – it's okay. I move my left hand instead.

"Frederick Keddie," I say. "I mean, that was... but not now... it's Brother Fridericus, really."

She cocks her head, either to show confusion or to make one perfect lock of hair flop across her face.

"Is your name Freddie or not?" she asks with a frown.

"Yes," I say. "It is."

She holds out an elegant hand and we shake.

Mother can you hear me? I am touching the spiritual plane. Her grip is very strong – but only briefly. Then it softens a little, as if her flesh is savouring the contact. Have to screw up my eyes and half turn my head. Her light is blinding at such short range. Then she suddenly leans even further forward like she's about to tell me a secret. I can smell the sweet night scent of her skin floating out towards heaven from the front of her robe.

"But iz zat your character name or your real name?"

"Character... ?" I start.

She waves a slender had at my habit.

"Oui, zis, crazy inventor-type person you are looking like. He iz very eye-catching."

"I'm not an inventor," I say, "I am a friar-"

"I am sinking," Lucy interrupts, "zat you will make a great partner for me."

My brain does one complete revolution in my skull and settles back a little squint.

"A partner? Um... what?"

"For ze pub crawl, silly. Together we will win, I am sure of zat. I am wanting to win, you know."

"Well, I was sort of going to go with-"

"Freddie! When ze book of ze world is written, is it better zat zey put 'on Friday night Lucy stayed in and perfumed her backside'? Or 'on Friday night Lucy went three-legged pub crawling, got so very drunk and had such fun!'?"

"It's not that-"

"So what is it?"

Her eyes are melting my brain.

"It's that I am a friar, I have taken certain vows..."

She grabs my hand again. Strokes it. Her skin is like cashmere.

"Freddie," she says, "I can see you are a pious man, so you must sink of zis as a pilgrimage."

"The pub crawl is a pilgrimage?"

"Exactamente! With pubs as ze stations and drinks as ze penances."

What an interesting perspective. I hadn't thought about that.

"Plus," she says, "you monks are always making booze – ze beers, ze chartreuse-"

"The Buckfast," I add. And she beams at me. Golden cherubic radiation tingles my skin. Thrills my blood. Want to point out that I'm a friar not a monk. But I simply can't answer. To be honest, my synapses are still completely fused by image of Lucy Sugar perfuming her backside.

"Well, says Lucy. "What is it to be, M'sieur Kederick? To crawl or not to crawl?"

'Well, I... uhh... ha-humm..."

My mouth dries up.

She smiles at me, eyes shining wet and blue. Her lower lip hangs a pouting half inch below her top lip.

I clear my throat.

'Sure. That is... um... yeah."

She shoots to her feet. With a flourish wraps her dressing gown up tight.

"Zen I will see you on Friday night – for a pilgrimage to partyland!"

And just like that, the light is gone.

I look out to the darkness. For a minute I'm blind. Then I start to pick out the hundred burning eyes that now glow an unearthly green.

The last thing I see before they close the doors is a pale face at the edge of the crowd.

It's Penelope.

She looks back at me sadly for a moment then turns her face down and to the side. Then she too disappears into the night.

~

# THURSDAY, 5TH SEPTEMBER 2002

It's a lovely morning.

Cold and windy certainly, and a bit grey, but glorious nevertheless.

Gulls wheel and scream abuse at each other as Dougal and I walk along The Bents, the oldest street in town. It runs from McIvor and the North beach up and along the top of the cliffs, past the university and up to the ruined cathedral that sits above the harbour and the start of the South beach. The town's ancient spine. On the landward side, narrow lanes branch like veins towards Central Street. On the seaward side a straggle of old houses clings to the fringe of the town. Every few years a storm gobbles another chunk out of the cliff and another building is condemned. Despite packing itself with youth every year, there's nothing the ancient town can do to stop it.

I'm like a hawk – I see everything in unbelievable detail. The sea air's so crisp it makes my eyes water. Every piece of crumbling stonework stands out. The sharp breeze waves every leaf of every plane tree. Even the grey gulls look wonderful against the grey sky. It's a great day to be alive. In the prime of life. In God's creation. In Lucy... Gah! Damn these foul thoughts. Must distract myself.

All this fresh air is too invigorating. Better off sitting in the dark in my room. Do a spot of praying or something. So I head off back to halls.

Between my desk and the window casement there's a little window seat. No cushions or anything, just bare wood. But it's nice to sit there and look out at the sea. At the moment, though, I can't see much farther than the start of the beach. There's a fog rolling in and a gentle misty rain melts onto the panes.

So I'm just sitting here, arms wrapped around my legs, cup of Bovril steaming on the desk beside me, staring out at the rain. The scene might sound peaceful, but I'm not very comfortable, if I'm honest. My habit is sitting funny. Keeps riding up my hips. The repairs didn't go as well as I expected. Something wrong with the needle, I think. Or the thread. One of the two.

"Got the costumes!"

"Huh?" I look round to see Dougal trotting triumphantly into our bedroom.

"Check these out!"

He whirls towards me and throws a pair of carrier bags onto my bed. Reaches into one, pulls something out triumphantly. Big smile on his little face.

I stare.

"What the hell is that?" Not sure why I cursed just then. Not like me.

"Flintstones, man!"

"No, it isn't."

"Well now, Mr Snap-Snap, of course it is. This is Fred for ye and yon fella's Barney for me."

"Dougal, this is an orange leotard with some patches of black fur sewn onto it. That is a lime-green leotard with some patches of black fur sewn onto it."

"I am aware of that. But it's all they had."

"Thought you'd booked us Yogi and Boo Boo?"

"Ach, I cannot believe that myself. But apparently some bandits took our booking."

"How-?"

"Claimed they were us. Fella in the shop swore they even looked like us."

"Unrealistic practical circumstances aside, Dougal, the main problem with the fancy dress you have procured is that it isn't going to impress Lucy. She dresses so modernly for a pious girl and..."

"Lucy?!" woofs Dougal.

He pulls his chair over and sits down at the end of the desk, facing me across the window.

"What are you talking about, 'Lucy'?"

"Ah. Did I not mention that?" I reply. "She asked me to accompany her on the crawl."

"No. Not at any point in the last three days, Freddie, almost every hour of which we have spent in each other's company, have you mentioned that you are going to the three-legged pub crawl with Lucy Sugar."

He breathes slowly out. Looks down at his feet. And in. He stays like that for a while. Though he's not saying anything, it certainly feels like he's yelling something antagonist. Got to break this silence.

"I didn't actively decide to not mention it," I say.

"Don't try to be fly, Freddie," says Dougal, and swiftly lifts his eyes to mine. A piercing gaze that shoots out from low under his bushy little brows.

"I was holding the belief that you were going with Penelope. And I would hazard a pound to a punnet of tripe that she'll be holding that belief too."

And here he looks sad rather than angry. Which makes me feel even worse.

"It's just," he continues, "that the two of you got on so well together that night."

"Well, umm... I don't think so... I mean... we didn't say a whole lot."

"Perhaps it was the case that ye didn't need to. Ye were like the heather and the hillside."

"She's nice. Don't get me wrong. Really nice. A sweet, sweet girl. But..."

Dougal stops me with a wiry little paw. There's a wind gusting in from the sea. It ruffles his hair as he faces me. A gull soars behind him.

"But what?" he barks. "But she's no Lucy Sugar?"

"No! I mean. I haven't talked to anyone like I've talked to Penelope – with the possible exception of you. It's just that Lucy is...

"Angelic."

"Now why did you use that word!?"

"Pretty. Beautiful. Gorgeous. A classic beauty."

"That's not the point. I know what the word means. The important thing is that you know what I'm talking about."

He sighs, shakes his head and looks out of the window to the sea. There's something strange out there... It's like someone has taken a B pencil and just shaded a little at the horizon, where water meets wind. Is it a storm? Too far to say for sure. But it's spoiling a perfectly good blue sky.

And then the wee furry fella looks back from the window, reaches a paw out, picks up a tin, opens it and offers me a Penguin biscuit.

"Go on," he says.

"The Lucy thing is more about the moment. I'm not good with moments."

"Who is?" says Dougal.

"Maybe. But I'm different here. Honestly. I have significant history. I always miss the moment. Some good thing can be coming my way, and then, guaranteed, it will just never get to me. The party train never stops at Freddie's station. I can see it approaching on the tracks, chugging along, and I'm on the platform waiting and I can see everyone on board, waving flags out of the window, smiling at me and laughing and drinking cocktails in the dining car and I'm so looking forward to it arriving, and it's getting really close now, 'cos I can see how pretty some of the girls are, only just before it gets to me there'll be some massive disaster. Every time. There'll be like a landslide that will wash the tracks away, or the points will change, taking it to a new destination. Or the electrical overhead power system will fail, or-"

"I get the idea," says Dougal.

"And I don't know why. I mean, I really want the train to get there. But a lot of the time the disaster that stops it will be down to me."

"Electrical failures aren't your fault."

"It's a metaphor, Dougal."

"And it's a confusing one, bonny lad. Can you give me a 'for instance'?"

"Okay. It's like, when I was on my Italian exchange trip, I was staying in this tumbledown old palazzo, which is a big villa kind of thing, outside Florence. With a farming family. I was there to practice my Italian, you see?"

"I know what an exchange trip is, Freddie."

"Course you do. Course. Well, I was there for a week. And they made me feel so welcome, the farmer and his wife. Every day, the old wooden table was practically bucking with the freshest and most delicious food. Tomatoes, bread, olives, fish, cured had, homemade wine, even. Thing is, they also had this... daughter."

"Nice?"

"So hot. Oh, you wouldn't believe. Fresh and rosy like she was grown in the fields."

"Sounds lovely."

"And she had the most massive tits. Really incredible. She had this tiny waist and these tits – each one was bigger than her whole head, I swear."

"That's not a very holy observation."

"I know, sorry. But that's the point. This is when it all came to a head. And I had my epiphany."

"Ah, go on. I want to hear about this."

"Well, all week I have been chatting away with them, learning my vocabulary, my little phrases. The farmer and his wife have been bringing this fruit and that meat in and telling me all about them. But the daughter, she hasn't said a word to me. Not a thing. I swear, she hated every inch of me. Blanked me for six and a half days. Her tits were still stupendous, really full, globular almost..."

"Aye, I've got the bit about the tits, go on with the narrative."

"Sure. So. Anyway, the last night of my stay. I finish yet another wonderful meal and I go outside into the cool evening to walk off the food. Insects are droning, the air is sleepy, the low sun is melting the corn into honey. Perfect peace. And there, on the terrazza, she is. Sitting on the low wall. Black hair shining in the light. She turns back. Looks at me. And instantly, it all makes perfect sense. All I have to do is step over and kiss her. She hasn't been talking to me because she's shy. As shy as me. All week. So here it is now. My ideal moment to step on up. But I didn't. I mumbled something – in English – about needing the lavatory, and went in to bed."

"And ye're annoyed because ye didn't take the opportunity to kiss her?"

"No, that's not it. Plenty of people wouldn't have kissed her. After all, it was such a perfect moment that the pressure was on. The real pain came later that night. It's gone midnight. I'm lying there still awake under a fine white sheet, beside this plain cool wall that must be centuries old, watching the spiders and thinking what an idiot I've been when... I hear this knock."

"A knock?"

"A little tap tap. At my window. I'm on the ground floor."

"What did ye do?"

"Just lay there."

"Maybe it was a wee birdy."

"Then there's another knock. Tap tap tap. Ever so delicate, but very definitely there. Still I lay there. Finally, a third knock. Very bold. Tap tap tappity TAP!"

"And... ?"

"And still I just completely lie there. Lie there, staring at the bloody spiders on the bloody ceiling until she goes away."

"Ye think it was her?"

"Of course it was her."

"It might not have been..."

"Hey, don't spoil my story. The point is that the tapping stopped. She went. And in the morning we had to leave and I almost killed myself with regret. Tore me a-fucking part. I blew a perfect moment. But then I had the chance to make amends – and I blew that too."

"Ach, has it ever occurred to you that you just didnae really want to get with her? Her tits were braw, I understand, but there's more to love than that."

"Oh, you're right. But still I had this yawning, churning sickness in my stomach and wished beyond belief that I could turn back time. And I knew that feeling would bug me every day – I'd constantly be wishing I could go back in time and get up off that bloody bed and open the window – unless I did something about it. So I took the bus into Florence, strode into the basilica of Santa Croce and told one of the brothers to make me a friar that instant. He pointed out that the process took quite a while. Years, apparently. I pointed out to him that I had to get a plane at three-thirty. The fool just beamed. So I took my vows in my own fashion when I came home."

Dougal munches on a Penguin.

"Things are making a bit more sense now," he says. "However, you are not alone. We all make mistakes-"

"But not again and again and again! Don't you see? Now I've gone and blown it with Lucy Sugar too. The train has left the tracks. The costume is a furry leotard."

"What are ye talking about, ye great haddock? It's not too late. The pub crawl hasn't even started yet."

"A mere technicality-"

He leans forward, places a gentle terrier paw on my shoulder. Says softly:

"Freddie, ye're working yourself up into a right stramash over something that hasn't happened yet. Something that ye can make happen. Now, I want ye to put yon Italian lassie oot of yer heid for a while. Leave her back there in Italy. And I want ye to imagine for a second that ye're a field."

"A field."

"Aye. A great big beautiful wide field. Ploughed and ready to be seeded. Now ye have to open yourself up, open yourself to the sun and the rain so ye can grow. And if ye do, ye will surely flourish, by God."

"I suppose..."

"Just do it. Ye doing it?"

"I am a field."

"Good. Now step into yon shower through there, and imagine it is the rain, moistening yer seeds, bringing ye to life. And imagine that when ye see Lucy, she will be yer sun, helping ye grow. In the meantime, I'll make a nice spot of tea. Then we'll make ourselves look all braw and dandy, go downstairs and flourish. Together. What do you say?"

Pause.

Little chap has an interesting way of putting things. Look at his soft brown eyes. So warm. So friendly. So wise. Like little pots of muscovado sugar at gran's house.

"Toast," I say.

"What?"

"Could you make a slice or two of toast with the tea?"

"Of course, bonny lad," he says, smiling again.

~

The hilarity begins in the Rec. Huge old hall that forms most of the ground floor of MacIvor. The grand ballroom when the place was a hotel. You could land a plane in it. Six floor-to-ceiling windows on either side, beautifully proportioned, disgustingly dirty. View of the beach would be heart-stopping if only you could see it. Wallpaper magnificent in colour, texture and pattern - less so in its ability to stick to the walls.

Place is now our Recreation Room - although there's not a hell of a lot to do. Two pianos, one at either end, neither in tune. Genuine Radiogram foolishly situated beneath the dartboard. Sweaty Grundig telly that can only get BBC2. Pool table with no cue ball. Last week's newspapers. Threadbare rugs stained with a thousand cider spills. Some poor stag above the fire with a comedy 'tache and only one eyeball.

Room is busy, buzzing. Must be a hundred freshers here, full of hormones and cheap alcohol.

"She's not here," I say, and stop on the threshold. "She's changed her mind, she's-"

Gently, Dougal takes my arm.

"Remember what I said in the room?"

"Yes."

"It's up to us to flourish."

"Right."

"She'll come. Ye just have to be patient. Come on, let's get ootside some of yon punch."

We make our way over to Glasses Matthew who stands behind a chipped grey table ladling watery pink liquid from a purple plastic bucket into polystyrene cups.

"How many?" says Glasses Matthew.

"Two," says Dougal.

Glasses Matthew hands two cups of punch to Dougal.

"And two for him," says Dougal pointing to me. Glasses Matthew narrows his eyes. But Dougal steps innocently away, sipping at the first of his drinks.

Glasses Matthew pours my cups. Hands them over. Curls his lip at me in an alarming way. I turn to join Dougal. He's slurping at his plastic cup.

"Nae bad. Try it."

Not sure about this. Punch looks and smells like the vomit of a kid who ate too much jelly at his own birthday party.

"Come on, laddie, down the hatch!"

He lifts his cup to his lips and raises his eyebrows expectantly.

"You can do it," he says.

Grimacing, I stick two fingers up my nose and gulp the foul liquid. It surges in my stomach, homesick for its previous owner, but I breathe slowly and swallow it back down.

"Good show," says Dougal, turning to the guy with the huge NHS glasses. "Two more."

"No, please-"

But suddenly I notice a vastly overweight girl cantering across the floor towards us. Monica. She wears a tutu, a tiara and tiny pink wings. In her right hand is a wand. In her left, a white cotton strap.

"Dougal, darling! There you are! How fucking dare you keep a fairy waiting!"

"Ach, Monica!" coos Dougal, his little tail wagging.

"Love your outfit," she says with a giggle. "You're quite the rugged caveman!"

"And ye are the most enchanting wee sprite ah've ever met," he says smiling. She laughs and grabs his arm as I marvel at his ability.

"Hey, Monica," he says. "You remember Freddie?"

"Oh, hey, Freddie," she says. "How's it going?"

Pause. Stare at her.

"My seeds are moist," I say, "and I'm ready to grow."

Monica doesn't say much for a moment.

She turns to Dougal. Holds up her white strap.

"Come on, Barney," she says, "we'd better get ready." And she takes his arm to lead him away.

"Aye, sure," nods Dougal. "Wait just a second, though." And he turns back, steps up to me. "It's not too late," he whispers, "remember that. Ye can make this happen."

And then with a whirl of her wand, Monica magicks him away. I'm on my own.

~

I shuffle my way through the chattering throng. People keep staring at me. One guy dressed as Superman nudges his Wonder Woman partner. Points. Together they laugh. What the fuck are you looking at?! Punch! Smash! Sigh. Wish I had the courage to forgo my peaceable promises and just hit out. But I don't have it. And I know I don't. Which makes it twice as bad.

Take up position below previously mentioned monocular mammal on a splintered cane chair to the left of one of the massive marble bulwarks of the fireplace. Exquisitely Italian stone towers beside me. Press my face to its white coolness.

A moment's calm.

There's a massive gold-framed mirror above me. Randy cherubim forever pursuing laughing seraphim round its perimeter. Poor cherubs. Bad enough being frozen forever in a state of frustrated arousal without some pretentious sculptor painting your arse gold and sticking you on the mantelpiece.

Place is really filling up now.

Suddenly the room goes strangely silent.

Normally when a crowd goes quiet, the noise dies away gradually. There are always a few people who are too thrilled with their own voices to notice or who simply can't stop themselves who continue to babble on until the silence gains enough weight to shut them up too.

But this is weird because it's instant. Everyone just hushes at the same moment. I shiver. Is there a draught in here? Can feel the hairs on my neck standing up a little. My skin is clammy.

Look around – everyone's doing the same. Pausing. Looking unsure. Trying to work out what's making them feel so creepy.

Then I see them.

Standing in the doorway.

Two guys in fancy dress.

Yogi and Boo Boo.

The thieves.

Everyone clocks them – briefly, then they look away. Because there's nothing sinister to see. They're perfectly normal, in a scruffy way. Yogi's about my height. His collar is wonky and instead of a trilby he has a beret. Boo Boo's suit doesn't fit that well. The guy inside is about Dougal's height, but a lot fatter. The pale meat of his belly bulges out at the waist of the pink suit. The material has a few brown splashes of dubious provenance.

Spats of rain clatter the windows. Wind rattles the casements. A collective groan rises from the crowd. Their attention is diverted. Chatter starts again.

Perfectly normal.

If a little cheeky. Them taking our costumes. Still, probably not their fault. Dougal told me that the guy who runs the fancy dress store is a retired North Sea roughneck who has a piece of exploded drilling gear embedded in his skull. Dresses each day of the working week as a different member of the Jackson 5. He probably got confused.

Yogi and Boo Boo already have their strap tied round their legs. Thought this was meant to be boy and girl. If one of them's a girl she has problems. As I watch they hurple across the room towards the piano. Takes them a while – Yogi's stepping normally, making it hard work for Boo Boo. Not very considerate of him.

There's really nothing extraordinary about them at all. But then, as they reach the piano stool, Yogi flicks a glance at me and I feel... I feel in my entire body what your stomach feels like when you drive over a hump in the road too fast.

Weird.

Anyway, forget them. Lucy will be here soon. Think field. Think sunshine. Better check my outfit in the mirror.

For God's sake, look at my balls. This Flintstone costume is a joke. The orange leotard would be tight on an eight-year-old girl. On me it's obscene. There's a patch of fur sewn into the crotch to cover things, but it's not very big. My plums are bulging right out the bottom. Some of the hairs are poking through the orange lycra. Be very surprised if I get through tonight without getting arrested.

Sense a few people staring at me already. Look down. Got my

hand stuffed into the bulge of the leotard. Probably shouldn't be there, in a public place. Take it out – carefully – don't to pull any junk out at the same time.

Stare out at the rain, now slapping heavily against the panes. What the hell was in that punch? Stomach feels all soapy, head all whooshy. This is even worse then Italy. At least then my misery was private. Now I have a hundred happy people watching me, all tied together, drunk together. Together together.

Man, I wish I'd persevered with Penelope.

Which is when the room goes quiet again.

Not totally silent like the last time. Now it's only the blokes who have stopped talking. The girls chatter on for a moment before looking round to see what has so completely taken their man's attention away from them.

Lucy Sugar is with us.

She sees me. Smiles. Waves. At ME! And my heart is a salmon, leaping and slithering in my chest. Fly to my feet. Smile. Wave back. Start to gallop across the room.

And then the salmon crashes back to the lower pool.

Not because of the tight brown boots she wears, with pointed toes, Mexican heels and fur trim round the top. Nor the leopard-print cowboy hat or soft leather gunbelt slung round her taut bronze midriff. It's not even the red satin bikini with more fur trim and silver tassels flying from the nipples that has me stunned.

It's the fact that she is tied, with a white cotton strap round one beautiful bare leg, to CLIVE.

In a dinner jacket. Shit. Have to admit, the fishy fucker looks almost cool. Christ, they're coming towards me. Moving together in perfect harmony. Her hips glide, proud legs strut, breasts bounce in their satin sheaths. Silver tassels sway. Hypnotic. Atomic. Room's still silent. Everyone else is probably staring at her too, but I don't know. I'm not taking my eyes off her to find out. angelic visitations certainly grab a crowd.

And who would have thought angels would be so shapely? Slender, but not skinny. Athletic thighs, very. As she moves the muscles flex and counterflex beneath the taut golden skin.

Suddenly she stops about ten feet away. Stares at me like

something's wrong. Puts her hands out at her sides. Half crouches, like she's a cat ready to spring. Cocks her head on one side. Sets her jaw. All the while staring at me. Don't like this. Don't like it at all. What's she doing?

Her hands fly to her hips – and grab two silver plastic cap guns from the soft leather gunbelt. She points them at me.

"P-kow! P-kow!" she cries, firing them at me in turn.

Pause.

"P-kow! P-kow!" she cries again, her shots echoing round the stunned room.

Longer pause.

Her eyes narrow. She stands upright. Drops her hands. Frowns.

"I hit you!" she shouts. "You're completely dead!"

A hard stare. Eyebrows really furrowed. She doesn't want me to... ? Oh God, I think she does. Don't want to do that. Not here, not in front of these people... Too late! My son of a bitch body is going ahead without me. Can feel myself crumpling lamely to the floor. No, stop it, you arsehole! But I'm going down. Somewhere, someone sniggers. And without looking I know that every man, woman and medical student is watching me, a sneer on their vicious, thankful faces. The last thing I hear as I hit the deck is the unmistakable sound of my dignity galloping for the hills.

The ceiling looks so white.

Breathe out.

With little black spiders crawling on the ancient plaster.

Breathe in.

Cannot believe I just did that. No way I'm getting up now. I'm just going to lie here until everyone goes away and me and my nine-foot shame can leave in peace.

Maybe I am dead, though. They weren't toys, they were real guns. She's gone ahead and shot me. "Sorry, son, you're too virginal to live. You have to die. Die! Die! DIE!" Hope so. Be better than getting up again. Can't face the sniggering looks of the mob.

So I'll just stare at this old ceiling until the demons come for me. Must be demons, because I'm going to hell. Wanked too much to go to heaven, I must confess. St Peter's got his accounting sheet up there, wanks on one side, prayers on the other and though I may be a friar, I am in serious wank overdraft. No way that dude's letting me in.

So, I'll wait for the demons right here. Just staring at the fading paint and watch the spiders and the phenomenal young breasts bursting from a red satin bikini with silver tassles-

She's standing above me.

I'm alive.

Her flawless belly sheers up to the jutting wonder of those tits. Her flawless belly also dives down to the taut crimson fabric of her bikini bottoms. So brief. So beautiful. Look at them, the way they've been cut so- Oh my fucking God, is that the curve of her fanny-?!

"What are you being Mr Lazy Bones down there for? Jump to it now!" I have to tie you up." She's dangling one of those cotton straps above me. Except this strap is different. It has a long thin piece of soft black fur sewn onto it. The same fur that adorns her toes.

It draws me to my feet.

"Wunderbar!" she cries. "Now tie yourself to me here."

Clive leans forward, his slimy eyes rolling in their hoods.

"Lucy, what, ah... what's going on?" I ask.

"Him? Oh, he ask if he can come too."

"Yes, but this is a three-legged pub crawl. Not a four or five. Or whatever."

"I know, but he kept going on and on. He said it was somesing to do with ze fire regulations. In ze end I couldn't be bozzered saying no. You don't mind, do you?"

Look over at Clive. His trout mouth is set. Skin is cold as the deepest sea. Clammy eyes are almost completely hooded. It's really very simple, he's saying, 'Tonight, you will die'.

"Good boys. Now you get busy with this, Frrreddie." And she hands me the furry strap.

Clive stares at me for a second longer, then-

"Darlings, can I have your attention please!" booms a voice.

Monica is standing on a chair beside Glasses Matthew. The chair moans in pain.

Clive hauls his eyes away from me as we all clock Monica.

"Now, my loves. You want to drink some beer?" shouts Monica. A few gentle 'yesses'.

"You want to crawl round every bar in town?"

Yes!

"You want to get totally fucked up and puke your fucking ring?!"

YEESS!!

"That's more like it! Now, in a second I'll come round and give you all a map. You can visit the bars in any order you like, as long as you..."

But I don't hear any more. The fur is soft in my fingers. I bend forward to tie it. Shit, there's her leg. Her actual leg. Skin so golden and smooth stretching for miles. Going to have to get the strap round it. But I can't actually touch the godflesh, so how-

And suddenly Lucy presses her bare leg against mine. Adrenalin catapults my heart from my chest. It's the first time I've ever properly touched a girl and it's a yard of solid contact. From ankle to thigh I feel her firm beauty pushing against me.

Nnnnnng...

Can't think.

Dooohhh...

Hands won't move.

All powers of locomotion have been instantly suspended by the mammoth erection that springs into existence within a second and a half of her touching me. Can feel it roaring at the seams of the leotard. Glance down. Oh God, it couldn't be more obvious. My entire crotch area looks like a gala-day marquee. How the hell to deal with this? Run for it. No, I will not blow this opportunity. Have a wank? Tricky - there must be a hundred people in this room.

The belt! Of course, perfect. With frantic dexterity I reach down and work my cock so it points directly upward. Then I hook my belt over the underside of my bell-end. The terrifying tenting of the leotard has now been replaced by a curious but not entirely offensive ridge that extends downwards from my navel. It'll have to do.

Brain comes on line. Hands are shaking, but they're working. Cotton strap flutters and flaps. Try to pass the end around behind her calves. My hand accidentally brushes her skin. So smooth...

My cock gives a mighty spasm.

"Hurry, Frrreddie!" she says, waving a route map. "We haff a great many pubs to go to."

Try again. Hold one end of the cotton against my leg with my left hand, pass the other end round, gather it up and pass it round again. Look at her boots. They're fucking insane. The way each strap presses its own niche in her flesh. Damn, I've dropped the cotton. Start again. Hold it here and pass it there and try not to think about how the top of her golden foot curves outwards as the stack pushes her heel up and shit, I've dropped the cotton again.

"Are you going to take all night?" snaps Clive.

"Yah, hurry up zere," adds Lucy.

What with the texture of the leather and the fur brushing her brown skin and the heart red splashes of polish on her toes, I believe that is a distinct possibility.

But before I can share my doubts she is bent over beside me. Her hands work the end of the cotton. Moving confidently, roughly even, they bind her leg to mine. As she ties a knot she pulls the cotton strap so tight it bites a little into my flesh. Pain makes me wince. Is that a smile she's torturing?

Slowly I stand upright. My belt holds. I manage a strangled smile.

"Buenissimo," she says. "Now we are ready to party."

~

Walking three-legged is bad enough when you're as tall and gangly as I am. But when you're going four-legged or five-legged or whatever it is with three people, it's twice as bad. And it's started to rain. A nasty, whipping squall that comes at us from all directions. Plus I have to do the whole thing hunched over so that my rampant prong doesn't spring free from his berth. Each time our legs move together I feel her skin slide against mine, her muscles flex and my cock twitch. Every limping step we take through the ancient town only cripples me more.

"What are you, Keddie, some kind of spaz?" says Clive as I

make us stumble for the twelfth time.

"I'm trying, alright?"

"Yes, I haff to say, you are moving like a stupid giraffe."

She says it with a smile, but there's a curl of impatience around her heavenly eyes that I don't like the look of.

"Where are we going anyway?" I ask. "Isn't there a closer pub?"

Clive snorts.

"You're new here, Keddie. Leave the route finding to me. If we go to the closer pubs now we spend half the night queuing with all the other fresher idiots."

Lucy stops suddenly.

"Hey... do not be calling me an idiot!'

"Just a joke, Lucy. Take it easy," slimes Clive.

"Don't 'take it easy' me!" storms Lucy. "Your joke it is not funny, okay?"

Hallelujah. Look at the way she's jabbing that finger. Making her breasts judder. She really means it.

Clive recoils into his shell.

"Sure, Lucy, I'm sorry," he says, eyes wide.

"Bueno," she says, easing a few stray hairs back under the rim of her cowboy hat. "Now can we allez?"

I know I shouldn't look at him, but I can't resist a cheeky peek. He catches me – and bares his teeth.

Mother Broon's lies on the Bents, deep in a basement. We get stuck in the door on the way in and I clatter my head off the lintel. I can feel a raw bump rising as we step inside.

A beautiful white marble bar runs the length of one wall. Oak panelling and leather stools. At one end is a platform which offers the well-placed scrum half a perfect view of incoming tottie. Slightly incongruously, an ancient tabletop space invaders game sits in one corner.

"See?" says Clive, sweeping his hand wide.

Dammit. He's right. There isn't a three-legger in sight.

Lucy looks around.

"Zat is clever thinking," she says. "I like it!"

Clive sneaks a grin back at me. "I'll get these," he says, pulling up a pair of stools. "A pint of eighty shilling for me, please barman.

Lucy?"

"Oo, that sounds lovely. What is it?"

"It's an ale," says Clive. "The 'eighty' refers to the old price of a barrel and it's now really a measure of the strength and taste. You get seventy, eighty and occasionally ninety."

"Paf! I don't know what you are talking about, but Lucy will try some."

He tries to smile this off, then turns to me.

"And what do you want?"

"Erm, just a half of lager please."

"A half of lager?" cries Clive. "What are you, ssssome kind of gay?"

"I have taken a vow of sobriety, as well as celibacy."

"Mein Dieu!" says Lucy. "You are a man are you not?"

"Well... if you say so."

"Of course, you have balls, yes?"

"Yeah..."

"Well a man with balls must have a drink wiz balls. You must be having an eighty pint too."

"But I don't like bitter."

"Perhaps you would prefer a cider?" says Clive. He's smiling, which is worrying, but I have to admit, cider's about the only thing I can drink.

"Um, sure. Thanks."

"Pint of Addlestones," says Clive to the barman.

The drinks come.

"Here's to you!" says Clive, his eyes on Lucy, and takes a big pull on his eighty.

"Salut!" says Lucy and quaffs almost half her pint in a oner.

"Hmmm! Lucy like!"

"Right. Um, cheers," I say and take a deep draught of my cider. It's not really that sweet. Tastes almost metallic in fact.

Urrrpp!!

And it roils unpleasantly in my stomach. Makes my belly contract.

"So, Lucy," says Clive, easing himself back on his stool. "Which department will have the honour of your presence?"

Why didn't he just ask her what she was studying?

"I am enrolled in Frrrrancais!" she says with a flourish.

Clive slides towards her a little.

"How fascinating," he says. "From your accent I presumed you spoke that already."

He has this quiet, slippery way of speaking which means Lucy has to turn completely away from me to converse with him.

"Bien sur. I speak many languages. Zat is why I chose zat course. So I can pass it easy and concentrate on important things."

"What's more important than your degree?"

She looks at him like he's dropped from Mars.

"It is ze acting of course."

"Oh, how simply sssensational!" he says.

"Zank you. Yes, I am also taking the Media Studies course in, how you say, a joint paper."

"Clever, as well as talented," he says.

Look at him, with his fake smile and silly grin. Can she not tell he's putting all this shit on? She leans right forward into his space, her magical face completely animated. I take another gulp of my cider.

"Mais oui, I am going to be a fa-moos actress!"

"I can see that," says Clive.

"You can?"

"In fact," says Clive, wagging his finger at her, "you remind me of someone..."

"Who?" cries Lucy, leaning right towards him. I cannot believe she's falling for this crap. More cider required.

"Hmmm, let me see. I can't... no... you know, it's not one movie star. You have too remarkable a face for that. It's more a combination... oh, I don't know..."

"Go on, please, how are you meaning?"

"No, I can't. You'll think me stupid."

She clasps his fin.

"Please no, you must tell!"

Suddenly I feel a draught. Turn to see the door is open. And Yogi and Boo Boo are standing in the frame. The biting wind whips rain round them into the bar.

"Well, it's like... like you have the class and grace of Audrey Hepburn, the strength and charisma of Lauren Bacall, and the powerful sexuality of Marilyn Monroe."

Christ in a catsuit. For fuck's sake, man, stop it. She won't swallow that.

But her eyes glaze and half close. She sways in her seat. And, I swear, she moans. Gently, and under her breath, but very definitely a moan.

Past her swaying left shoulder, Clive sneers at me. That's it. Eye for an eye time.

"I acted once," I say. Part of me knows this may end badly, but still I say it.

Lucy comes back to earth.

"What?" she snips.

"In a play at school. A Streetcar Named Desire. I got the lead."

"Oh," says Lucy, half turning to me. "Ze Paul Newman part?"

"No, ah, the other one."

Clive snorts with laughter. "You played Blanche DuBois?"

"It was a boys' school," I retort. "I was the only one whose voice hadn't broken." I turn to Lucy. "But everyone said I was really good."

Clive laughs harder. Lucy doesn't at first. Not sure she gets what Clive's laughing at. But she can see he's doing so, and she can see that I'm getting redder, and somehow that's enough to make her laugh too.

"Oh," says Clive, wiping his eyes with the back of a fin. "That's a great story, Keddie. A real cracker."

"Yes," adds Lucy. "How very funny!"

And suddenly Clive's smile is gone. Instantly replaced by intense concentration as he says to Lucy:

"So, you must have had some major roles yourself?"

His attention is like a tractor beam. It pulls her head right round from me to him.

"Why yes, at my first school, in Buenos Aires, zey gave me the role of second dairymaid. Very important to ze story. You see, ze dairymaid gets seduced by ze leader of ze banditos-"

Can't bear to watch him even listen to her. Swivel away from them and... Whoops! Almost slide from my stool. Suddenly a little wobbly... Definitely not steady. Better have some more of that cider. Yes, that'll help. Now where's my glass? There it is. Where? There! Get it, quick, before it moves again. Gotcha! Now let's have a lovely big glug and-

Shit, it's empty.

Sure I hadn't drunk that much. Weird. Really w-w-weird. Where did my lovely cider go? Not down there or over here or... Hang on. What's Yogi doing? Look at him. Standing no more than two feet away, looking as guilty as a giant nylon creature can look. Is that cider on his chin fur? Think it is.

"Hey!" I say.

"Hey yourself," replies Yogi.

"D-d-did you drink my drink? M-m-my lovely cider?"

He wipes his chin with a paw and leans back against the bar.

"Yes," says Yogi. "Now keep your voice down."

Outside, thunder rolls across the ocean.

"I will not. Not until you buy me another."

Yogi exhales loudly. Shakes his furry head.

"Are you g-g-going to b-b-buy me another one?" I manage.

"No."

How dare he? Outrageous! Not standing for this. Turn to the barman.

"Excuse me," I say, "this beer just drank my bear."

"Shut up!" hisses Yogi.

"Shut up yourself!" I say.

"I beg your pardon?" says the barman.

"Not you," I say. "Him!" and I point at Yogi, but he's too near. Hand goes right over his shoulder.

"For Christ's sake," hisses Yogi. "Put a sock in it."

"NO!"

"He's right," says the barman. "It would be for the best if you kept your voice down, sir."

"And just who do you think you're talking to? What kind of bar is this anyway? Giant fauna drinking my cider. Ridiculous."

"What's going on, Keddie?" says Clive.

"He is, how you say... topsy," says Lucy.

"I think you guys should go," says the barman.

"Not until this furry oaf buys me lovely cider."

"NOW."

"Oh, don't worry, Keddie," says Clive with a smile. "Plenty pubs to go. Come along, we'll get you more cider in the Crit."

And he starts towards the door.

"Well, okay," I mutter, glancing back at Yogi. "But something should be done."

~

The Crit is at the opposite end of town, just inside the old town wall behind the ruined cathedral. Have to say, I'm glad of the walk. Once my muscles get going, my head clears a little. In fact the cider seem to sink directly from my brain to my cock, which shrinks out of sight most gratifyingly.

"Have to apologise for that," I say. "Just not used to drinking."

"Oh, don't worry, Keddie," says Clive. "We'll soon make a man of you. Practice is all it takes."

And he winks at Lucy. Like a stab in the heart she smiles back.

"This bar is a fabulously dramatic place, Lucy," smears Clive as we approach the stone-fronted pub. "It's run by old Miss Milne, a sssort of Miss Havisham character, if Miss Havisham owned a pub and had an alcohol problem of rock star proportions. Shall we?" And he opens the door for her.

Inside, I'm annoyed to see he's right. Everything in the bar is as it was in the early fifties. Dust, ancient bottles and real candles create quiet an atmosphere.

"You can only buy spirits, stout and bottles of mild," says Clive, "and you have to serve yourself if Miss Milne is sleeping."

I look over to where Clive is pointing to see our superannuated hostess slumbering in a velvet chair by the fire. A half-drunk half-pint of what looks like sherry stands on a little card table in front of her. The thick make-up on her face has been eroded into rivulets by untold streams of tears. The only other person in the bar is an antiquated beagle farting in his sleep on the rug close to Miss Milne.

"My round," I say. "What would you like?"

"Nonsense," says Clive. "I'll get these."

"You got the last lot."

"Oh, I know. People often remark that my generosssity will be my downfall. But what can I do? I ssso love to give." And as he says the last word he stares at Lucy and runs a slippery tongue along his top lip.

Miss Milne is starting to sing to herself in her sleep so we choose a table at the far side of the bar. Clive unclips himself and moves behind the bar to get the beer.

"He's got it in for me," I mutter.

"What's ze matter," coos Lucy. "Can't ze daring mister SAS man take it?"

I stare. Can't believe it. Is she on his side?

Long pause as her eyes challenge me.

Then suddenly she laughs. Leans forward. Her soft mouth open, ripe lips budding.

"Don't worry," she says gently. "You have nussing to fear."

My world goes still. I'm lost in her eyes. What can she possibly mean by that?

SLAMM!

Clive puts three drinks on the table.

"Mild for us, and I thought you might try some of this." I look at the bottle in front of me.

Large, brown, dust-encrusted bottle. On the label is a picture of a heavily bearded sailor in full oilskins. He smokes a pipe and grins as he puffs. In his right hand is a brown bottle similar to the one I hold now. His left arm stretches out to embrace a tremendously busty but somewhat cock-eyed mermaid. Below the illustration are printed the words, 'Nathaniel's Old Particular'.

"What do you think?" asks Clive.

I take a drink. Cough a little. Hold back a splutter. Tastes very much like Nathaniel has been using the stuff to bathe his old particular.

Swallow.

Take a breath.

"Harmless," I say, smiling at Lucy, who sweetly smiles back.

The door creaks open. Three pairs of laughing three-leggers tumble in and approach the bar. Yogi and Boo Boo slope in behind them.

Boo Boo edges into the corner just to our right. Yogi stares across at me, then follows his little friend into the shadows. There's something creepy about them. Something unnatural that I don't quite like. He's uncanny.

Clive is still going. I lean towards him, feigning interest.

"Yes, last Tallowmasss I drank twelve bottlesss of this," he says, pointing to his beer bottle. "And I still made it to the Vindendraam."

"What is zis 'Talllowmas'?" asks Lucy.

Out of the corner of my eye I observe Yogi as he casually reaches forward out of the darkenss, picks up my bottle and downs three quarters of it in a oner. What is it about him...?

I turn completely round to face Clive.

"Have you not heard of the Tallowmas Fair?" says Clive to Lucy.

"No," she says.

He smiles and rubs his hands. Moves closer to her.

"It happens at the end of Tallowmas term, on the nearest full moon before the winter solstice. It's a festival to bring the community together against the coming cold – it's been celebrated since the middle ages. The townsssspeople have a carnival with a fire procession, while the university runsss entertainment in the ancient roman amphitheatre below the castle. Every year one hall is chosen to put on a 'Vindendraam' – which is kind of like a mediaeval cross between a play and a re-enactment of a historical event. This year it's McIvor's turn."

Lucy claps her hands together.

"Mein dieu, it sounds so very exciting!"

"The whole town will watch. And it's really popular with tourists too. Anyone who's in town for the golf will come and watch. It's a famousss occasion. And of course, it's a great honour to be in the Vindendraam. I'm on the committee, don't you know."

Lucy leans forward, eyes blazing. Christ, is that her hand drifting towards his leg?

Suddenly I feel something pressing against my fingers. I look down. Under my hand on the tabletop is a beermat that wasn't there before. I pick it up. Nathaniel smiles at me as he does from his bottle.

I flip it over.

The same picture adorns this side – apart from, scrawled across the mermaid's chest, the words: "Want to shut him up? Bogs, now, Yogi."

~

This is the lavatory of a million pisses. The victorian porcelain urinal has been stained with a yellow stalagmite design by a century of recycled booze. Smoked windows an inch thick keep the stale air in and most of the light out. In the corners, vast mutated spiders harvest cigarette buts.

Lighting flashes outside, revealing Yogi leaning against the rusted up condom machine, a bottle of stout in his right paw.

"About time, Junior," he says, tossing the bottle in the urinal.

"Who are you?" I ask.

He shakes his head. "What are you, thick?" He steps out of the shadows. "I'm Yogi fucking Bear, kid." And stares at me threateningly, face to face. How odd. We're exactly the same height.

"W-w-what do you want?" I stammer.

He moves back towards the sinks.

"I'm here to help you, kid."

"I d-d-don't need help."

"Balls. You're being totally outplayed. Half-cut already and that fucksack Clive is laying down primo moves on the golden wonder."

"Lucy says I have nothing to worry about-" I start.

"Listen, kid, if we don't act now you're going to get so staggering drunk that she cuts you loose on the way out to the Mashie, leaving you to piss all over yourself in a bunker while she gets snug with Clive."

"I'd never do such a thing!"

"Believe me, kid," says Yogi, "you most definitely would."

"I'm not listening. You're an illusory demon sent by Satan."

"What?!"

"You're in cahoots with my evil randy subconscious..."

"What the fuck are you talking about, you drunken tool? I'm not in cahoots with anyone. I'm doing this purely for your own good. Believe me, I want nothing more than to see you pump Lucy Sugar."

"Pervert."

"Can't believe I was this stupid," he mutters.

"What are you talking about?"

"Listen, it's better that we don't go into this right now. If it'll help, you can think of me as a good Samaritan. And if you do as I say, things will work out for you."

"No way..."

Yogi takes a step towards me. I take one back – against the clammy brick of the cubicle. I have nowhere to go. Yogi moves closer. Lays a paw on my shoulder.

"Junior, it's okay to be nervous. Lucy's hotter than a mile of hell. Clive's a highly practised tosser. Odds stacked against you. Always were."

Lightning flashes.

"Let me take your hits for you," he says.

"You want to drink my beer?"

"Most of it, yes."

"So you're a wino."

"Listen, you dumb fuck, I'm doing this because the most you've ever drunk before is the half a bottle of Merrydown you had on your eighteenth birthday that made you spew on the cat!"

I wilt a little.

"How do you know... ?"

"Give me three pubs."

"What?"

"If I haven't turned things round by the time you get out of Bar Central, well, you got a long night ahead. Plenty of time to do things your way." He pauses, looks through the grimy glass, as if there's something out there. Then he shakes his head to clear it and looks me in the eye. His voice slows. Drops quieter. "But please, give me that much time."

I think about this. He looks as sincere as a giant cartoon character can look. I breathe in.

Sigh out.

"I can feel the muscles in her thighs move," I moan.

Yogi puts his arm around my shoulders.

"Know you can, kid," he says softly.

Beyond the dripping brick walls thunder crashes across the heavens.

~

Miss Milne now lies on the rug, her arm around the farting beagle as she sings into his fur. Several pairs of three-leggers stand around, quickly quaffing their mild and trying not to look.

Back at our table I notice that Boo Boo has take up station at the next table to Clive. As I sit down, he picks up a spirit glass and swiftly pours a large dose of clear liquid it into Clive's mild. Ffflllooooop! The spirit swirls in the flickering electric candle light, mixing quickly.

Boo Boo lifts a paw to his lips in a 'sh' gesture. I nod. He peels away, the empty spirit glass in his other paw. I slide back into my seat at the table.

Lucy is sitting forward on the very edge of her stool, her left leg hooked high over her right towards Clive who lounges back with his hands clasped behind his head. Her arms writhe around each other like crazy snakes, her hands clasping and unclasping this way and that in front of her.

"...so how can I be in the Vindendraam?" she keens, bobbing a little in her seat.

Clive strokes his moustache.

Out of the corner of my eye I notice Yogi pick up my bottle and casually down three-quarters of it. A rivulet of beer courses down his acrylic yellow chin.

"One way," says Clive, "isss through the open auditions held in hall. Competition is fierce, of course, and-"

Yogi pops the bottle softly back on the table and moves round in his seat.

Lucy stops her arms writhing and slowly puts a honey-coloured hand on Clive's knee.

"And the other way... ?"

Clive sits forward, putting his hand to his chin in thinker pose.

"Well, as deputy warden, I am on McIvor's Vindendraam committee-"

"Come on you guys," I say. "Drink up."

Then I pick up my nearly empty glass and finish it.

Clive's scaly eyebrows crawl upwards.

"We have a lot of pubs to go to, right?" I add.

Lucy looks at me. Shrugs her shoulders. Downs her beer. Looks at Clive. He looks at his glass. Picks it up. Puts it to his lips. Sniffs. Can he tell... ?

"The night is yet young," I say casually. "Isn't that right, Lucy?" And I pat her on the knee.

Where the hell did that come from? A half-chill of panic shoots through me – surely she'll slap me for touching her like that? But she doesn't. She just laughs and tosses her hair.

"Yah, iss true. Stop being such a snail, Clive!"

He looks back at me. I stare him down, a big powerful smile growing on my face.

Then he shrugs, lifts his glass and drinks.

~

The Cathedral Inn is a quaint and rustic place. More American tourists having a meal than locals or students. Lucy gets the beers in.

The bears move fast. Clive has barely started banging on about the strings he might be able to pull on the Vindendraam when Boo Boo's got him dosed and I'm down to an inch of beer.

"What is it with you tonight? I thought you were an expert at this drinking lark?" I say.

His oily eyes roll and sneer with outright suspicion. But he doesn't get it. And down goes another double vodka.

On the way to Bert's Bar the heavens open. We try to hurry, but Clive's now too drunk to move fast. We get soaked. Which is awkwardly thrilling – Lucy's heavenly nipples show through the red satin of her bikini, perky and proud. Clive slips and stumbles for the tenth time; Lucy grabs my arm. We laugh. My cock threatens to rocket to Mars. Oh Lord.

Clive watches the barman pour his pint carefully. As we sit he never takes his eyes off me and for five minutes he stares at me intently, clearly suspicious, his right hand clamped knuckle-white round his beer. Which gives Boo Boo the perfect opportunity to dart in at his elbow and tip the spirit in.

Bar Central is buzzing. It's full of what Clive terms 'yahs' – the posh kids – with their crowing voices, forced laughs and deafeningly awful fashions. This is their usual hangout, it seems. But tonight the bar is also crammed with three-leggers. We have to stand in the corner. With all the braying it's like being stuck in a donkey sanctuary. Clive is noticeably starting to sway.

"How are you feeling?" I say to Lucy.

"What's that?" she says, cupping a hand to her ear.

I lean towards her. Lift my voice above the hubbub.

"I said, 'How are you feeling?'"

She smiles.

"I feel like-"

Just then, Clive leans forward and mumbles something in Lucy's other ear.

"Excuse me," Lucy says to me. She turns to Clive. "What did you say?" she asks.

Clive cups his hands to his mouth.

"Gorra g'forra piss!" he yells, so loud the entire pub hears.

He bends down and unhooks himself. When he stands up he topples sideways, clattering into a table of female yahs.

"I say!"

"Do be careful!"

"Watch it, old boy!"

"Sorry, sorry," mutters Clive.

"He iss so drunk!" says Lucy.

"I know," I say. "Disgraceful."

Yogi appears at my shoulder.

"Are we good?" he whispers.

I watch as Clive bounces from yah to squawking yah like a pinball.

"I thought he was a big drinker," I say.

"Lousy fucking amateur, kid," smiles Yogi, and downs my beer. "Now," he adds, "show no mercy. Push on through to the Mashie."

~

In Route 66 I offer Lucy a bottle instead of a pint.

"I w-w-w-wanna borrel, too," slurs Clive.

"I thought you were a real man?" I say, raising my nearly empty glass.

He grumbles and mutters and downs another dose as Yogi and Boo Boo peel off into the shadows.

Bert's and the Gowanlea Hotel – they go just as well. Then it's the Student Union, where I get two rounds in and Clive doesn't even notice.

By the time we head out to the Mashie, our final bar, I figure I've had the equivalent of about two pints of beer. Lucy is ten drinks down which, to her credit, she is holding pretty well. Clive, meanwhile, has had ten pints and nine double vodkas.

The Mashie clings to the world a mile out across the sleet-streaked golf course. A derelict railway line is the quickest path from the town. All around the pub lie the lumpen ghostly forms of the bunkers. Hollow and windblown, their cavernous shadows howl at the dunes and the sea.

This is where old caddies come to die.

It's slow going out along the railway track. Clive is having trouble walking in time with himself, let alone us and Lucy is getting tired. Plus it really is a filthy night. If this storm were a movie star it would be Christopher Lee. Dark, powerful and deadly serious. No cheap shocks here, this baby means business. Storms don't normally bother me, but there's something almost... unnatural about this one that's making my spine itch as we inch our way along the ghostly remains of the railway.

I have my arm round Lucy. She shivers. Stunning though her bikini is, it's no protection against the chill rain that's now driving in horizontally. I'd offer her my costume, but I only have cock underneath.

"Do we haff to go on?" says Lucy. "I am not wanting to be a quitter, but I am cold now."

I check out Clive. He's swaying around in the breeze like an old newspaper. "Uuurrrlllppp!" He lets fly a wet sounding belch. He has to drop soon. Please, let him drop soon.

"Last pub," I say. "Just keep going a little more. This is fun, right?"

"I suppose-"

"Whassat?" hisses Clive, suddenly ducking and spinning.

Lucy gasps and grips my shoulder.

I look round. Some of the heaviest clouds I have ever seen are rolling in from the sea, but there's nothing on the track. Not even Yogi and Boo Boo.

"Nothing," I say, trying to remain calm.

"Whalesss'r'comin'!" cries Clive, grabbing Lucy's arm. His eyes are hugely round, eerie in the faint light coming from the pub a half mile ahead. "Don'tcha sssee'em?!"

"Wh-wh-what's he talking about?" she asks, flicking her pretty head around nervously.

"He's stotious," I say. "Ignore him."

"Look!" Clive shouts, pointing out across the golf course towards the ocean. "Big whale fishesss comin'! Comin' to gerrusss!"

"He is scaring me," says Lucy.

"We gorra run!" Clive wails.

He tries to run and trips over. As he measures his length, his falling weight twists the strap round Lucy's leg.

"Ee-yow!" she cries.

"Take it easy, Clive, for God's sake," I say. 'You're hurting her."

"Gorra go," he slurs.

"You're not going anywhere," I say.

"Gorra gorra go!" he yells.

"We'll call you a cab from the pub. You'll catch your death out there."

"What's he doing?" says Lucy suddenly.

Clive is undoing his flies. Before I can react, he has his cock out and is peeing on himself.

"Gorra go!" he says.

"Dieu in heaven!!" cries Lucy, trying to back away before his fishy pizzler sprays all over her.

Moving fast, I bend down, reach over and untie her from Clive who rolls away from us towards a bunker, still peeing. The bunker's a deep one and he teeters on the edge for a moment before dropping with a muffled 'Oof!' and a groan to the sand below.

For a second there is silence. Then:

"Uuurrrlllllpppllllllooooaaaaaarrrrggggghhhh!" A wet belch that turns into the distinctive sound of a copious spew.

"Leave him," gasps Lucy.

"But-"

"LEAVE HIM!"

Cool blue fire flashes in her eyes.

"Sure," I say. And we walk in perfect three-legged style to the Mashie.

~

It's warm, but Christ, it's like the night of the half-drunk dead in here. Semi-animated bodies hunch over the bar, sipping beer and whisky and trading mumbled tales of golf rounds they've never even played.

A barman with gargantuan forearms stands polishing glasses. He's bald but for a hedgehog tuft of ginger hair on the crown of his head. To his left, at the end of the bar, an elderly woman sits doing a wordsearch. From her shock of carroty hair and equally vast arms, I presume her to be the barman's mother.

They, and every other person in the bar, stares at us as we come in. Sorry, glares at us. Students annoy them at the best of times; tonight's procession of drunken freshers in fancy dress looks to have tipped them over the edge.

"Take a seat by the fire," I say to Lucy. "I'll get you something warming."

I approach the bar.

Behind the barman above the optics are a fiddle, a guitar and an accordion. When an ancient caddie gets particularly morose, they take these instruments down and share their mood with the rest of the bar.

"Two halves of lager, please."

"Lager's off."

"Halves of eighty then, please.

"Halves are off."

I smile slowly.

"Okay, what can I have?"

The barman looks to his mother. She wrinkles her lips. Nods. He turns back to me.

"Whisky," he says.

I take the stingy measures and head back at the fire. Lucy is surrounded by drunken caddies. They strain their scrawny necks to leer at her.

"Excuse me," I say pushing past them. They keep their limbs firm and make it hard for me.

"Here you are," I say, putting down the whisky. "That'll warm you up."

Lucy picks up her glass. She tastes the spirit, spits it out.

"Lucy n'aime pas," she says. "Want to vamoosk!"

She gets to her feet.

"Stay!" I say.

"She wants tae go, son," sneers the nearest goblin-faced caddie. He reaches out a vile claw towards Lucy's thigh-

And just then the door opens. Yogi steps in, his fur soaking wet. Boo Boo moves out from behind him and they stand in the doorway. They see me. Yogi salutes. Boo Boo nods. I return the nod. Yogi and Boo Boo step inside and slip into the shadows. The crowd pays them no attention. Everyone's focused on me.

I turn back. The goblin-faced caddie is practically on top of Lucy. She looks terrified. Her wide blue eyes appeal to me; my heart lurches. Suddenly I feel something on my leg. The caddie with the rosy cheeks is running his hand up and down my thigh.

"Smashin' wee leotard you got on there, big man," he says.

For the first time tonight, I need a drink. I down my whisky.

"Wait a second," I say to Lucy.

Then I turn to the bar. "Give me that guitar!" I bellow, holding my arm outstretched.

Silence.

The barman stares at me. The customers stare at the barman.

"Those instruments are for customers' use, right?"

The barman looks to his mother.

"Can you play, son?" she says.

I look round at Lucy.

Take a deep breath.

I turn back to the landlady.

"I can play."

She holds my glance for a long moment. I match her steely witch glare. Then she nods at her boy.

"But-" starts the barman.

"Gie the man the guitar, Sandy," she states with a mother's simple power.

Grimacing, Sandy takes down the instrument. He comes round the end of the bar. Walks over to the fire. Its neck looks tiny in his meaty fist. Hands it to me. The caddies around us leer. Rosy cheeks moves a little closer.

I sit on the stool.

The bar hushes.

Completely.

I look at Lucy. She's watching me, wide-eyed, open mouthed, her cupid lips softly curving.

I strum a chord. A. The guitar's in tune. And sounds beautiful. I strum A again. Then A minor. Then an E.

Pause.

"This one's for the lady," I say. And start to sing.

> "All things bright and beautiful,
> All creatures great and small,
> All things hot and wonderful,
> The Lord God made them all."

Feeling a bit dizzy and my fingers are fudgy, but as I sing I can see the antagonism melting from their hard old faces.

*"Each little flower that opens,*
*Each little cat that sings,*
*He made their shiny colours,*
*He gave them pointy things..."*

Not sure I've got all the words one hundred per cent correct, but who cares? – a couple of old guys at the bar are starting to sway. Sandy the barman is nodding in time. His mum his humming along. Yogi stares disbelieving, Boo Boo taps his foot.

And best of all, Lucy is looking at me with unmissable lust.

*"The purple headed monkey,*
*Feels a little shy,*
*He rubs his tum at sunset,*
*And brightens up the sky.*

*So cold we lie in winter,*
*But the warming summer sun,*
*Will ripen juicy cherries,*
*To give to everyone."*

Don't know what my subconscious is banging on about, but the whole bar is on its feet now. They're joining hands and swaying in unison. Rosy cheeks is crying. Yogi stands in the corner swinging his arms and moshing in slow motion. Boo Boo is dancing with the landlady.

And Lucy walks over to me and sits at my feet.

One more verse, I think, then we'll call that an evening.

*"He gave us eyes to stare with,*
*And nice things to look at,*
*How great is God Almighty,*
*For giving girls a-"*

Suddenly the door crashes open.

Clive stands there, costume soaked and shredded.

"You screwed me!" he bawls. "You nasty slippery sod, you screwed me!"

"Hey, son, leave it. We're enjoying the music here," says Sandy.

Clive ignores him and clatters into the room, heedlessly shouting.

"It's not right, I was meant to have her!"

He reaches Lucy.

"Can't you feel it?" he squawks. Thunder rolls outside. "This isn't how things were meant to be. It's not natural. You should be mine!"

And he lunges for Lucy. Just as a giant fist grabs his paw and hoists him high in the air.

"I told you, son," growls Sandy, "we're listening to the music." And he hurls Clive against the wall. There's a crack and a groan.

I stop playing. Leap to my feet.

"Keep goin', pal, we'll deal with this guy. Cammy, Pete, take him round back."

Two heavy set caddies get to their feet and approach Clive who is staggering to his feet clutching his head and groaning. One caddie rolls up his sleeves, the other cracks his knuckles. They both grin menacingly as they approach Clive.

I look at Lucy. Fear fills her eyes. I look at Yogi. He very deliberately strums his hand up and down over an imaginary guitar.

I look at the menacing caddies. They haul the moaning Clive to his feet and start dragging him outside. I look once more at Lucy. Her mouth is slowly closing. She's going to let it go. And I would too, were it not for the strangest thought that pops into my head. For some reason I find myself wondering what Penelope would think of me if I did leave him. Bizarre. I want to ignore it, but I can't. It's too strong. And before I know it, the thought has taken over. It swells within me like a wave until I can contain it no longer and-

"STOP!" I shout. "He's with me."

I put down the guitar.

"Sorry everyone, that's it for tonight. Come on, Lucy." And I hold out my hand. She takes it.

We cross the floor to where Clive sags like a wet flannel between the two caddies.

"Hang on, old friend," I say and loop his left arm over my shoulder.

"Thanks, everyone," I say. "Goodnight." And I leave the bar. The last thing I see before the swing doors shut is, in the corner beyond a sea of sad faces, Yogi banging his head repeatedly against the dartboard.

~

It takes us an age to get Clive back. He's a mean, fractious drunk. Keeps swearing at me and lunging at Lucy. Plus the storm is unbelievable. Biblical stuff. The soft lights of McIvor are like beacons across the blasted wasteland of the golf course. Slowly they draw us on.

The place is locked up when we arrive. Luckily Clive has a pass key. I fish it from his sopping pocket. Together we drag him to the door of the subwarden flat. I open the door and we haul him inside.

"I'd better get him undressed," I say.

"I'll wait outside," she says. She turns towards the door. She pauses. "No matter what happens," she adds, "I just want you to know that I loved your song."

I smile.

She loves.

Christ, look at her arse in that bikini. The sweetest ripest fruit you ever saw.

She steps through the door.

And it's only as I'm undressing the rude, sprawling Clive that I start to wonder what on earth she meant by 'no matter what happens'?

I drop him like a stone and dash outside.

Gone.

Fucking knew it.

Just not going happen for me. Another lost moment.

Oh well, balls to Clive. Time for bed.

Trudge round the corner to the stairs. And-

There she is.

Asleep on the bench by the payphones.

"Lucy. Loooo-seeee." No response. I shake her shoulder.

"Hmmm, hmmm mm!" she moans dozily.

"Time to go to beh-head," I sing.

"Mmmph!"

And she flings an arm around my shoulders. Is she asleep?

I kneel down. Put my right arm around her shoulders. Slide my left under her legs just below her bottom. Lord forgive me.

"Where are you taking me?" she smiles.

Good, she's still awake. I can look into her eyes a little longer.

"Bed," I say.

"Mmmpphh," she moans and rolls tighter in towards my chest. My cock springs back to life. Snarling at its lycra cage like a wild dog.

Outside lightning cracks the blackness in two. The flashes illuminate the pale corridor walls and makes the coursing rain shine on the landing window. The thunder crashes close.

At the bottom of the grand staircase is the hall information board. I check her room number. D36. Is that where she lives or her bra size? Oh God.

I carry her up the single flight and along the twisting corridor. The occasional flash from outside illuminates the shadowy recesses of the passage.

Okay, here we are. I half bend down and turn the handle with my right hand, taking care not to bash her head. The door swings open.

It's very warm in here. And the sweet girl smell is incredibly concentrated in the darkness. Her roommate is fast asleep. I pad softly through the shadows with my heavenly burden.

Lucy's bed is rumpled. Like she just got out of it.

Ever so gently, I lay her on the tumbled sheets.

I take one brief last look at her.

Then I turn to go.

"No goodnight kiss?" murmurs a satin voice behind me.

I turn.

For a second, the boiling stormclouds part and a giant full moon powers her way into the room. Lucy Sugar stretches out on her bed, every divine curve and angle of her lithe young body coated in silver magic.

"Sure," I say, and step forwards.

I bend down.

"Take your time," she breathes, "take all the time you want with me."

My knees are suddenly balls of putty. My legs are going everywhere.

Got to get it together.

I put my right hand on the bed.

Then my left. On the other side of her body.

I'm in position.

My heart is like a gazelle in my chest.

There are her lips, sweet, pouting, curved – and open.

Waiting.

I lower my face towards hers.

Thunder growls.

I'm on the final approach.

Christ, I'm going to shake apart.

I can no longer focus on her face.

I shut my eyes.

Every nerve in my lips is stripped raw, ready for the sensation. I brace myself for electricity...

But it never comes. Her lips are soft, but they just kind of sit there. It's like pressing my mouth against a piece of fruit.

I pull back. Look at her closely. Smile to myself.

Lucy Sugar has passed out.

The tiniest girl-snore whiffles from her nostrils.

I pull the rumpled sheet up over her rounded shoulders and stand up. One last look at her beautiful face, then the moon disappears, the room is darkness and I leave.

Outside I softly close the door, turning the handle to ease the latch home. I turn towards the East stairway and:

"What the FUCK do you think you're doing?!"

It's Yogi. He looms in front of me.

"Going to bed," I state.

Yogi puts his paws on my shoulders and spins me round.

"Get back in there and shag her."

"What!?"

"Just climb into bed and put your cock in her pie."

I throw his paws off and turn to face him.

"Are you fucking insane? I can't do that!"

"You can make history here."

"I can get arrested here!"

"Put your tassel in her hand first, she'll soon wake up."

"I can't believe you're saying this!"

"You fucking hypocrite. You thought it."

"I did not... not like that... look, forget it, you're smashed."

"Or prod her awake. Then just slide him home..."

"And a lunatic. Smashed and a lunatic."

He clasps his paws together as if in prayer.

"Please..."

Suddenly Boo Boo comes hoofing down the corridor. Reaches us, puffing, sweating. Stabs his watch, which he wears outside his costume, with a stubby finger.

"Uh, Fre- I mean, Yogi, we only have ten more minutes of displacement. Better hurry."

"Shit!" yells Yogi. Turns to me. "Will you fucking get in there?!"

"No!"

He grapples my shoulders. I resist. We tussle.

"Get in there, you stupid scared young moron-"

"Yogi..." another stab at the watch.

"Goddammit!"

Yogi stops fighting. Points a quivering paw at me. Looks like some words are trying to find their way out past the anger. They don't come. Instead:

KKKRRRRUUUNCH!

Yogi punches the wall with an acrylic fist. Knocks a hole clean through the plasterboard. Jabs the dusty paw at me, blood seeping on the orange fur.

"This isn't the end," he says, voice rigid with emotion. "You're going to finish this."

Turns to his little friend.

"Come on, Boo Boo," he says. "We gotta rock."

And together they gallop down the corridor, Yogi veering drunkenly from side to side.

~

# SATURDAY, 21ST JANUARY 2016

Oooaaooooowww.

Pain.

Unbelievable fucking pain in my head.

Note to self – never travel through time when drunk. Hangover ten times as bad.

Roll over on the bed – something in my way. Turn round. Dougal sprawls like a great furry starfish behind me.

Poke him in the head.

"You alive?" I say.

"Nnnnggg..."

Forget him – more important things to worry about. Bursting for a piss.

Move to the ladder. Climb up and out the trapdoor. Stand in the hallway. Hang on, feeling a bit wobbly. Need to sit down. Head through to the kitchen and find-

Several hundred pastries.

What the fuck's going on here? Who cares, this shit looks good. Let's try one of those éclairs...

Woah!

What's going on? Oh, that's horrible. Put the éclair down. Brain feels like plasticine. Squelching and kneading itself in my skull.

Images are flashing up from my memory... me on the pub crawl... drinking too much... falling over and seeing Lucy go off with Clive... but now that memory squeezes in the middle, stretches, squashes back smaller, blows up again – this time the figures are moving, like a projection on a balloon – but they're getting thinner, fainter, and they're changing... there's Yogi drinking my drinks and Boo Boo spiking Clive's... and I'm not too drunk now, it's me looking at him falling into the bunker. I'm playing the guitar... she's looking up at me... we're walking home with Clive... I'm putting her to bed... I'm kissing her goodnight... she's sleeping... I'm leaving...

Son of a bitch!

Stupid, gutless little bastard. Why didn't he go back in there? Why didn't he just–

"Who are you?"

Turn round.

It's Pen.

She's wearing her favourite coat. Her battered little suitcase that reminds me of Paddington bear is in her hand.

God she looks so much older than when I last saw her. That was fourteen years ago, but still. You really notice the lines. They weren't there at all before. And there's a sadness now too. Bright hope slid to quiet desperation.

From her puffy cheeks and red eyes, she looks like she might have been crying.

"'S me," I say with a flourish.

"Who?" she says. What's she so scared for? Doesn't she recognise me? Shit, of course.

Start to pull off Yogi's head – the transferral has melted the fur. Hard work – have to tear my way out through his nose.

"Me, my little love trumpet!" I say, freeing myself at last.

Her face screws up. Like she has a thousand things to say. Old girl only got one mouth though.

"What... are you doing?"

Look down at my éclair.

"Eating," I say.

What's she so upset about?

"But where on earth have you been?"

"Oh, here and there, little mouse, here and there."

"Have you... have you been drinking?"

"Not really."

"Oh for God's sake, you smell like a brewery."

"We live in a brewery."

"This isn't the time for jokes, Freddie! You didn't come home last night. You don't answer your phone and Clive said you weren't at work. Then you don't come to the party, and–"

The party... of course, that explains the cakes. Shit.

"-Mummy said I should call the police and I had to lie to Daddy or he would have stayed and killed you and-"

"Mouse, I'm sorry I missed your party. Now give Freddie a cuddle."

"Get OFF!" She steps away. Pushes hair from her flushed face. Don't recall ever seeing the old gel this angry. "Freddie, you're not coming anywhere near me until you tell me where you've been."

"You wouldn't believe it if I told you."

"Try me."

Mouse has her hands on her hips. Looks serious.

"Okay. I invented a time machine and spent the last twenty-four hours in 2002."

"Doing what?"

"You do believe me! That's wonder-"

"Doing what, Freddie?"

"Well, I went to a few pubs and-"

"Freddie, unless you tell me the truth, I'm going to think the worst."

"What do you mean, 'the worst'?"

She turns to the sink. Drops her head. Takes a deep breath. Then she quickly turns back to face me. Fresh tears shine in her eyes.

"That you're seeing another girl."

Pause.

Breathe, man, breathe.

"How do you- I mean, what makes you think that?"

"Is it true?"

"Course not. Only room for one mouse in my-"

"Then tell me exactly what you've been doing!"

"Okay. I will. But, you see, it's complicated-"

"FREDDIE HOW CAN YOU DO THIS TO ME!?"

Shit the bed. Poor mouse has gone completely crimson.

"We've just got engaged! I spent the whole day looking at

wedding venues. I actually booked one, and-"

"Where?"

"What?!"

"Where did you book?"

"The hotel in Dairloch, but that's not-"

"The one below the castle?"

"Freddie, you have to listen to me." She steps really close. Can see how soft her skin is. Want to touch it. Want to kiss it. Soothe her. But have a feeling that would not go over well. Resist.

Pen flinches.

"I'm going to stay with my parents."

"Why?"

"Well for one thing, there's no bed here-"

"No, there is, I brought it back. It's just downstairs in the lab-"

"But the main reason is that I want you to think about things. I booked the church for the fourth of February. That's two weeks. More than anything in the world I want to walk down that aisle then and see you waiting for me. But..." she takes a step closer again. Holds my paw. "Freddie, I need you to be straight with me."

There's that fear again. God it makes me want to wrap me in my arms. Maybe I should. Think I will. But then I hear myself say-

"Here's straight – I went back in time, had a few beers-"

She places one hand over my mouth.

"Think about it, Freddie. Then, if you want to, come and get me."

And with that she picks up her little battered suitcase, walks down the hall and out the front door.

~

Only just found the Scottish Historical Biography section, high in the loft at Ballantrae's, when Dougal rushes up to me. His ginger hair sprays out from his head like insane wire. Big bags have formed under his eyes. His pallor is distinctly porridge-like.

"Why didn't ye wake me up?"

"Busy, old boy."

Pace down the aisle, my eyes on the shelves. He follows me.

"You made us late again. We really could lose our jobs here..."

"Bollocks jobs. There are more important things at stake here."

Pull a book from the shelf. Check the blurb on the back. Put it back.

"Like what?" says Dougal.

"Don't you understand, Dougal? That skinny twat failed. Kissed her lips and then quiched out at the Beach Ball. He still blew it. Circumstances twisted themselves so that I still ended up getting off with Pen. It appears, my little sausage of companionship, that the fabric of spacetime is denim. Very tough indeed."

"How do you know he didn't make it?"

"Because I have the memories!"

"I'm confused..."

"When we arrived back, my memory started changing. Could feel it morphing in my head like dough. At the moment it's like a double exposure. I remember getting drunk and screwing the whole thing up. But that's fading. It's been ingrained in my brain for fourteen years, but now it's slowly being replaced as my body catches up with spacetime. Because now I also remember Yogi taking my drinks, Boo Boo spiking Clive and me very nearly succeeding... I put her down on the bed, kissed her sleeping lips... and if it wasn't for the fact that my younger self was – is – a total tool I could right now be enjoying the memory of her naked breasts boynging up down in front of me. And I'd be successful. That too, of course."

He stares at me, his little brown eyes goggling.

A memory whizzes to the front of my brain. I smile and stare into the middle distance.

"Wasn't she stunning though? Even more gorgeous than I remember. So hot. And so young."

Pull out another large, dusty volume. Check the blurb.

Dougal suddenly jolts back to life. See him looking at me like he's worked something out."

"Freddie. What... what are you doing?" he asks slowly.

"Isn't it obvious?" I say. "Research." And stuff the book up my jumper.

He lifts the hem of the wool and grabs the book. Reads the spine:

"The Complete History of Mary of Moncur and the Black Prince of Balbirnie – what are you taking this for?"

Bend right down and look him square in the eyes.

"You know what for."

He steps backwards, banging against a stack of autobiographies.

"You're crazy. You're not... going back!?"

"Look, I'm running out of time. We have to return. Pen's gone and booked the church for two weeks today. Also need a copy of Scene That – The Millennium And The Death Of Visual Entertainment by Dr Trevor Poleshaft. Where will that-?"

"Woah, hang on. What's all this 'we' stuff?"

"Can't do it without you, Dougalicious," I say, patting him on the head.

"Oh no, I'm not going again," he says, and pulls the book from me.

"Bloody are," I say and try to pull it back.

He doesn't yield – just squeaks a little and rolls into a ball. Stretch out my arms – one round his head the other towards his belly. Try snatching, and when then that doesn't work, tickling. Still Dougal holds on. Am considering grabbing his nuts when he wriggles free with all his strength and blurts out:

"Freddie, it hasn't worked! You still didn't sleep with her! There has been no magical success story! Clive still took Lucy's virginity!"

What the...?

Can't believe it.

Cannot fucking believe it.

He took Lucy Sugar's virginity!?

Stare at Dougal.

"She was a virgin then... ? How in all that's unholy do you know that? Did she tell you?"

"Freddie, she told everyone! Don't you pay any attention at all to anything that isn't inside your own head? Come here." And he grabs my hand and leads me off down a book lined corridor. After a few rapid twists and turns he reaches a dusty display table and snatches up a book. Thrusts it under my nose.

An angelically sexy face is smiling at me. Above the picture is printed 'Life is Sweet! My Story by Lucy Sugar'.

Dougal stares at me, challenge brimming in his doggy eyes.

"It came out earlier this year in time for the Oscars. Hardly a literary sensation, but it had some interesting section." He grabs Lucy's biography from me. "Shall I read you some?" He flips open the book. Finds a spot. Reads: "'The night I was discovered was the night of the Tallowmas Fair. This night was to be a memorable night in more ways than one...'"

"Quality writing," I mutter.

"For," continues Dougal, "it was to be the night of the Midwinter Beach Ball – and the night... that I met my first lover, the fabled inventor...'" Dougal snaps the book shut. "I won't go on," he says, "If you have to make yourself even more miserable you can read it for yourself. Page 69," he adds. "That's providing you buy a copy, of course."

The gauntlet is down. He really isn't going to help me. All is lost. Frustration boils in my throat. Want to spark up a match and burn this whole ancient building down around me.

Then I look at him. And something occurs to me. A vision. Of him and Ruth at the rockpools together... him standing on the cliff, wanting to ask her something...

Lean in close. Whisper to him, slowly:

"Come with me... and when I'm done... I'll take you back... to her."

His brown eyes flash at me, the old spark burning brightly once more.

"You couldn't..."

"Course I could," I say with dark seriousness. "You think about that." Grab my book from him, stuff it back up my jumper. "And bring your black cloak, will you?" Then I turn and run for the staff exit.

~

Dougal arrives bang on six as predicted. Sticks his fat little head down the trap.

"The door was open," he says.

"Come down," I say through my visor, "I'm nearly finished."

He shuffles down the ladder, little paws padding softly. Christ, he's wearing that shitty tracksuit again. Poor sod. Can't help but feel for him.

Make my last weld and put down the oxy-acetylene torch. Take off my gauntlets and visor. Inspect the weld. Still glows a pleasing red. And it looks good.

Move over towards Dougal, picking up a bottle on the way.

"Claret?" I say, offering him a beaker.

"Can we just get on with this?" he says sullenly.

"Cheer up," I say. "You're about to make some more history. You got the cloak?"

He holds it up.

"Good lad. Check out these boots I got from the cancer shop – and this mask. Perfect, huh?"

"Please, Freddie?" he says, raising his bushy little brows in the middle so his forehead goes all wrinkly.

"Follow me," I say, then step over towards the bed. Dougal follows. "Now, as you will see," I continue, "I've made some modifications to our temporal machinery for this journey. As you cleverly discovered when your head caught fire, the transferrals generate significant levels of theta radiation. So I've hired these-" I reach into a canvas hold-all and pull out a couple of wetsuits. "Which I reckon, once I've soaked them in turpentine, will give more protection as we go through the singularity. Of course, they could spontaneously incinerate us, but hey – who said life was easy?"

Dougal's lower lip curls in glum dismay.

"I've also tuned things up a little," I add, pointing to the head of the bed. "To give us a more enjoyable ride."

Dougal wanders over to the bed and starts poking morosely at the equipment attached to the bedposts.

"What are these?"

"Those, my little elephant seal, are Wharfedale K10s. Kicking out 50 watts per channel."

"And what do they do?"

I smile at him.

"Play music, of course. The speakers on your laptop aren't up to much."

He turns. Stares at me.

"Freddie... is Penelope okay with this?" he mumbles.

"Pen-station? Ah, right. Yeah, um, she's cool."

"You haven't told her, have you, Freddie?"

"How could I? She's round at her parents."

"You could phone her."

Stare at the furball.

"Are you serious? We got work to do-"

"I'm not going anywhere until you call her."

Bastard.

"Alright. But I'm not doing this for you, you know. Doing it for her."

Find my handset in a wine case. Dial Pen's parent's house.

RING RING

Man, I hate speaking to her mum.

RING RING

And I really hate speaking to her dad.

RING RING

Come to think of it, I don't much enjoy speaking to Pen at the moment.

Hello?

Get in! It's the answer machine.

"Mr and Mrs Cotton are out at this present time, if you would like to leave them a message, please do so after this electronic noise... meeeep!"

"Oh hi, listen it's Freddie here. Hello Mrs Cotton, Mr Cotton. I, erm, hope you enjoyed the party last night, I'm sorry I couldn't be there. I was, erm..." I think of Lucy and the pub crawl. "...kind of tied up. Anyway, this message is really for Pen... um, hi honey... listen, I've just called to say I'm going away for a little bit, I'm..." I look around at Dougal, seeking inspiration.

"Tell her the truth!" he hisses, leaning a bit to close to the handset.

"...off on my stag do," I continue, waving him away. "Going to St Mary's. With Dougal. Now, um, we shouldn't be gone more than a couple of weeks, ah..."

"Two weeks?!" squeaks Dougal. "Penelope, listen-" And he starts grappling for the phone. Have to stick my hand over his mouth and pull his fat head under my arm.

"...but, ah, don't worry," I continue, "we'll be back in time for the wedding. Oh, and could you get my kilt cleaned? Got wine all down the front. Cheers."

And I put the phone down. Let Dougal go. He paces in front of me, eyes wide.

"What are you talking about, two weeks? We can't go for two weeks! We have work, and the wedding to organise, and-"

Can't believe he's kicking off about this. Turn towards him. Bend right down so my face is in his.

"You know what I have to do," I shout, "and you know how long it's going to take. And until I do that, I'm not going to take you back to... you know when. So you have to decide," and I jab my finger at him, "do you want to spend the next two weeks stacking books in an attic or do you want to get your answer?"

Dougal glowers at me, his brown eyes burning almost red with anger.

"You're a bastard, Freddie."

"Yes," I say, "but I get things done. Now put this on." And I toss him his wetsuit. "I'm going to find the turps."

~

With a drip and a splat, I pour the last of the turps onto Dougal's wet-suited head.

"This smells," he says.

"Final checks," I say. "You got the source material?"

Frowning, he holds up a large white seashell.

"Today's paper?"

He shows me that.

"My reference book?"

He puts the Mary of Moncur book on the bed.

"The outfit?"

Lifts up a Spar bag.

"And your shades?"

Dougal places a pair of aviators on top of his neoprene-covered bonce.

"Nice one. Let's go." And I take the seashell and drop it into the time reference hopper. Then I climb squelchily onto the bed and initiate the launch sequence.

Just because we know what's coming, doesn't make it any less terrifying.

WWWHHHUUUMMMPPPP! The bed springs into the air. The brasswork shakes and clatters.

"Hit play!" I shout to him.

Dougal reaches over to the laptop, presses a couple of keys.

A quick rolling beat on the cymbal, a rippling guitar riff and...

"It's been a long time since I rock an' rolled..." sings Robert.

"Here we go," I say.

And the orb springs into existence. Energy snakes hotter than the sun writhe in their conduits.

FFFFWWWWIIIIIIP!

The singularity tears an atmoscopic hole in reality. With a judder, a shake and some fine guitar work from Mr Page, the blackness grows. Dougal grabs my arm. Grab him back as the eternal blackness ripples unstoppably towards us.

And with a shudder and a rip and a gentle little hiss we slip through time.

~

"What on earth is that smell?" says Dougal.

"Freddie, you're the fucking man," I say, punching the air and leaping from the bed onto the sand. Turn to Dougal. "Look at this, will you?"

"All I see is blackness–"

"Come here, slugboy, your wetsuit has slipped down."

Peel his headpiece up from his eyes.

Dougal looks around slowly.

"So we're in a hole. I don't see what's so great about that."

"Well, firstly, you might notice that we have not even been singed by the transdimensional vortex, proving my wetsuit and turps theory, and secondly, look up."

"Holy shit, what's that? Is that bats?"

"They are indeed, my little jammy dodger," I say. "Isn't it wonderful?!"

"We're in the caves!?" he squawks.

"Yes. Cleverly, I have decalibrated the geographical vectors," I say.

He stares at me, eyes glazed.

"Last time," I continue, "we burst through the continuum right on top of the source material. Which almost got us busted by ourselves, if you remember. But with a bit of inspired tweaking I have projected us a little distance from the original location into a discreet area nearby. Namely the Castle Caves under the Bents. Perfect spot to hide the bed! Dead close to the beach and below the castle. And Ma Broon's is about two minutes away."

Dougal shakes his head slowly.

"Also, if you come with me through here..."

We duck under a low archway and crawl forward a few yards to where the cave twists sharply to the right then opens out. Ahead of us lies a tumbled floor of puddle rock and bladderwrack. Beyond that, the mouth of the cave shows the crashing sea.

Lead him forward to where the highest splashes of the tide reach. Out to the right now the sheer cliffs of the Bents rise up to the gnarled feet of the castle.

"…now look over there, you should see…"

Dougal follows my pointing finger.

"You again!"

"That's right. That skinny prick is moping because he didn't get a part in the Vindendraam and he can't think of a way to get into Lucy Sugar's knickers."

Sat on a flat rock fifty feet away is Junior. He stares out to sea, chin on his cupped hands. As we watch he picks up a sea shell and looks at it morosely.

"So soft and beautiful," we can hear him faintly sigh, "like her skin." Before slipping the shell in his pocket.

Wink at Dougal.

"The source material," I say. "There was a risk it could have taken us back to when the creature grew its shell, but the object only became emotionally relevant to me when I picked it up, so I figured it was worth the risk."

"Look, he's off!" says Dougal, pointing a scratchy little finger. He's right. Junior's traipsing across the rocks towards the end of the beach. "Should we follow him?" adds Dougal.

"Yes, but first, grab some of that seaweed."

"What for?"

"To camouflage the bed, of course. Come on."

~

It's a crisp, cold morning in early winter. The kind of day that St Mary's does best. The fresh sea air thrills your lungs and sings through your blood. Your cheeks are rosy all day long. Even the shortest hair is happily ruffled by a mischievous breeze. The low sun turns the crazy alleys and towers of the ancient town into a fantastic patchwork of mellow light and seductive shade.

"I really don't think they're going to let us in like this," moans

Dougal as we chafe our way down the Bents. "We'll scare the children."

"Bollocks the children," I say. "Say we've come to clean the penguin cage."

"I'm not sure they have any-" starts Dougal as I turn away and shuffle down the steps to St Mary's World of the Sea.

The white-haired old bat in the shabby wooden entrance booth looks down her nose at us, but, after a growl from me, sells us tickets.

The booth is connected to the main centre by a dipping, slatted walkway. Very dark. Slimy too. Feels like we're descending into some hulking leviathan, sleeping off a vast fish dinner on the shore.

After a hundred yards or so, the tunnel opens out into a black-walled cavern filled with blue and green tanks. The tanks are lit from above and the knuckly rock walls of the cavern shimmer and shine with reflected light. Hundreds of beautiful fish drift calmly to and fro.

"There he is!" I say.

And I set off past a grubby clutch of schoolkids fleshing their noses to the shark tank. Their petite teacher runs in circles after them, flapping her arms like a crazy seabird.

Round another tank and there he is. Look at him. He's met up with skinny Dougal who he's currently boring senseless in front of the angel fish. Staring into the water and moaning like a fanny. Can't get over how uncool the guy looks.

Walk over. Approach him slowly. Want to surprise him. Get to within a couple of feet before my squeaking wetsuit gives the game away. Junior turns and looks at me.

"You still can't believe you fucked it up, can you?" I say.

He stares at me. Squints.

"Excuse me?"

"How long you been whinging at him for now?" I say, pointing to skinny Dougal. "Eight weeks? It's pathetic, you do know that, yeah?"

"Do I know you?"

Smile. Circle round him a little.

"Let me give you a clue..." and I mimic: "'smarter than the average bear!'"

His eyes shoot wide, hands fly to his mouth.

The angel fish start to speed up. Go a bit mental.

"Yogi!"

"Spot the fuck on, Sherlock."

Junior turns to skinny Dougal.

"I thought you said they were a dream!" he moans.

"Dry up, you arsehole," I say. "I'm here to help you again."

Skinny Dougal turns square to me.

"What d'ye want with him?"

"None of your business. Now listen, Freddie-"

"No, ye listen, sir. My man here has been mightily confused since that night. He's been having dreams and all sorts-"

"Call Ranger Smith!" whines Junior, curling his hands around himself.

"So if ye're that Yoga fellow..." continues Young Dougal, "...I'm wanting some answers from ye."

The angel fish are really whipping up a storm now, thrashing and splashing the water.

Turn to fat Dougal.

"Can you have a word?" I say.

"I don't think-" starts Dougal.

"It's not him I want to talk to," presses skinny Dougal, rising from his seat. "It's ye. What d'ye want with my friend here?"

"To help him."

"Help him what?"

"Fuck Lucy Sugar, of course."

Skinny Dougal takes a step back. His caterpillar brows wriggle up and down like little waves.

"And why would ye want to do that?"

"It's complicated. Now listen, if I can just talk to him about Lucy-"

"Ye listen to me ye big pumpkin. Ye're not talking to him about nothing until ye explain yerself." For Christ's sake, why was I ever friends with this little biter.

"Quite right," says Junior. "And you can start by taking off that stupid suit."

Turn to glare at him. He faces me out, lips set firm.

The fish are going mental. Some children are starting to point and look fearful. The petite teacher glares over at us.

Right, you bastard, you asked for it.

Reach my hands up. Take off my shades. Peel the headpiece of my wetsuit back and down.

Stare at him.

For a second he does nothing. Just stares right on back. Then his left eye twitches. Forehead tightens. Brows knot. Now both eyes twitch, then widen. Colour dies in his cheeks, which sag like grey beanbags. Finally his mouth falls open like a drawbridge and his body goes rigid. He raises a palsied finger.

"Y-y-y-you're... m-m-me..." he manages.

Behind him the fish are rioting.

"That's right," I say.

He stares some more. Then raises another shaking hand to point.

"But that's impossible!"

"Keep your voice down."

"How can this be?! It doesn't make sense!"

"Will you shut up?" I hiss.

Some of the fish are leaping from the tanks around us. Flopping on the ground. Gasping. The children are getting scared. The petite schoolteacher gathers them under her flapping wings. Looks for someone in charge.

"Come here," I say and grab his elbow. Lead him right through the aquarium to the pools. These start deep in the cavern and extend right out into the open air. A low concrete wall keeps seals in while giving them a tortuously close glimpse of the open water beyond. The Dougals follow.

Sit my younger self down on the wall.

Above us the worn face of the Bents cliffs sheers up like a vast layer cake. To my left, a fat man in a blue boilersuit lobs fish to nodding seals. To my right, the Dougals watch each other in edgy silence.

"Yes, I'm you," I whisper. "The 2016 version. Invented a time-travelling bed, you see? How else could I shag Lucy Sugar? Can't be unfaithful to the Penster. So this way, I get you to shag her and I will get the memory of that shag."

My younger self knots his brows.

"Och Dougal," says skinny Dougal to his plumper self. "How did ye get yourself involved in this, man?"

"That's a good question," mutters my Dougal.

"Will you two be quiet, please?" I say. "He's trying to think."

My younger self knots his brows some more. Then nods.

"This certainly explains things-" he says.

"Good lad."

"-but I really don't think you have to worry. I'm going to make a big effort to impress her with my piety. I'm on the costume committee for the Vindendraam and-"

"You'll fail again."

"Don't say that..." he whines.

"You still don't get it, do you? This has already happened to me. The Vindendraam – Lucy's playing the part of Mary of Moncur, Clive has cast himself as the Black Prince. You didn't get a part. So you volunteered to sit around sewing sodding costumes hoping Lucy will notice you. Although, of course, you didn't have the bottle to acknowledge that you fancied her and you insisted it was all part of this religious charade that you're currently putting on."

He stares at me, eyes wide with desperation.

"My calling isn't a charade-" he starts.

Put my hands on his shoulders.

"You. Cannot. Lie. To. Me." I say. "I. Was. You. I know that you're a virgin and that you are so twisted up by this fact that you have prayed yourself into a corner. I know that, because I was that and I did that."

His face crumples at this volley of truth. Think he's about to cry. Forgotten how seriously he took himself. Myself. Better soften things a little for the silly young sod.

"Listen," I soothe, "if it helps, you can think of this whole Lucy-shagging-adventure as a holy sacrifice. Your penis is leading you in a fall from grace – just a teeny, totty little tumble – that is in a very noble cause, namely, your future mental health. Your purity for my sanity. I'm sure St Crustible would approve."

He looks up at me, eyes wet and red.

"Really?" he asks.

"Truly," I reply. "Your cock is on a crusade. Shit like this will get you canonised one day."

Something seems to click in his simple brain. He nods. Smears a skinny paw across his eyes.

"So… what happens next?" he asks.

A memory flashes into my brain and my wetsuit feels like it's suddenly been stuffed with nettles. Want to escape from my own skin. Can feel my face flushing.

"Is it that bad?" he says, cringing from me.

"The Vindendraam is a huge success," I grumble. "In the crowd is a tourist. Yank. Works as an agent in Hollywood. Spots Lucy, makes her an offer. She's so happy she jumps into Clive's pants."

"When?"

"At the Midwinter Beach Ball. The post-Vindendraam party down at North Sands."

"And what do I do?"

"You console yourself in the arms of Pen."

"Penelope," he nods. "Of course."

"You're not surprised?" I ask.

"Perhaps it was her you wanted all along," mutters my fat Dougal.

Turn to him. "If you're not going to be helpful, just keep your mouth shut, okay?"

Skinny Dougal leaps to his feet.

"Hey! Don't talk to me like that!"

"I wasn't speaking to you, I was speaking to him."

"Same thing."

"Oh, for fuck's sake," I say. Take a deep breath. Turn to Junior. "Do you understand or not?"

He gets to his feet. Paces a little way along. Watches the keeper throw a fish to a seal. "Sure I do. But what I want to know is... do I, you know...?"

"What?"

"Shag her?"

"I just told you, she pulls Clive-"

"Not Lucy, Penelope."

How annoying is this guy?

"Course you bloody do."

"I get laid?! Awesome- I mean, praise be! When?"

"Shit, I don't know."

"Come on, you have to remember how you lost your virginity."

Doesn't he realise what an immature prick he's being?

"In the holidays sometime. Easter, I think," I snap. "She invites you to a long weekend at her house and you get it on in the pantry."

"Really!?!? This is so cool!"

"No, this is poor. Yes, you get laid. But, you end up spending the rest of your life with her. Her and no one else. And because of that, nothing goes your way. Ever."

"She is kind of sweet. And very understanding..."

"Don't you want to fuck someone else before you die?"

"I'm just delighted I fuck anyone," he says with a smile. "In the pantry. By St Mungo that's hot..."

"Well, by the time you become me, that changes. I tell you. So, here's the plan-"

"Is it nice?"

"The plan?"

"Me and Pen. When we do it. Is it nice?"

"Um, yeah, sure it's nice-"

"How nice?"

"Well, so nice you shelve your chastity vow pretty sharpish, but-"

"Do we do it a lot?"

"This isn't the point-"

"Come on, have a little empathy. Do we do it a lot?"

Can't help grinning at him.

"Four times a night sometimes in the early days-"

He punches the air.

"YES!"

Put on a serious face.

"But then it drops off, believe me."

His eyes are shining.

"I won't ever let it drop off! Morning, noon, night – I swear I'll be doing it every hour, on the hour."

"It drops off."

"I won't let it."

"You will."

"I won't."

"YOU WILL."

"Freddie," says fat Dougal quietly, "listen to yourselves."

"Shut UP!" I snap at him. The rotund little fellow drops his eyes to the floor. His skinnier self leaps towards me, brows bristling.

"Hey! Where de ye get off talking to anyone like that, let alone yer best wee buddy?"

"Yeah, why are you so grumpy?" asks Junior.

Spin to face myself and stab my finger at him.

"You stay out of this, you virgin."

"Don't call me a virgin, you baldy bastard."

"Baldy?! Receding in a classy Christopher Lee way perhaps, but-"

"You're bald. You're rude. You're crazy." He stands up. Faces me directly. Eye to eye. "And I'm not doing your idiotic plan. It didn't work out for you, but it's not too late for me. I'll just have to try harder, that's all."

Lunge forward. Grab the collar of his green and black checked shirt.

"But you are me!" My virgin self's eyes go wide. I continue: "If it were different, and you were going to succeed now, then wouldn't I disappear or turn into a successful millionaire or something?" I beat my chest. "But I'm still here. You don't do it. You FAIL. And it smoulders in your soul like melting plastic. Burns right through you. Hollows you out. For fourteen years it hurts. Disappointment after disappointment. You flunk your degree. Decide, for reasons I don't clearly remember now, to be an inventor. Inventions don't sell. Live in a brewery. End up working in a crummy old bookshop trying to scrape by while slowly going FUCKING INSANE!"

Even the seals are looking at me now.

"And this is what you-" I poke him in the chest, "have ahead of you." Heave a deep breath into my lungs. Let it go a little. "Look at me," I say softly. He does. "I'm telling you, son, you're staring failure in the face."

Don't quite know where that came from. Didn't mean to say all that girly personal stuff. Just meant to threaten him a bit. Shit, now I've got that nettle feeling again.

Junior keeps on looking at me. Up and down, like I'm some sort of show pony. There's a look in his eyes now that just about kills me:

Shame.

The air stills. He pauses for a minute like he's thinking about something. Then he tightens his lips. Swallows. His eyes clear. The shame twists to pity and I feel even worse. Feels so hot inside this damn wetsuit. Want to get out. Want to tear a hole in it and dive into the blissful ocean. Also want to tear a hole in my younger self. What a twat. Look at him eyeing me with those sad, scared eyes. Who's he to pity me?! Boy's never even touched a fanny...

"Okay," says Junior.

"Huh?"

"Okay, you can help me win Lucy Sugar."

Clear my throat. Nod.

"Cool. Now the first thing we gotta do is get me into a lecture with Lucy. Then I can-"

"No, the first thing we gotta do is get you out of here."

He nods over at the far side of the pools. The guy in the boilersuit has found a crowbar. He's shuffling towards us clutching it like an ape holding a femur.

"Okay," I say. "Let's go."

And the four of us leg it up the incline, my wetsuit squelching with every accelerating step.

~

"Quick, get in here. Shut the door. Do you think anyone saw us?"

"Fuck's sake, Junior, take it easy," drawls my older self before flopping back full length on my bed. "Give yourself a damn hernia."

God he's annoying. Thinks he's so cool. And look at the state of him. Jesus. Do I really let myself go so much? Tufty shoulder length hair, clearly not been washed in an age. Stained wetsuit barely stretching round a bulging belly. Rickety legs and a pasty, bomb-eyed face.

"Damn, this room is small," he sneers. "Did we really live like this? If this was a dog kennel it would be condemned."

"If you've quite finished," I say, "perhaps you could explain-"

"The plan?" he says, "That's the spirit, Junior. Up for adventure. Okay, here's the breakdown – I become you. In your puny student life. Use my superior life skills to pull Lucy while you quietly carry on as if nothing has happened. It's important that we don't fuck up the space-time continuum too much. So keep hanging out with the costume committee. If you don't make her clothes, Lucy doesn't get to wear them, etcetera etcetera."

"Wait a second," I say. "What if people see us out together?"

"They won't. We'll co-ordinate our movements. Time it so we're never out at the same time. If there's an emergency, just give me a chirp on my mobile."

"Give you a what on your what?" I say.

He stares at me blankly for a second.

"I don't have a mobile phone," I inform him. "They're for show-offs."

"Christ, I forgot how crap 2002 was," he says. "Okay, forget that. Send your Dougal out to get me. They look so different it won't be a problem. If, for any reason, we have to go out together, one of us can wear a false moustache." He leans over, opens the bedside cabinet and pokes his nose in. "Got any beer?" he asks.

"No. Now why can't I be the one who tries to make it with Lucy?" I say.

He sits forward shaking his head. "We did that last time, remember? You cocked it up. 'She's sleeping'," he mimics in a girly voice, "'I can't touch her'." He glares at me. "Waste opportunities like that and you're finished. Christ knows you don't get that many in life. Listen, this may sound harsh, but I'm afraid it's the truth – you simply haven't got the balls for the job. Oh, God, don't look so fucking forlorn. It's nothing to be ashamed of. You're nineteen. Whereas I... I got fourteen years' experience on you. I know how this shitty mechanism we call life works."

"B-b-but where are you going to stay? There's no room here."

"There's a stairway that runs up just after the turn from A13c," he says. "At the top is a small attic flat. Used to be where the head porter lived when this was a hotel. It's not kept locked – it's pretty much forgotten about. You discover it next term playing a hall-wide game of drunken hide and seek. It's where Pen first lets you feel her tits."

"Really?!" I hear myself saying. "How cool!"

"Junior, you're a dork," he says. "It's a mystery to me how you ever got laid. Anyway, listen, we'll sleep up there. Now, the Vindendraam rehearsal is on Friday night. That gives me a little less than a week to impress Lucy enough to get her to kick Clive off the team and take me on instead." He lies back again. "Plenty of time. So why don't you make yourself useful and pop to the offy?"

He thinks he's so the man. Why can't he see what an old fool he's being? My hand drifts to a propelling pencil on the desk. I fiddle with it for a moment. Then I smile.

"It's not beer you need to be buying," I chuckle.

He cocks his head. "What are you smirking about?" he says.

I get up and lean down towards him. "The way things are just now... you're going to fuck this up worse than I ever could."

He sits back, surprised.

"What do you mean?"

I pace round the room a little.

"Lucy Sugar is never going to believe you're me."

"You keep forgetting – I am you."

And I point at him with the pencil. Really jabbing it in his saggy face. "Yeah – the demented hillbilly version of me," I say. "Your skin is like uncooked pastry, you're going bald-" He glares at me. "-sorry, your hair is receding, and you have a pot belly. I mean, Christ, what have you been doing for the last fourteen years? Sitting in a darkened basement drinking yourself stupid and eating junk food?"

He turns to his Dougal.

"Did you tell him?" he says.

His Dougal shrugs.

"You're currently sitting in a wetsuit soaked in petrol-"

"Turpentine."

"Who cares?" I say, waggling the pencil some more. "You don't have any cool clothes. And even if you did you couldn't get into them."

His skin isn't pasty any more. It's purple. He goggles at me with muppet's eyes. His body jitters with rage.

"You think Lucy Sugar is going to leap into your pants because you feel a little bit more sure of yourself?" I add. "Well here's the news, grandad – you're dreaming."

He goggles at his Dougal who shrugs and says, "He has a point."

I get right in his face.

"You say you have a week to win Lucy round. Well that might just give us time. If you stay off the beer and put some work in, with my help you could perhaps pass for a nineteen-year-old."

I lean forward and reach under the bed.

"Here," I say, sitting up and tossing him a pair of mucky blue Hi Tech training shoes. "You can start by running off some of that experience of yours."

~

Behind the dunes is a sandy little road that runs all the way out to the end of the beach. In the summer it's jammed with holidaymakers and golfers, but now it's dead. The perfect place to take your older self for a training run.

"Come on, you lazy old bastard," I shout, "get that belly moving!"

"Can't you slow down a bit?" he moans through his fake moustache.

"No," I reply. "In fact, we need to go faster. You're hardly running at all. More like waddling." And I press the accelerator a little. The car moves gently ahead. He has to work even harder to keep up.

"Move it, Grandad. Just imagine you're chasing a giant pie."

He wheezes in enough breath to respond:

"You do realise you're insulting yourself here, don't you? That says a lot about you psychologically."

"Shut up and get your fat legs moving!"

"Hang on a sec!" pants Grandad. And he stops running and bends over at the side of the road. Gives his breakfast a little air.

Older Dougal snorts with laughter in the back seat, then hi-fives his younger self.

The joke's on me, I know, but I have to smile.

~

I knock quickly three times then slowly three times. Older Dougal opens the warped door. My Dougal and I enter and move over to where Grandad lies flaked out on a camp bed in the dusty attic flat. He still wears my trainers and a sweat-stained Stone Roses t-shirt.

"Now you're trimming down I got you a set of decent clothes," I say, and empty a couple of carrier bags on top of him.

Puffing, he raises himself to his elbows.

149

"Fuck's this?" he snaps.

"It's called fashion."

"A Fred Perry polo shirt with a button-down collar is fashion?"

"Britpop culture, Grandad."

"It's bloody awful."

"Well, we're all out of frock coats, so you're going to have to get used to it."

~

"Ah'm no sure that's fitting right," says Dougal.

"Yes, I'm afraid you're still too fat."

"It's poorly cut, I think you'll find," whines Grandad.

"Afraid not, old man," I smile. "Dougal, break out the emergency measures."

"What the hell's that!?" shrieks Grandad.

"What does it look like?"

"A bloody corset."

"Spot on. Come here."

"Where did you get it?!"

"Borrowed it from Monica," says Dougal. "Look, it has lovely little furry bits and everything."

"Give me a hand, here, Dougal. Just pull on that and we'll tie it off."

"YOWW!!"

"Och, will ye look at that, his flesh is all squeezing through the laces."

"Slack slack slack! For God's sake, slacken it off!"

"Oh, stop whining, you old git. You look lovely."

"Aye, awfy pretty."

"Oh God."

~

"The hair is definitely a problem."

"My hair's fine!"

"Och, no, there's no enough in some places."

"Too much of it in others."

"Aye, and it smells."

"That's the turpentine."

"Right, come over to the sink. Okay, Dougal, you hold his head while you trim him at the back, there, Dougal. I'll put this on at the front.

"WHAT!? Gerroff! You're not putting a dead rat on my head!"

"Don't panic, we'll comb it in."

"Aye, ye'll look grand. Like Sean Connery in Never Say Never Again."

"You think?"

"Aye, definitely."

"Well, I suppose we could give it a try."

"Fine. Oh, listen Dougal, while we've got him by the sink, get the fake tan out, will you?"

~

"Now plant your feet. Clench your fists and put them over your nipples. And just... sway. Like you're a sea cucumber in a gentle ocean swell. No! Too much. You hardly want to move at all."

"Don't tell me how to dance," he snaps. "I saw Oasis at Maine Road, you know."

I stand back a little. Look at him.

"I didn't go to Maine Road," I say slowly. "Dad wouldn't let me. Do you tell people you went? What kind of inadequate are you?"

"What is this shit anyway?" he growls at the radio.

"Don't tell me you've forgotten Limp Bizkit!"

"Forgotten how pump it is. Put on the Bee Gees or something."

"Man, I can't believe I'm such a square."

"Tragedy. That's a good tune. Put that on."

~

"How do I look?"

"Like an old grump. Stop frowning."

"I mean, could I pass for nineteen?"

"Let's see what the Dougals think. Gentlemen, can we interrupt your chess for just one second?"

The Dougals look up from the board.

"What do you reckon?"

They stare.

"Is Freddie Senior going to cut it in 2002?"

And, ever so slowly, the Dougals smile.

~

Man, I feel like a tool. Look at this kit. Ridiculous. Can't believe anyone ever thought it was fashionable. Had I no taste? Surprised the damn police haven't arrested me for crimes against public decency.

Still, gotta run with it. Be cool. Act like a nineteen-year-old. How do I do that? Think about sex all the time. Hell, that shouldn't be hard.

Here we go. The entrance to the quad. Stop for a minute. Soak in the scene. How many times have I stood here? Hundreds. Thousands. Ancient uneven cobbles beneath my feet, slimy with last night's rain. On the right, the crumbling buttresses of the chapel. To my left are the stairs to the coffee-washed crypt that is the Old Refectory. Above, the square shoulders of St Anthony's tower loom, the numerals on the golden clock gleaming in the winter sun. Ahead of me is the archway that runs through the base of the tower. Yawning darkly like a gateway to hell. Deep breath. This is it. With my right hand I tousle my curtains some more, with my left I untuck my t-shirt. Another breath, and in I go.

The square is crawling with students. Look at them. Hundreds of the little bastards. A geeky guy struggles to control his bundle of books. It topples first one way, then the other – he trots to keep it balanced and just as he gets it under control his glasses clatter to the flags. Aw mate, unlucky!

A trio of goths loiters beneath the chapel arches, drinking milk and glaring at everyone who passes from under thick black brows. The girl goth in the middle looks up at me as I pass. I wink at her. She can't help herself smiling back – her pal sees her and scowls.

A gaggle of yahs stand round the 'No walking on the grass sign' having what appears to be a 'who can hold their cigarette in the most ridiculous way' competition. All the boys wear pink shirts and chinos and have lambswool jumpers slung over their backs. They pat and play punch each other with the casual heartiness bred of a thousand communal showers. The girls wear coloured jeans and puffa jackets. Be great to fuck them – not 'cos they're hot, just 'cos I'd love to see the look of surprise on their face as I paraded my manky old soldier.

Good news so far is that none of them look that suspicious. They're buying it. And why shouldn't they? What's fourteen years, really, when you think about it? It's all in the mind. And right now, I think I'm the coolest nineteen-year-old in this town.

Media Studies lectures are in seminar room four. Take up position by the steps outside the entrance. Lean back against the cold stone. Cross one flared leg over the other. Think groovy thoughts.

The quad is busy, but the second Lucy walks into it, I know. You'd have to be a corpse not to spot her. High-heeled black boots. Tight black trousers with a little Mexican kick-flare. White fur jacket. White fur hat. Her lips are blood on the snow. Shit, she looks like a fucking Bond girl.

Again, I witness the Lucy Sugar bow wave. As she moves across the quad the males sense her an instant before they see her, and turn to stare open mouthed. The girls see the men move and spin to follow their eyes. When they clock her, every single one of them gives a little involuntary snarl. Many manage to re-control their features and cover their animal hate with a civilised and apparently carefree smile. But for some, the brutal emotion remains twisted on their face until Lucy has come and gone.

She glides across the gravel and reaches the steps. As she

mounts the first one, a pen slips from her hand. One of the yah guys bends down to pick it up. For a glorious moment he basks in Lucy's grateful smile. Then the sun moves on. He's left in the twisted shadows by his fuming girlfriend.

Lucy trots up the steps and into the lecture hall. Wait a moment for a few more people to follow, then I also enter.

Ten rows of steeply tiered wooden rows. At the front a vast wooden desk, a blackboard with white pull-down section and an overhead projector. To my left, high arched windows. Watery winter sunlight shows up years of dirt and insect adventure. Very high ceiling – must be fifteen feet up. More room for big ideas.

Head right up the rows to the back. Lucy is near the front. Currently taking off her white hat and shaking loose her hair. Sit on the old leather and slide myself along to the middle. All around me, students are getting ready to learn. Bit of chatter. Rustling and flappings as they extract notebooks and pens from bags. Aw, look. There's an Asian girl in the next row with a tin pencil case. She pops it open and selects one of a dozen identical rollerball pens. Beside her a guy with a woolly hat on is drawing a margin in his notebook with a chewed ruler. Shit, they're all so earnest. Still, there's a buzz in the air. Kind of makes me wish I'd gone to a few more classes when it was my turn. Used to hate coming to lectures. Don't know why – this is kind of fun.

A door just to the right of the blackboard opens. Guy in his mid-to-late twenties struts in. He's short and slightly fat, with long unkempt hair. Too-tight jeans and baseball boots on the bottom half, a holey sweater and leather jacket on the top. In the hand nearest the class he holds a packet of Red Marlboro. Tucked under his left arm is a battered leather satchel.

He places the cigarettes right at the front of the desk, then lobs the satchel onto the surface. It skids a little and knocks the blackboard duster onto the floor. The man pretends not to notice and shrugs off his leather jacket. Lays it at the front of the desk beside the cigarettes. Perches his bulging bottom on the side of the desk and looks up at the class.

"Good morning," he says. "Can any of you cats remind me where we got up to last week?"

Now I remember why I used to hate lectures. Fucking lecturers.

The Asian girl with the tin pencil case puts her hand up.

"Yo, Amy," smiles the lecturer.

The girl flicks back through a blue folder of extraordinarily neat notes.

"We had just talked about the subversion of government propaganda into the plot-lines of Australian soap operas," she says.

The lecturer nods. "Oh yeah, right. Good stuff. Okay, well, this week, we're going to trot that trope on a little. You cats ready to roll?"

With a final flurry of pen clicking and pencil sharpening, the room settles down. The lecturer opens his satchel. Pulls out some transparencies. Turns on the overhead projector. Hits the light switch by the blackboard. Puts the first transparency on the glass, covered with a sheet of paper.

He looks round the room.

"Prepare to get wise," he says. And he looks at Lucy – the half-light of the projector throws her face into sharp film-noir relief. "I know that many of you are seeking careers in the media, but I feel I should warn you..." and he pulls the covering sheet from his transparency, revealing a single statement in large black type:

'By the year 2010, popular entertainment will be dead.'

Stunned silence.

The girl with the pencil case is scribbling furiously.

"You think I'm joking? Seriously, forget any dreams you may have of making it in entertainment. That whole rosy little worlderoo is about to implode."

All around the room you can see dreams popping like rainbow bubbles in the air. Lucy shifts in her seat. He's still staring at her.

"Television, film, the big studios, the very concept of stars and celebrities – they are all dying."

Lucy's lips are tight.

Amy lifts her hand. "Why is that?" she asks.

"A combination of factors," drawls the lecturer. "In the first instance, the undisciplined human brain is easy bored. It constantly seeks out the new and the unusual. And so we are becoming bored of the same old stories. The same old famous faces. We crave variety. And yet, as we desperately seek this fresh entertainment, so that entertainment satisfies us less.

"Secondly, the talent available in the industry is more meagre than ever before. Movie stars, TV actors, writers, directors – they are all simply not as good as they used to be. And as the talent becomes diluted, so does our enjoyment. Our boredom and the dearth of quality feed off each other and a cycle begins. We are at the alpha stage of this process now. Soon a vortex will form, sucking entertainment into unrecognisable forms. Eventually, we will be so unsatisfied with what we are watching that we will simply switch off. In our millions. This point I refer to as the Trevor Equilibrium. After its discoverer – me."

How old is this guy? Twenty-eight. Look at him. Thinks he knows it all. Eager student faces mooning up at him as he parades around like Indiana fucking Jones. They don't know any better. Big shot in here – but in the real world, a grade four helmet. Guy's never functioned outside of an institution. Gone straight from boarding school to uni to life as an academic. Has he lived in a brewery for ten years, drinking cheap wine and failing? Course not. Fuck does he know about life?

Lucy is almost boiling. The lecturer clocks her and smiles.

"So why should we bother studying it?" asks a frizzy haired bloke in the front row.

"That's an interesting point. We study it because what can be more important than understanding the decline of our entire Western society? That's what's happening here."

And again, the pencils wag. Amy is underlining like a mad woman.

"And so where do we go from the Trevor Equilibrium?" He reaches for a new transparency. "Well, the culture necessarily begins a stage of metamorphosis-"

"But how can you say ze stars are dying?!"

Zone back into the room. This passionate outburst came from Lucy. She's leaning right forward, her face flushed, fists clenched.

"Zere will always be stars here, just as zey will always shine in ze heavens."

The lecturer smiles.

"That's an interesting point of view, Lucy. But if you had taken the time to read my book on the subject" – he lofts a thick hardback volume entitled, Scene That – The Millennium And The Death Of Visual Entertainment by Dr Trevor Poleshaft – "you would know the answer to your question." He struts in front of her, wafting his book around his head. "This is required reading, people. It's going to be the bible of the new culture revolution. Get it. Read it. Try to understand it. Okay?"

"Rubbish," I say.

"Who said that?

"I did," I say.

"Ah," he smirks. "The gentleman in the Fred Perry shirt." A couple of girls at the front snigger. Amy turns. "What exactly do you consider to be rubbish?"

"Every single word you've uttered since you came in this room."

"An interesting point of view," he says. "Would you care to justify it?"

"With pleasure. You're spouting views that you think will be controversial so you can get your supposedly cutting-edge book onto a few university reading lists. But actually, as we both know, your theory is the worst kind of pretentious nonsense."

A slight gasp ripples round the room.

"In 2010, popular entertainment will be more abundant than ever. More channels, more programmes, more movies, more apps–"

"What's an app?" someone mutters.

"More celebrities," I continue. "And more money. The people in this lecture room are going to be at the forefront of an almost

157

grossly healthy industry."

"That's an interesting point of view-"

"Stop saying that." More gasps. "You don't mean it. It's a passive-aggressive way of discarding my opinion while maintaining your own over-inflated self-esteem. As a complete social and intellectual inadequate, the only way you can function is by coming in here and bullying unformed minds. While all the time you remain jealous of their potential, their youth and the chances they will enjoy. Chances to make it in a world where you so spectacularly failed."

In the corner of my vision I see Lucy. She's staring round at me, her delicious lips a little open.

"And I'll tell you something else I know. That girl there is right." Point to Lucy. "There will always be stars. In fact, she'll be one of them." Her eyes shine, her neck tilts back a little. Like she's going into a trance. Keep going, baby, keep going. "When beauty, style and talent die, that's when the stars fade. But as long as there are girls like her around, they will burn forever."

Stand up. Dust swirls in the light from the projector. "Now, if you'll excuse me, I've got more important things to do with my time. Like watch Neighbours."

As I pass the front of the class, I wink at Lucy.

She starts, confused for a second – then despite herself, she smiles back.

Then I'm gone. Scattered coughing echoes behind me then dies as I step out of the lecture hall and into the quad.

Where I slow right down. And wait.

And wait.

Wait.

Patt-patt-patter-patt.

Soon as I hear that I start again. Normal walking pace at first, then faster as I move across the middle of the grass.

After all, I don't want her to catch me too quickly.

~

Not sure about this. My skin is getting itchy. Every step I take down the stairs it's like there's hot sand in my clothes. Have to stop on the landing for a second. Hold onto the banister. Look out down the frosty, moonlit beach. Get calm...

I probably wouldn't have been bothered about going to see Pen if it was my idea. Except now that I know I have to get it on with her, I feel nervous. Somehow I have to that common room and be so nice to her that she shags me in a pantry. But I'm sworn to celibacy. Yet my future self is clearly not celibate. Anything but. So how do I reconcile these two inharmonious states of being? Oh, goodness what a lot of pressure I'm under. I expect in Grandad's past, I just did it casually without even realising – one minute we're talking away about costumes, the next – BAM! – she's got her hand down my pants.

Not that she'd be so forward. She's a nice girl. Sexy of course, in her way. Or rather, not sexy, but sensual. If I weren't a friar I can imagine it would be nice to lose my virginity to her – not embarrassing. Lots of kissing first. Little noises. Wriggles. Then, slowly, we'd lose our clothes. Her skin laying against mine, soft and sweet like the inside of a Bounty bar. I can reach out and touch her, nibble her deliciousness, wherever I want – and she'll want me to. She'll love me to. Every inch I cover will be an hour of pleasure. And all through it, her face so close to mine, her soft brown eyes smiling, trusting, loving. Yeah, that would be nice...

But hang on a minute, I'm not going to lose it to her any more, am I? If Grandad is successful I'll be popping my whatnot with Lucy Sugar. Then snogging Pen after that. Wow. Seems a bit of a shame. Don't know how, but it does. Can't smell her coconut skin. Can't see Pen's face so close any more. Still, I'll bet losing it to Lucy would be unforgettable. You've got those pneumatic knockers of hers for a start. The proudest caramel puddings in existence...

Anyway, better hurry going down the stairs before I miss the meeting. What will I say to Penelope when I walk in? We haven't talked much recently. In fact, now I come to think of it, I've seen her at meals and stuff, but we haven't so much as exchanged a word in weeks. I've talked more to the cleaning lady than I have to her. That's a bit weird. What's that all about?

Here's the door.

I look in through the glass. Six girls sit round the long oak table in the middle of the room. They have sketch pads. At the head of the table sits Monica.

Oh man, how can I get talking to Pen with them like that? Six girls, all bloody staring at me. I can't go in there. Hang on, Monica's getting to her feet. Going to speak. Can't hear. Ease the door open a little. That's it...

"Alright, gels," she starts. "Listen, thanks for coming along. We got a few jobs what need doin', so I've divided 'em up as fair as I can. Alex and Sally, can you do peasant outfits, please? Quite a lot to 'andle, I know, but keep 'em simple – one male design and one female, that ought to do it, alright, my darlings? Fiona, Becks – can you 'andle the guards. They can all be the same. Just make 'em nice and threatening. Big codpieces or something. Smashing. I'll do the Black Prince and the king. That leaves you, Penelope, to do the wailing children and Mary. Now, the primary school 'ave kindly offered the services of class 2B. So you might want to pop along there, darling, and 'ave a word."

Pen nods. She smiles. And what a smile it is – I'd forgotten how pretty it makes her look. The key to her face. Suddenly she's the most attractive girl in the room. I have a sudden urge to get in there and talk to her. My fingers reach for the handle – and stop. Damn. Can't quite do it yet.

"Alright, girls," says Monica, getting to her feet. First rehearsal's on Friday. If you can have some ideas by then, that would be great."

"Alright." "Sure." "Okay."

And they start to get to their feet. Shit. They're going to leave from the other door. Quick, turn the handle, in the room, walk across to them. Pen looks round – sees me – and her smile evaporates. Stops looking at me, starts staring at the floor instead. Now I'm here. Right at the table in the middle of them. Pen's not watching me, but all the others are. What now?

"Yes, darling?" asks Monica.

Not sure what to say. Wish Pen would look at me. Feel that might help somehow.

"Um, hi. I, uh, just, uh, came to see if you guys, um, need any help."

Monica looks me up and down like I'm some sort of prize pig.

"You any good at costume-making, darling?"

"Um... yes. At least I think so," I say. "I dressed as Blanche Dubois once," I add, nodding. And I look over at Pen. She still doesn't catch my eye. Notice she's gone a little red.

Monica stifles a laugh. Then she clocks me looking at Pen. Looks at her too. Does she see her red cheeks? Her laugh turns into a sly smile.

"What's your name again, darling?"

"Freddie."

"Well, Freddie love, I reckon Penelope over there could do with an 'and. Why don't you join her? Wailing children and Mary."

Penelope whips round and glares at Monica, who only winks once, very quickly, then writes my name on her sheet.

The other girls all leave. Pen stays where she is. Monica is the last out. She throws a last glance over her shoulder towards her room-mate, offers up another chuckle and is gone.

I edge over to where Pen sits, one leg crossed over the other, her A3 pad angled sharply up in front of her. Head bobbed forward, hair curtaining her proud little face, she sketches away with furious intent. Man, what now?

"Hi," I say. "You sketching?"

Twat. Course she's sketching.

"It's pretty good," I try. "What is it?" No answer from her – and no wonder. This is terrible chat. A three-year-old would be embarrassed.

I shift myself towards her a little – and she instantly coils herself away. What's that all about? Have I said something to offend her? Don't think so. Still, best give her a moment. Just watch her sketch for a bit. Maybe she's not ignoring me. Probably just getting an idea down on paper.

No, she's finished that one and gone onto the next one. She's definitely ignoring me. Why, I don't know. But I'm going to have to make conversation.

"So, ah, Penelope, what kind of outfit would Mary of Moncur

have actually worn?"

"You tell me," she fires back, "you're the costume expert."

Man, what's got into her? This is harsh. Feels a bit humiliating. Want to keep going, though. Want to see her lovely smile again.

"I mean, what would it have been made of? I guess they didn't have cotton, and silk would have been way too expensive for a peasant, so I guess it must have been wool, right?"

She stops sketching. Looks up at me. Dead in the face. And I see something strange there in her sea-storm eyes – the last thing I expected – not anger, fear or bitterness, but... hope. Despite themselves, her sweet eyes are full of hope.

"Wool, yes, that must be it," she snaps. Then she drops back to her sketching.

What can I do but watch? Her head down, hand plugged into her imagination, she sketches for ten minutes straight. And all the time I'm watching her. Not once does she look up. And suddenly an image flashes through my brain – of the last time I spoke to her.

The night of The Dangling.

When I went off on the crawl with Lucy and Clive. She'd thought I was going to ask her to the pub crawl. She'd looked like she was keen on the idea. Then I started showing off. Nearly killed myself. Agreed to go with Lucy instead. No wonder Pen's a bit pissed off. Poor gel's upset. Look at her there. Drawing away so neatly. Her delicate fingers moving so surely.

"Listen, I'm sorry about that evening."

"What evening?"

"The pub crawl."

She looks down at her sketch. Decides she's made a mistake. Rubs it out. Quite violently.

"It wasn't how I..." She draws over her erased mistake. Shit, how can I say this? "I mean, I didn't want to... that is... I didn't plan for things to go like they did. I mean, you can see it from my point of view – I'd just been dangling from a fourth story window. Which was kind of disconcerting. She asked me and I just said yes. I didn't mean to let you down."

She stops sketching. Looks back up at me – a piercing, strangely fiery glance.

"You did though," she says. Another furious rub with the eraser. And now she puffs the rubbings towards me.

Fair point. I suppose you have to see things from her point of view too. It must have been pretty shitty.

Pause for a second. Watch her draw some more. What can I say now? Hell, why not be honest?

"Listen," I say, leaning right forward over her pad. "I didn't come down here because I'm good at sewing."

Her pencil hand pauses.

"We both know I haven't a clue."

She moves her hand to the side of the page.

"I came down because I wanted to talk to you. Been wanting to for a long time. That night... I've been thinking about it, you know, and... if I could somehow turn back time, I'd say no to Lucy. I'd go with you."

She looks down at her drawing. Tries to sketch something. But it's an aimless line.

"Because, I had a dream."

Molten brown eyes look up to mine.

"The dream was you and me. In the future-" she's staring at me now, eyes wide, "-in the not too distant future, and we were on the beach. Dancing. Together. Just dancing on the sand."

I look away towards the six huge windows, dark now, with the winter night beyond.

"And I don't know what the dream means, but I know that if I didn't try to tell you about it, then I'd never have a chance of making it come true."

Turn my head back to look at her. Her face has dropped. She's staring at the badly drawn feet of the model she sketched. And then I realise – those feet aren't badly drawn, it's just that the charcoal is smudged. A wet drop soaked into the cartridge paper.

I breathe.

She hoists her moistened eyes to mine.

"Linen," she says.

"Huh?"

"I think Mary's dress would have been made of heavy linen."

And as I feel my smile grow, I see it doubled back at me in

her beautiful face and my heart feels as light as the moon on the beach.

~

My long legs stretch out down the Vennel, the high-walled lane that connects the quad with Central Street. For every one of my steps that canons off down the sheer stone alley, I hear two of hers.

"Hey."

Still twenty yards before I get there. Keep going.

"I said, 'hey!'"

More steps. She's almost running now. There's a tug on my arm.

"Huh?"

Slowly turn to see her perfect face beaming up at me.

"Are you not hearing me?"

"Sorry, I was... far off."

"What you sinking about, walking along so fast and mean looking?"

Cough a little. Narrow my eyes.

"Nothing. Everything."

Hold her eyes. Then look suddenly out over her head to sea. And back. Ten yards to go. Get moving. She follows.

"You gave heem a pretty rough ride in zere."

"Can't sit and listen to that rollox. Man says the stars are dead? Pah!"

Twenty yards to go.

"Oh, I agree," she says. "But... did you really mean what you said about me being a star? You seemed so... certain."

Ten yards.

"As sure as the sun comes up tomorrow, you, Lucy Sugar, will be a star."

"How can you be so certain?"

Five.

"Know quite a bit about acting, actually."

"What sort of sings?"

Another couple of steps and we'll be there. The recess at end of the Vennel. It ducks off left, dark and low. Leads to the basement of the tower. But there's something else in there today.

Here it is.

Watch this.

"Tell you over a drink," I say with a smile, and step past the doorway, just as two dark forms step out from it.

All in black they block our path. One is short and fat, one is short and thin. The Dougals. Their shoulders are hunched sinisterly in thick donkey jackets. Both wear black woolly tights on their heads, the legs hanging down like spaniel ears. The tights are thick enough to obscure their features, but I don't think they can see too well. They're both staring in opposite directions.

"What is zis?" says Lucy, her eyes flicking between the men in black and me.

They focus on the sound and face us. Please don't fuck this up, boys.

"G-g-give me your wallet!" says my fat Dougal in an atrocious American accent. Oh God.

"You mean her purse," I hiss.

"Aye, yes, her purse. Your purse. Sorry, I got confused."

Idiot's going to blow this.

Look at Lucy. She's starting to quiver.

"And if she doesn't want to give it to you?" I say.

Thin Dougal nods to his other self, who begins fumbling about inside his donkey jacket.

"Then..." he starts.

He fumbles some more. At last he pulls out... His Swiss army knife. Twonk. His fat hands can't get it open.

"Hang on..." he mutters.

Oh God, hurry up, you fool.

With a shower of crumbs, the blade comes free. The nail file blade.

"Then... we cut you up."

"Real bad," adds thin Dougal.

"Man," says fat Dougal with a nod, and he wafts the little weapon towards us like he's scared of it.

"Oh, mein Dieu!" squeaks Lucy and turns instinctively towards me. Move my body towards her.

"It's okay," I say softly. "Give me your purse."

She does, her hands shaking.

Draw myself up tall. Turn to the Dougals.

"You want this?" I say. They nod. "Then you're going to have to come and get it." And I slip her purse into my back pocket.

Lucy gasps. "No!"

Give her a wink, then face the Dougals once more.

"But I should warn you," I smile. "Got a sixteenth dan in Sudoku."

The Dougals look at each other. They take a step forward.

"HEEEYYYYAAAGGGHHHHH!!!!!" I suddenly scream and throw my limbs into martial convulsions. After a full ten seconds of stiff-armed windmilling and eye rolling, I come to rest, my fingers spread out beside my face like claws. My arms juddering with barely restrained fury. One leg extended like the Karate Kid.

My boiling eyes complete last lap of honour and come to rest staring at my nose.

The Dougals look at each other.

They turn as one and tear off down the Vennel, bumping into each other as they go. Turn to check out Lucy. Her lip hangs very, very low.

"You okay?" I say.

"Sure. I mean, my head it is a little wibble-wobble, but I guess so, yeah."

"Here." Hand back her purse.

She looks up at me.

"Zat was so impressive," she says softly. "I did not know you were such an expert at ze combat."

Which is when I break out my hugest smile.

"Never done a martial art in my life," I say with a wink.

"You were faking!?" she gasps.

"Acting, my darling, acting. Told you I knew a thing or two about it. Now, I don't know about you," I add, "but I really think we ought to see about that drink."

~

"Say good morning to Miss Cotton, class," orders the tweed-bound schoolmistress.

"Good-mor-ning-Miss-Cott-on," the kids chant back dully.

Miss Tweedie nods to Pen and beetles behind her desk.

Pen stands up in front of the blackboard. She's dwarfed by it. Could almost be a child herself, summoned to do long division. Almost. You don't see many kids wearing gypsy skirts and striped shirts. Nor many with breasts.

"Good morning, children," says Pen. "I expect you're wondering why I'm here talking to you today-"

"No."

Chuckles ripple round the room like floodwater. A boy with a million freckles grins at his sudden notoriety.

Pen smiles a little. Nods her head. Composes herself. Starts again. "Mr Keddie and I are here today because-"

That's the funny thing. I thought she was flat-chested before, but now she's wearing that more tailored shirt, I can see her breasts are really quite a nice size. It's because her back is so slim that it looks like she goes straight up. But from the way those dark blue stripes are distorting, I reckon her boobs are actually quite pronounced. Pert even. Not that it matters of course. To a man of my calling.

UUUURRPPP!!!

Million Freckle Boy rips out a machine-gun belch. Giggles echo in its wake.

"Who did that!?" snaps Miss Tweedie, rising to her feet. She turns to Pen. "Perhaps you'd like to get to the point, dear," says Miss Tweedie. The old girl readjusts her half-moon specs and descends into her hardwood chair. Fat lot of good she is.

"Well," continues Pen, "my friend and I are students at the

university, and we want your help-"

PAARRRPPP!!! Now he mocks a flappy fart. Laughter fills the class and heats the air. It's getting harder to breathe. Outwardly, Pen is calm, but her cheeks are reddening from within. Don't like to see her like this. Getting eaten alive. The little shits are about to run riot. Million Freckles is preparing something under his desk. Something that requires spit. Who do you think you're dealing with here, you wee nyaff? I invented that shit.

Pen gathers herself. Clears her throat.

Million Freckles winks at his pal. Takes a breath.

She opens her mouth.

He puts a biro to his.

"Can anyone tell me what a Vindendraam is?" I hear myself say. Shit I'm standing up in front of them. Twenty-eight pairs of eyes are on me. Twenty-eight faces scanning me like satellite dishes. But I'm glaring only at Freckles.

Daring him.

"I said, who knows what a Vindendraam is?"

Still I glare at Freckles. Walk towards him. Loom from an altitude of seventy-eight inches. Young scrapper pockets the pellet shooter. Wise boy. To my left I see a little girl's hand sneak shyly upwards.

"Yes, there. What's your name?"

"Eliza," says the girl – plump with bunches.

"Go on, Eliza."

"It's a play."

"Very good, Eliza. It's a play. A very special kind of play that takes place only at Tallowmas fair. Who knows what Tallowmas fair is? Yes, what's your name?"

I nod at a boy with no front teeth and unruly hair.

"Hugh."

"Go on, Hugh."

"It's the midwinter festival," says Hugh.

"Well done, Hugh. That's right. Every year on the first Saturday before midwinter, we hold a great celebration here in St Mary's. Everyone who works in the town joins a big parade – who here has parents helping out?"

"Me." Yes, mine are!" "Mine too!"

"Excellent. And that's not all the fun. Some students like me and Penelope over there-" I point to her. The kids look round. She smiles and waves. They look at her with wide eyes. Then back to me. "-we're putting on a special play, a Vindendraam, like you said, Eliza-"

Eliza flutters in her seat like a little sparrow.

"-which is always about a dramatic event from the town's history. Usually these events are grisly and horrific with lots of fake blood. Who wants to know what we're performing this year?"

"Me!" "I do!" "Me too!"

"I'm glad you're so keen," I say, smiling at a bucktoothed girl in the front row. Little lass's eyebrows rocket off the top of her face. "This year, we are doing a particularly wicked story about the burning at the stake of St Mary herself."

Childish jaws hit tiny desks.

"And we need some young people like you to play the part of Mary's pupils-"

"Me!" "I'll do it!" "Pick me!"

I raise my hands, calming them.

"Before I pick anyone, I need to know that you can act upset. So I want you to imagine that the lovely Penelope over there-"

Shit! Why did I say that? Came from nowhere. Look over to see how she took it. She's gone bright red. Dropped her face to the floor. Is that good or bad? Impossible to tell. Bugger. Better press on.

"-imagine that she is your teacher and some bad men want to burn her – right out there in street – what would you say?"

"No!" "Stop it!" "I'd scream!"

Check out Pen again. She's still looking up. Think I've blown this. "Er, that's pretty impressive, class," I say. "But it's not really up to me. What do you think, Penelope?"

She stares at her feet for another second. Then she looks up at me. Smiles.

"Not bad," she says. "Not bad at all."

"Good news," I say, smiling round the room. "You're all in."

HUGE CHEERS.

"On one condition."

"ANYTHING!"

"I need you to go home tonight and tell your parents to make you a mediaeval peasant costume. Okay? Why don't you write that down for me. Mediaeval-that's m-e-d-i-a-e-v-a-l. Peasant. Peas and an ant together. You got that? Great."

I don't need to look to know that Pen is laughing.

~

Merchants Café is a tangled warren of old stone store rooms dug deep beneath Central Street. Part coffee shop, part bar, total legend, the place dates back almost as long as the university. Countless generations of students have plotted politics, love and underwear raids in its cramped booths.

Our table is recessed into a huge old fireplace. An ancient iron soup pot dangles from black chains beside us.

Sip my coffee. Lucy absent-mindedly stirs her marshmallow into her hot chocolate.

"That was so impressive!" she bubbles. "You tricked him so well! Where did you learn to act like that?"

Shrug my shoulders.

"Just a gift, I guess."

"You know, I knew from ze first time I saw you zat you were like me."

Oh, I'll bet you did, you wise and sexy thing, you.

"Have you acted in many plays?" she asks.

"Never had the opportunity."

"I have always loved acting!"

"Is that the case?" I say, stirring a little sugar into my coffee. But I say nothing, waiting for her to fill the silence.

"Oh yes! I was obsessed with movies when I was a child. Of course, I had to watch zem in secret movies on my own, when my mama was out-"

"Why's that?"

"She hated me to enjoy anysing glamorous. Maybe she was

jealous. I don't know." She looks up at me, then away quickly, back down to her chocolate. "Anyway," she continues, "I remember ze first time I sought about becoming an actress. I was in ze house one day when my mama was out and I was watching zat famous romantic movie about ze doomed love relationship-"

"Casablanca?"

"No it was a more recent film – ze lead character, she was a mermaid..."

"Splash?"

"Yes! Splash! Oh zat is such a wonderful film, don't you sink?"

"Um, John Candy's pretty funny..."

"But se girl, Darren-"

"Darryl Hannah."

"Zat's right! Oh, she is so beautiful. When she comes out of ze water naked and everyone looks at her!"

"That is a good bit."

"Zat scene is probably my favourite in ze whole of cinema history! I just laff it! Every time I watch it I imagine myself as her – arriving in a new world so pure and free and innocent! Such a powerful image, don't you sink?"

"Very powerful," I agree.

"It is my ambition one day to be as big as Daryl Hannah."

She smiles. Stirs her chocolate some more. Then she picks up a little piece of half-melted marshmallow and brings it to her mouth on the long-handled spoon. Her lips part, then close over the moist confection. She slowly extracts the spoon. A solitary creamy drip escapes for a second and hangs glistening on her budding lower lip. Then her tongue slips out and hooks it into the dark silk of her mouth.

She swallows.

"Oh, I don't think you'll have any problems there," I manage, trying to deal with the rampant stiffy tearing its way through my trousers. "And now with the Vindendraam, you got a great chance to get noticed."

"Yes, only a few days to go now. I am so excited," she says.

"Looking forward to it myself," I say.

Then I pause.

Lean back.

Pause again.

Screw up my face a little like I've just remembered something.

"There's just one thing that worries me," I say.

She pauses, cup en route to her mouth. Cocks her head on one side.

"Yes?"

"About our play."

"Oh, I don't think there's any need to worry," she smiles. "Ze committee runs it every year. Zey have zat all under control."

"Yeah, but Tallowmas fair has been celebrated here for centuries. It's not just part of the town's history – it's part of people's lives. Every man, woman and child is going to be there. It's the only thing that unites the students: geeks, yahs, goths, surfers – for one night they're all part of the fair. Plus, there will be tourists from every part of the world. And we're going to be the focus for the whole event! Our hall will perform the Vindendraam. Two thousand pairs of eyes and every one with five hundred years of expectation."

Her face clouds. Pretty little nose twitches. Cheeks are going red. Puts her cup down.

"So, you do not sink I can do it??"

"On the contrary. The way you helped me fight those muggers – I know you're a great actress."

"I did nussing."

Lean towards her. Clench my fists for emphasis. "You made it look easy. That's what I mean, you're a natural. But... it's not just that." Pause for a second. Look from left to right like someone might be listening. Then whisper:

"I heard something."

She leans forward. Says in a low voice:

"What?"

Look around again and beckon her even closer into the

fireplace.

"One of the tourists... may be someone who can help you."

"What do you mean?"

"Guy from Hollywood. An agent."

"What?! Who?! How do you know zis!?"

"Sh. Can't tell you any more right now. But trust me, this information comes from a good source. So, you see, this isn't any old year. If that Hollywood dude is going to notice you, this has to be a special year. Everything should be fabulous. Your costume, the crowd and, most importantly, your Black Prince."

"My what?"

"It's a famous saying in the theatre, 'You're only as good as your co-star'."

"It is?"

"Absolutely. Now, Darryl Hannah in Splash – she had Tom Hanks, right? Very talented actor. In Blade Runner, Harrison Ford. Very handsome movie star. Who have you got?"

"Mr Sleevewort..."

Raise my eyebrows.

"But he knows so much about ze event. All ze history. He is planning ze whole sing. And he is the acting warden. He is in charge of acting."

Is she for real? Her wide eyes tell me she is.

"I think in this instance 'acting' refers to the fact that he isn't the full-time warden. He's stepping in, as it were."

It takes some doing to crumple Lucy's smooth golden forehead, but she manages it.

"He is playing a role," she says after a moment. "I like that."

Rats. Don't let this slip away.

"Ah," I say, "but have you asked you asked yourself exactly why he took this 'role' on in the first place?"

She puts down her cup.

"He wants to act with me. He told me so."

"Course he wants to. What man wouldn't?" I smile. "But maybe that's not his only reason."

"What do you mean?"

"Maybe he does want to put on a really good show. Wants you to be part of that. Or maybe he has another reason. Golly, I don't know, how can I? The real warden's overseas..."

"Warden? What...?"

Lean in towards her. "Well, it's no secret that he'd love the warden's job, right? So imagine if something were to happen to the warden. It probably won't but just say that were the case – then he'd be next in line for the job, right? And with everyone watching, it would be the perfect opportunity for him to impress the Dean."

"I suppose–"

"And if he's got that on his mind then, nice guy though he is, he's hardly likely to be putting you first, is he? And then that poor agent isn't going to be able to see past his crazy attention-grabbing antics to you!"

"I don't think he would do such a sing..."

"You're right. Listen, I'm probably worrying about nothing. I'm sure he'll be fine. It will all be fine and everything will be special enough for you to catch an agent's attention. Forget I said a word."

Stand up.

"You are leaving?" she asks, eyes fragile like glass.

"Lecturers don't insult themselves you know."

Shit, she looks so confused. Even so, she's still gorgeous. Her hair falls in a sad blonde comma over her crinkled blue eyes. Her lips are narrow and turned down. Her tits in particular look like they need a cuddle. All I can do to stop myself from reaching down and taking her in my arms right now.

Got to be strong, though. Reach in my pocket. Make a show of putting my money on the table.

"I'll get these," I say.

And that's when I walk away.

~

Penelope and I turn along the tree-lined avenue that leads to McIvor. Naked branches grapple the slate sky.

I walk on the outside. Penelope is to my right. Beyond her are the area railings of the once-posh townhouses. Now these buildings are all subdivided into student flats, their dignity quartered.

She's wrapped up well against the chill – duffle coat, mittens, furry boots and a woolly hat that looks like it was knitted by a very demented auntie. Bobbles and shit everywhere. I'm wearing my lopsided habit, and I have to admit, I am freezing. She looks so warm, I wish I were a squirrel. I'd climb up her leg, inside her coat and hibernate somewhere between her scarf and her lambswool poloneck. Not sure she'd like that, mind you. Not many girls are fond of things scampering up their legs. Maybe I could drop on her from a tree...

"I can't believe you got them to make their own costumes," she chuckles, her breath puffing into crisp clouds. "You just saved us about three days' work."

"Division of labour. Makes sense."

"But you had them in the palm of your hands!"

"Ah, it's not so hard. I'm still about twelve years old in my head, so I just talk the same sort of nonsense that I'd want to hear."

"I wish I could do that. Soon as I stood up there all these doubts and worries poured into my thoughts – what if I say the wrong thing, you know? Should I say this or that? Each choice builds up and builds up and in the end I get so paranoid I never know what to say to them."

She's really fired up. Stick a baton in her right mitten and she'd look like some Eastern European conductor.

"Well, don't worry about it," I smile. "You're not likely to be standing in front of the burping wonders again any time soon, are you?"

Blood drains from her skin. She looks round at me. Starts to gnaw on her lower lip.

"Uh... you are?" I say.

"I'm going to be a teacher," she says.

My first instinct is to laugh. But she's serious. Poor girl's really fretting this shit.

My hand moves towards her arm.

"Listen, you weren't that bad-"

"It's all right," she interrupts. But she presses my hand gently onto her arm. Rivers of electricity cascade over my skin. She starts walking again, but she doesn't remove my hand. "I know I'm bad. Terrible, in fact. But I really want to do this. Always have. So, I'm going to work hard and get better."

The main hall doors rear up in front of us. I push one open for her and we move into the warm.

Penelope takes her woolly hat off as we walk down the corridor.

"What are you going to be?" she asks.

"Me?" I say, opening the zip of my hoodie a little now that we're inside. "I originally applied to study Italian-"

"How romantic," she smiles.

"But as soon as I became a friar I swapped from Languages into the Divinity school. They seemed pleased to have me. The course seems a bit... theoretical, I have to say."

"And after we leave – what will you do?"

"Be a friar," I say. "What else?"

"Teach," she says, moving her hair from her face with her left hand.

"Me?" I laugh. "I don't think so."

"You're a natural."

"I was just helping you out-"

"No, you took control. Instantly. Effortlessly." Is she serious? "Part of me hates you right now," she adds. "You do realise that?"

Oh no, really? Stop. Whip round to see if she means it. That would be terrible, I don't want her to hate me...

It's okay, she's smiling.

"Which part?"

Silence.

Complete stillness in the air between us.

Shit did I really say that? I've taken it too far. What a twat. Here's her door. Thank God. Bloody blown it again. Time to run.

She stops. Turns.

"Listen, uh, I have a couple of fabrics in my wardrobe that I was thinking of maybe using for Mary's dress. I'd like your opinion on them."

"Really?"

She thinks for half a second. Then nods.

"Yes."

Hang on. She's asking me into her room. To look at fabrics. I couldn't tell a good fabric from a bad fart. She must know that. So why's she asking me-?

"If that doesn't sound exciting enough for you, I should say that I also have tea and biscuits."

Lord, she really wants me to come in. Bloody hell. This is great. Maybe I haven't fucked things up. Suppose I should accept, then. And sound grateful.

"Sure."

And she leads me back in to the oasis of teenage femininity.

By the holy incense of St Hilda, I can't get over the smell of the place. It's no mere aroma – it's an olfactory terrorist, clambering up my nose to detonate a scent grenade. I want to find out what makes that sweet perfume. Want to stay here all day. All night. Investigate every cushion and pattern and softness. It's all I can do to stop myself taking off all my clothes and rolling around on her woolly counterpane.

Penelope levers off her boots. Kicks them into a corner. Slips her feet into a pair of furry items that look more like roadkill than slippers. She steps to the sink. Bends down and picks up the kettle. You know, her arse isn't as big as I thought. It's actually quite nicely rounded. She turns on the tap. Places the kettle spout under the cantering stream. Takes down a pair of cups from a shelf by the window. Decants shortbread from a tin with a picture of a small white dog in a wicker basket on the front. Puts the biscuits on a small yellow plate. She sits on a tiny armchair opposite me and tucks her legs up underneath her like a cat.

The kettle fizzes very quietly.

"Takes a while to boil," she says.

"Right."

She stares at the kettle. I try to look out of the window, but my eyes are drawn back to her compact form, curled tight in her chair.

"So."

"So."

"Better show you these dresses then," she says.

"Okay."

She extends her legs and slips her feet into the roadkill again. I get up and together we walk to her wardrobe. Is it me or is it getting hot in here? Swallows. Think maybe she's feeling the heat too.

She opens her wardrobe.

A rack of dresses. What did I expect?

"Wow. Lovely."

Behind us, the kettle crescendos and clunks off.

"I'll pour the tea," she says, and darts backwards. I stare into the wardrobe some more.

"Nice colours," I say. "Where did you, um, get them?"

Penelope darts a look at me. Then drops her eyes and starts fiddling with the teapot.

"I made them," she says to the sugar bowl.

"What!? You made all these yourself?"

She nods.

"No wonder you volunteered for the costume committee," I smile.

Penelope leans forward, hands me a cup of tea.

"It's kind of like my hobby. Mum taught me. Before she died."

"Shit, I'm sorry. I didn't know..."

"Don't worry, it was years ago. I was twelve. Cancer. But she showed me how to cut cloth and how to sew and I just kind of kept it going."

"Wow. Can I?"

She nods and I put down my tea. Then I reach into the wardrobe and remove one of the dresses, holding it very gently by the hangar. It's a white number, cut very simply – it's really little more than a cotton shift. But somehow that material hangs like water tumbling over a precipice. It's unfussy, beautiful. And ever-so-slightly saucy.

"You're really talented."

"Says Mr Expert," she replies with a half-smile.

"Hey, don't put yourself down. I'm not an expert, fair enough.

But not everyone can do this, you know? You should be proud of what you can do."

She thinks about this for a while.

"Thank you," she says finally.

"I mean, really, this is stunning," I say, turning the white dress around.

"That is one of my favourites. The last one mum and I worked on together."

"Is it a ball gown?"

"A wedding dress."

"Who for?"

"Me, of course."

Shit. She's married. How crap. But why's it crap? Why can't the girl be married? She's over sixteen, isn't she? No reason at all why she shouldn't be a wife. Mother even. Why not?

"C-c-congratulations," I cough. "Who's the lucky fella?"

She laughs.

"Oh, I'm not married yet. I just made it for fun. For the future. Silly, I know, but little girls love to dream, you know."

"It's not silly," I say. "There's nothing wrong with marriage."

Not sure why I said that. Never thought about marriage in my life before. And I'm take a personal vow to avoid it. Anyway, it's another clanger and she drops into silence. She looks a bit awkward. Fiddles around until she finds the plate of biscuits. Offers them to me. I take one and thank her. I'm not entirely sure why she's uncomfortable, but the fact that she is makes me feel weird. Better say something. Bit of gibberish has to be better than this.

"Try it on." Who said that? Was that me? Jesus with a jam tart, what am I bloody thinking?

"What?"

"Well, I can't give you an honest appreciation when it's hanging on the shelf, can I?"

She looks at me.

"I'm not going to wear that until I actually get married," she says. "It would be bad luck."

"Then make it for Mary."

"What?"

"Use this as your design for Mary's costume. It's simple, it's beautiful and it's a dress for love. Isn't Mary's story all about love?"

"In the fifteenth century."

Can feel a good line coming.

"Beauty like this is timeless."

Yesss!

"Oh..." she says softly. Turns away. Goes a little red. A bit of her biscuit drops off into her tea.

"Well?" I say.

"I could do that," she nods. "If you like."

Outside, the grey sky splits and a late ray of winter sun floods the room. Her face is golden in the light.

"I would like," I say.

~

Vindendraam rehearsal's in McIvor's library. Seven o'clock. Library at the end of the north wing. Fact, almost is the north wing. Starts on the ground floor, but its walls rise beyond where the normal ceiling should be, right up through another level. Arch to an ornate wooden vault a full twenty-five feet above the ground. A dozen battered oak reading desks stand in formation below. Two storeys of books and an uncarpeted stone floor. Half-a-dozen stained glass windows. Hell of a space.

Place feels ancient. Almost holy. Stained glass images depict famous students from St Mary's past. Inspirational intention. Lord St John Macauley, writer of epic odes about sheep farming in the borders. Alfred Bumbleton, classicist, the first man to translate Shakespeare's works into Ancient Greek. Captain Stewart 'Happy' Appleton, discoverer of Fiji's native fertility cult. And, of course, Mary of Moncur and her paramour, the Black Prince of Balbirnie.

It's a big room, but it's full to the brim with bustle as I walk in.

Opposite the windows, half-a-dozen pasty-looking guys are laying out a selection of homemade weapons: broomsticks turned into poleaxes, swords borrowed from the fencing club, cardboard helmets that look like something out of the Power Rangers.

To their left, on the wide librarian's desk, is a large wooden model. Shows the set up of the castle and the old Roman amphitheatre where the Vindendraam is held. Dozens of little figures represent the action – the king and nobles, the guards, Mary on the pyre. Glasses Matthew stands proudly beside it. He may be Clive's slave monkey, but I gotta hand it to him – the model is cool.

Below the windows, Monica and a few other girls are fussing with a load of outfits. All sorts of clothes laid out on four desks pushed together. Their fingers tug and tease, snip and smooth. The costume committee. Man, glad I don't have to bugger about with that shit again. Start to walk past them, heading for the big table, when-

"Hello Freddie!"

"Huh?"

Spin to see the Penster. Except it's not the Penster. Well, I mean, it is of course. But she looks so young. And she's smiling. Makes a pleasant change instead of all that whinging and whining. Kind of forgot what a nice smile she had.

"Aren't you going to join us?" she asks.

"Uh, what?" Shit. Suppose I have to.

"Are you okay?" asks Pen.

"Er, fine."

"You look a little... tired. And your hair. Have you, uh... done something to it?"

"No. Why?"

"Oh, nothing," she says. "Must be the light in here. I just thought it looked a little... nothing. It doesn't matter." Her face suddenly flushes with excitement. "Listen, I've finished the stitching! Come over here and have a look."

Wait. Can't go over there. She thinks I'm him. God knows what tripe he's been coming out with. Situation potentially embarrassing. Don't want to get into that right now. But what can I do? She's waiting for me...

Suddenly I'm saved. The door at the back of the room opens. Here they come. Lucy enters first. She's wearing a woollen shawl that's slipping off one deliciously bare shoulder. No bra strap visible. Fuck, my cock's buzzing already. Below that she has on a long wraparound skirt and thick-heeled sandals. As she walks her firm legs press against the fabric of her skirt. A slit at the base reveals a slice of perfect calf with every step. Her hair tumbles around her face like Kelly McGillis's in Top Gun. Try to catch her eye through the unruly strands, but she doesn't clock me. Just walks quietly to the top of the room, head down, staring hard at the floor. Like she's thinking really hard about something.

Glasses Matthew and the geeks with the weapons all stare at her. She passes without seeing them. Sits to the right of the librarian's table. And still she doesn't look my way. Too busy thinking. And that's got to be good news.

Turn back to see Pen staring at me. Strange look in her eye. Think I've seen it before sometime. Little lines cut into her face. Nervousness? Who knows. Probably her time of the month. Cheer up, love. Don't worry, it's all going to work out fine for you. Just bide your time, don't interfere and you'll get your Freddie.

Anyway, don't have time to think about that nonsense because here's the door moving again. It hasn't opened far when Clive wriggles in. Behind him steps a tall man with a long silver mane, a hooked nose and the largest, hairiest ears ever seen on a human being. The guy walks with a calm nobility like he owns the room. A hefty purple and gold academic gown with a fur trim adds to his air of superiority. In his left hand he holds a delicate crystal glass. In his right, he caresses a nigh-empty bottle of port.

The Dean.

Clive walks ahead of the old gent to the head of the room. And just look at the prick go. Smiling and rubbing his hands like he's the fucking bomb. Yeah, we all see you mate. Get on with it, why don't you.

He steps forward. Extends his hands and wafts them to quiet the room down. Not that anyone's making any noise.

"Good evening, everyone," he simpers. "Thank you so much for coming to my rehearsal. Before we begin, I have a couple of formalities to deal with. First, I'm sure you'll join me in welcoming our very distinguished guest, and it therefore gives me tremendous honour to be standing in front of you now and introducing... Dean Killikrankie!"

"Do get a shift on, Sleevewort," says the Dean. "can't you see I'm running low on Garrafeira?"

"Yes, your Deanship, I can," nods Clive. "And I will. Get a shift on, that is." He hastily turns to face the room. "Just before we do start proceedings, I have some good – sorry, bad – news for you. Word reached us today that the warden has been badly mauled in the groin by a female gibbon. He will be unable to walk, work or indeed urinate for some time. This means he will be officially resigning his post here as warden. I am sure you will all be absolutely delighted to hear that I will continue as your acting warden until such time as a permanent replacement can be found. And, of course, if any names... jump out at you for the job-" Here he throws his arms forward, thrusts his hips and tries a laugh that sounds more like a frog vomiting. "-please don't hesitate to let our honoured guest Dean Killikrankie know."

Gathers his hands back in and rubs them together in front of his chest. Looks over towards Lucy. But she's not looking at him. She's staring furiously at the floor. Clive bobs and weaves like some demented boxer. Seems to be waiting for someone to say something.

The Dean shakes the last drops of port into his glass. Brandishes the bottle in Clive's face.

"S-s-shifting, yes," mutters Clive. "Well, as you all know, McIvor Hall has been chosen to perform the Vindendraam for the Tallowmas Fair this year. We are greatly honoured and have chosen the tale of the founder of this ancient university, Saint Mary herself. Indeed, what better story could there be for such a loyal, noble hall?" And he holds his toffee-shaped head aloft.

Checkout Lucy. She's flicked her eyes up and is staring at him from under frowning brows.

"Of course," continues Clive, "with such an honour comes tremendous responsibility, and there's a lot at stake here. Not just for McIvor, but for the whole university. That's why I invited the Dean along tonight, to see how my – sorry, our – plans are coming along."

Lucy folds her arms and deepens her stare.

"Noble sir, I'd like to start by introducing you to the characters of our humble drama. You will be pleased to hear that I will have the honour of playing the part of the Black Prince-"

And that's when I start.

"In many ways," I say, softly but very clearly, "the most important part in the drama, wouldn't you say, Clive?"

Clive gapes.

"Who's this?" asks the Dean.

"Not exactly sure," grinds Clive through his teeth.

Step forward. Walk right up to the Dean. Pump his hand.

"Frederick Keddie, your Deanship," I say.

The Dean looks me up and down.

"Good god, he's a monster, isn't he?" He downs his last gulp of port. "What altitude have you attained, young man?"

"Six six, your Deanship."

Dean frowns.

"Sixty six what? Metres? Cubits? Bananas?"

"Six feet and six inches."

"Never forget your units, boy. Where would Pythagoras be if he'd forgotten his units?"

"Don't know," I say.

"Nobody does," says the Dean with a decisive nod. "Now, what are you saying?"

"Just commenting that our acting warden Mr Sleevewort is taking on a very important role, sir," I say, half to him and half to Lucy.

"Yes yes, we know that already. Carry on Sleevewort."

"Of course, Dean," says Clive, eyeing me suspiciously. "If you come this way I'd like to introduce you to my Mary."

He leads the Dean over to where Mary sits, folded in on herself.

"How do you do, Mary my dear?" smiles the Dean.

She stands, slowly extending her limbs and tilting her head until her perfect nose is high in the air and her back straight.

"Very pleased to meet you, your worship," she says with a curtsey. "But my name iz Lucy." Then she shoots Clive a filthy glance. "Lucy who hates ze attention-grabbing antics." And she sits rapidly down and folds her arms again.

"My word. Good choice, Sleevewort. She's a battler, isn't she?"

Clive stares at Lucy. He has the look of a boy with his ear to the tracks who's just heard the runaway train coming. It's far off, but he knows it's on its way.

He tears his worried eyes away from Lucy and moves things quickly along.

"If you come this way, Dean. Over here are the costume and weapons team–" Clive sees me moving back to join the girls. Steers the Dean the other way. "–which aren't really that interesting. But if you step this way I can show you my scale model of the event."

Clive leads them up to where Glasses Matthew stands proudly by the model. The group fans out round the sides of the table. Glasses Matthew pulls his tie a little tighter and clears his throat.

"The scale ob dis moduw is one do dwenty-five," starts Glasses Matthew in a nasal monotone. Guy sounds like he has a badger up his sinuses. "Dis means dat for ebery inch on here, you hab do–"

"Will you get out of the way?" snaps Clive. Glasses Matthew's head drops. He slinks back behind the model like a kicked dog.

Clive leans over the table and beckons his guests towards him.

"Come closer, Dean. See, the pyre will be here, on the stage of the amphitheatre. The peasants will occupy stations here and here, while the nobles will actually sit here as part of the crowd. To involve the spectators more."

"Course some of the crowd won't be able to see Mary so well," I say, "but they'll get a great view of the Black Prince's entrance."

Everyone stares at me. Except Lucy. She's staring at Clive.

"Keddie, will you please be quiet?" snaps Clive.

"Just admiring your organisation," I smile.

Clive clears his slime-clogged throat and continues. "Mary will be brought through the proscenium arch and her sssentence read out. She will then be ssstrapped onto the pyre. Guards will take up position around the flanksss of the daisss here and here-"

The Dean's silver brows furrow.

"Seems a damn shame to set fire to the lass," he continues. "Burn all that lovely blonde hair off? Those full lips, turned to charcoal? Eyes, melted? Blessed waste, I say."

Clive looks baffled.

"Ah, your Deanship, we don't actually set fire to the girl," he says. "You see, when the pyre is 'lit', we actually just set fire to some kindling stacked well in front of the stake itself. We then simulate a burning with lights, some dry ice and a tape recording of a bonfire."

"She doesn't get burnt?"

"No, your Deanness, it's all an illusion. For entertainment."

"Well, thank buggery for that," smiles the Dean. "No idea how I was going to explain a barbecued student to the Burser."

"If we can get back to the model?" says Clive.

"Yes, yes. Press on, man. No dilly-dallying." His eyes are on Lucy.

"One question," I say.

"WHAT?!" yells Clive, spinning in fury.

"Let Mr Kedderick speak," says the Dean.

"Thing is this," I say. "We're going to have a big pyre, yes?"

"Seven feet high!" announces Clive triumphantly, wet eyes rolling and goggling at the Dean.

"And Mary will be on top of that?"

"Of course, Keddie! What sort of idiotic question is that?"

Pause for a second. Knot my brows.

"So, ah, how will you, as Black Prince, get to the top of the pyre to join Mary?"

Clive's eyebrows wriggle up his face in surprise.

"Are you a total oaf? With a ladder of course! Now can we just conclude the vote and-"

"Of course!" I cry. "Now I understand. Golly, I can be so dim sometimes. Climbing the ladder gives the crowd time to see you. If you leapt off your horse, that might show how passionate you were about the beautiful lady, but it would be over so fast. You'd just ride in, jump, get burned."

Clive's eyes flicker. He knows the train's getting closer.

"But this way," I continue, "you get to really make the most of your moment, right?"

Check out Lucy. She's scouring him with her eyes, waiting for his answer like a wolf for meat.

"Uh... yes," says Clive.

"That's fine. Just so's I know. Carry on."

And I turn back to the costume table and move some material around.

"Surrounded by bloody lunatics," I hear Clive mutter under his breath. "Gentlemen, if we can move on? Once I have ascended the pyre-"

"STOP!"

Don't have to turn to know it's Lucy, but I do move round, because I want to see this.

Lucy steps forward.

"Zis is no good," she says, shaking her head.

Clive stares at her, fish eyes staring.

The Dean smiles a little.

"What's the matter?" asks Clive through gritted teeth.

"Everysing!" she cries.

She turns to the Dean.

"Zis whole sing will be a disaster!"

"But my dear-" starts Clive.

"Don't 'dear' me, you stinky little jelly man!"

Oh, I like that. Stinky little jelly man. Girl's a genius.

"Zis is meant to be ze story of St Mary – ze woman who has

inspired millions over ze centuries. Who made ze king's son fall in love wiz here and sacrifice himself for her honour. And what do I have? A Black Prince crawling on some ladder like an old woman?! Five hundred years of history – paf! Five minutes of idiocy, I sink. I will be a laughing stock not a star."

They stare at her, jaws dangling. For a long moment. The only sound is her heaving chest and, if you listen very closely, my smile cracking.

"Great crusted corks," blusters the Dean. "Why doesn't he just do the leap?"

"Ah, not really possible," says Clive. "Remember, the pyre is seven feet high, and-"

"Not possible for your stumpy fishy legs," yells Lucy. "But he can do it!" And she whips round and points at me.

All eyes are on me now. Clive's are like black slits.

"Oh no," I say. "I'd be no good at this sort of thing."

"But you are!" she cries. Turns to the Dean. "He is just being modest. I have seen him act – he is brilliant. And look at his legs. So long – he will be able to leap like a giant jumping bean!"

The Dean surveys me. Narrows his leonine eyes. Scratches one huge ear. "Fellow could certainly manage such a leap. What about it, eh?"

And I hear the strangest thing. Outside, the wind suddenly howls. But the howl is kind of like in Pen's voice. And the eerie animal wail throws itself against the stained glass windows which rattle like the chains of the dead.

I say nothing.

Then the wind drops. All is quiet.

"Well, lad?" says the Dean.

"Uh..." I stammer, still a little astonished.

"Oh, please be saying that you will do it!" gasps Lucy, my balls tightening with every hoarse syllable.

"Sure," I say with a wink.

"Well there you go," says the Dean, smiling. "It's decided. Sleevewort, this overlegged fellow is your Black Prince."

"No!" yelps Clive.

"Get him togged up, won't you girls?" the Dean says to the costume committee.

"But the residents have already voted-" whines Clive.

"Then they can bally well unvote! Or do you want me to make one of those damned gorillas-"

"Gibbons," corrects Glasses Matthew.

"-gibbons the warden of this place?"

Clive recoils into his shell.

The Dean turns away. From the boiling fire at the edge of my vision I know Clive is glaring at me in betrayal. Glare all you like, you slimy whelk of a man. Fuck do I care? Right now I feel like I could fly. Move to the door on winged heels. Singing – here I go, here I go, here I go...

"One more thing," says Lucy suddenly.

We all turn.

"Zere is a problem with ze dress."

The Dean cocks his head. Lucy walks over to where the costume committee stand with their creations.

What the hell's Pen looking at me like that for? Like she's scared.

Lucy steps up to the white dress she was examining earlier. Stares at Pen. Young gel looks nervous. Nothing to be afraid of Pen, just lovely little Lucy.

"Where is ze glitter?"

"Glitter?" says Pen softly. "Mary was a peasant girl-"

"Zis woman defied her king! Zere must be boldness and excitement and... glitter!"

Pen looks at me.

"But... Freddie said this would be perfect."

What the frigging fuck?

Lucy swivels to me. Can feel her eyes like red hot coins pressed to my cheek.

"Is zis true?" she asks.

"Course not," I say. "Don't want Mary up there in this drab old

189

rag. Glitter's exactly what we need."

Pen colours. Looks like she's about to bubble. For God's sake. Know she's emotional, but this is a bit bloody ridiculous.

"There's no need to cry about it," I say. "You'll just have to start again, that's all."

Pen throws her hands to her face. Turns. Snatches the dress. Runs to the door.

"Pah! Forget it," snorts Lucy. "Tomorrow I will go out and buy one." Then she smiles. "You can help me choose."

The door slams loud enough behind Pen to burst an elephant's eardrum. Ah, don't worry about it. The old gel will be fine. Always is. Besides, I really don't care. Lucy's here, looking up at me, her beautiful blue eyes wide. And I'm staring back into my sun, happy and blind.

~

Golly, look at that. It's really raining now. Great heavy slabs of it. Clouds of fog sweeping down the beach like huge grey spectres. It's coming in so fast. Be here soon. Never seen clouds move like that. It's scary. Unnatural.

I turn from the window and shiver.

"Aren't you guys cold?"

My Dougal looks up from the board.

"Naw, we're toastie," he says, and moves his knight.

"Braw move, Dougal."

"Thank ye, Dougal."

The pair of them sit hunched in the other window, chessboard between them on the desk, the beach beyond. A large bag of doughnuts rests beside older Dougal. Every so often he absentmindedly inserts a pudgy paw and pulls a sugar-covered lump from within.

They make a strange pair: one fat, one thin; both calmly absorbed in the game. Happy in each other's company. Or perhaps they're just pretending to be occupied. Like I used to pretend to be asleep in the back of my parents' car. So I could listen to the mayhem.

But the Dougals are really watching me. Wondering why I'm pacing up and down. I'd like to know why I'm pacing up and down too. It's not like I care about what he's doing. I mean, it's his stupid plan, and-

Plat-plat-platter-platter...

And that's the rain on the window.

"Where the hell is he?" I blurt.

"Check," says older Dougal. My Dougal furrows his brow and stares even harder at the board. I huff and pace over to my wardrobe. Take out a sweater. Can't sit here in this cold. I put my sweater on and sit on the edge of my desk. Suddenly I feel a little queasy. It's not that I think I'm going to be sick. It's not really a physical sensation. It's deeper inside. In my mind as well as my body. Like there's something wrong with my soul.

KNOCK KNOCK KNOCK!

The Dougals don't even look up from their game.

"I'll get that then, shall I?" I snap. I don't mean to speak to them like that. But I feel so damn jittery, the words just tumble out. They react, looking up at me, surprise arching their brows.

I huff and stalk to the door. Sling it open.

"Hey beautiful."

"What have you been... ?" I cry.

"Meet the new Black Prince," says my grandad self, sweeping past me into the room.

"Exactly what have you been doing?!" I blurt.

"Being a complete fucking legend." And he spins on the spot like Michael Jackson in the Beat It video then flops backwards onto my bed which creaks and sags beneath him. He reaches into a plastic bag he's carrying and pulls out a can of Stella Artois. Cracks it open. "Junior, the whole thing ran like a dream. You should have seen Clive's face when she stuck her boot up his pipe. Oh man, it was fucking beautiful!" He takes a long pull on his beer and belches. "Here, get yourself outside one of these," he says, tossing me another can from his bag.

I catch the can but don't open it.

"Are you sure it went okay? Something doesn't feel right."

"Crack it, baby," he says, nodding at my beer. "Settle your

stomach."

"I don't have indigestion-"

"Then shut up and open your beer." He reaches into his bag again. "Beer for the Dougal dudes, too," he says, handing a couple of cans over to them. They put them on the floor unopened and silently refocus on the chessboard.

"Listen," I say, waggling my can at him. "I really need to know what happened."

Grandad watches my can then puts his hand to his face. Like he's trying to cover a laugh or something. He coughs. Makes his face go serious.

"Chill, Junior. Right now, you are a flaming fucking comet in young Lucy's heaven."

"Really?" I say, despite myself.

"Ho, yeah. You very much da man. And this time on Saturday..." he smiles and raises his can to his lips- "...you'll be conkers deep in Sugar. And I will be a success!"

He drinks, as if toasting himself.

"You reckon!?" I say, edging forward.

"Oh yeah. I just need you to do one thing for me."

"Uh, sure. What's that?"

"Don't leave this room."

"What?!"

He takes another pull of his beer. A drop dribbles down his chin.

"We're at a critical juncture right now," he says. "Need you to keep your head down until Saturday. Stay inside, you hear?" And he burps loudly.

Frustration clots in my throat like hot phlegm.

"But I can meet with Penelope. Talk to her, right?" I say.

"I'd rather you didn't."

'Why, what's happened!?"

Grandad leans forward, stares at me, eyes wild.

"Nothing, nothing, shit, what makes you think something's happened?"

"Things don't feel right."

He nods, grins sarcastically.

"Oh, they don't feel right. Well, they feel pretty damn alright to me. Shit, you got a lot to learn." He sits back a little. Takes a breath. "Need you to stay in because I'm going to be out and about from now right up till the Vindendraam on Saturday. To start with, Lucy and I have a date tomorrow." An ugly leer lurches across his face. "We're going shopping for a dress with glitter on it. Then there are the walk-throughs and rehearsals and stuff. Might take her for a drink or two. Who knows? If you're on the streets as well, we could be spotted together. Time like this that could be disastrous. Last thing I need is you wandering around out there like some dopey great giraffe fucking things up for me."

He takes another swig from his can.

I think about this for a second. No, something still doesn't feel right.

"I thought when you were me all those years ago you hung out with Penelope, though," I say. "Surely I have to keep doing that?"

"Shit, we didn't exactly do a lot. Trudged up and down the beach in the cold, mostly. Listened to her bang on about costumes while I thought of Lucy Sugar's backside. Trust me, you won't miss much. And as for Pen – listen, stop worrying. What's she going to do? Leave town? Forget it. Old gel's not going anywhere. She'll be at the Beach Ball. And that's where you'll snog her – after you've strained your potatoes here with our young Goddess, of course." He leans in close towards me. "Can you actually imagine that, Junior? Peeling off Lucy Sugar's dress in this very room... surveying her in her underwear... gently undoing her bra strap... liberating those breasts, seeing those breasts, touching those breasts... then pulling her closer... moving your mouth towards her blood-red pouting lips... slipping your hand inside her knickers..."

SNAP!

He clicks his fingers in front of my face.

"You got a stiffy, right?" he says.

I smile.

He laughs.

"Great. So put a sock in all this worrying bollocks, will you?" he says, waving his can at me. "Hunker down. Enjoy yourself. Get some wanking done. Don't worry, I'll buy you a stack of beer in. And I'm sure your Dougal can bring you some grub up from the refectory."

He finishes his can. Tosses it at the bin. Misses. Pulls out another one.

"All you have to do is be waiting in the bogs at eleven o'clock on Saturday. That still gives you time to get it on with her then get down to meet Pen before my time portal closes at midnight. So when you hear me bring her in, you get yourself psyched. While you're doing that, I'll be laying her down, getting her ready. By the time I come to get you she'll be laying down rubber. We switch clothes – although there won't be many of them –" he says with a wink, "and then you come back in..." He leans forward. Raises his arms. Throws his head back and shouts to the ceiling: "...and we make history!"

Pause.

The Dougals look from grandad, to me, then to each other.

Eventually grandad turns to me. Smiles. Lowers his arms.

"Now are you going to join me for a beer or what?"

Fffssshhhtt!! He cracks open his second can.

Look at him sitting there on my bed. So sure of himself. Doesn't he have any doubts? Am I the only one feeling like this? Can't he see the filthy rain smacking against the window?

Still he grins. I guess he doesn't. Oh well.

"To making history," I say, raising my beer.

"To making history," grandad says with a huge grin.

And I pop my can.

Beer foam jettisons all over my hands. It pours stickily onto the floor before I can get to the sink. grandad whoops and thumps the bed. Wipes tears from his eyes.

"Like I said, Junior. You got a lot to learn."

~

Soaked. Been raining like a bastard all night and it's still nailing it down. This parka may be high fashion but it's a little low on waterproofing. Surely it's got to stop soon. How much rain can one sky hold?

Who cares? Stop whinging. Any moment now, Lucy Sugar is

going to walk round that corner and take me shopping with her. Wonderful.

Quick, under the awning. Gaze in wonder at the scantily-dressed mannequins. Press against the glass. God, can you imagine – that garter belt on her? Jesus. Can you imagine, really?

Shit, there she is again, the grumpy proprietrix with the nose shaped like Norway. Staring back out at me like some goggling old waxwork. No, madam, I'm not a hooligan. Yes, I'm waiting for someone. Girl so stunning and young she'll make you sick with envy. Sneering out at me with your Scandinavian proboscis. Bugger off why don't you?

She'll be here. Nearly an hour late, but she'll show. That girl's just daft on old Freddie. Always knew I had it in me. Fucking rock, so I do.

Unless... what if Clive's somehow got to her? Man, that would be unfair. Went to all that effort. Hours I put in. Meticulous planning. Inspirational ad libbing. Plus I had to handle Junior's scaredy-cat bullshit.

Kill Clive, so I will. Cut his ugly fishy balls off. Do fish have balls? Pouches, I think. Or sacks of eggs or something. Anyway – balls, pouches, sacks, whatever he's got down there I'll cut the bastards off. And you know what I'll do then, fjord-face? I'll stuff them up your snooty nostrils, that's what-"

"Bonjournee, my prince," sings a voice from over my shoulder.

Spin.

Wow.

Brown cords, a thin cream jumper and puffy beige bodywarmer. Burberry umbrella. Christ, even her cold weather clothes give me the horn. Hair held back in a ponytail. Lips somehow a light fawn, like the softest, sweetest rolls of fudge you ever saw.

"Hey, Mary," I say, smiling.

"Talking to yourself is ze first sign of madness, you know."

"Certainly crazy for you," I add with a wink.

Throws her head back, laughs, and in a far-off fairyland, the bells on the elves' merry-go-round ring out.

"You are so funny."

Nod at her, grinning. After all, she's right. Hilarious bastard. so I am.

"Please accept my apologies for my lateness–" she starts.

"Not a problem," I say. "Shall we?" And I extend my arm towards her.

"Yes, of course–"

And she moves a half step closer. But doesn't take my arm. Pauses. Her brow wrinkles. She swallows.

"You okay?" I ask.

"We will go to the shop in a minute, but first I haf a qvestion for you."

Rain's dripping into a crevice I never knew I had. Would rather be inside, but...

"Uh, okay. Shoot."

Her face tightens. Her eyes drop. She looks somehow less... radiant than a moment ago. Like the rain got to her. Dampened her sunshine somehow.

She runs a brown gloved hand over her brow.

"Why did you not come to see me after ze pub crawl?" she says.

What the hell? What does she mean by that? She's looking down at her boots, but when her eyes dart to mine, I see they're as sharp and grey as flints.

"I saw you all the time," I soothe. "In the refectory. The library–"

"But you did not talk to me. Not for weeks. Zat lecture was ze first time you even came near me. And I had to follow you."

For God's sake, woman, what does it matter?! Here now, aren't I? Can we not just get on with it? Divert her.

"Guess I didn't think you'd be interested in hanging out with me," I manage.

"Are you sure zat is ze reason?"

The dog is not letting go of its bone. How can I tell her? Feel like saying, "Ze reason, my dear Lucy, is that I was a dopey young prat." But that's only going to muddle things even more.

Maybe she senses my confusion. Or maybe she doesn't really want to make me sweat. Whatever her motivation, she adds: "Perhaps it is really because you were not interested."

"Not interested in what?"

She looks away. "In me."

Holy crap. You're joking. Can't believe she's insecure. Are they all insecure? Jesus, if she is they must be. Hardwired into them at birth.

"How could I not be interested in spending time with you?" I smile, opening my hands wide.

"Maybe you just didn't like me."

"What-?!"

"Maybe you like someone else more?"

Shit, look at her. That expression on her face. This incessant rain is really drawing her out. For one crazy second I think she could be any young girl caught in a Scottish downpour.

"Who?" I ask.

"You tell me."

Man, how do women do it? Turn a simple conversation into this multi-levelled spy talk. The bullfighter has left Turin. Tell Mama he will be holidaying in Canton with his nephew. Just don't understand. Going to have subvert this emotional crap. Employ my cock to do some thinking. Go on, boy, see what you can do.

"Lucy. You are the most beautiful girl I've ever seen."

She starts. A little warmth. Her face melts a touch. Well done, lad. You plough on:

"And I can honestly say that if I could be anywhere in the world in space and time, I'd choose right here, right now, with you."

Like the ice thawing on a mountain brook her expression warms and tinkles into a smile.

"How about right in zere, right now," she says pointing into the shop. "I am getting dribbles all down my body."

"After you," I say, with a bow. And I follow her in out of the rain.

197

~

I don't believe it. Listen to that. Is that... ? I think it is – two different kinds of rain at once. Big bass drops smacking into the pane in front of my nose and, under that, a light but insistent tenor constantly drumming into the day. Depressing as it is, you have to admire the Scottish weather gremlins for that one. It's taking rain to an entirely new level.

Sigh.

God, it's wet out there. You can't see the end of the beach. It just blurs into mist like some dodgy episode of the X-Files. On the course to the west, a couple of golfers huddle under an umbrella like leprechauns beneath a mushroom. But they won't be out there long. Giant streaky puddles are forming on the rippled turf. Soon they'll join up into a grey lake and the fat grumpy starter with the hat that's too big for him will waddle out to kick everyone off. "Ah've come all the way from Montana to play this course." "I dinnae care if ye've come frae the bloody moon, pal. Clear off!"

Sigh.

It may be wet but I wish I was out there. Having to stay indoors is rubbish. Eerie disappearing beach or not I'd love to feel those drops on my face. Man, if I was out there it would be so great. I'd just put on my coat and hat and wellies and splash along. Maybe find someone to go with. Someone to talk to. So I wouldn't notice the weather. We could step into the mist together. See where it took us.

Sigh.

Look at Dougal over there. Bristly ginger head bent over his jotter. A curling, ink-stained paw clutching the pen. Tip of tongue poking over a pink lip like a mischievous mollusc. How can he think about poetry at a time like this? My future self is wandering about town threatening the very structure of spacetime. Reality could fracture and tear itself apart into hideous infinity. Plus he's making me look stupid. I'm the one who's going to have to live with what he does. He can zoom off back to the future and it'll all be a memory to him. I'll be the one people will be pointing at. Got three more years in this place. All for the sake of a shag. Inconsiderate bugger. Tell you what, she'd better be worth it...

~

Madame Norway is confused. Part of her wants to look down her considerable nose at me. Another part of her can't help fawning over this truly exquisite creature that has found its way into her shop from the enchanted forest. And since I'm with Gorgeous, she's having a bit of a bottleneck in the thoughts department.

"And what can we help you with today, madam?"

"I am wanting to appear as a mediaeval Scottish peasant girl. But I also must look fabulous."

Norway's eyes widen. She nods like a wooden doll. Stares dully around like she's lost in her own shop.

"Right..."

"And it has to have glitter," I say. "That's your starting point right there."

Norway scowls.

"Come with me," she snaps, and leads the way to a rack of dresses. She walks like she's had her legs amputated and replaced by stilts.

"Here we have a simple black design. Very classic lines, it could be from any era."

Lucy takes it off the rack.

"What do you sink?" she says, holding it up to me.

Survey it for a moment. Rub my chin with one hand.

"Dull," I say, "dreadfully, drearily dull."

Madame Norway looks like her blood has started to effervesce. Lucy desperately tries to hide a smile. "Do you have anysing else?" she asks.

Norway flicks several hangers along the rail. They clack into each other like gunfire.

"This is a very flamboyant dress," she says, holding up a gown constructed of a patchwork of material pieces sewn together with beads and shiny bits.

Lucy raises her eyebrows to me.

"Flamboyant," I nod, "in the way a transvestite gypsy is flamboyant."

Lucy blurts out a laugh. Tries to turn it into a cough. Norway's eyes are live coals stuck in her head. Her elongated conk is throbbing. She spins on her heel and stalks further through the shop on her awkward stilt legs.

And then I see it.

"How about that one?" I say.

Lucy follows my eyes. Delight sparkles on her face like the sun on a waterfall.

"Now zis is more like it," she says. "I will try it on," she announces to Norway. The dress hangs on its own on the back wall. Norway extends her stilt legs and gets it down. Hands it to Lucy. She steps towards the changing rooms.

Stops.

Looks back over her shoulder.

"Well, come on. I can't do zis alone, you know!"

Get. The. Fuck. In.

With a skip and a hop and a big thumbs-up to Madame Norway I walk with Lucy into the changing area.

~

Hang about.

What's that? Out there in the rain. Is it... I think it is.

Penelope.

She's walking out of the back door of hall. I only see her face for a second before she puts the hood of her duffle coat up, but I know it's her. Where's she going in this filthy weather?

She reaches the corner by Auchentoshen's Golf Shop and turns left. Golly, she's heading for the beach.

Suddenly my stomach lurches. My vision goes fuzzy as reality shifts an inch. There's a rumbling crack deep within me, like a chasm opened up in my soul. Something's not right here. A young girl going for a walk on a rainy beach – nothing out of the ordinary there. Hell, in this town a lot of them do nothing else. But... but... I feel there is definitely something wrong...

I feel like I should be with her.

"Think I might go for a bit of a walk," I say.

I really don't know why I said that. It just kind of popped up inside me.

Dougal looks up towards me briefly.

"It's peein' doon," he says, then goes back to his work.

"Refreshing," I say. "Been cooped up in here for hours."

He stops writing. Turns.

"Ye know what yer man said-"

"He's not my man," I snap.

"Easy. Then ye know what ye agreed to. Yer no tae leave here till Saturday. That's only two days. Why don't ye try writing a wee poem or something?"

"But-" and here my silly eyes betray me, swivelling briefly towards the window. Dougal follows my glance. The duffel-coated figure is clearly visible striding out onto the sands.

"Ah..." he says, nodding. "It's like that, is it?"

And suddenly a wild wave of emotion crashes through me. Feels like the wind is pushing the rain right through the window and into my bloodstream. It's like the universe is shaking apart and I'm at the epicentre. Gotta hold it together. Insane claustrophobia grips my bones. I'll do whatever it takes to get out of this room. I simply have to get down to that beach.

"Look, it's alright for you, you've got someone," I blurt. "But how would you feel if you didn't? What if that was Rose out there? And your future self came back in time and told you not to go and see her. Would that stop you?"

"If he had a good enough reason-"

"What if he was wrong? I mean, aren't you even curious?"

He puts down his pen.

"What about?"

I stand up and pace up and down the little space between the beds.

"You know perfectly well what about," I say sharply. "Why your future self is so fat and miserable!"

"Hey, that's nae way to speak about me-"

"It's clear he's not with Rose any more. And that's obviously fine with you. You just sit around playing chess together, never talking. But what if this pair aren't any wiser? What if they mucked up their lives once before and now they're back they're only going to muck them up all over again? I'm not sure I can sit around and watch that happen. But maybe you can. In which case, get the chessboard down from the shelf. He'll be back any minute."

Dougal's brown doggy eyes are wide with astonishment. His ginger brows twitch up and down a couple of times. Then he looks quickly down at his jotter. Picks his pen back up.

"A wee walk might be just the thing," he says softly.

And he writes another line of his poem.

~

There's a tiny gap between the black velvet curtain and the jamb of the changing cubicle. It's not big, but through it I can almost see heaven.

Lucy Sugar is starting to undress.

Does she know that when she stands there I can see her in the mirror? She must. All she has to do is look up and she'll see me. And surely she'll do that any second now.

But she hasn't noticed yet and I'm not going to tell her. Just going to sit right here on this padded, rickety chair and watch.

Here we go. She's taking off her bodywarmer. A shrug of those delicate shoulders and it's gone. She hangs it on the little hook. Christ, look at the way that creamy jumper caresses her curves. It's like a second skin, moving round her flesh like-

Creeeeck! goes my chair.

"Are you zere?" she says suddenly.

"Huh? Oh yeah."

Shit, is she going to look round. Man, she MUST be able to see me from there. No, she just turns a little and starts kicking off her boots.

"Zis reminds me of ze time I was at finishing school in Lausanne," she says. "Ze girls and I used to go down to ze basement and play at dressing up wiz some of ze old cloze we found zere. All zese lezzer aprons and felt hats wiz ze fezzers in. Zey were so ridiculous. We used to laugh so much."

"Sounds like a fun school."

"Oh no, it was very strict. We were never meant to be down zere. Strictly verboten. Ze girls and I had to do our dressing up in secret."

Wait, shit, where's she going? She disappears to the other side of the cubicle out of my line of sight. Bring her back, quick. Get her talking.

"So, uh, what was Lausanne like?"

"Oh. it was a fabulous place. All ze mountains in ze background behind ze school buildings. We were at ze edge of ze forest and in ze night, you could hear ze wolves howling!"

You beauty! She moves back into view. Her delicate fingers move to the front of her cords. Yes, go on girl…

Creeeak!

Shit! She half looks round. Her fingers stop. No, keep going…

"Sounds incredible."

She shrugs. "To some people, yah, maybe. But to me, it was just my school, you know?"

"Yeah. Kind of. That is, not really."

She laughs. But her fingers are still poised. It's like she's waiting for something. There's something I have to say.

"So what was your school like?"

Should I bullshit? Nah, might as well tell her the truth. Then again, that would be involve emotions. Could be problematic.

Shrug. Bullshit it is.

"Ordinary school in the city. No mountains, no forests – apart from the odd conker tree. And I don't remember wolves, but there was this one time when a dog ran into the playground."

She laughs. And her fingers start to move. With the tiniest eek and stretch of leather she undoes her belt. The buckle tinkles as she pulls the loose end free. "My school was girls only. It is hard, I am sinking."

"Why did your parents send you there? Travelled a lot, or something?" I ask.

"Oh yah, my fahzer he was a diplomat, and my muhzer an opera singer, so I was always moving from zis place to zat place."

Her hands move to her fly.

"Lisbon, Athens, Gothenburg..."

One, two, three, those immaculately strong fingers pop the buttons of her fly. Come on, woman, move faster!

"...Egypt, Rio."

Four, Five. Done. Now slip them down. Go on. No, she isn't going to. She moves her hands... crosses them over her body at her waist... grabs the bottom of her cream sweater... oh, she's going to take it off over her head! This is beautiful.

But again, her hands wait.

"But you will have travelled a lot, too, of course?" she asks.

Again, for a half second, I think about telling the truth. But something in my gut tells me not to. what's the point? "Oh yes," I say. "You many not know this, but I have been to North Berwick and Berwick upon Tweed."

She laughs.

"Both Berwicks?"

"Both Berwicks."

And like a spring uncoiling she extends her arms, arches her back and whips her jumper over her head.

Both Berwicks indeed.

As she lowers her arms and tosses the sweater aside her breasts jostle like naughty puppies. Her cleavage is high and ripe. Full. Oh fuck, it's full. Gently bulging over the top of a white lacy bra that's jutting out so proud and firm it looks like it was cantilevered by Balfour Beatty.

CREEEAKK!

Don't care about the damn chair. All I can do to stop myself moaning out loud. Beneath her bra, her torso is slim and delicately tanned. It bends as she moves her arms back and the skin pulls trimly over taught muscles. For a second I see that pristine belly lying horizontally before me on a bed, every square centimetre of goosepimpled skin crying out for a kiss from my lips, a taste from my tongue.

"I knew you were a cosmopolitan man, ze first time I saw you," her voice continues, from a million miles out in space. "When you were acting like a crazy inventor."

"Uh-huh," I grunt.

"Mais oui!" she coos. "I look at you and sink 'zere is a man who lives for ze stage. He does not care for washing or looking nice. Excitement is in his blood. Danger is his friend'."

Not sure what she means by that, but she's moving her hands back to her cords, so I don't really care.

"Um, thanks," I say.

Then with an almost petulant little shove, like she's pushing away a bully in the playground, she thrusts her hands down and her cords drop to the ground. One sweet step, then another, and Lucy Sugar stands in her underwear.

It's like, like... I don't know. Perfection's so hard to describe. Michelangelo couldn't capture that sweet skin texture. Stephen Hawking in his computer turbo brain chair couldn't define the curve of that arse. Words desert my head. Replace themselves with images of my hand moving over those exquisite thighs, tracing the curve of the flesh, circling, teasing, moving ever upwards until they touch the fresh white of her knickers...

White knickers... white bra... how odd. For some reason I'd expected black underwear. Why? Don't know. Imagined all sorts of black thongs and G-strings. But both her bra and panties are plain white. Very nice and delicate and soft-looking, but perfectly ordinary.

How odd.

Shit, where's she gone? Out of my line of sight. Did she clock me? Is she shielding herself in the corner, shamed and invaded by my grubby peering.

Cla–clack–clack.

No, that's the hanger resting back against the wall. She's just picked the dress up ready to put it on. Wait. Want to watch her some more. Delay her. Think of something to say, you twat.

"Er, um, did you ever go to that famous Swiss theatre? Where they do all the avant-garde stuff. Going on stage and barking at each other. Meant to be a riot."

There's a gentle slipping, whispering sound. Think that was the dress going on. Oh well.

But she doesn't come out right away.

There's a pause.

And a tiny crackle of static. Then she says:

"Uh, no, honey, Switzerland is one of ze few places I have not been to."

Hang on.

"Yeah, but didn't you say you were at finishing school in Lausanne?"

Zzziippp!!! comes through the curtain. Bugger goes the preview.

"Zat is right."

"Well, Lausanne's in Switzerland," I say.

Dead silence.

And then the strangest thing happens. Through the gap Lucy's face appears in the mirror. And suddenly she smiles to herself. Not the worried tic of someone caught in a lie or moment of stupidity. But an open, relieved smile, of someone who has shared a burden.

"Now," she says softly. As much to the mirror as to me. Then louder: "You ready out zere?"

Swallow. Holy fuck, am I ever ready.

"Uh, yea–" my voice cracks. Clear my throat. Try again. "Huh-huh! Yep, all ready out here."

"Zen here I come."

Very, very slowly the curtain slides along its rail. It gets halfway then stops. Then, even more slowly, Lucy sidesteps through the gap. Like she's trying to take up as little room as possible. Then with a little spin on her bare heel, she turns to present herself before me.

And there she stops.

Breathes in.

Tosses her head a little.

Breathes out.

"Here I am," she says. "What do you sink?"

How can I tell her? My lungs have shut down. So too has my heart, my blood and most of my brain. Only my senses remain alive. And they're jammed to overload.

She's a red satin bullet between the eyes.

The dress hugs her curves just enough to hint at the exquisiteness below. A little tightness around the outside curve of her breasts. A languorous tension in fabric across her belly. Then it flares away, running with your eye through airy folds and ripples, the movement perfectly counterpointing the tightness of the fabric holding her body.

And then I see something else. Something beyond the dress. It's weird, but there's something in the way she's standing with her weight mostly on one foot and her hip cocked like that. Her head a little dropped and shoulders raised. There's... uncertainty there.

Didn't expect this. If you'd asked me before how Lucy would come out of a changing room I'd have said prancing like a pony. Professional model style. But that's not how she moved at all. She's somehow vulnerable. Like a child in a play.

And the way the sublime material lies so close to that vulnerability. It's almost like she's more naked than if she had no clothes on at all. Maybe it's the poor lighting in here, but I feel that I could almost see through her clothes, her skin and bone too – right down to her soul. Like her feet, coyly twisting themselves into the carpet, she is bare.

Bare before me now.

"Turn for me," I whisper.

She spins neatly, once.

The dress soars up like a flame in my heart.

"Now please tell me," she breathes, her voice cracking in its intensity. "Do you like what you see?"

Clear my throat. Force my lungs to work again. Sit forward. Try to steady my voice. Say slowly:

"Don't exactly know what mediaeval Scottish peasant girls looked like..." I start.

She bites her lip.

"...but if they looked like this – I'm going to build myself a time machine."

And she claps her hands together repeatedly, quickly in front of her beaming face. Happiness surges through her limbs. Energy commands her. She spins again and again in front of me, her dress flaming my heart to a crisp. And as she twirls she bounces on the spot. Like a little red rubber ball.

~

Even if it fitted me, my paper-thin Peter Storm cagoule wouldn't be up to rain like this. But since I got it to go on a field trip to Galashiels aged thirteen, and it extends no lower than my navel, I'm getting absolutely soaked.

Not that the cold water dripping through my undergarments and the wind chilling my skin really bother me. I'm part of this scene – the universe is in me. The notion of personal discomfort is absurd. My body is a machine, transporting my soul to where it can join once more with Penelope's. Then and only then will my bones rest.

I start to run.

Penelope had a start on me, and thick misty rain obscures all but the twenty yards in front of me, but I know I'll catch her. Not that I've got a clue what I'm going to say. All I know is that I have to be here on this beach with her. Really with her, talking about stuff. Costumes, wellies, rain, anything.

A stronger gust of wind buffets my face, whips my cagoule into rippling waves like Roger Moore's face in Moonraker. The wind pushes the sheets of rain and the thick grey atmosphere lifts a little.

And there she is, a hundred yards ahead of me.

I'd recognise that duffel coat anywhere. She's pacing slowly along the high tide mark, a smudged brown thumbprint on the wide seascape. To the left, two dark figures huddle under a brolly in the dunes. Couple of depressed surfers having a joint, no doubt.

For a moment she pauses. Looks at the sea. Then she walks down the beach to where the waves beat the sand into muddy slurry.

Then, as she passes the surfers, one of them digs his hands deeper in his pockets, leaves his colleague under the umbrella and scurries out into the rain.

After Penelope.

Who the hell's that? What's he doing? Going to mug her? Assault her? Shove her in the sea, what? Quick, got to get to her. I up my pace.

She stops right by the water. Tiny waves emboldened by surging nature foam over her wellies. The dark figure is right behind her, getting close. His head is weirdly angular, like horns are protruding from his scalp. Shit, I'm not going to make it, he has a full fifty yards on me.

"Hey!" I shout, "Penelope!"

But the roaring surf is too powerful. She doesn't turn. The black spectre is right at her back. He reaches his arm out... a finger extends... and like some satanic sneak he taps her on the shoulder.

"Noooo!!" I bellow into the wind.

She jumps at the touch. Turns in shock.

Then smiles.

What... ? Smiling at the devil doesn't make sense...

A few more frenzied steps and I stagger to a halt, unsure whether to go on or not. Because now I can see that the dark figure doesn't have horns. His head looks angular because he's wearing spectacles.

The dark figure is Glasses Matthew.

~

Bloody fantastic. That's what this is. Ma Brown's, 2002. Probably my favourite place anywhere, ever. And here I am again, for the second time in as many weeks. With Lucy Sugar – and she's buying all the drinks. Bonus.

Wouldn't have imagined she'd have chosen to come back here, but here we are. Sitting in the bay window seat enjoying a post-shopping drink together. A loving young couple scoff surf'n' turf burgers at the table to my left. On the right, a scrum of rugby guys sit round a couple of tables expertly playing drinking games.

The rain floods the glass behind me, but I don't care, because she's laughing at every crappy joke I come out with, slapping my thigh, touching my hand – and getting rapidly pissed. Only had two pints myself – she's just ordered her fourth double G&T. Girl's drinking like Oliver Reed's goldfish.

Like I said, bloody fantastic.

Lucy takes a hefty gulp of her drink and clatters it clumsily back on the table.

"It is so much fun to shop wiz you. I haf never had anyone to shop wiz before."

"Thought all girls went shopping with their mothers," I say, sipping my pint of Theakston's No. 3.

"Hah! Not mine. Maybe if she was shopping for cakes for her fat face and needed someone to help her carry zem all home. Yah, maybe zen."

Uh oh. Mother topic obviously not such a romantic one. Steer her clear of it.

"So, uh, is there anything else you want to shop for? We could maybe go again tomorrow-"

Lucy sways towards me a little.

"You know what she did ze time I bought some make-up?" she slurs.

"Ah, no-"

"It was just after my sirteenth birsday," she continues, waving one elegant hand around. "We were living in Rome and I had been saving my birsday money and zen one day when Mama was rehearsing, I sneaked out to ze Via Condotti to buy myself somesing."

Her roving hand stops gesticulating and clutches a salt cellar from the table of the dining couple next to us.

"Oh, it was such a wonderful day. I wandered around ze streets like Audrey Hepburn in Roman Holiday. Except of course zere was no Gregory Peck to fall in love with me."

And she looks at me from under cloudy brows, like somehow that was my fault.

"You want to play space invaders?" I suggest. But she rolls on over me:

"I found ze most fabulous store, Madame Mantalini's. Nervously I crept in. Stood zere in awe at all ze fabulous sings to wear. Oh! It was like heaven. And zis beautifully dressed older woman came across – ze angel of zis heaven. She was so slim and sophisticated. And I was so gawky and tomboy-like, I must have been quite a sight. But she was so polite to me."

"'Buena sera, senora,' she said, 'what can I help you wiz today?'

"'I-I-I want some make-up,'" I said.

"'Of course,' she said. 'Lipstick, mascara, rouge...?'

"'I do not know!' I cried and burst into tears. Well, even zo I was so young and naïve and what seemed like a lot of money to me was probably nussing to her, Madame Manatalini was so helpful to me. It was like having a real muzzer all of a sudden."

Will you look at the way her fingers curl round that salt cellar? Are there children in here? Get them out. That's sheer pornography.

"So I took my purchases and went home – to find ze fat bitch whore waiting for me as I sneaked in my bedroom window! She saw my bags, grabbed zem and looked in. Her wicked face lit up like a pumpkin lantern. Zen she took out all my new make-up, clutching it in her flabby fist like zis–"

She reaches back to the table next door and picks up a handful of the loving couple's sauce sachets.

"'So you want to look beautiful, do you?' cried Mama in a voice like a banshee. 'An ugly little dog like you! What a waste of time. And you know we must not waste our time, must we?'

"And she took every single lipstick, every powder and cream and she srew zem into ze dustbin in front of me."

Lucy hurls the sachets to the ground. The couple look at each other. The girl glares at her man. To my right, a couple of the rugby boys are starting to giggle.

"Zen she sent me to bed wizzout any dinner," continues Lucy. "So you know what I did? In ze night I went down and I got zem from ze dustbin. And I scraped all ze powders and ze paints into a bowl and I mashed zem all up together. Then I added flour and butter and sugar and I baked the whole thing up into a great cake which I covered with icing. Then, ze next day, I went to my mama with ze cake. 'Here Mama,' I said, 'I want to say sorry for my bad behaviours. I haf made you zis.' And of course, she was so fat and greedy zat she could not resist. She took ze biggest slice you have ever see and she began to eat. It was perfect! Every bite made me laugh inside so much, I could not believe she did not tell. But she gulped her mouthfuls down fast like a pig in ze mud, and she did not even notice until she had eaten a huge chunk of ze foul sing. And zen, all of a sudden, she began to go a funny colour. She went pure green! Like a great fat vegetable. Of course, by zis time I was laughing so much she knew it was me, but what could she do? She felt so sick she had to run for ze bassroom. Hours and hours she was in zere, puking. And I can honestly say, zey were ze happiest hours of my life."

"What happened then?"

"Oh, I was beaten horribly, of course. She srew me around ze room until I was black and blue."

She takes the girl at the next table's napkin. Uses it to wipe away some tears that are starting to flow. Blows her nose on it. Puts it back on the girl's lap. More glaring. More laughing from the rugby guys who are now all watching.

"Shit, that's terrible."

"Yes, I sink it was terrible. I was very unhappy for a very long time. But-"

She leans forward, like she's about to say something.

Pauses.

Jesus, love, I'm not a damn psychiatrist. Get on with it.

"But you know ze really strange sing about zis story?" she continues.

"Uh... next day you got abducted by yetis?" I say, trying to lighten the mood.

"No," she says softly. "What is remarkable is zat-" and here she puts her hands down and stares straight at me. A new expression is blooming on her face. "-I have never told anyone zis story before."

And there she waits. That new expression is in control of her features now. Simple, honest, vulnerable. She's like a baby daisy, opening to the sun for the first time. And I tell you it's fucking sexy.

"Amazing," I nod.

"Yes, it is most amazing. You are a surprising man, Freddie."

The daisy girl is staring at me again. She downs the rest of her gin. Shakes her head. Raises her shoulders. Get the feeling she's about to say something-"

"Will you hug me?"

"Uh, what?"

"I would very much like it if you would hold me."

You beauty. This is it. Breakthrough. All aboard the express train to Fuckadilly Circus. Thought I'd have to wait till after the Vindendraam, but never mind. Can get hold of Junior somehow and bring our timings forward-

She stands up. Her daisy head bowing slightly as she looks down at me.

"What, here?"

"Of course," she nods and stands up. Holds her arms out.

The rugby guys are loving this. But what can I do?

Stand up. She moves towards me round the table. Opens her arms wider. Open mine. She wraps herself around my torso. How small she looks against me! Almost like a child. Her slim limbs twined around my great lanky body, she presses her head into my chest. The top of her head rests between my nipples. Then I put my arms round her shoulders and pull her in closer.

As our bodies come flat together I suddenly feel her breasts. Expected they'd be firm, but not this firm. Like bloody Christmas puddings. They don't squash or shift or spread one bit. Just press into the flat of my groin just above my pubes.

Ah, now don't think like that. The last thing you want right now is a damn erection. Because if you did get an erection, and if you were both naked right now, the old boy would right now be lying straight between those outrageous mounds.

Too late! My traitorous testicles have ram-raided my brain. Fuck! Here he comes. Shit, how embarrassing. Going to have to try to manoeuvre my arse a little to pull him away from the contact zone. Shift my weight onto the other leg, shimmy my hips and twist 10° anticlockwise, a quick jerk to change his position relative to my underpants and…

Total failure.

Boy's up like Nelson's bloody column.

She must know by now. How can she not? But she doesn't say anything. Or flinch. She just pulls me closer.

And so there we stand.

Cuddling in the pub.

Rugby boys are in fits. Even the couple on the left are smiling.

An hour we stay like that. Well, that's what it feels like. Eventually, she takes a deep breath, gives me one final squeeze and releases the tension in her arms.

She steps back and looks up at me and it's like she's suddenly become one of those seventies posters, all soft focus with the evening sun glinting through the trees and flaring on the lens.

"Sank you, Freddie," she says.

"Uh, we could go back to my room and hug some more, if

you like?"

She laughs.

"Oh, Freddie, you make me smile so."

"I'm deadly serious."

She tinkles her elvish bells some more.

"Zere will be plenty of time for zat. Now I have to go and buy conditioner for my hair. I will see you tomorrow for the rehearsal."

She kennels her breasts in her bodywarmer. Picks up her bags. Clatters them into the girl. And with a smile and a nod of her shining head and a little swaying stagger she is gone.

And I'm alone.

With half a flat pint.

And a fucking bundle of thoughts. 'Plenty of time for zat.' What does she mean by 'zat'? Hugging? Or red-hot-cock-between-my-breasts action? Difficult to say. Think she was on my wavelength, though.

"Mate."

Turn round.

Rugby guys looking up at me. Trying hard not to laugh. One on the left nods towards my crotch. Says:

"You got something on your mind?

Look down to see my trousers tenting proudly.

Rugby guys fail to stifle their hilarity.

Have to smile. It is kind of funny.

Step towards the bar. Can cover my embarrassment there. Plus I can buy another beer. Because I suddenly realise I really, really, really fancy another one.

~

What the hell's he saying to her? Wish I could hear, but the bloody wind's knocking out any chance of that. Feel like going right in there and stopping their conversation, but I'm also desperate to know what he's saying.

Glasses Matthew pulls something bulky from his left-hand coat pocket.

What is it? A gun? A dildo?

A thermos flask.

He unscrews the top of the tartan cylinder. Hands it to her to use as a cup. Unscrews the inner stopper. Pours the steaming liquid.

Christ, I can smell it from here. Lentil soup. The world's dullest foodstuff, but right now, on this beach, I know it would be the most divine delicacy ever tasted by mortal man.

Her face widens and crinkles with gratitude. He bobs his head at her, encouraging her to drink. She lifts the cup to her face. Sips down the golden goodness. Lowers the cup again.

And suddenly starts crying.

Sobs burst from her like little sneezes.

He takes the cup from her. Says something. Can't hear what. The brutal waves are roaring to my left.

She wipes her eyes with the back of her mittens. Looks up at him.

Don't like the way this is going.

He screws the thermos back together. Stows it in the deep pocket of his well-made coat.

Then he puts an arm round her. Bastard!

He starts to walk her along the beach, shortening his stride to match her little wellie steps. What can I do but follow?

As they walk, he talks. I strain to hear. But I get nothing more than snatches of syllable. Is that "...each" "...all". What the hell's he got to talk to her about?

To my left a wave crashes, fizzes, and is sucked back to its death.

God damn this ocean!

And then there's a sudden eerie silence. Lack of noise is somehow louder than the crashing of the waves. Great, I think at first, I'll be able to hear what they're saying now. But then some deep animal brain takes over. Why, it says, is there such a silence? How can that be? It's not natural. My stomach flips like a pancake. My heart jitters. And I'm suddenly very, very scared indeed. I turn to my left-

-to see a foaming black wall of water looming over me.

A millisecond. That's all I have to take in the terrifying sight, then it hits me like the biggest, meanest flanker that ever peeled off a ruck. Wham! I'm down. For another millisecond – then I'm picked up like I was no more than an empty shell on the sand and whirled into the dark heart of the wave.

Air is totally knocked out of me. But even if I wanted to breathe I couldn't – the water is colder than anything I've ever experienced and my muscles are rigid icicles. Plus, of course, I'm underwater. So breathing wouldn't be a great idea anyway.

Are my eyes open or shut? Doesn't matter, it's utter blackness either way. But I'm sensing a change in pressure. It's increasing all around me. It's like I'm wearing a bodysuit of icy concrete that's getting heavier and heavier, impossibly heavy. Shit, I think I'm getting sucked out to sea. Deeper and deeper I'm going. And although the pressure increases, the rage and fury around me lessen. The black depths seem to promise peace. All I have to do is go with this flow and all my pathetic little worries will be smoothed by the dark pressure around me like wrinkles in silk...

Sod this. I'm not dying a virgin. And I kick against the pressure.

Oh, bother, now I really wish I could breathe. My limbs want to work, but my body has no fuel. Every pull I make pumps iron-hard blood through my head. My muscles are balls of crushed glass grinding against my bones.

But still I kick on.

The current tugs at my hands and feet like an evil puppeteer. My brain is a lump of magma throbbing and pounding against my skull. Somehow the utter blackness begins to swirl and become streaked with a vile red, without being any less black. My lungs have ceased to exist. My senses are blunt. The raw blackness is coming for me... but not yet, it won't take me yet, and I make one final agonising pull with my arms. The blood shrieks in my ears, my muscles rip like frayed hawsers and...

A wall of wind hits me.

Hoooooooaaaaaaaaaaa! I breathe.

Open my eyes. The lights of the town string out to my left. Make me want to cry for some reason. Can feel the tears rising hot within me.

SPPPLLLAAAPPP!!! I'm slammed onto the beach and the breath is once again knocked out of my lungs. Blackness. A surge from behind tries to rip me back – no, not now, I said. And I thrust my clumped fingers deep into the sodden sand and haul myself forwards.

Breathe again. Another wave tugs at my foot. But it's less strong this time. Like a frenzied turtle I scrabble up the beach. Gasping, heaving, shaking with cold, I finally flop down, away from the tentacles of the growling sea. And there I lie on the high water mark, a gulping fish on a bed of kelp.

From the corner of my vision I see a dark shape. Slowly I let my head loll round. A figure stands between me and the lights of the town. A figure with an umbrella. I can't be sure, because it's silhouetted, but from the weak line of the jaw, I'd swear it was Clive.

Before I have a chance to know for certain, the dark figure turns and walks away.

I look back up at the ghosting sky. I can feel the rain on my face. It pit-patters on my icy skin, and mingles with the quiet tears that are running there.

~

The rain has stopped. The sky is clear. You can see all the way down to the end of the beach and beyond – right out to the huge sandbanks that lie like idle whales in the shallows. Beautiful to look at, but a hell of a place to be. Kid went swimming there in my second year. Drunk at his own twenty-first birthday party. Pulled him out two weeks later down in Westruther harbour. Fishermen thought he was a seal he was so bloated. Shit, maybe I should go and warn him. Think he was in Melrose Hall. Nah, he wouldn't listen. Know I wouldn't. 'Next autumn you will drown when nightswimming out by the Grand Banks.' 'Yeah, right, you freak.' Probably make me drink even more.

Now the clouds are gone it's bitterly cold – the coldest day of the year. Coldest day of any year, it feels like, but I don't mind that. Gets the blood pumping. A bit of cold never did anyone any harm.

Apart from all the people on the Titanic, of course. But that was because of the lifeboats and the class system. Anyway, what the hell does that matter? Not on the bloody Titanic. Shit, got to focus. My moment of triumph is at hand.

The week-long downpour has given this old rooftop flat a right shoeing. The angry leak that was pouring in the corner of the window casement is now an icicle so sharp and hard you could use it to commit murder. The condensation on the window is a thousand frigid diamonds. Have to scrape off the flinty shards with a piece of floorboard. Need to use the window as my mirror, you see. And boy, am I looking good.

Boots, leggings, undershirt, tunic, cloak, mask – from top to toe I'm swathed in beautiful, brutish black.

Leave my 2002 clothes on the floor where I cast them off. Never need them again. Shame. It was kind of fun. Maybe I could take them back with me...

No. Fuck it. The future's all that matters. Better get on with it. Move towards the door and reach for the handle and-

Woah.

What the fuck is that?

A giant woosh of giddiness sloshes through my brain. Christ, feel like I'm capsizing in my own body.

Crunch! My shoulder slams against the jamb. Another sickening surge and my knees give way. The air around me begins to warp. A humming rattles my innards and the room begins to pulse. What the fuck? Is this the vortex again? How can that be... ? – and then, with a burst of pure pain, like a bolt of lighting slamming directly into my brain...

I remember.

The water.

~

Uuurrrghgghh...

The groan comes from miles away. Who was it? I wonder. Open my eyes to find out.

Whassat? Swimming above me. Beady eyes. Nose. Little, pointy.

Tufty hair. Ginger hair. GIANT BLOODY DOG! Under the covers, quick!

Hang on, not barking. Words. What's it saying?

"...eeling... ny... etter?"

Peek out again.

Features swim in wobbly Sixties visual effect. And resolve...

Hairy ginger face also friendly face.

Dougal. Did he groan?

"Ye feeling better?" he smiles at me.

What's he talking about? Not really sure how I feel. All I know is how incredibly hot it is in here.

Ugghhhh...

Golly, there's that groan again.

"Sh!" says Dougal. "Dinnae ye fash yersel'."

And he reaches to a table beside my head. My bedside table. So I must be in bed... and he must be sitting on the edge of my duvet.

"The worst is over," he says, "but ye're still awfy poorly."

And now he has a bowl of water in his left hand, a flower-edged flannel in his right. He takes the flannel and dabs it on my forehead. Oh, it's so wonderfully cool. Never felt anything quite so deliciously refreshing. Want it to go on for ever.

"That's it," smiles Dougal, "ye're doin' just grand."

KNOCK KNOCK KNOCK.

Think that must be the door. But I don't want this cool moment to stop. Look up at Dougal. Plead with my eyes.

KNOCK KNOCK KNOCK!

This time the door rattles in its frame. Dougal sighs. Glances down at me. His warm brown eyes shine comfortingly.

"I'll handle this," says Dougal gently. Then louder to the door: "Come in!"

The door crashes open.

A man in black stands there. Think I know him, but not sure where from...

"The fuck's going on here?" bellows the intruder.

"Sh! He's not well," says Dougal. "He has a fever."

The man in black stalks into the room.

"How the hell did he get that?" he snaps.

"Uh, ye see there's a lot of it going around just now, and-"

"Bullshit."

"You let him go out. Told you not to let him go out and you fucking let him go."

"No, he-"

"Don't fucking lie, you little ginger bastard. I am him, remember!"

Want to get up and help Dougal deal with this crude interloper, but the duvet is like a burning weight on my chest.

"The things he does, I remember," continues the man in black. "They come back to me through the vortex, you understand? So I know he left here following Pen and I know nearly drowned himself, because I'm the one who he nearly drowned. You savvy?"

"Er-" starts Dougal, his flannel dripping onto my pillow.

"You shouldn't have let him go. Bloody told you not to. Could have jeopardised the whole thing." The man in black leans in close to Dougal. Jabs his finger towards me. Snarls:

"Last time round he fucked up a once-in-a-lifetime opportunity and I didn't shag Lucy Sugar because of it. Well, now thanks to me, we got another shot at it. But this time I'm in charge and I'm not going to let him fuck it up a second time, you understand?" Foamy shards of spittle have collected at the corners of his mouth. "So here's what's going to happen. You're going to pour as much Lemsip down him as is inhumanly possible. At eleven I'll be back with Lucy and he needs to be ready with a stiffy. You understand?"

Dougal backs away from the jabbing black finger. Looks to me. Swallows.

"I'll try-"

"No. To paraphrase fucking Yoda, don't fucking 'try'," roars the man in black, "just fucking 'do', okay?!"

He turns to me.

"And as for you," he drawls. Then he reaches down. Rips the flaming duvet from my body. "Look at yourself."

I do. Skin's all mottled and clammy, like sour cream. My limbs twitch and shiver. Brain feels like navy warships are using it for target practice.

Urrrrrghh.

There's that moan again. Golly. It must be me.

"Bollocks your moaning," says the man in black down his nose. "Stop being so pathetic. No wonder I never got laid. Bloody wimp."

I recoil from his words like a slug from salt, trying to get back into the duvet. His black gloved hand pushes me back. Pokes my clammy chest, hard.

"At eleven o'clock you're going to be fucking Lucy Sugar whether you like it or not. This is my night, comprendy?"

And with a final flick of my ear and a low moan, he turns on his booted heel and sweeps through the door.

~

The air is ice in my lungs. The chill tears at my eyes. Drills into my skin like a thousand steel wasps. And my head still aches a little. After-effects of the vortex, probably. But despite the pain I'm happy. In fact, the pain makes me happy. Raw, pure sensation. Love it. Haven't felt this fresh, this alive, this... young in a long time.

The streets are a lethal patchwork of iced cobbles and pockmarked puddles. In a couple of hours they'll be rammed. But right now they're empty. It's just me and the reflected, shimmering lamplight as I hurry through the ancient alleys.

Bloody Dougal, though. Forgotten what a tool he could be. Never there when you need him and when he is there, he's buggering things up. Nearly ruined everything letting Junior go out after Pen like that. Talk about selfish! Tell you, if he dares to fuck things up for me and Junior again... Don't know what I'd do. Rip his ears off. Shove them up his hoop. But that's just to start with. Then I'd pour glue down his pants. Mess up his stupid ginger pubes.

As for Junior, he's just an idiot. Prick doesn't seem to realise that he's the one I'm doing this for. All this effort so he can rod a princess. Bonehead hardly deserves it.

Forget him. He'll come good when it matters. On with the job at hand. 'Cos suddenly, in front of me, looms the castle. It sits atop the far end of the cliffs, crumbling like an old tooth. Below it on the landward side lies the plucked gum of the Roman amphitheatre. Behind, the entrails of a weak winter sun feebly blood the sky. In the ruins, the shadows swarm.

Here's the drawbridge that leads from the end of the Bents over the deep grassy moat to the castle and amphitheatre. Soon, like the streets, this will be thick with people. But, for now, mine are the only footsteps that echo around the dark gully. And it really is dark. Though there are no clouds, the stars are faint and there's no moon. Not obscured – it's like they're hiding. Still, it all adds to the atmosphere, and that's gotta be a good thing.

Moving into the courtyard of the castle I have to pause and take a breath. It's some place. Crumbling towers shoot up high into the night sky and sway above me like huge drunks. Amid their feet black doorways lead to warrens of rooms.

As I move to the rear, to the seaward wall, I pass the Bridge. This narrow strip of banked earth links the castle with the amphitheatre. Rises almost thirty feet from the moat, and is only a couple of feet wide at the top. In the busy summer season, tourists are limited – only one at a time can cross. Occasionally one stops to take a picture, loses their footing and tumbles down the slope. Usually they break an arm and complain, but I like the fact they keep on using it. It's not a namby-pamby kind of place.

The Bridge leads directly to the stage area of the amphitheatre. From here I can see right down into the arena. Some archaeologists believe that the amphitheatre isn't Roman at all. They think it's much older than that. On a night like this, you know they're right. Volunteers from the town pace slowly along its perfectly preserved perimeter, placing flaming torches in lofty holders. Hooded like monks, they move slowly and seriously. Give the place a primitive, magical feel. Like it's somehow more ancient even than land from which it is carved.

Keep going towards the black mouths of the store-rooms. Here the solemnity ends. All is busyness. Volunteers rush to and fro. Some carry logs, some torches, some piles of costumes. Others just rush aimlessly. The ones with logs are heading to the right to a wider walkway that leads from the castle's great hall round to the back of the amphitheatre. Must be setting up the pyre. The costumes are being placed on long trestle tables. One is marked 'peasants', another 'guards', a third 'nobles'. Behind the tables, two of the dark store-rooms have been lit with torches. Gas heaters have been placed inside. Above their arched entrances are signs: 'changing – male' and 'changing – female'.

Several nuns oversee the process, prodding and guiding the

volunteer runners. The costume committee.

As I pass, one of them glares at me from under her wimple. Monica. Lift my head. Nod down at her. She snorts and turns away. Hah! Disrespect me all you like – I'm about to make history. Give them one more look – checking for Pen. Not because I want to see her. Want to make sure the old gel isn't here. Less chance of a dangerous interaction that way. And... there's no sign of her. Good.

Move past the costume gang to a roofless room with an enormous tumbledown fireplace. Glasses Matthew and some of his fellow geek guards are sorting weaponry into stacks against the irregular stone wall. Broomstick pikes. Fencing sabres with the tips corked. Hatchets with thick tape on their edges. Still, in the flaming torchlight they manage to look quite sinister. Like the nuns, the guards are already in costume. Have to say, they've made quite an effort. High boots. Leather leggings and jerkins. A couple of them have got some chain mail from somewhere. And helmets. Bloody hell, Glasses Matthew has pulled a whetstone from his breeches. He's sharpening his sword. That's going a bit far boys, I think. Pass their evil little cloister and all six of them look up in unison. Hold Glasses Matthew's stare as I go past. His face is a dead blank. Then suddenly a sneer appears beneath those gargantuan black frames. Not a man I'd normally be scared of. But here, in the dark, a sharpened sword in his hand, it sits strangely ill with me. The pain in my head revs like a motorcycle engine.

"Hey!"

Whip round.

Ghostly white face looms at me.

Christ, run!

"Wait, it's only me!"

Recognise that voice. Turn back.

Bloody Dougal. The fat version. His pudgy face splits into a dopey grin.

"Wow, ye look terrific," he says. "All in black! Amazing."

"Dougal, I'm the Black Prince," I say. "Not going to show up in pink bloody feathers, am I?"

Ginger face drops a little.

"I'm just saying you look cool..."

"All going to plan, is it?"

He wobbles his furry great head in what I assume is a nod.

"Show me."

"This way," he bubbles, then turns and waddles off through the bustle. Follow him to a doorway in the base of the north-east tower. The place is deep in shadow.

The arched doorway has been divided into a makeshift stable with a split door, the top half of which is open. But it reveals only thick blackness. An eerie quiet rolls out from within. Presses like moss on my skin. Suddenly I feel like a million insects are creeping through my blood. My brain pulses against the front of my skull like it's trying to escape. Surely the vortex should have subsided by now. Something is wrong here.

We face the inky square. The darkness is like a window into space. A cosmos where something huge and wicked lives between the stars.

"Well?" I say, staring at Dougal. He lifts a quivering finger and points at the void. Slowly I inch forward. Peer into oblivion.

Suddenly jets of steam shoot past my face. For a hideous second the blackness surges forwards, ready to swallow me whole. Then the thrusting dark stops and, with a shrieking whinny, reveals itself as a horse's head.

"This," says Dougal, "is Diabolo."

The creature's coat is dark as a collapsed mine. Rolling eyes boil an infernal red. Nostrils flare and snort. Sinews twist over iron-hard bone. It's William Blake's worst nightmare.

"This isn't a horse," I hiss. "It's a damn dragon!"

"I think he's an awfy bonny boy," witters Dougal. "Watch this." And he pulls a carrot from his pocket. Holds it towards the hell creature which curls back its foul black lips, snorts two more jets of steam and extends teeth like a complete collection of woodworking chisels to sheer the carrot off right by Dougal's pale meat fingers.

"Where's the damn pony?" I say.

"What pony?"

"Don't you remember? When Clive did this first time around, he rode out on some fat old donkey. Half blind, half deaf, completely lame. Thing just waddled in then sat down. How come he got that and I've got this satanic monstrosity?"

Diabolo snorts again. From the other side of the split door comes the skreek and clatter of a heavy metal hoof pawing stone.

Dougal shrugs. Shakes his stupid fat head.

"This is the only one they had. All the others were booked."

"Who booked?" I demand.

He squints like a cartoon mouse. Furrows his brow. Puts a sausage finger to his lips.

"That's the weird thing. There were other wee horsies at the stable. The groom chappie just said that this was the only one he could hire me."

For Christ's sake. Had just about enough of this. Lungs feel like they're icing over. Feel my bones starting to shiver. Every word he speaks pounds on my frozen ears like a brass hammer.

"Now listen," he continues, "I was thinking we could head up to the battlements, you see-"

Shut up.

"-when I got here I saw someone hanging around behind the corner of the north-east sea tower, and-"

Shut up.

"-they looked a bit dodgy, so I thought maybe we should check it out and-"

"SHUT UP!" I bellow.

He stares at me. Pale lips slack around his gaping mouth.

"Shut your empty balloon head for one damn second. Had it up to here with you. Christ! Thought your younger self was a fanny, but you surpass him in every measure of uselessness."

Dougal blinks but doesn't move. His mouth still gapes.

"All you had to do was get a pony and could you manage it? Arse you could!" Pain pulses in my brain. "Christ's sake, my head is banging with your bullshit!"

Dougal starts back. Like I've poked him in the eye with a stick. His shoulders crumple.

"Here's how it is," I say. "There's simply no way I'm going to let you fuck this up for me."

His mouth slowly closes. Eyes drop. He mumbles:

"What are you saying, Freddie?"

"Fucking hell, you goofy bloody spaniel! Do I have to spell it out?"

Dougal looks at me for a half a second – and it's like the spark in his once-bright eyes is dimming. It flickers once more, then dulls. He drops his head.

"No," he says quietly. "I understand."

And he moves off softly through the crowding shadows.

~

Out on the sands the torches bob and sway like a firefly disco. Three hours they've been gathering, clustering close against the dark pit of the sea. The annual call to every man, woman and child in the town. Thousands of them have answered and they dot the night with their quiet brilliance. Slowly now they begin to maze their way along the edge of the golf course and up onto the Bents. Soon they will all be in motion, a whole snake of tiny fires heading towards the amphitheatre half a mile away.

Watching from my glass eyrie, it's a beautiful but remote spectacle. Wish with all my heart I could be down there. Be a part of it. Let the sights, smells and sounds fill up my senses. Or rather, let the strange spirituality of the event seep into my soul. Revive me. History tell us it's a powerful thing indeed, the Tallowmas parade. Not a soul speaks. No spectators are allowed on the route. Leather-booted feet barely shuffle. Breath curls softly into swirling vapour ghosts that fade and die in silence. Even the winter surf is flattened to the faintest of rustles on the sand, the sea lying on the beach like a great sheet of black satin.

And so the people of the town walk from wild nature along the cliffs to man's prehistoric shelter. There they file into the steep-sided arena and take their place for the Vindendraam, the ancient play enacted by the students. Town and gown in a mystical, midwinter act of pagan communion. The only witnesses the gulls and the bats and the few tourists brave enough to sit out all day on the cold grass banking behind the tiers of the amphitheatre. And, somewhere among all those thousands of people, Penelope walks. Probably with that speccy wretch. What's he doing now? Could be holding her hand, looking at her arse, anything. It's just not right. Oh God, what was that? A sick-filled swirling crashes through me, like I was back under the waves. A cough savages my chest like a wolf. Oh man, I have to get down there. I get to my feet...

"Woah, where ye off to?"

"I'm fine," I gasp.

Dougal shakes his head. Steps towards me.

"Ye look like shit."

He reaches out and places a cool little paw on my forehead.

"And yer temperature's ragin'." Shakes his head again. "Just when I thought ye were getting better." Then his face quickly tightens. Beady brown eyes dart out at me. My heart flinches. It's like those eyes are piercing right into my soul.

"What's on your mind?" he says.

"Huh?"

Leans right in towards me. Can't resist that stare...

"Just thinking about the people. All the people down there-"

Dougal barks out a triumphant little laugh. He leans back, his eyes sparkling like the torches in the night. He smiles and says softly:

"Did I ever tell ye about the summer Mr Harvey-Jamieson moved onto the island?"

"Uh, no-"

"Rich type, don't ye know. Made a bunch of cash wearing one of them coloured jackets and waving his hands about down in London town. Decided he'd got enough money and enough London in him and came to retire on the island. Only twenty-

229

five and retiring, can ye fathom that? Anyway, this boy he moves into an old croft complete with peat fire and vegetable patch and a goat. But the silly bugger had this fancy car." He laughs. "Come and live on a Scottish island and bring your Maserati." He chuckles some more. Wipes a tear from his eye. "Anyway, the lad had this car. Only one on the island if you don't count old Angus's tractor. So Mr Harvey-Jamieson used to drive around the lanes all by himself. Until the day he was driving past Rose. She was coming up the hill with a can of milk. Mr Harvey-Jamieson offers her a lift. Rose accepts. Enjoys herself. Next day, he sees her again, further down the slope. Enjoys herself some more. Soon she's not carrying the milk at all. Soon pretty much all she's doing is driving about every day."

"That's pretty shitty, man," I say.

He shakes his head.

"Aye, I wisnae a happy laddie, I can tell ye. A whole month, this went on. And all that time this feeling was boiling within me like poisonous lava."

"She didn't like him though..."

Oh, I'm sure she did. A handsome boy like that."

"So what did you do?"

"For a long while, nothin' at all. Couldn't. The boiling lava was makin' me ill. Real sick I got. Couldn't eat or sleep. Flushin' hot and cold all the day and night. Then one day I was pacin' about on the beach, half delirious. Didn't know which way was up, who I was. Started thinkin' about how nice the sea looked. How maybe I should walk in there an' lie down in her rockin' arms. An' that's when I see them drivin' over the headland, her hair flying in the wind, her laughter ridin' the air to me. They drove down to the harbour. He parked up an' they walked out along the pier. Stood at the end. Then his left arm starts twitchin'. And I knew – he'd taken her there to kiss her. This was it. This was absolutely it. And that's when everything went clear. The illness fell away. I walked up from the beach to the harbour wall. Climbed the jutting stone steps up to the pier. I paced along the walkway towards them. When I was fifty yards away they saw me comin'. I remember she turned first. Then he flicked his head round to see what she was lookin' at. They both just stared as I got closer. Ha! Every step I took, her eyes got wider, and his got narrower. By the time I got there, she was staring right up at me, her face shining and open like a beautiful flower, while his was all twisted up like a fist of dirty money."

'What did you do?" I gasp.

He smiles. Looks out to sea. His bright eyes mist a little, like April clouds over the sun. He goes on:

"I said simply and calmly: 'You and I are meant to be.' Then I turned round and walked away again."

"And what happened?" I blurt.

He smiles.

"She followed me. Followed me out to the dunes where we made love in the open air."

Quiet – apart from a gentle wheezing in my chest.

Dougal lays his hand on my shoulder. Looks dead in my eyes.

"If you and Penelope are meant to be, you will be. And when the time is right, you'll know what to do."

~

Fuck me, look at that crowd. Hoo-ee, there must be two thousand people in there! The arrow slit in front of me is narrow, but well positioned. From here I can see the Bridge and the entire amphitheatre. Burning torches transform the earth ridge into a flaming spine. At its head, a halo of larger torches surrounds the top of the grass banking. Below them, the small brands of the multitude glow like gems from some fantastic lost world. Together they carve the ground of the arena from the darkness.

On the left as I look is the pyre. No Lucy yet, just a seven-feet high stack of wood and the stake itself. Must be fifty yards away over here, but I can tell the silence is deadly. Even the tourists are spellbound by the atmosphere.

Check my watch. Ten o'clock. Not long now. Look up at the stars. They're just coming out. Nestling in the blackness. Never seen them so beautiful. This is it. My time has come.

And there's a tiny ripple in the night. From the right hand side of the amphitheatre comes a figure. Dressed in monk's habit and hood. Stalks slowly into the centre of the arena. Stands alone before the mass, head bowed. Turns lifts his head. It's...

Glasses Matthew.

But his glasses have gone.

"Tallowmas Fair," he booms in a deep, clear voice suddenly devoid of any nasal twang. There's a strange new self-confidence about this prick that I don't like. "Five hundred years ago. On this very spot. As one woman and one man died, a legend was born. People of the town, students of the college, I present... for this year's Vindendraam... the burning of St Mary of Moncur."

He walks offstage. Crowd murmurs ever so slightly. Time for me to get ready.

Run across the castle courtyard. Icy air hacks at my lungs. North-east sea tower leers above me. Below it, Diabolo waits in the black of his stable. Can see him from here, his eyes glowing like twin furnaces. Got him saddled earlier. Thought he'd play up. But he let me put it on like he was a little puppy dog. Didn't even flinch. Strange, but hey – I'm not going to worry.

Open the stall door. Step inside. Diabolo's eyes roll madly – and a good job too, if it weren't for those eyes, I don't think I'd find him in here. Walk up, take hold of his bridle. Lead him out. Still he does my bidding.

Suddenly my guts clench. From beyond the castle walls comes the deep sound of drumming. Sticks pounding skins. Makes me stop. Shiver. The primeval beat riding the night air straight to my soul.

Wish Dougal was here... No, what am I thinking? Fat idiot would find a way to fuck things up even more.

Put my left foot in a stirrup. Hoist myself up. Again, Diabolo stands as I ask, a rock of a horse, making it easy for me to climb aboard.

"Walk on."

Diabolo paces in perfect controlled steps across the castle

courtyard. His pace in time with the thumping, booming drums. The only other sound a steady, rasping breathing from his flaring black nostrils.

The ruined doorway that leads to the Bridge.

"Woah."

Pull Diabolo to a halt in the shadows. No one in the amphitheatre can see us, but through the tumbledown rectangle, I see all.

A dozen drummers flank the pyre. Ahead of them, a platoon of guards is marching to the beat. No-Glasses Matthew commands them, now dressed as an armoured mediaeval officer. He forms them up into rank and file. Around the side, the peasants swarm, uneasy. Above this, the Dean sits in the centre of the first row of spectators, dressed as a mediaeval king. Happily pouring a colossal draught of sweet wine into a goblet from a magnum bottle of port.

Where's Clive? I wonder for a second. But then No-Glasses Matthew snaps his gauntlet to the heavens and I refocus. The army stops in an instant. The drumming ceases.

Silence.

No-Glasses Matthew bows to the king.

The king dispenses the briefest of nods. Then signals – get on with it.

No-Glasses Matthew turns. Points at a lieutenant. The lieutenant marches to the front. Another command. The rank and file split to form two banks, a gangway in-between leads to the pyre. The lieutenant reaches the pyre. Stops. Again, No-Glasses Matthew snaps his arm in silent order. From the opposite end of the gangway, two more guards step forward, between them holding-

Lucy.

Fuck me, will you look at her.

Blonde hair flowing. Her strong, tanned limbs golden in the lamplight. That red dress. God, she was so right. Every single piece of glitter reflects a thousand torches. Every sparkle is an electric shock to my heart. She's an island of colour in the grey sea of guards and peasants.

Two guards haul her out into the arena. They treat her roughly, tugging at her bonds. She wants to go with dignity. They want to drag her. Look at her move. Like they're really handling her roughly. You can feel a thousand men in the audience half rise to their feet. Can imagine the tourists are starting to get nervous now. Whole thing looks more real than I remember it.

The guards pull her up to the front of the pyre. Nod to their lieutenant. He signals. They take her up the steps at the side. Pulling hard at the leather straps attached to her wrists. God, she really looks like she's in pain. Never thought she was such a good actress, but she is. Even from here you can tell she's got something special.

The guards tie her to the stake. They retreat.

No-Glasses Matthew speaks:

"In the presence of his divine magnificence, King Donald Hammerfist, as punishment for the crime of high treason, I hereby pass the sentence of death by burning upon you, Mary of Moncur. Prisoner, do you have any last words?"

Lucy lifts her head, hair flowing. Sucks in a breath, her bountiful chest swelling. Somewhere on the grass banking I'll bet that Hollywood agent is getting a stiffy in his wallet.

"Let my death tonight not be in vain. Let no woman ever fear an untrue man. And no true man ever fear a woman!"

No-Glasses Matthew snaps his gauntlet to the earth. His lieutenant lights the pyre. Flames leap up almost instantly. Lucy writhes. The peasants begin to moan in horrified unison.

Kick my steed hard in the ribs.

"Right, you satanic motherfucker, let's rock."

And Diabolo goes mental.

A terrifying, brain-bursting scream howls from his hellish mouth. He rears almost vertically. Once, twice, three times, his massive muscles tossing me around like a bit of fluff. Sinews like razor wire. Mane slashing my face. Somehow I cling to his neck.

Then, his front hooves still slashing at the air, he begins his charge across the Bridge at full gallop.

Can't focus. Can't breathe. Barely know which way is up. Every hoofbeat sends the saddle smashing up into my bollocks. His neck thumps into my clinging face like a battering ram. On either side the sloping grass drops off to the dank depths of the moat. Thundering vibrations from his hooves jar my bones. Rattle my teeth. Batter my brain against my skull. The Bridge is a flaming runway, Diabolo a screaming F-16. Fucking hell, we must be doing a hundred miles an hour.

Diabolo corners at full tilt, swinging me out wide, barely in my saddle. Hang on by my fingernails and we thunder into the arena.

The steep rows of spectators rear above us, every level packed. Flame-lit faces loom out like creatures in some primeval forest. My heart is doing its best Mike Tyson impression against my breastbone. Blood booms in my ears. Ahead, the gangway between the soldiers, beyond that the burning pyre. Shit those flames look realistic. Thought it was just the kindling they lit. That can't be lights and a smoke machine.

Who cares. Got to hang on.

No-Glasses Matthew sneers. Lifts his gauntlet. And in one perfectly drilled movement the guards reform. The gangway is closed. Blocking my way.

"What the fuck are you doing? This isn't what happens!" I yell. But I know my voice is lost amongst the machine gun smashing of hooves.

"Get the fuck out of the way!" I try. But the guards only kneel and lower their pikes. Christ, we're going to be impaled.

Yank as hard as I can on the reins.

"Slow down you psychotic bastard!!" I scream, but Diabolo thunders on. Holy fuck. We're rocketing closer. A hundred steely deaths sparkle in the torchlight. This is it. We're only inches away. And then...

We fly.

Oh sweet Jesus. Cobbles disappear. Torches streak like motorway tail-lights. Guards astonished faces zip below. Pikes clip my heels. Cold air slams into my face like a bolt. For a blissful second I am as light as the freezing air, at one with the black calm of the night.

Then we land like a car crash.

My chest slams onto the saddle pommel. My balls crunch. Limbs shoot out like a starfish. And Diabolo keeps running. Now the pyre is dead ahead. Can see Lucy, her face wild with terror. She opens her arms. But Diabolo isn't stopping. Slow down, you bastard. Going to rocket right past. She's so close now I can see her bosom heaving. Slow DOWN! But he just doesn't stop. Lucy jolts closer. Swear I can smell her.

"Come to me, my lover!" she cries.

And Diabolo drops anchor.

Sparks rip from the cobbles in four screaming showers. My feet tear from the stirrups and I take off on a solo flight. As I soar towards the pyre the world slows right down.

Tumbling, dropping, over the crackling, roasting pyre. Lucy's beautiful face looking up at me. Blue eyes shining in the night. Her arms stretching towards me. Her skin shining with sweat. Want to reach down and touch her so much it hurts.

But then I'm past and the world is speeding up again. The pyre is gone. Sky is below me. Stacked wood rolls past my feet as I tumble on.

SMECK! I faceplant wet cobblestones, my breath smashed from my lungs. Pain seizes my body. Sucking at the freezing air I roll in agony. Then SLAMM! I clatter into the banking.

And there I lie.

When I open my eyes I see Lucy standing on the pyre. Panting, screaming. Her face contorted with confusion. Her beautiful breasts bobbling with terror. Sense the crowd getting restless. This isn't right. Jesus Christ, what's going on here?

Then, in the corner of my eye, a shadow moves. So faint. Not sure I even saw it. Then:

SWISH...THWOCK!

Shit, is that a crossbow bolt? Quivering there in the wood of the stake above Lucy's head. And what's that glinting in the firelight? A metal wire. Where does it go? Follow it into the night. All the way up to the battlements of the north-east sea tower.

And then I see a terrible thing. A figure in black. Sliding down the wire like some filthy great bat from the rafters of hell, the figure zips straight onto the top of the pyre. Beside Lucy. She grabs him in her terror. He swirls his heavy black cloak around her. Stamps his black-booted foot. A trapdoor springs beneath them. They start to plummet. But in the millisecond before they drop to safety, I swear I see the man in black turn and grin at me. And then they're gone, and as the flames lick the stake above the trapdoor and ten thousand voices raise the heavenly roof in relief, and all I can think is:

Clive, you complete cunt.

~

Ploiink!

The cistern above me drips and echoes round the vast bathroom. I shiver. It's freezing here in the stall. The ancient ceramic WC below me is like an iceberg. The sickly linoleum intensifies the cold. Outside the stall by the sinks the Victorian radiator stands, broken, like an iron war machine rusting in defeat at the side of the battlefield.

God I feel ill. Over an hour now since Dougal left. Pulled on his little sheepskin jacket, wished me luck, then went. Soon as he was gone, the nausea returned. I'm sure he could see I'm in trouble. Don't think he wanted to go. He paused at the door and looked back, like he was feeling sorry for me. And I wish he hadn't. When that door clicked shut behind him I felt a thousand times worse than before. And I didn't feel that great to start with.

Ploiink!

Check my watch. Gone eleven. Any minute now grandad will come in here. And he'll expect me to get up, walk next door and shag Lucy Sugar. To lose my virginity. Sacrifice my pure self for him. Send my cock on a crusade. Well, ring a ding ding. Hardly the erotic bonanza of sensuality I once thought it would be. I mean, does he expect me to just walk next door and stick it straight in her? Or would that be rude? Maybe I have to wait until she gets my charlie out. That can be my cue. But then who takes off her knickers? I feel I'd have to wait until she said I could before I did. But then she'd be taking the lead with both my charlie and her pigeon and I'd be looking like a right amateur. I think maybe I should take care of my end of things, so to speak, and leave her to handle hers. So I'll wait until we've kissed for a minute or so, then I'll take my pants off. Yeah, that should do it.

And what will it actually feel like? The same as a wank? Can't do. Must be better. Otherwise everyone would just sit around tossing themselves off. Species would die out. No, intercourse must be more enjoyable than wanking – Darwinian rule.

Anyway, who cares? Moment she takes her top off I'll spunk my breeks. Whole thing's a colossal waste of time. Specially since what I really want is to be down there on that beach, dancing with Penelope. Be such fun! The Vindendraam is over. The locals are back in the warmth of their front rooms. And the students hit the north sands and party. The Midwinter Beach Ball. Can hear it now – out in the dunes, the bass of the sound system starts to bang like a drugged-up heartbeat.

Soon, somewhere out there, he'll be buying her a beer. Asking her to dance. Dammit!

BLAMM!

I punch the side of the stall. It should be me. What if I get down there and it's too late? What then? Grandad hasn't thought of that, has he? Can't bear to think of him. Thanks to him I've got a pile of explaining to do. Not that she'd believe me. Whole thing's fucking madness. 'Hi Pen, I'm really sorry I was rude to you, it wasn't actually me, it was my thirty-three-year-old future self'-

SLAMMMMCRACCKKK!!!

The door flies back and smashes into the wall. Grandad stands glaring.

"Levis!" he bellows. "The cosmos wears fucking Levis!"

He steps into the stall beside me. Lord, he looks a mess. Black outfit ripped in a dozen places. Patches of blood soaking through the material. Hair wild. Hands waving like an epileptic conductor.

"It's the only explanation," he rants. "The fabric of spacetime – it just does not want to rip."

Don't want to enrage him, but got to know what he's on about.

"Er, what?"

He turns on me.

"Clive of course! That unbelievable fuckface has got her again. Just like he did before."

I smile to myself.

"You mean you messed up again," I nod.

He stabs a quivering finger at me.

"Shut your fucking mouth. Fucking did not, okay?"

And for some reason, I have to laugh. Long and loud and hard.

"What's so fucking funny?" he snarls.

But the harder he rages, the more I want to laugh. He's just the funniest thing in the world. Soon I'm doubled up. We're both going purple.

Suddenly, he grabs my collar with his fist. Slams me up against the stall wall. I stop laughing.

"Listen to me, you immature little shit. You need to do exactly as I say," he barks. "She's gone to the Beach Ball with him, so I need you to get down there and-"

"No."

His eyes narrow.

"What?" he says, he voice spiked like barbed wire.

"I said... no."

"You'll do as you're told."

"No, I won't. Don't you get it? It's not meant to happen. The only thing I'm going to do now is go down and dance with Pen."

Try to move past him.

He pushes me back.

"Get off me, you lunatic," I snap, and shove his hand away.

Suddenly something very weird happens. The side of the stall rushes very fast to meet my face.

BLAMM!

Ow. That hurt. Now here comes the floor. Ooyah! That hurt even more. How strange. Think I should roll over. There we go. What's that big blur above me? Is it grandad? Think it is. What's that he's holding in front of him? His right hand, I think. And it looks... yes, it looks like it's bunched into a fist. What the hell? Did he just? He did. Bloody bugger hit me.

He's reaching down for me now.

Quick! Roll through the gap under the stall side.

"You little bastard!" he bellows from the other side. And I'm up on my feet and heading for the door, but he's quickly after me. Get the door half open when it's slammed shut before my face. Desperate hands claw me backwards onto my arse. I spin, grab one his legs, whip them sideways. WHAPP-OOFF! He topples to the deck.

I'm up again, sprinting. Then it's my turn to have my legs taken out – the paper towel bin slams into me from behind. SMECK! My face cracks onto icy lino. Dirty towels rain down like dying birds.

Sit up. I'm facing him. He's reaching for a toilet brush. Grabs it by the handle. I'm half on my feet when he flicks it towards me. The plastic casing shoots off and catches me square on the forehead. OW! The lights go blotchy. I go down again.

Once more I try to get up, but-

OOF!

He leaps onto my chest. Straddles me.

I whip and writhe like a demented snake but I can't get free. Then-

EEEUURGHH!

I retch and recoil as the thick odour of the brush clogs my nostrils.

"You want it? Huh? Do you?" he snarls, jabbing the brush millimetres from my face.

Stop.

Still.

I've lost. I've given my all, and been defeated. This should be my ultimate despair. But I feel no pain. No shame twists me. Instead, a sudden calm floods my bones. Fills me with strange elation. And I'm instantly free. In my heart, I don't care any more.

"Okay," I whisper.

He leans back. Wipes the blood from his mouth with filthy

fingers.

"Good," he says.

And my calm hardens like bone.

Because you know what? If that's what he really wants, well, maybe it's time I got it for him.

~

Look at these twats. I mean, really.

Hands clutched to their chests, they sway and bob on the sand. The less movement the better, until occasionally one will start windmilling in slow motion, as if throwing imaginary flowers around.

And they're not even on drugs. They're pretending that they're on drugs. Which is pathetic. If they were on drugs you could excuse the dancing. But this is just indulgence.

And look at those twats. The band. There in front of the dunes on a tiny temporary stage. Chunking out yet another drony minor key dirge. The Baggy Spirals. Christ, they think they're so cool. We're from Madchester, mate. Yeah, well, get over yourself, mate. You're going nowhere. Two years' time you'll all be stuffing kebabs in Oldham.

Cut our way through the party. Junior's just crashing through people. When they don't see him coming that is. Guy looks like shit. Strange stare in his eyes. Glassy, but intense. Like he's died and been possessed. Bit scary.

Soon as people clock him they move. And when they see me they do a double take. Probably shouldn't be seen together, but right now, who cares? This is a fucking emergency. Any minute now she's going to cop off with Clive and the whole thing will be ruined. Can't let that happen. Cannot let that happen...

Lean over to Junior.

"Listen, we have to clinch this. When you get her, take her down to the Castle Caves, okay? My bed is in there. It'll be perfect. You got that?"

But he doesn't say anything. Just stops suddenly. Throws out an arm. His pale index finger pointing like bony death.

"There."

Follow his bug-eyed stare. A fat guy in a baseball cap is waddling determinedly through the hordes of shoe-gazing students. Very short, can't be more than five two, but he walks with a swagger like he's the biggest cock in town. Got the most violently orange tan I've ever seen. Like some radiation victim from a cheap sci-fi flick.

"That's not him," I say, "tourist-"

Junior's bloodshot eyes swing back to me. Swear I can see hell in those fearsome orbs.

"Agent."

"Oh," I say. "Of course."

His head swivels back like a tank gun turret. Eyes zero on their target. And without another word he lopes off across the sand like a giant wolf.

Well, who'd have thought it? At last! The boy finally looks like he's up for the job.

Junior's moving fast. Have to jog to catch him. Together we follow Baseball Cap through the swarm. Then I see her.

More stunning than ever. A white fur coat covers most of the red dress. Makes her look like some exotic creature of the night.

Tug on Junior's sleeve.

"Hey," I say. "Easy. Need to stay out of sight." Lead him into a holding position behind a genuinely stoned shoegazer.

Clive and Lucy are talking as Baseball Cap approaches. He's holding her arm. She's saying:

"Are you sure it went well? Waz it not confusing zat zere was two Black Princes... ?"

Clive slimes back:

"Sssertainly not, oh no. Two princes are better than one, you sssee-"

Baseball Cap taps her on the shoulder.

"Miss, can ah have a word of your time, please."

They stop. Turn to face him. He thrusts out a great ham of a hand. She takes it. He pumps her hard.

"What's your name, honey?"

"Luciana Sugar. But everyone calls me Lucy."

"Lucy Sugar?! Oh hell, yah got to be kidding me?"

"No," she says with a smile and shake of her head.

He whoops and thumps his thigh.

"And you are?" says Clive.

Baseball Cap calms down. Pats his cheek. Takes a breath.

"Name's Max T. Lieberman." Produces a card. "That was one hell of a show you put on back there."

"Thank you," says Clive.

Baseball Cap takes Lucy's arm. Turns her away from Clive.

"Take a look at that card there, sweetheart. What does it say?"

"Max T. Lieberman..."

"Below that, honey."

Her eyes suddenly widen.

"Talent agent!"

"Now, some folks, they're good at judging horses or cats or goddamn Pekinese. Me, I know talent. And that's what you got, honey. Raw talent to fuckin' burn."

"You sink?"

"You ever been to Hollywood, honey?"

Lights from the stage dance in her shining eyes.

"No-" she breathes.

"Well, the place is a shithole. But it's also the only place to be when you got talent like yours. So you got to get yourself there. And when you do, you give me a call."

"You sink you could get me in a movie?"

"Honey, with..." looks at her chest, "...abilities like yours, ah have no doubt whatsoever that ah can get you up on that silver screen. Got to work on that accent, but hell yeah."

She claps her hands quickly in front of her chest and does a few tiny bounces.

He smiles.

"Who'da thought it? Come over here to get maself a little golf and what do ah end up finding but the most talented goddam actress ever!"

She bounces some more. He goes on:

"So you take mah card and when you're in town, you promise me you won't call anyone else first?"

"Oh, I promise, yes, I do!"

"Well, y'all enjoy your night. You sure deserve it."

And with a touch of the peak of his cap, he's gone.

Lucy turns to Clive.

"Wasn't he ze most wonderful man?"

"Actually, I though he wasss-"

At which point she throws her arms around Clive and hugs him. He gathers in his eyebrows, grins and continues without missing a beat:

"-indeed the most wonderful fellow. We should ssselebrate immediately!"

"Oh yes!" she cries, hugging him again.

He moves his face closer towards her.

"Tell you what, my sssensssational darling, why don't you wait here and I'll go and buy us a little bottle of fizz?"

She hugs him. Clive beams. Can practically see his trousers tenting as he moves away to the bar.

"Going now," grunts Junior in my ear.

Look round at him. His stare is ferocious. Wow. Junior seems to be up for it.

"Uh, right," I say as he paces away after Clive, eyes black, shoulders hunched.

Turn away from him to look at Lucy. God, isn't she just amazing? Standing there on the sand, gently shimmying her righteous arse to the music. Her gorgeous face beaming. Every inch of her screaming joy and sexual excitement. And soon, I'll have the memory of shagging her. Almost can't believe it's really going to happen. Could stand here drinking in this moment for ever...

Oh oh. Lucy's turning this way. Can't have her see me now. Best not hang around here too long. Could get tricky.

Right, where's what's-her-name?

~

Follow Clive to the bar. He goes straight to the front. Pushes in front of a tiny girl with bunches. Snaps his fingers at the boss-eyed barman.

"Hey. Champagne," he barks. "Two glasses."

The guy's pouring a pint for the tiny girl with bunches. He looks about nervously.

"Are you deaf?" snaps Clive. "Hurry up."

Boss-eyed barman looks at Clive. Then at the tiny girl with bunches. Back at Clive. Boss-eyed barman bottles it. Puts down the pint glass, reaches towards the fridge.

Tiny girl with bunches huffs and shakes her head.

"There's a queue," she says.

Clive turns. Tilts his head back so he can look right down his codfish nose at her.

"I didn't see you down there," he says.

The tiny girl with bunches flushes scarlet.

"Well, you see me now. Who do you think you are, barging in like that?"

"The warden of MacIvor Hall."

The tiny girl with bunches thinks about this for a second.

"So?" she says.

"So, cretin, I'm on official university business."

The barman puts the wine and the glasses on the counter.

"Six pound fifty."

Clive throws down a fiver.

"I'm not paying more than that," he says, his nose in the air. Then he picks up the bottle in one hand and the glasses in another. Throws one last condescending glance to the tiny girl with bunches, then turns away from the bar.

Straight into my fist.

Not sure if it's actually possible to hit someone harder than that.

He rockets a yard backwards onto the bar, makes a single muffled bark of exclamation, like a dog with its muzzle bound up, then starts to slide to his knees in the sand. Bending forward slightly, I take his bottle in one hand and the glasses in the other. Then I walk away. As I go I hear him flap face first to the deck. I don't look back, so I can't be sure, but I think I also hear the unmistakeable sound of a small girl with the bunches bouncing up and down and clapping her hands together.

~

There she is, at the side of the speakers. Look at her. So awkward. Not even dancing. Just standing with her fat mate who glared at me before the Vindendraam. Martina? Morwena? Monica, that was it. God, she was annoying. Anyway, forget her. Better go and chat with old Penster. Just for a bit. Buy her a drink maybe. Keep her talking till Junior takes care of business. It's half eleven now, so say that takes him twenty minutes, he can be back here, snog her at say, ten to, giving me time to get back to the caves before the singularity closes at midnight. Job done. Fine. Let's get on with it. Slip past yet another windmilling arsehole, step towards the speakers, gather my cool, and...

"Look at these pricks," I say. "Call that dancing?"

Monica and Penelope look round. But they don't acknowledge me. They just stare. Faces perfect blanks.

"I mean," I chuckle, "this guy looks like someone poured glue in his knickers."

They don't laugh. They don't do anything. They just keep staring at me like I'm from fucking space. What's the bloody jackanory? This isn't the plan at all.

"Your drinks, ladies," rolls a confident voice behind me. Turn. That fucker Matthew. Still no sign of his glasses. And he's looking all trendy. Don't remember that. Has three bottles of K cider in his hands. Gives one to each of the girls, keeps one for himself. As they take their drinks, they don't for a second stop looking at me.

He follows their eyes. Clocks me. Smirks. Lifts his chin. Clears his throat. Says in a plummy tone:

"Would you also like a cider, Frederick?"

Feeling uneasy now. Penelope's stare has intensified. Feel like it's probing me, questioning. This is a key moment. Desperately need to say something clever. But nothing comes to mind. Think, dammit!

"No thanks," I hear myself say. "I just put one out." Fucking hell that was feeble.

He smirks some more. "Okaaay," he smiles. Turns to the girls. "Care to dance, Penny?"

Her eyes are still on mine.

"Absolutely," she says and takes his arm.

And in a second they're gone.

Monica leans towards me. Winks. "Looks like you fucking blew it, darling," she says.

~

Plough through the crowd. Dancers bounce off me and spin into the night. There she is. Move right up behind her. Tap her on the shoulder.

She turns.

"Zat was qui-" Her eyebrows take off. Lips split into the widest, ripest smile. "Freddie! Oh, I am so happy to see you!"

"Let's go."

Press her forwards.

"Go? Where to?"

"Caves."

"What for?"

"Celebrate," I say, holding up the champagne.

She looks over my shoulder.

"But what about Clive?"

I smile.

"Clive will not be partying with us," I say.

She smiles back. Takes my arm. Together we leave the music

behind and pace quickly up the ever-darkening beach.

~

The fuck's going on here? What's she doing with that idiot?
Christ, Junior really screwed this one up too. Surrounded by
cretins. Have to do everything myself.

Edge of the dance area. The band are kicking out their one
great hit, 'Twisting Acid Lemons'. Big fat bassline. Crowd goes
wild. Penelope and Matthew step into the dance area. They move
together. Oh no, that's hideous. Got to stop this.

Run forwards.

Jump in between them.

Dance.

"What are you doing?" he yelps.

Ignore him. Dance with her.

"Don't you get it, you lunatic? She's not interested."

Just keep dancing.

He squares up to me. Bit broader than I remember him being.
Suddenly, her tiny frame is there between us.

"It's okay, Matthew. Please excuse me for a moment, won't
you?"

"But-" he starts.

"It's okay," she says. "This won't take long."

Then she takes my arm and leads me away from the music up
the ever-darkening beach.

~

Lead Lucy over the rocks. Snowing now. Slippery underfoot.
Have to hold her much of the way. Body feels firm to the touch.
Oh, grandad you're going to enjoy this.

Cave now dead ahead. A hollow maw in the cliff. The wind
whips the sea over the mouth. The space behind echoes and
breathes. Lucy stops. Turns to me. Eyebrows steepled. Lips tight.

"Are you sure zis is a good idea? It looks so dark and slimy..."

Wink. Slide my arm round her waist. So slender.

"Come on in," I say. "You'll love it." Move with her into the cavern.

A vast space hewn by ancient storms. Rough-chiselled walls loom from their own shadows. Lucy looks up at me. Half-smiles. Shivers a little. How strange. Warmer in here than it was out there in the snow. She presses herself even closer to me.

Guide her across streaming black seaweed and tumbledown rocks. Champagne glasses clink and echo as we pick our way. At the rear of the cave, beyond the reach of the highest tide there is a low, rough arch.

Lucy pulls up. Again she hesitates. The whites of her eyes shine wide in the half-light. She swallows. A lock of blonde hair falls in a curious curve across her face. I brush it away with my fingers. She smiles.

Then I get down on my knees. Take her hand. And together we crawl through the small gap.

We arise in an almost perfect hemisphere. Soft sandy floor ten yards across. Smooth walls curving overhead to a hole in the centre – a natural chimney letting in fresh air. The cavern is lit all around by a soft, twinkling phosphorescence in the rock. A million tiny creatures creating a new heaven here in the heart of the earth.

And, in the middle of it all, sits a large brass bed.

~

That's strange. Don't remember her moving so well. Always thought she stooped a bit. But tonight... maybe it's the frozen sand, or the faint backlighting from the stage behind us. But there's real elegance in that walk.

There's something in the way she holds her head too. Confidence of a sort. You might call it alluring. Never noticed that before either. The coat helps, I suppose. Looks like the kind of thing a Polish general would wear. Long, black, tapered waist, gold buttons, large fur collar. Unbelievably masculine and yet, oddly, it highlights the subtle curves of her frame.

We're walking now along the water's edge. Far ahead, at the end of the beach, the town sits twinkling on its dark rock.

Snow has started to fall. Not surprised. Fucking cold. Don't realise it when you're in the body of the party. The dancers and the band and the booze are insulating. But further out the air is bitter. To combat it, the party-goers have built fires, nestling in the rolling shoulders of the dunes. Around each one a separate activity: this one snogging, that one guitar playing, all those ones smoking dope.

Now we've passed the last of them, and it feels like we're alone in an icy wasteland.

Penelope stops. Looks out at the flat black waters.

"God," she says, "I love the sea. You know, I heard about this place up on the west coast... Dairloch, I think it's called. It's meant to be the most romantic spot. There's just this tiny little hotel and a beach. The sands are so white and the ocean so blue, it's like the most beautiful tropical island." She looks at me and laughs. "Except it's freezing cold of course." She turns. Looks out across the water once more. "Apparently it feels like you have the world to yourself..."

She rocks a little. Snow flurries gently round her, caressing the smooth lines of her coat.

"What are you doing with that idiot?" I say.

She twists round sharply.

"That 'idiot' has been very nice to me," she says. "Unlike some people."

"What are you talking about?" I snap back.

A swift darkness descends on her features. For a second I think she's going to yell at me. Then the cloud passes. Her face settles. She moves a step towards me. Peers closely at my face.

"What is it?" I say.

Her brows furrow slightly. She continues her inspection. Then pauses and says softly:

"You have these little lines around your eyes. Tiny cuts almost. It's like sadness and like, like..."

"Like what?"

She looks directly at me.

"Like fear."

"What could I be afraid of?"

"You tell me," she says.

Long silence.

About to say something when suddenly she points over my shoulder towards the ocean.

"Oh!" she cries, "look!"

Turn to see where she's pointing.

Rising silver above the black glass of the sea is a pair of dolphins. They're so close, so real, so sublimely beautiful that I gasp. For a whole breath they defy gravity and hang in the moonlight, then they dip below the water with barely a ripple. My breath escapes. A pause. A few gentle snowflakes caress my cheek. Then they rise again, a pair of curving stars.

"Come on!" cries Pen, and in one swift movement she slips open the bottom button of her coat and skips away up the snowy sand.

"Where are you going?" I shout after her.

But she only laughs and runs on.

Look at her go! What a sight, her nimble legs running up the moonlit beach after the dolphins. Makes me want to...

Oo, hang on, what was that? Suddenly feel very strange in my gut. Like something wants to burst out of me. Oh this is weird. An alien like in that film. Oh shit, here it comes...

"Ha!"

Was that...? Think it was. Bloody hell, think I just laughed.

Look once more at Penelope up ahead. She's looking back at me.

"That's it!" she cries, her boots kicking up snow. "Come on!"

"HA HA!" bellows the alien.

Shit, this is incredible! The alien has complete control. But I don't mind. Far from it in fact. Go on, boy, let him loose. And with a mighty whoop I take off after her.

~

The bed creaks and mutters as we sit. Linen looks a bit singed. Hand the glasses to Lucy. Grip the top of the bottle. Fingers are a little numb with cold. Takes me a minute to tear the gold foil. The glasses rattle. Check Lucy. Her hands quiver. Eyes glisten in the phosphorescence. Lower lip hangs, trembling. She must be cold too.

Free the foil. Turn the bottle. Cushion the cork with my hand to control the explosion.

FFWWIIPPP!!

A tiny burst of vapour curls into the still air. Like smoke from a gun.

"Ha!" Lucy gasps. Her smile is back, eyes dancing.

I pour.

So still in here. Can hear the bubbles jostling in the light gold liquid that settles in the glasses like silk.

Screw the bottle safely into the sand. Lucy hands me a glass. We raise them together. Faces close now. Her eyes are living blue jewels.

"To the future," I say.

"To the future," she smiles.

We drink. Down in one draught.

Then I take her empty glass from her, set it down on the sand beside the bottle, and reach for the buttons of her coat.

~

She tears up the edge of the sea, her feet splashing in the icy water. Try to catch her, but she's too fast. Like a wild spirit of the air she runs, the thickening snow powerless to slow her. Don't remember ever running so hard and I never get closer than ten feet. My breath heaves in my chest, my muscles burn, my feet are numb, the snow stings my eyes. Every step is racking agony and yet – this is fun. In fact, haven't enjoyed myself this much in years.

Now, ahead of us, over the darkened castle the moon has risen.

Her perfect shining face dances on the water, shimmers on the snowy beach. She brings a strange thought into my head. How nice it would be, I think, to run like this forever. Penelope ahead, the water snapping hopelessly at her heels. Me following, every step a leaden agony. And beside us all the way, the dolphins rising and dipping, rising and dipping, running their silvery stitch up the dark hem of the beach.

Suddenly, Penelope leaps up in the air. She's reached the rocks in front of the castle caves. A stretch and a grab and I follow her onto a gnarled head of an outcrop.

Finally she's stopped. Her head is turned out to sea.

"Look," she says, pointing once more at the dolphins. But I cannot take my eyes from her profile. It's like some spell has fallen with the snow, freezing me in wonder. All I can see is her face. Lit from above by the moon, reflected from below by the crisp new whiteness. Her eyes glistening. Skin shining. Lips parted, her breath coming strong between. Never have I seen her so alive. So young. So beautiful.

A full minute we stand. Still she stares out across the waves. And still I cannot move my eyes from her face.

"Isn't it beautiful?" she says.

"Magical," I say, my eyes not moving.

"Oh," she whispers, "they're going."

And the spell is broken. My eyes follow her gaze. The dolphins have stopped leaping and have turned their shimmering backs to us. They glide away for a moment, slicing the moonlit waves, then they dip for the last time beneath the black water, and are gone.

For a long time we do not move.

Then at last she turns to face me. Her eyebrows suddenly crease in concern.

"Are you okay?" she asks.

Not at all, I want to tell her. Completely confused, I want to say. But the words are like snowflakes in my head. The moment I try to catch one on my tongue, it melts and dies forever.

She gives herself a little shake. A sort of mini shrug.

"Well," she says, "you'd best get in."

"Huh?"

She points towards the caves.

"There."

"W-what for?" I stammer.

"Oh, Freddie," she says, her voice cracking slightly. "You know why I brought you here."

What's going on? None of this is making any sense.

"Brought me here? But we followed the dolphins."

She smiles. Looks out to sea.

"A happy coincidence," she says simply. "They went where I wanted to go."

She nods to the cave.

"Hurry. Go to her."

Is this some sort of weird dream? Feels like I'm trying to do long division in my head. Can't hold on to the sense of things. Nothing adds up...

"What are you talking about?" I say, baffled further by the sound of my own stupid voice.

"I saw her come along here earlier. She was with another man, but if you hurry, you should still have time."

Still I flail after meaning.

"Who was with another man? Time for what?"

She takes a deep breath. Smiles a sad little smile. Then her face calms. She says softly:

"Lucy, of course. And time to tell her how you truly feel."

Then the wind swirls suddenly, ripping snow into my face like machine gun fire. And so I understand. My legs have been turned into giant strips of liquorice. My knees buckle. All I can do to stop myself crashing to the hard rock below.

"Don't fight it, Freddie," she says. And she pushes me towards the cave.

Oh God, no. This isn't right.

"Why are you doing this?" I manage, groping around on all fours.

"Because it's what you want," she says, gently taking my arm and moving me forwards. Then she adds: "You love her."

"I don't love her!" I bellow.

"Of course you do, Freddie," she says patiently.

"I don't love her at all!" I cry, "I only want to shag her!"

And I shoot to my feet, grab Penelope by the shoulders, pull her towards me, and kiss her.

Full on the lips and hard.

~

Run the fingers of my right hand through the white fur of her coat. From the front of her waist round to the small of her back. My skin flares with electricity. Pull her gently towards me. Her head rocks back a little as she moves forwards. But her widening eyes never leave mine.

Move my left hand between our bellies. Slide it just inside the opening of her coat. Lift it to the first button. Grasp the leather toggle firmly and flick it loose.

She gasps a little.

Raise my hand further up to the next fastening. Twist it free.

Another gasp. A little louder.

The third and final toggle. The third and loudest gasp.

Now with my right hand I grab a handful of coat in the middle of her back and pull firmly downwards. The fur runs over her shoulders like a waterfall. She moves her head forward and points her arms backwards so I can pull it free all the way. Her face is millimetres from mine. I could lick her lips.

The front of her coat splits open revealing sparkling red beneath. Can't pull the coat any further back so I bring both of my hands up to her shoulders. Grasp the furry lapels...

...pause for a second...

...then slip the coat off her. It drops and curls on the bed like a sleeping arctic fox.

She shivers once, briefly, as the air hits the skin of her arms, shoulders and neck. The glitter on her dress shimmies in the half-light. Her nipples press hard through the near-sheer fabric of the dress. Around them, the dress hugs the firm roundness of her breasts. And I can smell her too. Warm and honeyed.

Two slender straps run over her shoulders. Lift my hands, one to each. Flick them away to the side. She utters a little cat-like noise, half moan, half squeak and for the first time she takes her eyes off mine, shutting them for a long second.

But the dress doesn't drop.

It's too tight. Just clings there to her fabulous form.

"Stand up."

She does so. Still the dress hugs her curves. Stretch out my arms. She looks at me again. Her eyes flicker. Muscles in her throat quiver. Can see the blood pulsing hard and fast in the flesh of her neck.

Reach for the top of her dress. Grip the material.

Take a breath. She too draws one in sharply.

Then I slowly peel her dress down, like I would a ripe fruit.

We exhale.

And her naked body stands before me. A whole new world. She is the moon. I'm Armstrong.

Now she moves. Reaches for me. Toned muscles move together in harmony. She removes my clothes. Presses herself against me.

Hard.

Her skin flows beneath me. Liquid velvet to the touch. Then moving firmly like a wave.

We lie on the bed.

At last she's there beneath me, quivering. Waiting.

A gazelle. To my tiger.

Fear flicks in her eyes. Passion too.

"Be gentle," she says, voice wavering.

"Fuck that," I snarl, and pounce.

~

Pen snatches herself away. Glares at me. Eyes like lasers.

"What are you doing?" she hisses.

"Kissing you."

"Why?" Her face is crumpled in confusion.

A horrific sickness hauls at my guts.

Kiss her again.

She pulls away again.

"Stop it!" she yells.

A wave of nausea rolls in my belly.

"I thought you liked me," I say.

"Like you..." she echoes faintly. But then all sound dies on her lips. Now she's the one struggling. Like there's something huge in her that can't find a way out. Her cheeks blood themselves, her lips quiver, her expression crumples and crashes.

For a tiny second there's silence.

Then the giant tears free.

"I LOVED YOU!" Her voice cracks and wavers, the words ripping her throat as they pass. "You stupid... boy! I loved you from the first moment I saw you!" she cries. For a long second she just huffs and sobs as I stand frozen on the snow. "Oh, I had such dreams!" she gasps at last. "Silly, girlish dreams, but they were... lovely. Then when you went with Lucy to the pub crawl I stopped dreaming. It was obvious. She was gorgeous. Any man would want to be with her. But nothing came of that and we were working on the costumes and the dreams came back. Stronger. Lovelier. And I was so happy." She laughs, but there's no humour in the sound. Her face tightens into a mask of sadness. "But then, at the costume fitting..."

"That wasn't me," I blurt.

"Oh, Freddie, I've never seen someone so clear-eyed. So determined. You made it quite plain. And your words were needles stuck in my heart."

The wave has me swaying on my feet. Feel like I'm going to topple off this rock. Want to stop myself, want to say something, but the words choke and bubble in my throat.

"Next thing I knew, Matthew is with me. And I didn't want to be with him. God, I hated him. Every minute was a lie. When I was walking with him, all I could think about was walking with you. It wasn't like I was imagining he was you, it was stronger than that. Like I was remembering being with you. I'm not sure you can understand what I mean-"

"I do!"

"-but the more he walked with me and the more I thought about the hurtful words you had said, the more that memory faded. Until it was nothing but a dream of a dream." She looks out across the flat black ocean. "And then all I could really see... was how in love with her you really were." She sniffs. Looks up at me. Such seriousness in her eyes. "And I'd rather you were happy than both of us miserable. Go to her now. Please."

Tears are budding like little stars in the corners of her eyes. She turns away from me.

"Stop!" I shout.

She pauses.

"Don't torture me," she says, pulling away.

Grab her.

"No!" she cries. "Let me live!"

And she smacks my hand violently away and breaks free. Before I can reach her she has jumped down from the rocks and is trailing footprints fast up the snowy beach.

About to leap down to follow her when I hear a gasp. The unmistakable sound of female pleasure. Drifting out on the icy air from the cave. Stops me for a moment. Shit. Is he going to... ? Think he is. Oh no. Not now, you fool! Can't you see, it's all gone wrong?! Need to stop things for a minute. Get Pen back. The gasp slides into a moan. Oh Christ, no! Got to get in there. Got to stop him.

Leap-

No, got to get to Pen.

Try to change direction, but I've already started going left. Shit. Feel my boots shooting from under me. Suddenly I'm toppling backwards like a roll of lino. Try to twist in mid-air. Strain every muscle. Get one hand out. Forearm connects with barnacled rock. Fucking ow. Elbow gives. Shoulder too. Rock coming at face fast. Not going to-

BLAMM.

And once again, the world is black.

~

She gasps one last time then stretches her body like a cat. Slowly the tension in her muscles dies and she melts beneath me.

A moment of breathing.

My shoulders feel stiff, my arms tired, my body heavy. I heave myself to the side and collapse beside her.

Our breaths curl together in the icy air of the cave.

Quiet.

Then she reaches out a hand. Touches my chest. Very softly. She moves closer. Lifts her head. Rests it beside her hand. Feel her hair like a mass of silk against my skin.

"I always knew," she says.

"What?" I sigh.

"You and I are meant to be," she replies.

And I put my arm around her shoulders and pull her closer towards me.

~

My face is wet. Warm and wet. But my body is cold. My clothes stick to my skin with icy dampness.

Sit up.

Shiver. Shit, I'm still on the rocks outside the cave. It's raining.

Touch my face. The rain there is warm. That can't be right. Look at my fingers. The wetness is dark. Blood. My forehead is cut. How badly? Who cares? Look up. The cave.

Got to stop them.

Haul my shivering limbs upright. Run for the cave, staggering like a drunk. Across the rocks, stumbling, panting, smashing my knees against the cold stone. Snow coming down now like the end of the world. Whipping across my face, stinging my face. My eyes swimming. Blunder on oblivious. Got to stop them. Into the cavern. Lurch and slide across the weed and rocks. Can feel the blood pouring down my legs. Got to move faster! Here's the archway. Dive to my knees. Crawl through.

Into the soft light of the inner chamber. There's the bed. Quick. Run. Got to stop them. Stop them! STOP THEM!

They're not there.

Just some crumpled sheets, the quiet, and a strange glow about the place. Like the rocks are leering at me.

AAAAAARRRRGGGHHH!!

Every atom of my brain screams in sudden agony. Drop like a sack to the sand. Clutch my head. Of course, the memory is coming.

But that's not all.

OOOOOOOHHHHHH!!!

The rocks around me pulse in a huge, savage wave. They ripple back and forth, focusing the energy into my mind. Oh Christ, it's the singularity. It's midnight. It's closing.

How can I stop it? Got to stop it!

Stagger to my feet, but sickness fills my belly, floods my heart, surges through my soul. Collapse on the bed. My limbs flail like tissue paper.

KKERRRRACKKK-ZZT-ZZT-ZZT!!!

The bed leaps in the air. White-hot snakes crack into existence. They writhe over the orb. Which is shrinking. In massive concussive waves centred on my brain. Once more, the universe is imploding upon me.

Wild with pain and fury I buck and snap my body.

NOOOOOOOO!!!!!

The orb presses on me like a neutron star. The singularity is here.

And suddenly,

as reality dies,

everything comes back to me.

~

# SATURDAY, 6TH FEBRUARY 2016

Remember...

...Lucy's breasts, firm beneath me, nipples pressing into my chest. Her belly curving in taut expectation. My hand sliding down between her legs. She gasps...

"Freddie!"

Who said that? Nevermind. Back to dreamland... Don't be afraid my beauty, I won't hurt you. Move my hand farther, touching the heart of her warmth...

"Is that you in there?"

There does seem to be a voice coming from somewhere. But it's very distant. Like it's coming at me down a tunnel. Quick, press on before the dream fades... Now I move my body over hers, caressing every inch of her skin, pressing my hard cock against her soft belly and...

"Where the hell have you been?"

It's louder now. Ignore it, ignore it, ignore it, the dream is too nice...

"If you're in that bed you'd better get up right now!"

Too late! It's no good. Not in the cave anymore. In bed. Can feel the duvet around me. And still the sound intrudes. Footsteps now – the clack-clackety-clack of heels on solid floors.

"You hear me!?"

Please. Let me wank in peace...

White light explodes in my eyes as the covers are torn from me. Curl into the smallest possible ball.

"It is you!"

That's odd. Pen's accent sounds a bit... American.

"You'd better have a pretty amazing explanation for this!" she cries.

"For God's sake, Pen, you don't have to yell, I'm right here!"

Pause.

"Pen?!" she says quietly. "Who the hell's Pen?'

Hang on...

Sit up. Open my eyes. Takes a while, the light's so bright. Finally shapes begin to filter through the whiteness. The end of the bed... the bedside cabinet... the chest of drawers... the French wardrobe... the door to the ensuite bathroom... the balcony... the Picasso... and there, at the side of the bed, the unmistakable form of...

Lucy.

Woah. What's going on? This doesn't seem right. And yet, it does. It's perfectly fine. This is my bedroom. Could tell you where my socks are. Remember sleeping here a hundred times. But...

"You've got a lot of explaining to do, buster!"

Why's she talking in an American accent? Thought she was weirdly continental. No, of course, when we came to LA she went for speech lessons... how could I forget that?

"What have you done with our bed? Where did you get this piece of junk?"

God, she looks a bit thin, doesn't she? Can see the bones of her shoulders through the lace of that white shirt. And her tits! Where have they gone? Sure she used to have lovely great full breasts. Can hardly see them now. And what there is seems to droop.

Oh, of course, she went on that diet. Ate polystyrene balls every second meal. Studio insisted. Lost three stone. Squeaked a lot.

"Don't you have anything to say for yourself, you asshole? Two weeks you've been gone and you just fucking lie there!"

Two weeks? Have I really? How interesting. Thought I was just asleep. Dreaming I was back at St Mary's. Maybe I was really there. On a holiday perhaps. But how can that be? Shit, feels like my brain's been turned to marmalade.

BAMM!

She stamps her foot. Poor girl's face has gone purple. That's despite the makeup. Wow she's wearing a lot. How long's she been doing that? Always thought she had the most lovely natural skin-

"Freddie, you better answer me!"

Girl looks seriously on edge. Her meltwater-blue eyes eddy and cloud.

"WHERE WERE YOU?!!"

"Um... looking up some old college friends," I mutter.

Her eyes twitch. Like she's about to cry. Rubs her hands together. Round and round. Over and under. God, her fingers look bony. Always thought she had soft hands. How odd.

She takes a sudden deep breath. Draws her shoulders up tight. Then says, speaking each word like it's acid:

"You weren't... with another woman?"

Smile. Can handle this one.

"Absolutely not. Couldn't be farther from the truth."

She suddenly smiles, throws her hands open. Leaps forwards to embrace me.

"Oh, Freddie, I knew it. I knew you'd come back to me. My darling, I'm sorry for shouting, but I didn't know what to think. You weren't answering your cell, the media have been going crazy, I got the press girl to say you went up the Amazon. My life has been hell!"

"Up the Amazon?"

Her over-plucked eyebrows steeple.

"Hunting tigers."

"Right."

"Freddie, I had to tell them something!"

"Okay, okay. Take it easy, old gel. Freddie's here now. Didn't find any tigers, but I'm here."

She chuckles. Clasps her hands behind my neck and pulls herself in tight.

"That's all very well," she says in a low voice, "but you're going to make this up to me." And she slips her trouser-clad knee under the duvet. Slides it between my legs. Begins to rub it against my cock and balls. But she's not very coordinated. It hurts.

Flinch. Pull my groin away.

"Not now, honey," I say.

Her face crumples. Shoulders wilt. For a second, I see pure weakness.

Then somewhere far below a bell chimes Mozart. The muscles in her face pull together. Her body snaps upright. She smiles.

"Then you can pay me back in another way. Get dressed."

"What's going on?"

She winks.

"The girl from the magazine is here."

~

This house – my house? – is full of light. We walk down vast curling marble stairs into a similarly floored lobby. Above, the tiles in the vaulted ceiling gleam like movie star teeth. Atomic sunshine pours in from a domed skylight, flooding the stairwell and hurting my bed-eyes.

It's absurdly bright. Man, there's too much light for reality to cope with. A fuzzy glow suffuses beyond the edges of things. Lines are softened and distorted. This is painful. Not sure I can handle it...

Ahead of me, Lucy blends perfectly in her white lacy shirt and white satin trousers. Outrageously expensive art lines the white walls in an irregular flow. Can I really afford this? I think, passing a Reubens, a Warhol, a Lichtenstein. And all the way down, Lucy's tiny white shoes echo like pistols in a church.

At the bottom on our right is a huge wooden front door, bolted shut. To our left, a cavernous hallway stretches out towards far-off French windows. Lucy stalks down this corridor, I'm just a step behind.

As we approach the French windows I see sunlight flooding a pale stone terrace with a vast swathe of rich lawn beyond. And a shimmering crystal pool. Of course, my pool.

Now Lucy turns to the right into a long garden room. Six huge arched windows are defined by cathedral-like shafts of warm yellow light. A vast suite made of white leather forms a wide U beneath three outrageously large chandeliers.

And still that odd feeling is with me. Every step of this place is completely familiar, and yet at the same time, totally strange.

Lucy ricochets across the richly varnished parquet towards the suite. And now I notice the girl. She sits in a huge white leather armchair. Milky, lightly freckled skin. Cascading auburn hair. Upturned nose, twinkling eyes. Quite a beauty. Standing beside her is a guy holding a large SLR camera. He has the squarest jaw and shoulders I have ever seen. Looks like a damn superhero. The girl sees us. Stands up. Her figure is outlined against the sunlit glass. Very shapely. She wears a low cut black dress that hugs her curves. Now she takes a pace forwards and holds out her hand.

"Hi. I'm Red. From Jealous Bitch magazine."

"Red, honey," says Lucy, "you look divine."

"You think?"

"Not everyone could carry that outfit, but you pull it off wonderfully."

Red's eyes narrow. She half looks back towards Captain Camera.

Lucy takes her hand. Kisses her on both cheeks.

"Red, you know Freddie, don't you?"

She smiles at me.

"I haven't yet had the pleasure," she says, and steps towards me. Kisses either cheek. Is it me, or did she make that second one linger? Just long enough so I could feel her silken hair on my neck. Inhale her rich perfume, wafting warmly up from her pronounced cleavage.

"Love what you've done with the place, Lucy. You mind if we take a few pictures?"

Lucy waves her hand like she's trying to throw it away.

"Course not, honey," she smiles. "Be my guest."

Red turns to Captain Camera. Points him towards the windows. He moves off, lifting his lens.

A tiny woman, more hen than human, enters. Who... ? Of course, Constanza. Our maid. How could I forget that? She carries a tray with drinks.

"Lemon tea?" asks Lucy.

"Please," says Red.

Constanza pours out the tea.

"So," smiles Lucy. "Shall we start?"

"Sure." Red lays a Dictaphone down. Clicks it on. "Let's start, if we can, with your latest movie. Broken-hearted Symphony. Your co-star is Brad Rock."

Lucy's eyes flick to me very quickly. She shifts in her seat. Behind Red, Captain Camera snaps a volley of shots of Lucy.

"That's correct."

"There are reports that the two of you share a remarkable chemistry on screen. What was it like working with him?"

Lucy clears her throat. "This isn't a tittle-tattle movie, Red. This is a very serious piece. My character becomes a concert pianist despite overwhelming odds-"

"Yeah," smirks Red to Captain Camera, "she only has four fingers, we know."

"Three fingers and a thumb," interrupts Lucy.

"Whatever." Red rolls her eyes. "Did you enjoy shooting with Brad?"

Now Red stares at me. Lucy shifts her weight from thigh to thigh. Captain Camera fires off some more shots.

"Red, I'm a professional actor. Shooting those scenes is not 'enjoyable' to me. It feels the same as acting sad or upset." She looks at me. "It's a part of my daily life."

Again Red is eyeing me as she speaks. Like she's watching for something. And behind her, Captain Camera circles firing all the time.

"But," says Red, "you spent three months in Tuscany Italy together this summer. Surely you must have got to know him a little."

Lucy flicks her eyes to me briefly again, then looks down at the floor.

"Brad's a wonderful actor and very good company. I have nothing but happy memories of the time we spent together. It was one of the smoothest shoots I've ever been on-"

"How about you, Freddie?"

"Huh?"

Red turns to me, eyes like darts.

"Did you mind that your fiancée was sunning herself in the Italian countryside with the world's most desirable man?"

"Uh, not really..."

"You didn't mind. How interesting," says Red.

Lucy flinches. She leans forward. Says:

"I wasn't sunning myself, Red, I was working. And if we can get back to the movie..."

But Red is still looking at me. Captain Camera is shooting like a drunken squaddie.

"Just a quick word about your career, Freddie?"

"Mine?"

"Your inventions."

"Oh, yeah, sure."

"The Unboiler."

"Aha."

"You think it should have gone through more testing before taking it to market?"

"Absolutely not," says Lucy. "Freddie is a genius."

Red turns to her.

"And you're not upset that you lost $8 million on this project?"

Lucy freezes rigid for a second. Cheeks drain to the colour of off-milk. Then suddenly she tosses her head back. Laughs.

"What's that? Half a horror movie? I don't think so."

Red's eyes narrow. She nods slowly.

"Wow. Can't imagine many relationships strong enough to take that kind of hit."

Lucy grabs my hand. Lifts it up. She's shaking.

"Fourteen years together!" she cries.

Red cocks her head a little.

"And still no wedding bells?"

Lucy solidifies again. A full minute she stays there. Any longer and she's going to crumble away. Like a sculpture made of sand. At last she fixes on another smile. Swivels it to me, then back to the interviewer. Seems to have decided something.

"Well, actually, Red, you can be the first to know. Freddie and I are engaged."

"You are?" Red jumps forward, thrusting her Dictaphone even closer.

"We are?" I ask.

"We are," nods Lucy with a squeeze of my hand.

"My Gawd! When is the ceremony? Where will it be? Who will you invite-?"

Lucy stands up. "It's going to be fabulous," she says. "Hundreds of guests and champagne. But-" She holds her palm out towards Red in a 'stop' gesture. "-all in good time, Red, honey."

And Lucy takes my hand. Starts to lead me towards the terrace.

"Can I at least see your ring?" squawks Red.

Lucy smiles over her shoulder.

"We're going to get it this afternoon. You can send your photographer round tomorrow."

And with a swish, we're gone.

~

We get as far as the arcade before I can stop her. Grab her hand. Spin her back. Press her back against the low tiled wall that serves as a balustrade. Past her shoulder the brilliant fountains patter in the sunshine.

Stare at her for a long moment.

"What's going on?" I snap.

"Freddie, I can't stand it any longer!" she cries, her moist blue eyes fluttering like the water behind. "Fourteen years we've been together. The whole world is wondering why we aren't married. Things have to change. We haven't made love in months. We have this wonderful life, but you seem like you're... somewhere else. We have to either part or get married. And I don't think I can handle leaving you. I love you, Freddie! You're the only man who ever saw more than my looks."

"Don't say that..." I mutter.

"Why not? You wanted to be with me, not some selfish idea of what I am. They think I'm a fool because you're not some famous millionaire, but I know better. Who befriended me when I was a lonely student? Who helped me get my first break? Who moved to America and stuck by me when things didn't happen for so long. I know you really love me. You always have. Isn't that so? You have always loved me, haven't you, my darling M'sieur Kederick?"

"Oh, Lucy," I say. "You're so beautiful–"

She cocks her head on one side.

"That's not what I asked," she says abruptly. "Do you love me?"

And I want to say yes, but no sound will come.

Lucy's eyebrows crinkle. Her face reddens. Her mouth drops.

"Freddie... ?" she whimpers.

God, I want to say it. But the word sticks in my mouth, like a glob of dirty glue on my tongue.

Now she's looking really upset. Christ, think she's going to have a fit. Her face is stretched to breaking point. This is it. Going to get it good and proper. The storm is here... all I can do is hunch my shoulders and wait for the waves to break...

"Madame."

We both whip round.

Constanza. Bobbing and rubbing her wings together.

"Not now, Constanza!" snaps Lucy.

"I am sorry, miss Lucy, but zere is a strange man here."

"Strange?"

Constanza turns up her lower lip.

"Man not smell so good."

"Send him away!" orders Lucy.

"I tried. But he say he no go until he talk to Meester Freddie."

Lucy turns to me, watery blue eyes boiling.

"Nothing to do with me," I say.

The muscles in Lucy's jaw tighten.

"Alright," I say to her. Then I turn to Constanza. "Where is he?"

~

The figure standing by the shelves looks like a giant gobstopper on legs – but instead of layers of sugar, he's comprised of layers of straggly, dirty clothes. Muddy red hair sprays wildly from an oily collar at the top of the clothes. The creature's head, I presume. Its face is turned away from me, towards the wall of books. It appears to be intently watching a filthy black finger which the creature is running along the spines of some leatherbound volumes. And even from here, I know Constanza was right. This thing smells.

"Can I help you?" I say.

The figure doesn't turn round, just moves his arm down and presses his dirty digit along more pillars of immaculate leather.

"Some of those volumes are very valuable," I say. "I'd rather you didn't-"

"Are your college books here?" it says. "Tell me you haven't thrown any out."

Uh, what?

"Uh, what?"

"Your college books. It would be nice if you had kept them..."

"Who are you?" I ask.

"Ah! Here we go. The very fellow. Lives of the Obscure Saints," he says, and pulls a volume from the shelf. He opens it briefly, checks for something, then snaps it shut and lifts his head to heaven. Still his back is towards me.

But there's something familiar about that figure. And something very odd about it too. Don't understand what's going on here at all. Not sure I like this. Starting to feel distinctly wobbly.

"Listen, I don't know who you are or-" I start.

But then the figure turns to face me and I lose the power of speech.

"Would you mind if I borrowed this one?" says Dougal.

~

"Vodka and lime?"

Dougal smiles and shakes his head. Bits fall out of his beard.

Open up the little fridge that sits in the shade behind the diving board. Pull out my half-pint tumbler. Crack some ice into it. Toss in a couple of lime slices from the jar. And pour in the Stolly. Right the way to the top.

"You sure you don't want one? This is very beneficial."

"No, really."

"Would offer you something else, but that's all there is."

"Honestly, I'm fine."

Take a long pull of my drink. Nasal passages smart a little but the spirit goes down sweetly. Turn and walk over to the pool edge. Taking care not to spill my drink I climb on my inflatable Yogi Bear. Lay back with my head on his tail.

"You can take Boo-Boo if you like," I say, pointing to the other inflatable which bobs in the deep end.

"Not much of a swimmer," he says, sitting on a lounger at the side of the pool.

"Suit yourself," I say, secretly glad. Don't want his filth all over my pool toys.

Push myself off from the side. Lying back, I drop my shades over my eyes and float in the sun. Take another slurp of my drink. Turn to face Dougal. He's still clutching the book he took from my library, hugging it to his scruffy chest like a dead baby.

"So," I say. "You're looking good."

"Don't lie, Freddie," he smiles. "I look terrible."

He's right. So right. We all change, I know, but this is ridiculous. Last time I saw him he was this sparky little guy. But now... where once his brown eyes shone brightly, now they lie dully in his head. Like there's a cloud hanging constantly in his soul. Confidence and creativity no longer fizz from his features. Guy looks beaten.

Timid. His skin is pale and straining. Once he was slim – athletic almost. Now he's simply fat. Poor bugger. Would reach out and give him a hug. If he wasn't so damn smelly.

"When was the last time we saw each other? University, was it?"

"The last time you saw me was fourteen years ago," he replies. "At the airport. When you and Lucy left to come here."

"Of course," I nod. "When she came out for her audition. Was only tagging along for the jolly and now look at us," I say, splashing myself out of a cloud shadow.

Dougal smiles. In a strange, inward way. "But," he says quietly, "the last time I saw you was twenty-eight years ago. In the castle."

Take a sip of my drink.

"What are you talking about?"

"Just before the Vindendraam, don't you remember?"

"Woah. Hang on. To start with, you said twenty-eight. That's a mistake. Twenty-eight years ago I was five. And second, I wasn't in the castle before the Vindendraam. I was... waiting in my bedroom while... my..."

"Your alternate self."

Wait. What's happening to reality? Everything is starting to ripple and float like the sunshine on the water.

"Th-thi-this doesn't make sense..."

"I'm afraid it does. Don't you remember how you ended up shagging Lucy?"

"Down at the Beach Ball... got Clive out of the way... went to the cave..."

"But who helped you?"

Try to think hard. But it's like wading through treacle.

"Uh... there was this guy... scruffy, a bit mad... looked a bit like..."

"You."

Shit he's right. There is a memory there. But it's fuzzy and slippery. Like it wants to stay hidden.

"Yeah, I suppose..."

Dougal leans forward on his lounger. Points a grubby paw at me.

"It was you, Freddie. Your older self come back through time to get you laid."

"But... I've never invented a time machine."

"Not in this reality. But you did in another reality. Otherwise this reality wouldn't exist. Your randy alter ego would have had nowhere to come back from. Do you see?"

"No. Need more vodka," I say, reaching for the mini-fridge.

"I'll bet you do. It took me eight years to even get close to understanding this."

He leans forward. His eyes narrow. Start to roll a bit. Nostrils flare.

"Get this. Freddie, I'm forty-seven years old."

"Forty-seven! But we were in the same year..."

"Listen to me, Freddie. I was only in 2002 because I was dragged there by your alternate self where he then left me. Whether he did this out of lust-induced frenzy or simple malice is still up for debate. Either way, I have been living the fourteen years since that date for a second time. This has not been fun. They were not good years for me. To start with, there are two Dougals still in the world. My younger self, who this version of you last saw when you stepped on the plane to Hollywood – he's currently living in Edinburgh. Working in Ballantrae's bookshop. And there's me. The interdimensional tramp. Trying to avoid my younger self and get by waiting for this day. Which I did, because I knew that you had to return. My only variable was your location, but I guessed right – she really did fall in love with you."

Tip the bottle into the glass. Take a hefty swig.

"Wait wait wait," I say, waving my arm at the house. "I've been here for years."

"Yes and no," he says. "Before you arrived-" he checks his watch, "-by my calculations around an hour ago – this reality that you 'know' had never existed. But now you're here, well, that's all changed too."

"But then how can you be here? Just as this version of me hasn't invented a time machine, so you can never have travelled in it, so you can't have been stuck in the past, so you can't be here now, right?"

"Wrong. Your reality has changed. Because you're the one who just went through time. Mine is still the same."

"But they're incompatible..."

"Yes. It's a paradox and it's not a paradox. A pararadox, I call it." And he sits there, nodding to himself proudly, like he's just invented the corkscrew. "Thing about a pararadox is it's not stable. Don't you notice how this reality is a little wobbly round the edges?"

"Yeah, sort of..."

"You see, Freddie, you were right. Like you once said, the cosmos wears Levis. The fabric of spacetime is very hard to rip. Reality doesn't want this. It wants to settle back down."

"Will it?"

"Remember, both realities exist in your soul at the same time. That's where the damage is going to happen." And he leers at me. In his filthy clothes and straggly hair.

"There's nothing wrong with my soul," I say, and take another cool slug of spirit.

"No?"

"No."

"So you won't want to hear about Penelope, then?"

"Penelope?"

"The girl you left in both realities."

"Shit, Dougal, I'm sure she got over it."

"Twice."

"Yes, twice!" Pause for a second. Shit, he's infuriating. Have to say, don't quite know why, but I sort of do want to know... "So, ah, what did happen to her?"

He smiles.

"She married Matthew."

"Glasses geek?"

He nods.

"But he was a complete fuckhead!"

"They're happy enough, I suppose. No kids, though. And the last time I saw her she looked a little... lost."

"Hah!" I snort. "That's it. 'Sall clear now. That's why you're here, isn't it? Lay a guilt trip on me. Make me feel sorry for her, or something."

"Freddie-"

"Well it won't work, you hear?"

Dougal's getting up...

"Lucy Sugar wants to marry me and that's what I'm going to do!" I continue.

...he's walking slowly round the pool...

"She's beautiful!"

...bending down to the mini-fridge...

"Rich!"

...taking a lime from the bowl on top...

"Famous!"

...walking towards me...

"The whole world's in love with her!"

...leaning down and what's he doing now... ?

"So I don't need you poking about trying to help me and – Mmmppfff!"

Bloody hell. He's stuffed the lime in my mouth. Now he looms over me, his vast bulk blocking out the sun.

"You really are rather self-centred, aren't you?" says Dougal, half to himself.

Bloody hell. Don't remember him ever speaking to me like that before.

"Have you even considered," he goes on, "that maybe I'm not here to help you?"

"Mmmmmmmmfff!"

He drops to one knee. Jabs a meaty finger at me.

"Freddie, you made me a promise once. Now I'm here to redeem it." He rocks back on his haunches. Draws his shoulders high. "Get off that inflatable bear and show me your bed."

~

At first it's cool inside. Refreshing after the heat outside. But by the time we pass the Lichtenstein at the top of the stairs the air is wobbling. Face feels clammy. My stomach sways and lurches. Wish I'd slowed down a bit on that vodka.

"This way," I say, leading him into the calm whiteness of the bedroom.

Dougal waddles in beside me. Stops. "There it is," he mutters, nodding gently, eyes focused. And he starts edging towards the bed like it's a wild animal.

"Fourteen years I've waited for this," he says, his voice shaking. "I can't believe it's going to happen."

Poor sod. He's clearly mad.

"Right," I say. "So we really travelled through time on this?"

He nods, his eyes cold.

"I wish I could remember-" I smile, and then suddenly the world starts to wobble. Great ripples flow down the walls and across the floor. Dougal starts to pulse in and out like a giant hairy heart. And the bed... the bed suddenly looks like a time machine.

"Christ, that Stolly kicks," I mutter.

"That's no hangover," smiles Dougal. "You remember, don't you? Your secondary reality is returning to your conscious brain. You see, it's still in there."

Why does he have to be so right? It's true, I can sort of remember. Travelling between times, but why? Oh forget it. Humour him.

"Let's just get on with this," I snap. "Got the wedding of the century to organise. Where do you want to go?"

He reaches in to his jacket pocket. Takes out a tatty blue piece of paper. Eyes it for a second. Is he about to cry? No. He recovers. Hands it to me.

"Here," he says.

Look at the piece of paper. It's a letter. A love letter. Starting, "My dearest darling Dougal". It is unfinished. There are dark spots of mud or something in the corner.

"Okay," I say, clearing my throat. "Think this goes in here." And I put it into the timeframe reference hopper. "Now we need to work out how much displacement you need so you can return..."

"Oh don't bother with that. I'm not coming back."

"Er, what?"

He stares at me, face calm.

"Fourteen years is quite long enough in this reality. I'm going to stay there until... well, let's just say that this will be my last journey."

"But how am I going to get the bed back?" I cry.

He shrugs.

"Buy another one."

KERRLAANGG! Bang my fist against the frame so hard the whole bed shakes.

"Don't want another one!" I bark. "This bed has... history."

"Of your alternate life. You don't need that any more, right?"

What the hell does he mean by that?

"Are you trying to upset me?" I snap. "What do you care why I want the bed back?"

"I don't," he says calmly. "You're the one getting uptight."

"Not fucking uptight, okay?"

"Okay," says Dougal with the most irritating smile I ever saw.

God, he's winding me up. Did I really promise him this in some alternate reality? Can't believe I'd be so stupid. Feel like telling him to fuck off right here and now. But the weird thing is, I sort of do remember. Plus, he's so convinced, it would now be more hassle not to help him. Best go along with it.

Glower at him. "Coming with you," I say.

"If you like," he replies, "but please remember that this isn't on my account."

"Yeah yeah," I say. "Now, we'd better move this out of the way."

And I reach under the bed. Pull out a stack of muck.

"That's a lot of porn," says Dougal, eyes wide.

"Yeah well, if you don't get any action for a year, you have to improvise, you know?"

"A year?!" he says, wiry eyebrows rocketing up his forehead.

"And when was the last time you got laid, Casanova?" I snap.

Hold his eyes for a second. He shakes his tufty head then looks away.

"Oh Freddie," he says softly. "I think we should go now."

"Fine. We're all set. Now all we have to do is climb aboard..." We get up onto the bed. The springs sag and moan. "...pre-amp the zeiss gates... and turn it on–"

"What are you doing?"

Dougal didn't say that. Neither did I. Came from behind us. Slowly turn round.

Shit, it's Lucy. Standing in the doorway, her hair wild, fists shaking by her sides.

"Nothing, my sweet," I say, but my right hand has already flipped the switch. There's a hefty roar and the bed starts vibrating. Clatters and clanks echo off the pristine white walls, doubling and redoubling their sinister volume as they maraud through the house.

"There's something going on here," she says, advancing towards us.

The shaking increases in violence. The bed's brass feet eek and scratch on the tiled floor.

"I-I-I-If I told you, darling, you really wouldn't believe me."

"Freddie," says Dougal quietly over my shoulder. Spin to look at him. "Tell her the truth," he says, his dog eyes solemn.

"You're leaving me, aren't you?" she says, her voice level, her eyes angry.

"What?" I say, turning back to look at Lucy. Her eyes seem more lined now than ever. Her skin pale and slack. Her bones cold and brittle. "Don't be silly," I say.

"Where are you going!?" she shrieks, suddenly advancing

towards the bed.

Laugh a little. But I don't think it sounds that funny.

"Not going anywhere, my lovely. It'll all be over in the blink of an eye."

"Freddie, don't leave me!"

"How could I leave you, you beautiful thing..." but the words die in my throat as sadness crashes over me like a wave on St Mary's beach. It spins me round – but also washes my mind clear. It's a heavy wave of truth. For the first time in a long time, I see things as they are. Written there in the torn lines on her face. Poor, poor Lucy.

She's really in love with me.

"She deserves more than this," says Dougal.

Whirl on him.

"Will you shut the fuck-"

KRAA-ZZINNNGG!

The bed leaps into the air. Huge snakes of white-hot electricity whip out from the bedposts. Form a writhing orb around the bed. Dougal and I sprawl on our backs. Lucy is thrown spinning to the floor.

The orb begins to shrink.

Lucy hauls herself onto one elbow. God, look at her. That beautiful face scarred with tears. Crystal eyes dull as lead. Her skinny body cracking with strain.

Want to be nice to her. Want to make it better. But I can't say anything. Words won't come. Want to tell her the compassion I feel, but my mouth has trouble with these strange new forms.

"We can go and get the ring this afternoon," I hear myself say.

And infinity collapses on us.

~

Birdsong.

Simple, clear and sweet. Above the drowsy sigh of the wind. And a quiet ocean swell, plashing on shingly sand. Now a smell –

279

the bright yellow aroma of spring pollen.

Open my eyes. Blue sky. In it, nothing but a black dot. Hovering. The skylark who's making such lovely music. Hello, my friend. What a nice song. So happy, I think... think I'm going to cry. Poor Lucy... what a waste...

"You ready?"

Look round. Dougal is standing by the side of the bed. Behind him is a hillside, sloping down to a small cliff. Beyond that, a beach of the purest white sand. Turquoise waters with the gentlest white breakers. Bed looks so odd out here. Unnatural.

For a second he stares at me. There's a bluey sadness in his eyes. And he seems to be shaking his head with the tiniest, almost imperceptible movements. Like he's so disappointed in me he can't bear to show it.

"Sea Horse Bay," he says softly. Then he turns from me to look out over the ocean. "Come on," he says. "Got a little walking to do." And he strides down the grassy hillside.

Without a word, I rise and follow.

~

Ahead of us the building crouches on the hillside like a sleepy squirrel. An old grey stone building of two floors and maybe six neat little windows. Perched high on a twig-like lane right up on the headland. Below us, toy fishing boats bob in the jealous arms of the harbour. On the other side of the water, crazy houses cluster in straggly groups like kids in a playground. Beyond them the sun flares on the frighteningly blue sea.

What the hell is it? Fisherman's mission? Manse? School?

Here we are at the doors... a brass sign... what does it say?

Shit.

"COROSAY ISLAND CLINIC."

Suddenly Dougal stops in front of the door. Turns back. Crosses the road to the tumbledown wall opposite. Scans the crowded spring verge. Drunken bees sway through the air around him, singing their pissed pollen songs. He reaches down. Plucks a pair of bluebells. The flowers look tiny in his pudgy ham paw.

Dougal steps back over the road towards me.

"Come on," he says, and leads the way in through the front door.

A small reception corridor. Nobody at the reception desk. A single door opening off on either side. Ahead, a worn stone staircase beneath a large window. Hanging from the ceiling, three signs with three arrows: 'Dr McLeish's office - left', 'Nurse Lenzie's office - right', and 'The Ward - upstairs'.

Dougal doesn't hesitate. Paces straight for the stairs and starts to climb. Follow him up. At the top of the stairs a landing turns to the right. After five paces we reach a door. Dougal pushes it open.

Four white metal beds. Four windows set high in the stone wall. Each bed lies in its own calm bolt of brilliant sunlight.

First three beds are empty.

The last one lies by the far wall. Can't see whether it's occupied or not. It's surrounded by a huge, hulking mass of strange machinery.

Dougal judders to a halt. Sweat shines on his forehead like dew. His face is silhouetted dark against the first bright window. Lower lip trembles. Eyebrows twitch. He takes a sharp breath in. The air snags in his throat. He coughs. Gulps once. Twice. Three times. Breathes again. The air flows in a quavering breath. He limps forward. Slowly. Like a cat that's just been hit by a car. Follow behind him.

A dozen heavy paces and we're beside the machine. A pair of tarnished metal trolleys form the base. Stacked on them is a series of large black boxes. A giant worm of evil spaghetti connects these to a dull grey control panel crammed with dials, switches, old fashioned LEDs. To the right of this, a large glass tube hangs from a gallows-like stand. Inside is a strange cloth and rubber valve. It's both coldly artificial and horrifyingly organic. Folded like an accordion it rises and falls within its see-through sheath, clunking and panting as it goes. Pssshtttt-hoooo. Pssshtttt-hoooo.

Dougal steps, ever so slowly, past the machine to the end of the bed. Moving on tiptoe, I edge behind him – and into him, for suddenly he has become a rock. Not moving, not breathing. Just staring down at the bed before him.

Because now, for the first time, we can see that the sinister mechanical monstrosity is attached to a patient.

At least, I think it's a patient. It lies in the bed under ice-white cotton sheets. It is shaped like a body, bulging and swelling like a frozen ocean. But there is no sign of life. Just a white wasteland of bandages and tubes.

Look down at the chart at the exposed metal of the bottom of the bed. Check the chart. The name at the top is...

Mackay, Rose.

Rose.

Ah.

PSSSHTTTT-HOOOO. The metal tube clunks and wheezes loud in my ear.

Dougal is still immobile. Doesn't say anything for a long, long time. His body is static. His features dead. Then, finally, he lifts his hand, straining like it weighs a hundred tons, and points to the bandages. To where a face would be.

"Isn't she beautiful?" he breathes.

Nod. Try to smile.

"The most beautiful creature I ever saw."

PSSSHTTTT-HOOOO.

"What happened?" I ask.

"She fell," says Dougal softly, without turning round.

Want to ask how, why, where, but the words swell in my throat and won't pass. Dougal seems to sense my difficulty. He goes on, still facing the bed:

"Sitting on the cliffs, she was, looking out to sea. Over to the mainland to where I was. Writing one of her lovely letters to me."

He says nothing for a long second.

"And... she just fell."

PSSSHTTTT-HOOOO.

He looks away from the letter up to the window. Sunlight streams on his ancient face. "Fishermen saw her on the rocks. Brought her here. Soon as they told me, I came. You remember? It was just before the end of term. May. First year. But it's a long way, and... I was too late. I didn't make it in time. She..." he takes a breath, "...she was gone before I arrived."

PSSSHTTTT-HOOOO.

"But why come back now?" I blurt. "We could have gone back to yesterday! Warned her about the loose rocks. Then maybe-"

He turns to me, smiles the saddest smile you ever saw.

"Freddie, what's done is done. What's gone is gone. I'm not here to save her."

He takes a step to the left. Pulls over the grey plastic chair that sits wonkily beneath the next window. Sits by her side. Lays the two bluebells by her bandaged arm. Just looks at her for a while. Then finally:

"Hello, my love," he whispers.

Clears his throat.

Drops his eyes to his scruffily clad body. "Guess I look a little rough to you." Glances back at her. "I... I... I've found it hard, you see, getting old on my own." He leans in closer. Talks faster. "It would have been so easy with you, my darling Rose. Taking the years together. Seeing your face change. Watching as the lines came. I would have loved to see your lines! They'd look so funny. We could look at them together in the mirror and laugh. And we'd grab each other's chubby bellies and laugh at how silly and old we both looked!" He stops for a second. Catches a breath. The sunlight glints off the wheezing machine.

"But now... now... now you won't ever grow old and fat like me. Forever nineteen. That's what you'll be. Always slim and bright-cheeked and happy..." his voice fades. He suddenly lifts his head up, a huge smile shining on his face. "You know what? It's just occurred to me − I'll be forever nineteen to you too!" He chuckles a little to himself. "It's nice that I'll be like that. What a happy thought. Yes, I'll be forever young to you, my love. And you to me."

PSSSHTTTT-HOOOO! goes the huge metal tube.

Dougal drops his double chin onto his chest.

Sighs.

Then reaches one grubby paw into the inside pocket of his battered old jacket. Pulls out an the dusty piece of paper he put into the hopper. Holds it like it's holy.

"I came today for a reason. I came because there's one thing I wanted to ask of you. Before I left the island. You said I'd see you soon, but, well, twenty eight years I've been waiting and I know you can't hear me, but I want to say it anyway." With extreme delicacy, he unfolds the piece of paper. Once. Twice. Three times. "This is the last poem I ever wrote. I finished it the day before your accident." He looks down at the raggedy paper in his hand. It shakes as if in an imaginary breeze. Then Dougal begins to read:

### "A DOG WHO'S LOST

*Like rhubarb without custard*
*Or ham what's got no mustard*
*Like a skylark without wings*
*And a playpark with no swings*

*A door without a latch*
*Socks that do not match*
*Fingers without thumbs*
*Or sticks what's lost their drums*

*Like Bond with no Martini*
*Or a king without his queenie*
*Like Tom apart from Jerry*
*A Christmas that's not merry*

*A singer with no song*
*A ding without a dong*

*Lemon minus lime*
*A poem with no rhyme*

*Ying away from yang*
*A whiz without a bang*
*Skiing without snow*
*A Frenchman sans chapeau*

*Like a jigsaw short a piece*
*Athens without Greece*
*A sculptor shy a chisel*
*Scotland wi' nae drizzle*

*The wind that blows no willow*
*The bed that has no pillow*
*Like a house without a roof*
*A dog who's lost his woof...*

*What I mean, my darling bride*
*Is, without you by my side*
*Like all these things and more*
*I'd be less*
*Than what I was before."*

He casts the paper to one side. Drops to one knee on the linoleum. Takes a deep breath and his voice shakes as he says:

"Rose, will you marry me?"

PSSSHTTTT-HOOOO.

PSSSHTTTT-HOOOO.

PSSSHTTTT-HOOOO.

Who knows how long we stay like that. Dougal leaning by his unconscious girl, head bowed, his tears pit-pattering on the pristine sheet. Me, staring at them, feeling my own love coursing hot and shameful down my face. The machine breathing. The sun shining.

After a million years, maybe, Dougal lifts his head. Gets to his feet. Bends forward. Leans in very close to her, his lips almost touching the bandages. He whispers: "Sleep well, Rose, my pretty island flower. Sleep well."

A final, single tear plops from the end of his nose. Then he stands up. Turns. Starts to walk away. Move after him.

"You okay?" I ask.

"Oh, couldn't be better," he smiles. "I've found eternal youth."

And then I see the strangest thing, just as he moves past me into the corridor. For although his deep brown eyes are flooded with tears, the cloud in them has lifted. They glisten freshly, like rain on a summer bloom.

~

We walk along the edge of the cliff. Far below our feet, the sea smashes its creamy brains out against the rocks. Gulls circle the carnage, cackling.

Behind us, a little higher up on the rolling hillside, the bed stands on its own. At first it looked weird out there in the field. But now a couple of rabbits have hopped closer to investigate. They nibble clover by the edge of the rumpled sheet that dangles off the side. Now it looks as natural as anything else.

The really weird thing now is how calm Dougal seems. Looks completely content, just staring out to sea. The wind tossing his hair around. Tugging at his beard. His eyes as level and bright as the horizon.

Must be thinking about Rose. Times they spent here on this beautiful land. Looking at the sea together. The spot they always sat, maybe. The plans they made here. Poor bitch. Poor bugger. All he wanted to do was marry her. Live out his years with her. His one girl. Then she goes and dies. Falls right off this edge here. They probably sat here a hundred thousand times. Then once she just falls off. Onto those snaggled rocks down there. Shit, no wonder he lost the plot.

And then suddenly reality lurches.

Clouds scud over the sun. Superfast they stream. Like the world is being spun on the finger of a cosmic basketball player.

Giant images swoop into being in the swirling sky before me. Each one rushes towards me, is crystal clear for a second, then zooms away into ether to be followed instantly by another...

...it's Pen... walking along the beach with me in St Mary's... a foggy day in winter... the lights of the town are soft and diffused... the sea is flat grey... she's a splash of colour with her green eyes and red wellies... she's smiling at me... laughing at one of my shit jokes... no one else ever laughs at them... she does...

And now it's like some supernatural sluice gate has opened. A torrent of memories pours through...

... her paddington coat... the woolly sock-slipper things she wears around the house... the cheery way she talks to her fish... her endless, endless patience... her love of meatballs... the way she sips her tea... her smile... her smile... her smile...

Now there's a sickening twist in the motion. The images change. They come tearing up from the sea in a black, infected cloud. Swarming and roaring they zoom in at me like spectral nightmares, and at the head of the horde is...

... Lucy, but not young and beautiful, instead her face is twisted in pain... she cries up to me... the agony is melting her skin into flesh into bone she swirls and screams... the years are wearing away her beautiful face... no make up, no diets can stop this... and now the pain is the cloud itself, a swirling amalgam of silences, absences, rumours, the endless, endless loneliness... and through it all her ice-blue eyes are crying... crying... crying...

It's too much! There are so many! So black and hideous! Swooping at me, filthy dark ghosts of desolation. Oh God, no, got to get away. Got to run. There's Pen on the beach. She's smiling. Her arms are open, she's laughing now, the waves are splashing her wellies. Her simple brown hair is bouncing in slow motion. Want to run my fingers through it, bury my face in her neck. Bathe in the sweet scent of her. Go to her now. Got to.

The phantoms are closing.…… got to go… move forwards… leap… now!… LEAP NOW!!

"WOAH! Hey. Where you off to??"

Huh?

Look down. Dougal grips the front of my silk shirt in one iron paw. Two inches from my right foot, the cliff sheers away into sickening emptiness.

"You come back here, okay?" he says and gently but very firmly, he hauls me back from the edge. My bones suddenly turn to water and I collapse to the ground.

"You alright?"

My chest heaves up and down. An angry bee sways round my head like some tiny Liverpudlian drunk.

"D-D-Dizzy," I whisper.

He nods.

"More memories?"

"Hundreds… scary… had to go to her… "

He kneels down beside me on the daisy-strewn grass. Feels good to have him there. Like the earth below me. The faint rhythmic crash of the sea. The wind in the tall grass. And, high above, the skylark.

My breathing slows. Blood cools.

"Have they gone?" he asks eventually.

Look up. The white clouds and blue sky are back. But the whole world has a dark tinge about it, like the shadow of the spectres is in my head. Just behind my eyes.

"Can't go back to California," I say.

"I know."

Lift myself up one elbow, facing him.

"Maybe I can go talk to Pen now…"

"No, Freddie," he says gently. "She's married. Why would she leave her husband for some crazy old guy who broke her heart at uni?"

Think about this for a moment as the skylark is joined by his girl. The pair of them are belting it out now, hovering right above us.

"You know," I say, "that's pretty much what I did to her."

"And would she do it to you?"

"Never in a million years."

"Well," he says, "there you go."

God, I feel so ashamed. It's like I'm a scar on this hill, a black unnatural thing. An open cast mine on a paradise island.

"This is it. Stuck here forever. In a reality I deserve. Forever."

"Not forever," he smiles. "You'll die in forty or fifty years."

Glare at him.

"That was a joke."

Glare some more.

"Sorry. Not very funny."

"If only there was some way I could get to him... "

"Who?"

"You know."

"Oh, him. You really want to?"

"Man, what would I give to be able to go back and give him a good talking to. What a fool. What a bloody wasting idiot..."

Roll over. Bury my face in the soft grass.

WHUMMP!!

Something heavy drops on the grass by my head. Throw myself sideways.

Keep my eyes screwed shut. Nothing bad happens. Open them slowly.

There on the grass, inches from my eyes, is a book. A large, square, heavy textbook. On the spine I can see the title:

Lives of the Obscure Saints.

Sit up a little. Look at the front. An ancient illumination of St Mungo having his chin bandage blessed. A bolt has been drawn through his neck with felt pen. He also has a giant Tippex cock that loops out and back to his face. Tippex spunk splashes his tonsured head. Can remember the lecture I did that in. Drinking premixed gin and tonic from a Flintstones flask. Sad, infantile, but somehow I can't help but smile.

"What do you want me to do with this?" I say.

"What you've never done before," he says. "Open it."

Lift the volume. Start to thumb it – and the book flops right open to the centre. To where, pressed flat in the pages, is an object.

A yellow rose.

"Is that... ?" Can't be.

He nods.

Take the ancient flower out. It's fragile and strong at the same time. A concentration of beauty. So perfect. So real. For a second I feel that a whole life is contained in its dry and curling leaves and the weight's too much to hold. It's all I can do to keep it in my quaking fingers as I drop forward onto my hands and knees as if in prayer.

For a long minute I do nothing. Just stay there, hunched, my hands on the ground, cupping the flower. My face hovering just above, catching the essence of the tired petals. My body pointing out to the high sun that glows over the shimmering sea.

The rampaging hordes have gone. One image alone hangs in the blue sky of my brain. A girl in a restaurant. A lonely, scared girl. Sitting opposite me and a million miles away.

And then the tears come, violent and white like the waves below, and for a long long time I can do nothing but be washed and beaten by them.

Then at last they dry. My breathing is no longer choked. Now I sit up. Dougal is looking down at me. He also seems to have been crying.

"Thought it might come in handy," says Dougal under the breeze.

"Thank you," I breathe almost soundlessly. "Thank you, thank you, thank you."

Get to my feet.

"Come on then," I say, turning towards the bed and holding out my hand.

"Oh no," he says shaking his head. "I've had quite enough time-travelling for one lifetime."

"You're staying here?"

He nods quickly.

"Needs a lot of looking at, does this ocean."

"But if this doesn't work... I won't see you again... "

"That's true," he says.

And for a moment the wind drops. The skylarks stop singing. The sea ceases to crash or even sigh. There's no noise in the world between us now.

We take a step towards each other at the same moment. Put out our arms. We hug. Not for long. As long as it takes to know you have a friend. An hour, maybe.

Then we separate. Over his shoulder I see the bed tilting on its clovered slope. It's now completely surrounded by rabbits.

"See you soon," I say.

"I hope so," says Dougal, with a smile.

Then I walk past him up the hill towards the bed, reach it without looking back, and climb on for the second last time.

~

Can hear him coming before he even comes in. Muttering and swearing down the little corridor that connects the body of the restaurant with the gents.

"Twelve fifty. Can you believe it? Twelve pound fucking fifty... "

Climb off the bed and shake the cosmos from my hair.

The door slams opens. And in he comes. God what a mess. Hair all over the place, skin pasty and spotty. Purple hammocks slung under his eyes. And his clothes – a tramp would be ashamed of that outfit. He's just made no effort at all.

He stalks straight for the zinc trough on the right hand side. Throws his eyes briefly towards the sinks where I sit on the edge of the mattress. He clocks my feet, but doesn't notice the bed.

"Can you believe what these fuckers are charging for a fish?" he says, as he undoes his flies.

"Twelve pounds fifty," I say softly.

"For a fucking fish!" he bellows, and starts to pee into the zinc trough.

SSPPLLLLPSSSPLSSSPPSSS...

"I'll bet it's very tasty," I say.

"It would fucking have to be," he replies.

"Why don't you find out?" I say.

Pause. He tries to turn round, but he's still peeing.

SSPPLLLLPSSSPLSSSPPSSS...

Manages to get his head halfway round over his shoulder. Clocks the bed.

"Usually the weirdos in bogs are sat on stools and they charge me a quid to dry my hands. What are you going to charge me for?"

"My purpose today is to point out to you that it's okay to be scared."

"What the...?"

SSPPLLLLPSS–

He stops peeing. Shakes. Tucks. Buttons. Turns.

Sees me for the first time. Takes a step back as my image filters onto his brain. Bumps his backside against the urinal gutter. Puts his hand out to steady himself. Nowhere for it go but against the zinc wall. Into the water that gently dribbles from the slender pipe. With a curse he pushes himself away. Stares at me even harder.

"Who the fuck are you?"

"Who do I look like?"

He doesn't say anything for a moment. The snarling snappiness that was such a permanent part of his features slackens. His face calms.

"You look like... me."

"That's right," I nod.

He takes a step towards me. Examines me closely. Suddenly it feels hotter in here. He's feeling it too. Diamonds of sweat creep from the pores on his forehead.

"What are you, some kind of long-lost relative? That pervert uncle Keith who no one talks about. That's it–"

"You know who I am."

He swallows. My mouth is dry, so his must be getting unbearable.

"No, I don't–"

"You're staring at yourself, Freddie. An alternate version of yourself from a parallel time dimension three weeks in the future, but still yourself."

He steps sideways again. Cocks his head on one side. Quickly jerks his sleeve across his dripping brow.

"Some sort of fucking wind-up... " he murmurs.

Shake my head at him.

"Does this look like a wind up?" I say, pointing to the bed which hums and growls behind me like a Rottweiler. "You invent this tomorrow. So you can go back in time and shag Lucy Sugar."

For a second his eyes brighten. He leans forward.

"Really? How cool!"

Ignore him. Take a step forwards.

"You want to shag Lucy Sugar because, deep in the heart you keep from the world, you're terrified."

He crinkles his brows together. Barks a short laugh.

"What have I got to be terrified of?"

Take another step towards him. My face right in his. Can see the sweat running with the dirt. Smell the stale wine and the nauseous food seeping out of his sickly-white skin. He backs away from me.

"There's no point in lying to me, Freddie. We're the same person. What you feel right now, I have also felt. Only now, I recognise it."

He narrows his eyes. Can hear him start to breathe faster. A tiny pause, then I press on, my voice echoing off zinc and porcelain.

"You want an example?" I say. "You've spent half the meal so far fretting about the Unboiler. Even though you know in your heart it is a stupid idea that will never, ever, work and that Clive was right to make a fool of you."

He sucks in a huge breath. His eyes widen. Each white looks like a satellite map of the Amazon basin, the tributaries running wild with lurid blood.

"The other half," I continue, "you've been staring at your girl, wondering at the fear on her face. But you've not helped her. Not been there for her. You've given her nothing. And in the end, you're going to make that brave woman beg."

Now his head starts to shake. His body recoils like a snake. It's unbearably close in here now. Like a jungle. Can feel my own sweat start to flow. His clothes are starting to darken.

Suddenly I shoot out my right hand. Grab his shoulder. He yelps in surprise.

"Come here," I say, firmly.

"No... " he wails, shaking and quivering.

My fingers close on his wasted muscles like pincers. With easy violence I pull him over towards the mirror.

"Look at yourself."

We both face the mirror. Our identical yet different faces framed by a poorly painted view of Naples.

"Look at your eyes." But he won't look. Forces me to grab his chin. Grip my other flesh hard. Make him look.

"Out there just now you were looking at Pen. At the lines by her eyes. You thought she looks old. And scared. But look at these lines," I say, jabbing my finger to the corner of his eyes. "How's that for scared?"

And suddenly all resistance drops from him. He stares at himself, transfixed by some horrific self-realisation. He lifts a grubby hand to his own face. Touches the lines which cluster like graves on his face, deeper and more savage than hers will ever be.

His eyebrows arch in silent panic. His mouth opens but the scream never comes. For a second all colour drains from his eyes. In its place spins a vast and bottomless nothing. A vile cavity has opened right into his selfish soul. Terror grips me now. The urge to run is strong. This man is utterly lost and it's almost too much to bear.

But I must face it. So he can.

"You see it now," I say. "The fear."

His nod is barely there, but I see it.

"Fear of failure, disrespect, inadequacy, monogamy, but below it all, swallowing them all in its foul vastness... the fear of honesty."

He stares on into the abyss. Cringes from it like a kicked dog. Any second now he's going to be lost in it forever...

Take a deep breath. Lean in close to him.

"But you can make it go."

He twitches a little.

"All of it. Every last fear could drop from you now. And you would never see those lines ever again."

He swallows – tiny cracks echo in his throat like flaking paint.

"How?" he manages.

And then I reach over to the bed. Remove the dried rose from the hopper. Hold it up in front of his eyes.

"Now take out yours," I say.

"What?" he croaks.

"It's in your pocket. Where you stuffed it."

His eyes never leave the mirror. He moves his hand robotically, like it doesn't belong to him. Into his pocket.

Slowly, mindlessly, he pulls out his yellow rose and...

...we both instantly recoil as its golden flame lights up the entire room. Our faces bathe in its burning glow. The breath is sucked from our bodies. For a long time we just stare at the magnificent flower that burns like a sun before our mirrored faces.

Then at last I move. Hold up my own dried specimen. Like a shadow it can only be the same object; like a shadow, it is so very different.

"Every star," I say quietly, "will one day fade and die."

Then I turn to him. With my other hand I gently stroke his forehead, wiping away the last of the sweat.

"Time is passing. Nothing can stop that. But you can make every second yours." Then I throw my dead rose in the wastebasket. It sits on a high pile of used paper towels, a sacrificial victim.

"Light up her life, my friend," I say.

And then the weirdest thing happens. He starts to smile. Like a crack in the earth itself it splits across his dirty face. His lips turn up like rolling waves. The creases round his eyes dance with each other. And from his heart there comes the lightest, most joyous sound – laughter.

He laughs and he laughs. Doubling his great height up he whoops and yips and hollers. He guffaws and chuckles and hoots and sings. Tears cascade down his face. His cheeks shine pink.

At last he stops. Breathes. Pants. Hoots a couple more times and recovers.

Then he looks at me. And it's like every muscle in his body is filled with electricity, his limbs poised like an athlete's. His eyes gleam with happy fire. His skin is rich and healthy.

He looks young.

"Think I'll go now," he says with a smile, and he starts to head out.

"One thing, Freddie," I say.

And he turns, his boy-eyes wide, his flower clutched out before him.

"Yeah?" he says.

"Wash your hands," I say.

~

Who the fuck am I?

Not sure.

Something major has happened to my head.

There was darkness. Endless terrible darkness. And then a light. A light I must walk to. As now I do. Along this little corridor, back to the body of the restaurant, my rose out in front of me.

It's so strange. My thoughts are frothy and hard to hang onto. Like my brain has been whipped into Angel Delight. But at the same time, things are clearer and more focused than they have been since I was about twelve and spent an entire summer completing my Panini sticker album. It's like I've been driving through life with a foggy windscreen and now the aircon has kicked in. My destination is in sight. And I'm driving hard to get there.

Ambrosetti's is full to bursting... the noise and heat are incredible... the smarmbag waiters are poncing – but I don't notice any of it. It's like I've been shot through the chest with a harpoon gun and am being reeled in heart first.

Pace back from the loo with steel in every step. Past red-checked table after red checked table. Fat diners, laughing diners, braying diners. Shouting waiters, swearing Italian chefs. Clattering cutlery, crashing plates, banging doors. Plinking, whining music. It all flies past me like mist.

Can see Pen now. Only ten feet away. Her face a shining beacon in a wild, empty sea. Something in my guts surges to my mouth. The soup? No, I think it's a sob. Bloody choking up here. Got to get to her.

Nearer now and she's seen me. Smiles. Oh boy. Her face comes together into one brilliant, true and beautiful whole.

"The desert trolley's here, Freddie," she says softly. "The apple tart isn't too expensive. Or maybe we could share some cheese-"

"Fuck the desert trolley," I say, and boot it down the aisle at Mach 2. It whumps into a chair. Cakes take off. A perky waitress offers a startled "EEEP!" and stops them bravely with her breasts. Punters look round. Waiters set their eyes forward and their shoulders back. Could be in trouble here.

Got to move fast now.

Pen is looking up at me. Her beautiful face confused. Got to bring that smile back. Bask in it forever. But just before I move, I look around for the briefest second. Because I know, without a shadow of a doubt... my time has come.

Then I get down on one knee.

"Freddie what are you-?"

"Penelope," I start. She stops talking. Not surprised. Haven't used her full name in... ever. But then she looks straight at me in the strangest way and I know it's not about the name. Eager, like she can't wait to hear what comes next, but also calm, like she's not afraid. Pressure surges up within me like a tidal wave. A huge and terrifying wall of green water. But, rather than running, I reach for my surfboard. Hardly pausing, I leap on, catch the wave and now it powers me with its infinite energy. Strong as a storm I reach for her hand.

"Penelope, life is short." My voice is loud. The restaurant bustles no more. "Too short for me to treat you like I have been. But I had... well, I had a good long talk to myself and I sort of made myself see how it really is. If you know what I mean. Maybe you don't, but it doesn't matter. Listen, I'd like to apologise for being such a selfish, scared shithead all these years."

"Freddie-"

"Wait! Not finished yet. You could take every movie star and add them together and multiply them by six and they still wouldn't have half the beauty that's in that gorgeous smile of yours. You're the most beautiful girl in the world. You always have been and you always will be. Every day, from the moment we met, you've got more and more stunning until now the only thing equal to your beauty is my love for you."

Press her hands tighter. Her eyes are emeralds. Her face is alive – like my every word is charging her with electricity.

"Yes," I continue, "life may be short, but my love for you isn't. It deepens and widens and gets richer and stronger with every passing day. It's an infinite, mighty thing, higher than all mountains, heavier than all seas. It's beyond space. Past time. And, I truly believe, that if you can find it in yourself to feel the same, then our love can last forever."

Take a deep breath.

"Penelope. Will you marry me?"

Long pause.

Her lip quivers. Tears leap into her eyes. Then her smile shines like the midsummer sun.

"Oh, Freddie, of course I will."

Spring into her arms like a spaniel into the ocean. Whisk her up to her feet. Spin her round and round, kissing her and kissing her. Again and again until, when we're so dizzy we can't take it any more, I pull back.

How odd.

Place is silent. Look around. Entire clientele on its feet.

Staring.

And then, at exactly the same microsecond, every fucker in the place explodes.

Clapping and cheering. Whooping and yelling. And I'm happy too. Not because of the applause. But because my girl is smiling back at me, her green eyes shining bright.

"Hey, smarmbag," I shout to the waiter. "What are you staring at? Break out the champagne."

~

Haven't blacked out this time. The last trip and the only one that I don't lose it on. Obviously getting too used to this shit. Can feel myself spinning down the vortex. A billion realities swirl past me like fleeing stars. Every time and every place shooting through every atom of my brain and body.

So the bed and I are going back to my present – 2016. But where – who knows? Just as my present had changed from Edinburgh to California because of what I did in the past, so now I hope it will once again alter because of what he decides to do. In time, of course, I will remember it. But it's not with me yet. Not yet...

Look at all these possibilities... millions of them good, millions bad. But only one as it should be. Only one...

Oh, please not California. It hasn't shot by yet. Maybe it's coming up now. The lies and the cowardice and the loneliness. Surely not now. Couldn't bear it. But nor can I bear to hope where it might be. Oh God, I hope he had the balls to do it...

ZZZZPPPPPPRRRRPPPPPWWHHHHAANNNG!!!!

...and suddenly reality flips, the orb contracts and the cosmos births the bed and I drop...

...into an octagonal stone room. Small. Old. Lit by one high window. An arched window of coloured glass. Stained glass, flooded with sunny daylight. In front of me, a row of white and purple garments hang on intricately carved hooks. At my left and right, on either side of the room, dark wooden doors.

Reach out my hand. Grasp the ancient iron handle. Turn it and pull the heavy wood back to reveal...

A beach. Ivory white sand. Green-blue water. Right now I'm looking from one headland of the tiny curved bay. On the opposite point, a square stone building. The word 'HOTEL' written on the side in crisp white lettering. Shit, this is Dairloch. Up on the West Coast. And if that's the hotel, that means I must be in the...

Look down at myself. No longer naked. Instead, I'm wearing my kilt. Oh my God, can it be? Run back into the room. Just about to pull open the other door when it opens. Facing me is a short man with black floppy hair and a neat black beard. He wears a white and purple robe embroidered with long golden crosses. Around his neck is a white and black collar.

"You're a minister," I say.

"Of course I'm the minister, Frrrederick, but for goodness sake, what arrre ye doing in herrre?" he says in a rolling highland accent.

"Um... " I shrug, "trying to find the loo?"

"I told ye it's this way, just past the – hang on, where did this bed come from?"

"Not altogether sure," I say.

"How very odd," he mutters. "Nevermind. She'll be herrre any minute. Come on."

And he disappears back through the door. The segs on my ghillie brogues clatter a rapid tattoo as I scurry after him.

Along a little corridor, round a tight left turn, then a right, down a couple of steps, another left, up some steps, then through a larger wooden door, we step into...

...the nave of a tiny church. Both sides are crammed with guests in fine clothes. Frocks, dresses, trouser suits, kilts, morning suits, jackets. Flowers in buttonholes, hats, on pew ends and in excited hands. Hats sprouting like little shrubs. And, in the front pew on the left, sitting there with a cheeky grin on his face is..

Dougal.

Grinning broadly I step down past the altar and stand beside him. Shake his hand.

"Dougalicious," I say with another smile. "How very good to see you again."

"Ye're late," he says, winking one lustrous eye. His accent lilts and sings once more. His hair is wiry, his eyebrows bushy. The weight has gone. His limbs are sprightly. If a rabbit ran in here, he'd chase it. It appears I have a giant Yorkshire terrier for a best man.

"You look well. Slim."

"Thank ye, Freddie. What a nice thing to say. Ah'm back to mah fighting weight. Nine and a half stone. Course, got her to thank for that," he says, nodding over at a slightly chubby girl on the other side of the aisle who wears an emerald green dress and holds a bouquet.

"Best of fucking luck, darling," shouts Monica, giving me a big thumbs up. Then she waves at Dougal and blows him a kiss.

Nudge him.

"Hey, you old dog," I say. "How long's this been going on?"

"Since the launch party for my book," he says.

"Your book?!"

"Aye. My poetry anthology."

"Wow," I say. "Things going well then?"

"It was only a matter of time," he says.

Smile at him.

"Anything else I need to know?"

He points down the church.

"You may want to say hello to those two."

My eyes goggle. Dressed in suits and with hair slicked back, Clive and Glasses Matthew are waving at me from the last pew.

"Who the hell invited them?"

"Ye did, ye great daftie. Healing auld wounds and all that. Go on, gie them a wave."

Clive gurns and flails his oily fin around even faster.

Ah, what the hell. Give them a wave back. They smile and nudge each other in happiness.

In front of them are three pews filled with children. They look very excited. Some of them bounce on the spot. Some wave to me. All are chattering like crazy.

"Who are those kids?

"Pen's class," says Dougal.

Nod.

"How nice to have them here," I say and wave back to the pogoing youngsters.

Turn back to face the altar. Take a breath. Stare deeply at a gold cross on the Minister's robe.

"This feels right, now, doesn't it?" I say softly.

Dougal pats me on the arm. Winks one bright doggy eye.

"Just you wait."

And at that moment, somewhere up on high, an organ strikes up. Mendelssohn. The notes cascading over and past each other like the shivers in my spine.

"Now, please, gentlemen," says the minister, raising his hands in front of his body. Dougal and I get to our feet. We turn to look back down the church. Everyone is watching me, eyes glinting.

There's a pause.

Then, at the rear of the church, there's a clunk, a clank and a sudden shaft of sunlight fills the nave. Sounds enter with the light, blending with the music – the call of a gull, the whisper of the breeze and the gentle wash of the sea on the beach.

Then, an ivory shadow.

The congregation gasps. Old ladies nudge each other. Dab their eyes. Male jaws drop.

Because here she comes. Down the aisle. Penelope, my beautiful, beautiful girl. My one and only love. Her smile is bursting out of her. It's all I can do to stop myself exploding with joy. Even her bloody father looks happy. The whole world is watching her as she floats down the sunlit flagstones towards me.

And every step she takes lasts a thousand love-filled years.

~

I open our front door and walk into the hall. Take a brief look at the mail as I throw my keys on the little tray with the cross-eyed dog on it.

"Hun?"

"Out here, sweetie!" she calls faintly.

I head through to the sitting room. The doors to the little balcony are open. She's standing out there, silhouetted against the trees. God, she looks so big now. And so round. Like she swallowed a little planet.

I walk across the room and step out onto the balcony beside her. Give her a kiss. Look down at her. She smiles. I stroke the little crinkles beside her beautiful green eyes. Her skin is warm from the sunshine.

"Good day, hun?" she asks.

"Yeah, not bad at all. Not bad at all. You know that student I was telling you about?"

"The one who failed maths three times?"

"Adam, yeah."

"Aha."

"Well... he passed!"

"Oh, that's great news!" she cries.

"Yeah, he was made up. Gave me these."

I hold up the box of Roses. Show her the little card attached to the top. She reads the message – "Thanks for being such a great tutor. Cheers, Adam."

"Oh, how sweet," cries Pen. She throws her arms around me. I can barely reach her over the bump. "Well done, hun."

"He did all the work," I say.

"Yes, but he couldn't have done it without you. You were brilliant with him."

I shrug.

"Just doing my job. How you two been?" I say, patting her belly.

"Oh, we've had a very busy day. We went to not one, not two, not three, but four coffee mornings."

"That must be a personal best," I say.

"It might even be a national record," she says. "Then in the afternoon I met Monica and we had a nice chat."

"Sounds fun."

"Yeah, it was. They've decided on a venue."

"Where?"

"Dunkeld."

"Oh, that's fantastic. We used to go climbing there. And the golf course is great. Really high up at the back of the town. There's this mental hole where-"

"The cathedral is also lovely, Freddie," she says, her eyes crinkling.

I smile.

"I know, I know. I'll give them a call later on. Remind me, will you, 'cos I've also got to talk to the Dougmeister about the stag."

"Sure, hun."

"Great. Listen, are you hungry?" I ask.

"Always," she says with a smile and the tiniest glance at her bump. "What you thinking of?"

"Sofa picnic," I say. "Been dreaming of it all day."

She nods. "Perfect."

"Okay. I'll do snacks, you see what's on."

I give her a kiss, take her hand and lead her in off the balcony into the sitting room. She heads for the sofa. I move through to our little kitchen. Pull down a tray from on top of the cupboards. Open the fridge. Start to stack dips. Humus. Tsatsiki. The pink one.

She picks up the TV guide. Looks down the listings.

"CSI?" she suggests.

"Which city?" I ask, chopping some carrots.

"Miami."

"God no. Are there any movies on?"

"Uh, there's the Godfather part 2."

"Classic, but a bit long. You'll fall asleep."

"I will not!" she cries.

"Hey," I smile. "You can kid yourself, but I'm not falling for that one."

She laughs. Goes back to the paper. I pull out some fishsticks.

"Liar Liar?" she asks after a moment.

"Jim Carrey?"

"Yeah."

"I don't know," I say. "Not sure I'm in the mood for silly either. Is there nothing, you know, with a bit of... oomph to it?"

She looks down once more at the listings. I pour a couple of glasses of Ribena. Get some on my fingers. Suck it off, one by one. Man, it tastes so blackcurranty. Then I put the glasses on the tray beside the snacks and walk back through to the sofa.

I sit down. Put the tray on the little table. Pick up a carrot baton.

"There's this one about the four-fingered concert pianist," she says, her finger pressing on the page in her lap.

"Sounds lame. Who's in it?" I reply, dipping the carrot in the humus.

"Brad and Lucy."

"Brad Rock?" I say, crunching.

"No, Brad McShoogle from Niddrie." She looks at me deadpan. Then her face breaks into a smile and it's like the sun has come out. "Yes, silly," she says, "Brad Rock." She removes her hand from the paper. Reaches for a carrot stick of her own.

"And Lucy who?" I say, licking a stray blob of humus from my thumb.

"Lucy Sugar, of course."

"Is she the dark haired one?"

"No, daftie, the blonde. His new wife. They met on the set. Where on earth have you been? It's all over the papers." She dips her carrot.

"Um... "

"Freddie, for God's sake, she was at university with us for a term. You must remember her!"

I take my wife's hand. Lift it to my face. I kiss it. Then, with a quick bite, I steal her carrot.

"No, beautiful," I say with a food-filled smile, "I don't think I do."

$\sim End \sim$

*About the author*

Richard Happer is the author of two novels and several books of non fiction. He lives in Edinburgh with his family and a cat. He only goes back in time when he absolutely has to.